Rex Miller was
broadcasting bu
hand as a nost
order business
kind. Rex Mille
capist daydrear
merchants. The series of Eichord novels, of which
this is the second title, reflects his obsession with the
on-going, larger-than-life battle between Good and
Evil. *Slob*, his previous book was nominated for a
Bram Stoker Award as 'Best First Novel'.

Also by Rex Miller
in Pan Books

SLOB

FRENZY

REX MILLER

PAN BOOKS
London, Sydney and Auckland

First published in 1988 in the United States of America
by New American Library
This edtion published in 1989 by Pan Books Ltd
Cavaye Place, London SW10 9PG
© Rex Miller 1988
ISBN 0 330 30593 X
Printed and bound in Great Britain by
Cox and Wyman Ltd, Reading, Berks

Publisher's Note

This is an evil among all things that are done under the sun, that there is one event unto all; yea, also the heart of the sons of men is full of evil, and madness is in their heart while they live, and after that they go to the dead.

Ecclesiastes 9:3

PROLOGUE

Another tear splashed down on the expensive wood. It was hard, orange-and-black-grained cocobolo with alternate inserts of dense, reddish-tan tulipwood from Brazil. A trickle of tears had caught in the lashes at the corner of her eye and now they spilled over, dripping down her cheek and onto the arm of the love seat in her richly appointed bedroom. The tears beaded up on the arm of a piece of furniture that had cost more than some men bring home in a month. Yet, to her, the elegant surroundings were nothing more than a comfortable prison.

Her name was Tiff. She was fourteen years old. She was crying because she was sad, hurt, angry, frustrated, and frightened. She was a good girl. Why was this happening to *her*? How could her mother have deserted them? How could her father have treated her the way he had? One day everything had been so nice and overnight it all went bad, and what had she done to deserve this? I'm all alone now, she thought, and her shoulders shook with convulsive sobs. Crying her eyes out, as the saying goes . . .

Part One

TIFF

LAX was a bitch he could live without. He thought of it as a she, thinking of her as one might think of a lady of the night who appeared sexy, flashy, bright from a distance, but proved to be soiled and unpleasant-smelling up close. Some airports were the essence of their respective cities. Rome and Paris, Dallas and D.C.—but none more than LAX.

Fresh off a contract hit, Frank Spain took in a cautious lungful of L.A.'s airport perfumes and detected traces of a life-supporting pungency. That good ole allotropic, triatomic, Southern California fresh air. He hated L.A. and thought of the airport as nothing but an overpriced hooker who sucked when you came and sparkled when you left. And he'd never been happier to kiss the bitch good-bye than this morning.

She looked rough without her makeup—the glitz of the night-lights and the drama of darkness to cloak her in velvet and sparkle. Now she just looked busy and used. He was glad he was leaving. In fact he couldn't wait to get on the TWA flight, but he had stopped and bent to retie a lace that didn't need retying. Something a little out of place. Something tickling his nose a little. At first he mistakenly thought it might be coming from the clot of cops obviously greeting some VIP at a nearby gate. He could sniff out copper the way some animals can smell a hunter. He tied the shoe and walked into a small shop at the edge of the concourse. Lay back a bit, he thought. Just check it out.

11

Natural to be a little tight. The thing he'd come out for had been problems from square one and he'd had to jump back and put somebody between himself and the target. Ended up jobbing the Greek out to a couple of local kids. Airheads. He told the one on the phone:

"You don't want to make anybody nervous on this," and the kid goes, "Shit. Ain't no nervous about it. Let's rodeo."

"Just don't come up shy," he'd said to the kid. Let's *rodeo*? Jesus. That should have told him right there. And sure enough they just about screwed it every which way but straight up, and Spain wanted nothing but lots of distance between himself and the gig.

Southern Califucking Fornia. Everybody running around getting "deeply into" whatever the latest thing was. Greek dude. Name like popcorn cooking. Something—plop—pop—populous. Heavyweight in one of the multilevel sales things like Herbalife or Amway. Makes lots of dough. Goes into this and that. Gets too big too fast for the banks. Borrows a wad from family people. Winds up busting out. The Greek had been "deeply into jogging." Now he was deeply into the fucking GROUND.

Spain had smelled it when he saw the cops. Knew what it was when he'd taken a big breath of that hydrocarbonous delight that is laughingly called air in Lala Land. Equal parts of sleaze, sludge, smog, smoke, diesel, deals, Perrier, Pérignon, mimosa, mass flatulence, and—somewhere in there—ozone. But he'd also sniffed out the unmistakable scent of trouble. Smelled it right then and there. Smelled that sucker coming off the tarmac. And his beak never lied.

He pretended to be absorbed in a rack of paperbacks by the window of the gift shop as he watched them. Two in uniform. A guy in plainclothes shaking hands with a dark-haired guy, also obviously heat. He watched the way the first uniform cop put the one dude's bags in a car backed up to the gate. The way

the plainclothes cop glad-handed the dark-haired dude
as the other uniform came in and showed something
to an airport official and they moved toward a waiting
car.

A voice said, "Can we help you?" and he mumbled
something to the woman about a birthday card for his
daughter, turning as she directed him to the appropriate section so that he didn't see the dark-haired cop
say, Wait a minute, and come inside to get a paper.

When he looked up to see the eyes of that same cop
staring at him through the glass, it was a surprise and
he had to work not to show it in his face as he slowly
let his own eyes travel back to the card he was appearing to study. He had no way of knowing he was
looking into the eyes of serial murder detective Jack
Eichord, only that he was looking at heat, and Eichord
saw the man glance back at a card, appearing to be
totally absorbed in a caricature of the "see-no-evil"
monkey.

But Jack had seen something else. Eichord had a
habit of looking hard at everything. Cop habit. He'd
come back in to buy a newspaper and seen a guy look
up and make him for a cop. It was something cops and
wise guys could do. A cop could spot the read. The
flicker of recognition in wise-guy eyes that you didn't
get off a straight Joe. You didn't have to be up close.
State rods could catch it sometimes clear across a four-
lane interstate. Eichord moved away but watched the
man a bit longer from behind a magazine kiosk. He
appeared to hear his plane announced, paid for the card,
and quickly moved toward the boarding gate. It was
probably nothing. Jack stored the scene away in his
mind and dismissed it.

But as he went back to the waiting car, he had that
tug that he had learned to listen to or give in to. A
firm pull at the sleeve that said, Hey, Jack. Get with
it. It's the copper's version of that little shot you get

when you suddenly realize you're about to lock your keys in the car.

Jack Eichord was no genius cop. He'd solved the "Doctor Demented" thing, and the so-called "Lonely Hearts" killings in Chicago, and it had given him an international rep that bore scant relation to reality. He'd found himself to be the unwitting beneficiary of the imputation of super-sleuth, a rep his fellow detectives knew was ridiculous. Because of some luck, and a giant media spoon-fed by the Chicago brass, his involvement in the high-profile sex murders and mutilation killings had shot him into the hot limelight.

The press loves to pick up on ascriptions like "serial-murder expert," however imprecise they might be, and Jack Eichord had found himself to be so elected by the media mavens. They talked about his genius for crime solving and his Sherlockian brain, and like his colleagues who knew better, he laughed at the bullshit. He was lucky. He had a gift. Something. He got hunches. Whatever. The thing he had now. He thought of it as his shit detector. It was purring away and he didn't know why.

The one called Frank Spain had the same kind of instinct or intuition, only in reverse. Like two ships passing in the night, each shrugged off the cold feeling inside, but Spain had more difficulty getting the smell of trouble out of his nose. It dogged him as he left the concourse and climbed the stairs to find his seat in first class.

It was the troubling smell of a whore. Just professional paranoia, he thought, and the tired, heavy-lidded man with the LA/ST L ticket under the name Frank Spain closed his eyes and snuggled down as best he could into the seat.

He deplaned at Lambert Field at 12:21, and he had not adjusted his wristwatch to Coast time because he hated the way the long trip out was only a couple of hours long if you did, and then it just added to the jet lag when you came home. His car was still there in the lot. That was something, anyway. The feeling hadn't left him. It was building. Like he'd forgotten something. A little detail left to come and kick his butt later. In his business that was not good. The paranoia was mounting.

Early afternoon he was on the top of the hill next to their home in Ladue, and he could see Buddy Blackburn's car in their drive, but he didn't think anything about it. Pat was always calling or writing the insurance companies about something or other. He tried to show her how it was all a big humbug, but she insisted that they have insurance out the kazoo, and mostly for Tiff's sake he let her do her thing.

He'd stopped at the top of the hill to rearrange some things in the attaché case on the seat next to him and he saw the door of the house open and Buddy Blackburn come out. Just for a second, tired as he was from the trip, he thought he'd seen Buddy kiss Pat goodbye, which made no fucking sense at all. He shook it off and rubbed his eyes. Christ, he thought, Pat didn't even kiss him good-bye. Much less Buddy. Much less their insurance man, whom she could barely stand to talk to and . . . Oh oh, that's when he had the little zing and it dawned on him that he was back a day earlier than he'd told her.

Buddy was only three or four years younger than Spain but he wore his hair like a guitarist in a rock band, and Spain knew he had at least a couple of semi-platonic, flirting relationships with the younger married women among his clientele—but Pat? No fucking way.

He waited until the red sports car was out of sight and he shot down off the hill and into the drive, sprinting out of the car and into the house, fully intending to confront his wife in the bedroom, but there was no need. She was standing at the sink in the kitchen, looking out the window at nothing, standing there in high heels and a very sexy teddy he'd never seen before and wearing nothing else, her back to him, turning slowly as he burst in the door catching her in her fuck clothes in the early afternoon.

"I believe the phrase is *flagrante delicto*," he said coolly.

"You weren't supposed to be back today," she said, showing what he thought was an exceedingly good grasp of the obvious.

"Sorry about that." He was not having to fight to remain calm. That's what was surprising him. He was so calm even as he sensed everything crumbling about him. His life disintegrating, crashing down around his ankles. "I could go out and come back tomorrow if you think it'd help."

"Funny," she sighed, somewhat impatiently, and turned away from him.

"Oh. Sorry if my material isn't up to snuff. I could work on it and—"

"I don't want to fight," it sounded like she said, her back still to him. He hadn't even looked closely at his wife for a month or so. Oddly, she looked quite sexy to him at this moment. He said it before he thought.

"I don't suppose I could have sloppy seconds?"

She just sort of let her head move to one side and he saw her breathe deeply under the flimsy teddy, and with considerable grace she walked out of the kitchen.

"You owe me an explanation, bitch. Why, of all people, Buddy BLACKBURN?" he said to her moving back.

She said nothing and he followed her, catching an arm and spinning her around, still having no desire to slap her, which surprised both of them.

"Why Buddy Blackburn?"

"You'd never understand."

"It can't be because we didn't have great sex together."

"See what I mean?" She turned and he grabbed her again.

"Will you talk to me, goddamn you. *Why?*"

"Why? You must be kidding."

"It's always been good for us—" He was shaking his head.

"Sure," she said with heavy irony, at which she was past master.

"You never said it was bad—you acted like you enjoyed it between us. We had a great sex life."

"You call a two-minute quickie twice a month a SEX LIFE?" She laughed.

"That isn't fair."

"What do you mean, it isn't fair?"

"It isn't fair to me to say our sex life consisted of a two-minute quick—"

"See! It's a debate now. Okay, you win. Three minutes four times a month, eight minutes nine times a month. You win. It was great."

"Why BUDDY BLACKBURN?"

"You never cared if I was satisfied."

"What?" he asked, incredulously.

"You just wanted a fast wham-bam, and good night. When's the last time you did anything romantic or acted like you cared about me. Never. That's the last time. You don't care about anything or anybody except yourself."

"That's not true, Pat. How can you—"

"Why Buddy? It could have been anybody. A man. Not a wimp. You're not the kind of man who needs a woman. You should have been a . . . You should be gay or something. You don't even like it."

"You're crazy," he said. But the preposterousness of the situation, the ridiculousness of being inserted into the center of such a domestic cliché, had begun to numb him out. "You're nuts," he told her without an ounce of conviction.

"I want out."

"At least give us another chance together. I can change. I want to—"

"See what I mean? A WIMP! Why don't you slap me around. Scream. Break things. You want me to stay. You catch me unfaithful and you want another chance. Chance to what? To be more of a wimp? You want to watch me and Buddy from the closet, is that it?" She moved right in front of him, looking up at his reddened face, daring him to lash out at her. "You want me to tell you what it was like with Buddy? HUH? Will that get you off?"

"Pat. Come on." He could barely speak.

"You want to know if his is bigger than yours? It is, you know. A lot bigger. And he's a lot better. Better in the sack, Mr. Hotshot. How's that grab you? Is that what you want to hear? You want another chance at it—uh? *Jesus!* You make me sick." She stomped into the bedroom and slammed the door, indignant, as always the offended party, he thought.

Nice welcome back. He tried to swallow. There was a certain perverse gratification in discovering her infidelity, since it confirmed his secret fears of wimphood rather incontrovertibly. But the comfort was cold and fleeting.

He was dashed. That's the word. Dashed by it. And confused by the way his body chemistry had suddenly become independent of his brain in the face of the confrontation. Instantly benumbed, a growing hard-on had stiffened in counterpoint to the anesthesia of the dialogue. Undeniably, finding her desirable to another man had produced the curious effect of making him want his wife the way he hadn't in years. God, he *was* some kind of wimp.

The rest of the process of disintegration was rapid and heartless. She wanted out, goddammit, and the dissolution of the marriage was as much to blame on his coming home a day earlier than expected, as it was on his wimpification. It was *his* unforgivable indiscretion and *his* weakness and *his* lack of manhood that had destroyed what they had. She wanted out now. What could a wimp do but tearfully acquiesce?

And so she left him. And if you think there is an inconsistency in Spain's passive willingness to eat, as it were, such a dish of humble pie, considering his vocation and track record, you have understood the facts without knowing the truth.

The truth is that workers are just like you and I. They suffer from toothaches and the common cold. They sometimes become overdrawn at the bank and their cars won't start. If, like Spain, their life is compartmentalized to any degree, they can be quite ordinary-appearing family men who live the most prosaic and common home lives. The guy in the brake shop gets snotty with them, they don't whack him out; they go home and complain and suffer just like anybody else. They get fucked over just like we do.

And so he let her leave. And the idea of whacking Buddy Blackburn, or Pat, or the both of them, simply never occurred to him. What the hell would be the point? Besides, he knew that it hadn't been his ineptitude in bed nor his diminutive dick nor his wimpy ways that had turned them sour. It had been there in the cards all along.

The places where her clothes had been taken from closets, in the master bedroom and in the big walk-in closet, left gaping, black holes that sucked the juice out of his heart and mind. And each time he let himself be pulled by those forces, it took more out of him. For days everything in the house around him sapped his energies, and the most mundane act—opening a refrigerator and seeing a certain food—was enough to make him bleed inside.

It was all Eichord could do not to cry. He was not a man who spilled his tears easily. And the funny thing about it was there was absolutely nothing wrong.

Career-wise he was firmly at the reins of an upwardly
mobile skyrocket. And when they brought him out to
Los Angeles on the case media had tagged the "Eyeball Murders," it was all carte blanche and first class
all the way.

"You're a *star* in this business," the liaison guy had
told him. They actually spoke that way out here. It
was wild. Everybody in Southern California seemed
to be plugged into the entertainment industry in some
way. One of the detectives in the central bureau office
had a book on the best-seller list and Jack had overheard him talking to someone on the phone about pass-
through payouts and a second-lead store display, and
for a second he thought he might have been taken to
the wrong office.

They had VIP treatment ready for him at the airport
and a car waiting; standard. Two street cops had been
with the liaison guy and they took him to Studio City
first, so the cops could walk him through the most
recent crime scene on busy Ventura Boulevard. It was
one in a series of what happened to be three gangland
whacks, not enough to qualify as serial kills, but to
prompt reaching for Jack because of the attendant notoriety. He found the LAPD people crisp, flawlessly
groomed, hip, very smart, and insincere. Again, it
was the movie business. All of California seemed to
have it, a contagious virus of the ethics or something.
It depressed him.

It depressed him that he *was* a star. He was welcomed as if he was somebody out here to plug a movie
instead of to work on a murder investigation. He'd been
on talk shows. "Very hip," somebody told him. He
could sense there was nothing he could do here. It was
all too sprawling, too mobile, too California. It was
nobody's fault, it was San Andreas' fault. It was just
Lala Land.

They took him through the Studio City thing, jerked
him around for a couple of hours, and coming back,

took him to lunch; not so standard. The meal had to have set somebody back two bills for the four of them, had there been a check presented at the end of it. Waiters hovering around threatening to burst into flame at the very suggestion of a cigarette—one of those kinds of meals. The food adequate and unspectacular. Eichord conscious of his out-of-style threads and aloneness in this crushingly strange place.

"Have you ever seen the Pink Pussycat?" Questions about what was on his agenda for the night. Never mind the investigation. That told him everything he wanted to know right there. They were as thrilled to have him as he was to be here. It would be one of those things where "a special agent of the Major Crimes Task Force aided in the investigation—" They would feed him to media if he didn't watch them tomorrow.

"Want to see the town tonight?" The liaison man said, resplendent in a blazer sweater and gray slacks, the two blue-suited cops and old Jack looking absurdly out of place in the fancy eatery. Eichord sipping chilled chablis like an idiot, feeling sorry for himself. He'd *seen* the town, thanks.

He'd begged off the Strip and the rest of it, and hoped for a quiet motel room, but someone he knew slightly had insisted in no uncertain terms that he be fed a home-cooked meal, and he let himself be more or less led by the hand to this darkening, alien California suburb, where he was overwhelmed by the déjà vu of feeling himself in the grip of forces over which he had no control.

Eichord, who seldom had either the time or the temperament to sit motionless in front of a television in prime time (he was an addict of ancient *Late Show* whodunits), was in someone's home half-watching a set and waiting to be called to dinner, watching a show that was supposed to be a "roast" of some elderly comedian, and the comic called upon to make the keynote speech began by spitting pea soup out in a mock-vomit. When the shocked laughter of the grossed-out audience subsided, the comic smiled innocently and said, "It just seemed like the right thing to do."

Eichord leaned back and shut his eyes for a moment, thinking about all the awful, gross, inane, fatuous, imbecilic, terrible, and stupid things that Eichord the man, as opposed to Eichord the cop, had lived to later regret. Burning humiliations and prickling embarrassments that had proved to be mercilessly unforgettable.

Always when he asked himself, Why—the same answer. Because it seemed like the thing to do at the time.

Eichord sat with his eyes and mind squeezed tight to shut out the memories as the television set of a relative stranger roared in his ears, and he felt a momentary icicle of fear for his own mortality jab him with a cold point, and suddenly he was overwhelmed with sadness and self-pity. He had to laugh at himself.

He was laughing at the absurdity of his thoughts. Feeling so fucking sorry for himself—so sorry that he had to die one day. Feeling so sad about the way everything had gone, about the way his life had gone, about the way Edie's life had gone. He wished he could call her right now.

And this is what his host saw when he walked into the room to ask about salad dressing. Did Jack want vinegar-and-oil or Thousand Island? There was Jack watching a has-been comedian whose toupee appeared to have been spray-painted in place, laughing and enjoying the television show.

His host was heartbroken Jack wouldn't accept a ride back to his motel. Never mind that it was forty minutes away and *that* at 90 miles an hour, bumper to bumper, traffic moving at its usual mad pace. But Jack was adamant, and after profuse thanks for the home-cooked chow, he was in a Los Angeles cab and headed for nowhere or oblivion or neither of the above, whichever they hit first.

The cabbie intruded on his thoughts with sudden silence. He realized the driver must have paused in his monologue and asked him something.

"Pardon me?" he said.

"The Springs. You ever been to Palm Springs?"

"Not for years."

"Yeah, well, my brother-in-law and me did some work on Frank's home there. We're in the pool business too, see. And we did a job on his pool. He was doing a picture for the director John Frankenheimer. It was the one where he costarred with Janet Leigh, who I had in the cab once. Anyway, this was at Frank's house in Palm Springs and. . ."

Christ in heaven. Even the fucking cabdrivers out here were in show biz.

Dinner had turned into another family fiasco. Inside his head the man was Frank Spain, contract executioner. But to the girl at the dinner table he was only "Dad."

"Dad," she whined, giving it two syllables.

"Tiff, don't whine," he said as he chewed.

"You know I'm no whiner."

"No. You're no whiner. So please don't start now, okay?"

"Dad, why can't you like Greg? You didn't like Jeff. You don't like any boy I like."

"I like him fine."

"Come on, Dad. You know you hate Greg. And he's a good guy and all. He's from a nice family. How come you don't like him?"

"I like him already. Give it a rest, please. Let's eat in peace, can't we?"

"It's the only time I have you let me talk to you anymore. You won't ever talk to me. Dad. Please. I just want to go with him to games and shows and stuff like that. It's not like we'd be going out on real dates or, you know, staying out late and stuff.'' She was fourteen and flowering and he didn't know what to do.

"Do we have to think about it right this second while I'm trying to eat?"

"Can I see Greg, then?"

"When you're fifteen you can see Greg or any other nice boys just like we discussed. But until then I don't want to keep hearing about it, Tiff. Now that's it. Eat you dinner. Please.''

She sulked in silence. This girl who was neither a whiner nor a sulker. And she wondered what would become of them.

The *Archilochus colubris* had not yet joined the avian migration southward. The young girl who was the daughter of the one who called himself Spain stared out through the elegant curtains where a pair of brightly iridescent hummingbirds darted and soared and dove in an incredible air ballet. The female was airborne, zooming up and out of sight, and the tired male stopped to refill from the nearly empty feeder outside the window. As he began to drink, the female sped down from out of nowhere driving him away from his hovering feed-position and they began their elaborate aerobatics again. But the girl saw none of this as her unfocused eyes welled up with tears.

She paid little attention to the splendor of her surroundings as she sat perched on a love seat in her expensively furnished bedroom. Her parents' house was a fine home, and their exclusive residential area was beautifully maintained, free of any offensive ugliness, a haven for the local wildlife, almost a miniature park. But having known nothing but the finest, she had little frame of reference with which to appreciate the elegance of her environment. Nor would she have cared.

Her eyes filled with tears and overflowed in a salty

trickle blurring her vision and dripping down her tanned cheek, and she wiped at the little flood with the back of her hand and snuffled into a tissue. She wept in sadness and hurt and anger at her mother, who had abandoned them, and wept for her father, who was so devastated by what had happened and who, grief-stricken, had closed out everything else in his life—including his daughter. And yes, she wept for herself, at the shame and the bitter unfairness of it all. And as she sobbed she thought how ridiculous she must appear right now, curled up on the love seat wallowing in self-pity.

Outwardly she was a lithe, tanned, attractive teen-ager with long legs and the soft, lovely curves of wom-anhood beginning to flower and envelop the angular planes, and a stranger would believe her to be sixteen perhaps, and not fourteen. But she was a troubled fourteen-year-old, Spain's daughter. And as she sat oblivious to her richly decorated room, not seeing the courting dance of the hummingbirds, she felt an an-cient fourteen. Ancient and lonely.

She snuffled and wiped her eyes and blew her red-dened nose again and uncurled the long, tan legs from the cushions, got up, walked out of her bedroom, and went downstairs. Her dad's office door was not com-pletely shut, and she pushed the door open soundlessly and peered in at him sitting at his desk, unmoving. She nearly jumped out of her skin at the sound of the phone ringing upstairs, and she ran back up and snatched it off the hook on the fourth ring.

"Hello."

"Tiff."

"Oh, hi." It was Greg. She'd been hoping he'd phone her all day. She felt her breath catch a little as she said, "I've missed you."

"Same here. I wish I could see you right now."

"Me too."

"Touch you. Just hold you. I could cuddle you for

hours and never get tired of just holding you. You know that?'' She loved his voice.

"Greg. I wish we were together right now too."

"Well, why can't you meet me somewhere? Can't you get out of the house?"

"Dad doesn't want me going out anywhere, you know, with boys. He says not till I'm fifteen."

"Oh, wow. Well, can I come over there?"

"Um. I guess you'd better not. He just doesn't understand that I'm grown up. I can't do anything. It's like being in prison since Mom . . . left. I miss you so much."

"Go over to Amber's and I'll pick you up over there. I got Roger's car, man, come on. He'll never find out. No way." Roger was an older boy who let Greg drive sometimes.

"Well, I guess I could get Amber to go with us and we could let her out at Herman's."

"Yeah, okay, let's go. Okay?"

"I'm so lonesome for you. I . . . Oh, all right. I'll be over there about three."

"See ya."

" 'Bye." She hung up and realized there was a thin sheen of perspiration under her hairline. She got all hot and flustered talking to Greg. He was so beautiful, like a movie star, with all that unruly hair and those eyes like two little blue pools. He belonged in Hollywood. Greg always reminded her of the one on that soap she used to watch. What was his name—the one with the unruly, curly hair? Except Greg was a whole lot better-looking.

She wished she could talk to her dad about him, but when she tried, he got furious with her. And Greg was so great. He was gentle. Soft-spoken. A well-educated boy from a nice home. Everything you could ask for.

She was not pretty in the conventional sense but was the sort of girl who would grow into a woman that other women would describe with envy. Eyes were just a bit too far apart. Nose not quite delicately enough shaped, chin just a bit too square to be pretty ever, but an interesting-looking girl with the beginnings of a great body. She wore her hair in a kind of sleek, feathery cap that she spent hours and hours working on to get it just so—and once someone had told her that her hair and eyes made her look like a cat.

She liked cats and had since she was a little girl. In fact, she had copied her current hairstyle out of a magazine because she had misread the caption under the picture. She'd thought it said "Layered Cat" style, when it had been "Layered Cap," and she'd copied it and then later read it correctly, liking it better when it had said cat. She did have a little of the feline look about her, and she knew it and saw it as a strength, rightfully enough, and played to it a little. This kitten was a pretty good cat. A nice kid. And she was going through a very tough time.

She still couldn't believe her mother had actually run off with that . . . that thing . . . and left them. She'd refused to talk to her on the phone each time she'd called the house to talk to Tiff. She despised her mom for what she'd done to them. Especially to Dad. He was ruined by her leaving them like that. She wanted to help somehow, to come to his rescue. It had brought out all of her latent maternal instincts and she'd tried to comfort him, to do things around the house to help him and she couldn't reach him. It's like he was in shock.

"Dad?" she said, sticking her head in the door of his study. "I'm going over to Amber's. I'll be home early. Okay?" He looked up with heavily lidded eyes and nodded yes, and she took off.

She remembered back about a couple of years or so ago, one day her mother had been brushing her hair and they'd started talking about that time of the month, and her mom was talking about why you bleed when you become sexually mature, and she'd said, just kidding around with her mother, "I don't see why we were made like that down there. Why would God want you to bleed every month?"

And her mom had been real serious and she goes, "God made us different from man so we could procreate, and make love, and have babies. And someday you'll be with your husband and you will conceive a baby together, and then in nine months your little newborn child will come out down there."

And Tiff had gone, "Down *here*? Oh, sorry. No way."

And her mother had been so amused by that. She'd laughed real hard. She thought that was really funny.

Back inside the study, the one called Spain felt the fog lift from his thoughts for a fraction of a second and he absentmindedly realized that his daughter had just stuck her head in the door and spoken to him, and he had looked up from his preoccupied stupor and seen her oval face in the doorway, framed there like a madonna, and the sunlight through the blinds had just for that instant settled around her head like a golden halo.

She knew she was going to let Greg go all the way with her the day they were washing the Trans-Am and Roger left them alone to go riding with some girl who had honked at him as she cruised by. Roger's folks were gone, as always, and she almost went for it right then but she had enough sense to hold him off until she could get The Pill. They'd been fooling around while they were soaping off the car and she was in real short cutoffs and a little T-shirt knotted in front and bare over her midriff, leaning way out over the hood with the shorts hiked way up on her butt and Greg came up behind her,

"AHHH!" She jumped when he pushed into the back of her. "You rat, you're getting me wet."

"Is that right," he said, letting her savor the double entendre as he reached around and cupped her breasts.

"I'm soaking."

"I'd like to soak you good, you know." He was pressed into her and she could feel him hard and insistent,

"OOOOHHHHH, shit!" She flipped the hose back and squirted him with it and they wrestled around, drenching each other in soapy water as they slid over the car's slick surface.

"I'll get you for that." He was nuzzling her gently now and she stopped struggling a little and enjoyed his embrace, and they laughed.

"You're a maniac," she said.

"Yeah, Absolutely," he whispered behind her, his lips in her hair.

"That feels good," she said.

"That does?" He was making little circles with his fingertips, little feathery circles, barely brushing his fingers up against the wet shirt.

"I like the look of your ass like that," he told her, his hand moving down and cupping her right cheek.

"Wet, you mean."

"Ummmm."

"If you're trying to poke a hole through me, you're doing a pretty good jo—" She was turning and his lips shut hers with a soft, velvety kiss.

"Who do you love?"

"Ummff."

"What?" He let her answer.

"You know who."

"Say it." He kissed her and pulled her close again.

"You."

"Yes?" Kissing her so gently.

"Yes."

"YES."

"Ummm."

"You taste good."

"Let's go inside."

"We'll get everything wet."

"Not if we leave our clothes in the kitchen."

"That's an idea."

They went in, shedding wet shirts and shorts and kissing some more, and with their arms around each other they tumbled onto the sofa in the Nunnalys' living room, still moist. And he began his usual ritual that was the next step whenever he got Tiff to undress with him.

"I do love you so, you know that?" Had she been older or wiser, with some mileage, she might have seen through the practiced, toothy artifice as the bogus, manipulative con that it was. But she was fourteen and experienced not at all. And when he opened his mouth and those full, seductive lips of his smiled at her, she could feel her heart miss a beat and her breath caught as she was dazzled by the white smile and perfect mouth—blinded by the light, you could say.

"I love you too, Greg," she said as they kissed. She saw what she wanted to see when she gazed deeply into those pretty-boy Hollywood blues, and she would sort of let herself go and feel her insides falling into the depth of them, splashing down into those sexy, delicious pools.

"Do you really love me?" he'd ask.

So desperately did Tiff love the idea, so total was her commitment to the concept of romance in general, hers in particular, that she began to give herself to him in direct proportion to her desire to be loved in return. And that is a dangerous mistake when you're dealing with a slick little stud like Greg Dawkins. An only child who'd been spoiled rotten, fussed over and pampered, made to feel he was better than everyone else, given too many compliments and too much spending money, and too few rules. A kid with good looks and too much time on his hands and a wide and nasty mean streak.

"Come on, doll. Don't," he'd say as she closed her

legs, trapping his creeping fingers in the spreading warmth of her inner thighs, "don't stop me, please. I gotta have you." And the fingers would start moving again, insistently, creeping gently over her, up her long legs toward payday and bit o' honey.

"Please, Greg." She'd try to stop the fingers. "Please," she'd beg him with that hot, wet mouth of hers, her face all puffy and slack with desire, red through the tan, wanting him to please please please. "Please," she would say over and over.

"Please what?" he'd say, biting her a little as he kissed in all the right places where he could sense a heartbeat, kissing her racing pulse with that Hollywood mouth, putting those California-star lips all over her and searing her skin with the flame of his expert kiss as he laid down his con.

"Oh, please," she'd whisper back, urgently, letting him explore the newly discovered, uncharted regions with those adventurous fingers of his, and he would tell her, "Please, baby," pleasing her right back, giving the old please right back to her. "You gotta let me, angel, I'm gonna be sick if I don't get off." And his favorite standby, "Please let me show you the highest form of love," he'd say.

His con would echo in her ears and she'd remember his bullshit later. Later when it was too late. Later, when the most romantic thing he'd ever say to her was "Let's do lines."

But for now she was caught up in his carefully crafted romance. Greg had been put off over and over. There was a limit to how long he'd stand for it. He was the cutest boy in school and all the girls were doing it now. Lots of better-looking girls than Tiff would hop into bed with Greg in a second if he even blinked at them. And she was afraid if she said no much longer she would lose him.

"Please, baby. *Please*." Those hot fingers were moving and she wanted him. Why lie to herself?

"Don't." She pushed him back a little. "Just listen for a second, honey. Remember last time? How we got so hot and everything and you said it made you sick 'cause I wouldn't let you go ahead?"

"It's not fair, baby. I mean I'm so hot I'm gonna ex-*plode*." He breathed the flame out on her like a young dragon. "Please let me love you."

"Don't you know I want you to?"

"You don't act like it."

"I love you and I want you bad, believe me."

"Show me, then," he said, fingers moving again.

"Honey, listen. I can't take a chance of something, you know, going wrong."

"I won't let anything go wrong. I'll take care of it."

"I've got to be careful. Not yet, PLEASE. Just be patient a little longer. Greg, sweet, I want you too." She kissed him tenderly and he didn't respond. "After what Mom did to us, to Dad, her going off like that . . . God. If something would happen. It would totally bum Dad out for good. I can't take any chances. Just be patient."

"I don't know if I can," he said, darkly, with just the right degree of urgency. And the next morning they skipped classes and Tiff had him take her all the way downtown to the Free Clinic so she could get some birth control pills. It was the beginning of bad times.

She would be a long time forgetting that day. She could feel her face burning every time she thought about it for weeks afterward. She'd gone out of the house like she always did, heading for school. And Greg picked her up in Roger's wheels and they took off for downtown.

"Wow. It's truly gnarly." The Free Clinic was right out of Dickens and in a rough neighborhood. "You want me to go in with you?" She could tell by his tone he wasn't about to.

"No. Just wait for me, okay?"

"Yeah."

They kissed and she plunged ahead. You had to answer all these questions and this woman was going on and on telling her about everything and she sat there with a slowly building feeling of dread and apprehension creeping up on her, hearing the lady talk to her with half an ear—

". . . and this is called an IUD, which means . . ." —and wishing it would all end. And wondering what it would be like between them. The dark cloud of her mother's guilt hovering over her all the while.

". . . and this is a diaphragm . . ." And be sure to chew each bite 32 times, and look both ways before crossing the street.

And then it was over and she had The Pills and Tiff was excited and scared and very much fourteen years old as she hurried out of the Free Clinic and ohmigod, OH, NO, DAD!

Greg was nowhere in sight. Her dad, looking about ten feet tall, about to boil over with anger, was waiting for her.

"What are you doing here—"

And he cut her off with a thumb jerked at the car, meaning get your butt in here now. "Get in," he snarled.

"Where's Greg? What are YOU doin' here?"

"GET IN."

"Dad." Nothing. The car starts and he whips away from the curb and into the downtown traffic. "Dad? What's this all about?"

"That's really choice, Tiff. Shouldn't I be asking you?"

"Did you follow me, Dad? I mean, man, that's about the lowest—"

"No, dear. I didn't have to follow you. I knew exactly where you were going this morning."

"Did Amber—"

"Never mind how I found out. I could have picked up the phone and started to call out and heard you say birth-control pills and overheard by mistake, couldn't I? I could have seen you were acting suspicious as hell the last couple of days and I might have caught you in a couple of lies and I might have found out you were seeing this punk Greg when you were supposed to be at your friend's house—I mean, there's a hundred ways I could have found out. When you lie all the time you can expect to get caught. No?"

"Greg's not a punk. Don't call him that."

"Oh. I think he's a punk, all right. I think that is precisely, exactly, and absolutely what he is. A snot-nosed, lying, sneaking, no-good little punk who is about to get his butt in some serious trouble for molesting a fourteen-year-old girl. *AM I MAKING MY-SELF CLEAR?*"

"You don't have to scream. I'm sitting right here next to you, Dad."

"You little lying whore!" And before he could control himself he lashed out at her, backhanding her and hearing her head crack against the window on the passenger side, hitting her a lot harder than he meant to, slapping her involuntarily, lashing out at her before he could think to stop himself, slapping his errant daughter, slapping Pat, slapping her lover Buddy, slapping the stewardess who had touched him on the plane, letting all his anger and rage and frustration whip out at his little girl.

"I *HATE* YOU," she screamed at him between sobs. It was a slap he could never take back. Not the smack with the back of his hand or the tooth-rattling headache. That was nothing. It was what he called her. No matter how much she would ever want to, she knew that would be the one thing she'd find the hardest to forgive.

"Do you know the kind of thoughts I had about you on the way down here? The things I thought about while I was parked over across from the clinic waiting for your to get your little slut pills so you could give yourself to that—that boy? It was like realizing for the first time that I'd never known you. You were a total stranger living under our roof. My roof," he corrected. "And now I'm going to have to treat you as if you were a stranger. I'm going to have to make rules. Firm rules."

"I hate you, you know that," she spat, glaring at him with her narrowed cat's eyes, still sobbing and out of control.

"And I *love* you, and that's why—"

"No you don't," she sobbed ruefully, "you lying old *bastard*," and the word *bastard* was the last word she spoke to him for a long, long time.

He went ahead to lay down his new, iron-clad rules, so ridiculous they made his previous constraints seem positively reasonable by comparison. The rigidity he'd shown toward Tiff since Pat ran off to be with her real lover man would appear benign when compared to the stern measures he was going to take to "control" his wayward, delinquent fourteen-year-old.

Spain continued talking, commanding, when he should have been listening, asking. Instead of understanding or gentle guidance, he was making demands she knew she couldn't swallow. He'd taken a loving daughter and used her as a release for his bottled-up anger. And the harsh abrasiveness of this confrontation slammed the door on her once and for all.

"How you could do something like this to me when you know this sort of crap is the last thing I need right now and . . ." She only heard a blur of words. But wasn't that just like her father? The last thing HE needed. Never mind what anybody else needed. He could go to hell for all she cared.

She'd tried so hard to give him extra love when Mom had left. The little extras. Worked so hard to be home for him. Clean up after him. Feed him nourishing meals. Do all the things her mother had done around the house. She tried to talk to him, and he didn't want any part of it. When she was solicitous and sympathetic, he'd responded by pulling himself inside the shell of a shattered ego where she couldn't get at him. Now this.

They rode in silence for another half-hour and each kept their own raging counsel, sitting there unspeaking, seething with anger and frustration and self-pity, fuming with bitterness, and the hacksaw edge of their actions and words severed the last of the bonds between father and daughter.

When they pulled up in front of the house, she was out of the car and the front door was slamming before he's reached for the automatic garage-door opener up on the sun visor. And by the time she heard him come in the house, she'd already run upstairs and put some of her mother's old medicine in the case of birth-control pills and hidden her goodies safely away. Eventually he'd get around to asking for them. Or more likely, he'd open her purse and confiscate them without saying anything.

As soon as she heard him back in his office and she'd double-checked that the door to the office was shut, she quickly dialed the Dawkins number.

Greg's mom answered, "Hello?"

"Hi. Is Greg there?" she asked quietly.

"Sure, hon. Oh, do you know what your dad wants with Jerry?"

"Huh?"

"That's okay. I thought maybe this was about the other call. Just a second, Greg's on his way." And she heard him take the phone away from her.

"Yeah."

"What happened?"

"Came along while I was parked," he said in that abbreviated way he talked when he wanted her to know somebody was listening. Speaking so softly she couldn't hear all the words.

"What?"

"Said to get out of here or he'd call the cops on me. Underage. Throw me in. Get it?" He was whispering and not making sense.

"But we haven't done anything. I'm still a VIRGIN," she said, louder than she meant to, the word echoing in her bedroom like a pistol shot.

"Said if I did. Go to jail 'n' that. Going to tell my dad. See I never drive again. He thinks it was Dad's car. Called here and left word with Mom. You gotta stop him."

"I can't stop him. He's a madman. He hit me on the way home and called me a whore and a slut and all this stuff. Told me I was a stranger from now on and all this junk. And I can never see you again." She was sobbing again in spite of herself. "I told that bastard—" She heard the door downstairs. "Gotta go. I'll call you tonight," she whispered, and hung up quietly and waited for the footsteps on the carpeted stairway.

She said nothing when he knocked on the partially open door.

"We have to talk this out, Tiff. May I come in? There's no point in you sitting there not talking to me."

She sat perfectly still. Saying nothing. Looking at nothing. Trying not to show him anything. Let the bastard talk and then get out.

"I'm very sorry I slapped you but you pushed me too far, is all. I've never raised a hand to you in my life, as you well know. But I'm not sure that was the best way to raise a young lady, seeing how things worked out.

"Still. I love you very much, whether you want to accept that right now or not. I hope you'll understand that it was a combination of seeing you about to make a mistake that could ruin your life"—she allowed herself a smirk as he said this—"and the bad timing of it, coming right in the middle of what I think of as a marriage accident. I mean, here we are sitting in the middle of the wreckage of our home life, Mom leaving and all that, and you pull something like this." He shook his head in disbelief.

"I meant every word I said in the car. You've become a stranger to me. You're willful, self-centered, and this thing now—you've become wild. Dangerously so. And all the money and the luxury and no siblings—it's been a mistake. And we're both going to change.

"I'm going to have to start being a father to you for real. I'm going to start laying down the law, and even though it's for your own good, I know you're not going to like it. I allowed your mother to make the rules before, and she didn't care enough about you to do it, and I was too busy with my work. And you've been allowed to reach your teenage years without any parental controls. It isn't your fault. It's my fault. But all that is over now."

She took a deep breath, letting it out real slowly to show him how boring he was.

"We're going to start with the telephone. I don't want you to call Greg again. Is that perfectly clear? You just called him a few minutes ago, didn't you? I mean, even after what we just went through, you couldn't stand to not hear his voice, eh? So I can't trust you anymore with telephone privileges." He walked over to her bedroom phone and took out a large pocketknife.

She turned away while he sliced through the cord. She made her mind an absolute blank.

"I'm sorry I have to treat you this way. But you obviously are unwilling to meet me halfway. I can no longer allow you to have money of your own. You'll be given a small weekly allowance for your school

things. I don't want you going out of the house except
for . . ."

She had tuned it all completely out. She let herself
think about Greg and those eyes and those soft hands
and sweet ways, and let her mind daydream about how
it would be that first time. It was going to be soon,
she promised herself. No matter what she had to do.

". . . while I'm at it I'll take the pills and whatever
they gave you in the clinic today."

And she heard him searching for her purse and
opening it and going through it and taking things, and
she had to fight to keep from laughing out loud.

She had terminal cabin fever by the time the weekend rolled around, and her dad finally left the house
for the first time in days. She ran downstairs and
phoned Greg's number and held her breath, fingers
crossed, praying he'd be home. She heard him pick up
the phone and say hello on the second ring.

"Don't ask questions," she urged him breathlessly.
"If you want to make love to me, hurry over to the
house and pick me up. I'll be down by the highway
where you turn off, okay?"

"Huh? Oh, oh, yeah. Okay. I'll be right there."

"Hurry," she said, hanging up while he was saying,
"Don't worry. I will." And she dashed back upstairs
and put some fresh lip gloss on, which she didn't
need, and a little eye shadow, which she almost never
wore, and checked her hair, and sprinkled some more
perfume on, and made sure the pills were in her purse,
and scampered off across Ruffstone Terrace to the
highway. One great-looking fourteen-year-old virgin-
but-not-for-long.

"Hey," he shouted through the open window.

"You got here fast."

"I don't mess around," he said as she ran to the car
and got in.

"You got your dad's car." She was surprised.

"He's not home. I didn't ask. He and Mom took the wagon."

"Where do you want to go?" She said it almost absentmindedly.

"Huh?"

"I want to make love to you," she said, turning in the seat beside him, snuggling as close as she could. "Now."

In less than five minutes he was pulling off the road behind a motel-and-restaurant he knew about, and popping open the trunk. He gestured for her to get out. "Come on," he said. He'd produced an old army blanket.

"Where'd you get that?"

"We keep it in the trunk. For medical emergencies." He smiled.

"Is that what we are—a medical emergency?"

"It is for me, angel," he said, helping her step over the barbed-wire fence at the edge of a little triangle of woods.

"I'll nurse you back to health," she told him saucily, taking his hand.

"Yeah," he said, husky-voiced, looking at the way the soft cords gathered around that beautiful, high, perfect ass of hers. He crushed her against him. "Let's get you out of those pants."

"Ummmmm."

"God."

"Oh."

"Jesus."

'Ooooooooooohhhhh." Suddenly it all burst loose like a damn being dynamited. All the weeks of wanting and waiting. And he was trying to get her clothes off, pull the damn pants down, she was tearing at his shirt, and the traffic was whizzing by in the distance, and they fell down on the old blanket in the woods behind where the motel-and-greasy-spoon dumped its garbage, which was at this moment in the scheme of

events just about the sexiest, hottest, most wonderful
and lovely spot in the wide world of sports.

"You know how . . . long—"

"Nnnnnn."

"How long . . . I've been—"

"Oh. Oh, God." She'd waited so long for this. She'd
always known that they were going to be together
someday; she just hadn't dreamed it might be so soon.

"Oh, baby." His mouth was a hot fire and she let
him burn her tongue with it and tried to match the
inferno with her wetness.

"Jesus, God, oh." She was smooth and golden tan.
He loved the feel of those long, sleek, perfectly smooth
legs and he eased into her for the first time. Was there
anything like a cherry, sexy-legged, tight little fourteen-year-old pony who was in love with your ass. Oh,
she was so tight.

"I'll be gentle baby." Oh, yeah. I'll bust that cherry
for serious. Oh, yes. Ram this big mother home. Man,
a cat could scratch on that hard-on.

"Oh."

"You're so beautiful," he told her, kissing her gently now as he banged into her, "you're—so—beau-tee-
fullllll."

"I've wanted you for so long."

"Kiss." Her tanned skin was flawless, velvety,
baby-soft, and so incredibly smooth.

Their lips touched, he kept brushing up against her
mouth lightly with each stroke, pile-driving her back
into the mashed bed of weeds the blanket was covering, driving into her, over and over, putting it to the
foxy little lady.

". . . wanted you so long I've . . ."

"Yeah."

". . . I've . . . I . . ."

"Oh, yeah."

"Yes." He was running his soft hands over those

little childlike breasts with their small nipples. Little hot circles on the flesh.

"Ahhhh."

"You like this."

"Yes."

"Oh, yeah, baby."

"Unnnh. Greg."

"Kiss. Give me that hot, wet tongue." He speared down into her mouth, tonguing her, frenching her as he slid in and out.

"God. Oh, I love you."

"Come on. Oh. Come ON, DO IT OHHHHHHHH-HHH."

"AAAAAHHHHHH." He was almost laughing into her mouth. Into her hot, wet fourteen-year-old mouth. Burning his cock in that fiery, mellifluous tightness.

"Awwwww."

He didn't have to hold on for long. She came like a damn runaway train. God, he loved it all. Everything was coming together, in more ways than one. And they cuddled and snuggled and nuzzled, and before long, he was getting turned on by the situation, by the girl and the legs and the tight pussy and the bloody smear on the old blanket, and he was hardening again, and as he kissed her, he reached for the long, tanned legs and she opened herself to him, wetly.

"I need you," he whispered, gently, running his hot fingers down the fourteen-year-old chest. She could feel the burning heat all the way to her heart.

"I need you too."

"Are you mine?" He kissed her and then she answered.

"You know I am," she vowed.

"Tiff, I need to *know* you love me as much as I love you," he whispered in his soft but urgent way, his fingers moving down to her long, bare legs.

"I do love you," telling him between the kisses.

"Show me how much," he said to her. "Do you

want me, Tiff?" He was playing Hal Hunk again now
and guiding himself back into the cherry bowl.

"Yesssss. Oh, be easy, ohhhhhh. Oh, God, I'm so
hot." Her cat's eyes closed in ecstasy.

"Tell me. Show me. How much."

"I want you. Now NOW *NOWWWWWWWWWW-*
WWWWWW."

"Say it. SAY IT."

"NNNNNNNNNNNNNNNNNNNN." He'd settle for
that.

After the second time. Lying there spent. Soaked.
Bodies cooling in the open air. Listening to the muted
traffic noise and thinking. Was there anything as good
as that nice, fresh fourteen-year-old snatch. Hot damn,
Sam. I am jam—and Chocolate Thunder, he said to
himself, smiling.

"What's so funny?" she said, trying to cuddle.

"I was just remembering something else we could
share." And with the big Hollywood grin on his good-
looking puss, he brought out his blow. "Ever do any
of this?"

"What is it?" Her cat's eyes open wide again.

"It's the Real Thing," he sang off-key. He wore a
little gold thing on a chain and he used it to take just
a little bit out and he said, "Do it like this," and
snorted it.

"I can't do that."

"You can eat it, too."

"God."

"Try it. It's wild. Come on. We're going to share
goodies, right?"

"Right. Okay." He put a little on the spoon and she
cautiously inhaled. "Ooooooofffff. Oh! *GOD*, Greg.
GROSS!" She sneezed.

"You'll see," he said, one of the only true things
he'd said that day.

And she looked over at her hunk and laughed hap-
pily.

* * *

Frank Spain, who was then still just a kid named Frank Spanhower, had never been much of a cocksman. His childhood had been typical but sexually neuter. He also had a minor speech impediment that had not been any great asset with the young ladies. And when you're a kid, a speech problem can put you pretty far down in the pecking order. Even the severe acne cases, the freckle factories, the fat kids, the out-of-synch nerds, can look down on somebody with that sort of a defect.

As he matured, his initial sexual experiences had been embarrassing fiascos. Drawn to girls, he knew he was normal, just inexperienced, and this lack of self-confidence made him unduly shy. The work had a way of changing all that.

In the beginning he had been a gofer. The mob then operated from the fresh-vegetable storefronts along Produce Row in St. Louis, using their legit fronts to launder racket bucks. Frank started working for Mr. Ciprioni because they liked the kid, felt sorry for him, and had him run errands around the office. The kid knew nothing from mobs. But they paid him well, and he and Vince Ciprioni, the youngest son of The Man, were school chums and fellow gun nuts. Vince was always trying to get him to teach him how to shoot.

"Damn, you're good with a rifle," he told him one day. Frank had talked his mom into letting him finally junk his Red Ryder BB gun and get a .22, and within a week there wasn't a living shitbird within ten blocks of their house.

"Not too bad, I guess," he said. He knew he was good. He'd gone to Boy Scout camp one year and beat all the other boys easily first time he'd ever shot skeet.

He never bragged about it, but when the boys found out they shared a genuine interest in and fascination with weapons Frank admitted to Vince that he'd started packing.

"You're carrying! In school?"

"Yep." He explained his cousin had "got beat up real bad" by a gang who ran the streets near his house.

"They fuck with me," he said, taking care with the difficult consonants, "I'm ready." He patted his pocket.

Vince's eyes were rivited to the pocket where the hardware rested.

"Were you in school when Jarrod's revolver fell out in art class?"

"Yeah. I 'bout shit." They laughed over the kid who'd moved to Missouri from San Berdoo, and who affected the California teen-gang style replete to out-moded D.A. and the much discussed pawnshop .38 he carried with him to class.

"I don't think Old Lady Shindleford ever even caught it," Vince said, laughing, "the fuckin' thing dropped out like a damn bomb. I'm surprised it didn't go off." They both roared. "Can I see it?" he said with eyes glued to the pocket.

"Umm." Frank smiled and pulled out the piece. A Smith & Wesson with the short barrel and the hammer filed off.

"Can you hit anything with it?" Vince asked, aim-ing the gun.

"Once inna while," Frank said quietly. And that was the only time Vince Ciprioni ever saw the gun until the day Frank shot the four boys who'd jumped Vince down in back of the Rialto. Four of them. All with metal pipes. Frank shot the four of them deader than dogs right there in the alley down in back of the Rialto. And he didn't know what to do with the gun, so Vince made him give it to him and he took it to his father and told him what had happened and what Frank had done, and his old man just took the piece from him and told the boys never to say anything about it again.

The Man called Frank in by himself. Frank figured he'd tell him how grateful he was for saving his son's life and that shit, but all he did was say, "You're a good kid. But can you keep your mouth shut?" Frank nodded yes. "Okay," he said, the hard Ciprioni eyes boring into him for a long time until he'd seen whatever he'd been hoping to see. "Take 'er easy," he said, and that was all. No thank you for saving Vincent's ass. Nothing. Ehh. Frank shrugged and went about his business.

Vincent, on the other hand, couldn't shut up about it. Vince would tell him thanks about five times a day until after a week or so Frank finally had to ask him to please for crissakes shaddup about it. And the event didn't make him feel tough, or recklessly invulnerable, the way it affects some people, nor did he have any desire to clip out the stories about the killings and start a scrapbook. Oddly, it meant nothing to him. He handled it the way some kids would climb a tall tree or knock a softball over the left-field wall. He was a shooter. But soon after the incident he started calling himself Frank Spain.

Secretly he figured one day he'd be hoisting a box of fresh lettuce and the boss would come up and slip a hundred-dollar bill in his pocket, but it never happened. What Mr. Ciprioni gave him turned out to be something much more valuable. He gave him his trust.

A few months after the shooting The Man called him back into a storeroom and told him he was having a problem. A guy was creating some problems for him. It was a situation that required a solution. A final solution, he said. A piece of work like Frank had done in back of the Rialto. That kind of work.

"Well, now, then, there," Spain said, in his best James Dean.

"You understand what I'm saying to you?"

Frank nodded that he understood.

"I need somebody good. Somebody who can keep his mouth shut and do a piece of work like that. The

money I pay for that is . . .'' He pulled an envelope
out and started counting. He'd never seen so much
money in all his life.

"I'll do it," Spain said.

"You sure about that? I know you're good but you're
very young. It's one thing to stop some punks hurting
a friend of yours, another thing to clip somebody cold.
If you're not sure, don't take it.''

Spain said nothing, but he returned Mr. Ciprioni's
stare for a full beat and reached slowly for the envelope. He let him take it and put it in his pocket, and
then he told Frank the name and where the man lived.
It was a downtown hotel. And that night Frank went
down to the Milburn and walked in and took the elevator up to the fourth floor and knocked, and when
the door opened, he asked the man if he was who the
contract was for, and the guy said he was, and the kid
pulled out the hammerless Smith and put a round right
in his heart, turning and going down the emergency
stairs, deciding this time he'd get rid of the piece himself. And from then on he became Mr. Ciprioni's
shooter.

Gaetano Ciprioni was not in Tony Gee's family,
which was the St. Louis mob of that time. The boss
man explained the hierarchy to Spain.

"This is nothing here. It's shit. All the action is in
Kansas City far as Missouri goes, and Kansas City
doesn't have shit. St. Louis isn't anything serious in
the organization. It's all run by Chicago anyway. The
big man there is gonna retire soon. When he does, the
man gonna inherit the whole middlewest country is my
main man. He is to me what I am to you, you understand?''

"Yeah.''

"He's gonna change things. When he does, I'll be
moving up to The Council. You don't know what that
is, do you?'' Frank shook his head no. "It's the head
of all the families. *ALL* the families, even the big New

York families. The Council controls everything. I'll
be working there. I'm going to be needing someone
here I can trust. To do jobs of work for me. Mostly
here in the Midwest. The pay will be outstanding, I
can promise you."

"Okay."

"Okay, we understand each other." They shook
hands. Spain never could get used to how the Italianos
liked to shake hands all the time. But one thing about
The Man: if he told you something like this, well, you
could take it to the bank.

Spain was what his sainted mother would have called
a late bloomer. He'd already worked his way to the top
level of his chosen profession by the time he met Pat,
and his new self-confidence allowed him to approach
someone for the first time.

She was an ordinary girl, although he saw her as
quite beautiful. Mary Pat Gardner, who worked for his
neighborhood dry-cleaner, which—many years later—
he wanted to tell her had been a family operation, a
family laundry for money as well as clothing, but he
never told her about his work. He "traveled." He was
in "sales."

One day he walked in and she looked especially ra-
diant and he told her so.

"You look real pretty today."

"Thank you," she beamed. "How's life treating
you?" She took his dry-cleaning sack and started writing on a pad. "I'll get your things in just a second."

"No hurry." He'd seen her in there when he brought
his clothing in each week for a year or so, and finally
he'd worked up enough nerve to ask her out. His
speech impediment was almost gone. Frank no longer
stammered if he concentrated on what he was saying.
He was prepared to say, "Would you like to go to the
movies with me Friday night?" That's what he planned
to ask her. But what he said was, "Mary Pat?"

And she looked up from the order she was writing and said, "Uh-huh?"

"Would you like to know to the noovie, MOW to the noovie, GO to the MOVIE WITH ME?" Christ christ christ, is there no mercy no justice no rest no slack?

He could still recall how he shriveled with the hopelessness of it as she smiled at him and said, "Sure. When?"

"Mmmm. Okay," he mumbled, starting to pick up his dry-cleaning, so nervous, so blown away by his bungled attempt that it took a few beats before he realized she'd said yes. He couldn't believe it. It was a major victory of his life. The only conquest he could remember being genuinely proud of. More challenging and frightening than a dozen contracts.

She hadn't said "I guess so," even. Nothing tentative or halfhearted. A big smile and a warm, quick "Sure. When?" He loved it. He fell instantly in love with her. To him she was beauty, smoldering desire, femininity, and sex incarnate. And he thought she liked him too.

He proposed to her on their second date, surprising her with a ring he'd been carrying with him. She accepted, surprising both of them, somewhat bemused by the size of the stone, which she suspected was glass. The next day she was walking by a jewelry shop and just happened to take it in.

"Mr. Plotkin?"

"Yes?"

"Remember me? Mary Pat Gardner?"

"Shirley Goodell's cousin?"

"The same. Mr. Plotkin, I want your opinion on a family heirloom." She thrust a hand under his wrinkled puss. "My aunt left me this. I was told it had some value." He screwed something into his eye and peered at it, holding her hand.

"*Oi veh*. That's about five karats of perfect diamond

you got there, child. Yes. I'd have to say that had some value." He looked again. "Nice color. Not a bubble. Nothing. It's a show-stopper," he said.

They were married not long after. Within a year Spain had fathered a little girl. Outwardly he maintained a family life of seeming normalcy. A salesman or consultant or troubleshooter (he loved that one!), depending on who he was talking to, with a checkable "legend," a complete fake background that had been prepared by experts to withstand fed-level scrutiny, with the appearance of upwardly mobile, upper-middle-class wealth. A typical, if atypically rich, American mercantile transient.

Had he been a normal man to begin with, or even in a normal profession, it might have been different. An accountant with seasonal work overloads, a car dealer with long hours, every line has its occupational drawbacks. But Spain's vocation took him out of the city unexpectedly, sometimes for long periods, and the nature of the business made him secretive.

"You never talk to me," Pat so often would say.

"I talk. I just don't have that much to say."

"I don't even know what you do. Most men share their work with their wives. It can't be that boring."

"Believe me," he say, shaking his head in exasperation, "you don't know how lucky you are. Just be glad I don't bring my work home with me like some guys." Wasn't that the truth? "I decided a long time ago I'd seen too many marriages sour because the guy was always taking his job to bed with him. I leave my work outside. I'll take care of the selling, the money to put the food on the table. You take care of making us a good home." And so on.

And time has a way of passing so quickly. And before you know it, if you aren't careful, you can dedicate yourself to your calling but sacrifice your personal life in the bargain. He let his family slip through his fingers.

"I like a dedicated man. That's one thing about you, Frank," The Man said to him. "And you keep your mouth shut. It's a rare commodity in this day and age. Even my own guys. I hear 'em goin' around putting their mouth all over themselves, callin' each other guinea this and greaseball that. And worst of all, this son of mine talks about *wops*, which is a word sets my teeth on edge. I don't even like to hear the colored called niggers. You—I don't think I ever heard you say dago even, am I right?"

Frank shrugged. "I just don't think like that."

"My son. My youngest. He looks up to you so much. Ever since that time you whacked those boys. It's all I hear. Papa, Frank shot all four of 'em, he'd say. Hit four moving targets and *three head shots*. How many times I've heard that when the kid and I talk about you. You never said shit to me. You never asked him for nothin'. Never asked me for a dime."

"I was glad I was there that day."

"Yeah. Me too," It was a father talking to his son after the baseball game. Telling him how proud he was of the homer the kid clobbered in the bottom of the ninth. And the kind of dedication he gave to The Man was the kind you only give to family. Perhaps, when you think about it, that was his real family. It was certainly the one he devoted his time and energies to.

First, when he failed to hold his wife, it was as if the bedrock on which he was standing suddenly cracked open, and now . . . the thing with his daughter, he felt himself slipping into the abyss.

He was sitting there in the living room in the darkness, waiting for his little girl and thinking about what he could have done to keep Pat, and he heard her coming up the steps and opening the front door.

"You could have had him drive right up. No reason for you to walk all the way from the highway. I wasn't going to go after him with a ball bat. Of course it's not a bad idea."

She didn't even look at him, just started up the stairs.

"That's the last time you'll be allowed out," he said to her. "You get three strikes like everybody else. You've had two. One more and I call the juvenile authorities and turn you over to them. I can't chain you in your room. If the authorities can't take care of you I'll have to hire special guards. Whatever it takes, we'll make sure—" And the sound of Tiff's bedroom door slamming shut on his words put a period to his thought.

Inside her room, Tiff made her decision. She had asked Greg about what they were going to do and he wanted to cut out for Florida. She said, Let's sleep on the idea and they'd talk at school tomorrow. Roger Nunnaly had his fill of school and they could go with Roger in his car. They'd all take off for the South. Lots of fun in the sun. Lots of wild scenes on the beach. It sounded great to Tiff. She started packing and then realized she'd never get the clothes out of the house past . . . him. She dumped her books out of her voluminous book bag and began to pack the essentials into the bag and her biggest purse.

She had some money saved. Quite a bit, in fact. And there was the jewelry. She packed her dowery in silence.

And downstairs, the man who calls himself Spain sits quietly in the shadows.

"Are we really going to leave? I just can't believe it," she had asked Greg, her cat's eyes blinking as she looked at her white knight.

"Believe it," he told her, starting to load the car. Are we really gonna turn out a sweet little pussy like this? Does a snake have lips? he thought to himself, grinning and whistling softly as he packed the last of their meager belongings in Roger's car. He'd put this little fox to work for him.

Within twenty-four hours of the kids' departure everyone involved in the respective families knew they'd

left together, including Pat and her insurance lothario,
not to mention the cops. Too many people were involved in this. Whole families had suddenly been
turned upside down. Spain had ended up having to talk
to the police several times, which to him was the
equivalent of repeatedly plunging his hands into boiling water, but anathema or not, his daughter had disappeared. He had to find her.

"They'll catch them before the day is out," Roger
Nunnaly's father had assured everyone, "that car will
stand out a mile."

The private Spain had suddenly become very public,
sharing secrets with perfect strangers, not to mention
the cops, all of whom were now involved in his personal decision-making.

People he'd never seen in his life were seated in his
living room telling him ridiculous things about runaway hotlines and dope and how young girls can use
sex to ensare a poor, innocent boy like Greg Dawkins,
whom Spain had nailed for what he was first time he
saw him, and some kid named Roger who sounded
like a crackhead known to everyone but his own parents. And Spain sat there letting it all lap over him as
they talked about how his wife and daughter had *both*
run away from him, and almost overnight life had become a steamroller that was crushing the shards of
what remained of his shattered ego.

But there was no loving wife to take him aside and
say, There, there now, honey, it's going to be all right.
You tried your best, Daddy. You just forgot that fa-
thering is a skill as well as an art. And it's a skill that
demands practice as well as good intentions. And nobody was there to tell him that Tiff was hurting too.
That when you're fourteen years old, frustrations and
humiliations are deep knife wounds. Wounds that can
be fatal if not treated in time.

He was alone to take it all and deal with it. And
that next night, after all the Dawkinses and Nunnalys

and police and juvenile authorities had cleared out, he sat there in the dark feeling like he was having a heart attack, and it all came to sit on him with its enormous weight of guilt, and he sat there sobbing and hurting in the darkness of his fine home and began paying dues with currency he didn't even know he had.

And he was still there the next morning, sitting there on the carpeted stairway, racked with the dry heaves, on the edge of breakdown, consumed with guilt, nailed by despair, and absolutely, painfully, heartbreakingly alone.

And half of him was sorry for himself and the other half wasn't, and slowly, like the hard, seemingly stout heart of a diseased gum tree, he began to crack apart deep inside.

So Spain sits there on the edge of his reality, in the gathering debris of his life, well and truly screwed, blued, and subdued.

And the shadow of death edges closer.

Eichord fingered the edges of a few cards and scowled slightly. Christian's Cards and the ritzy mall in which it was situated—both brimming with purposeful, moneyed Californians and a smattering of ordinary commoners like himself—were as far removed and remote as the constellation of Andromeda. Another distant and far-removed spot on the planet, Chicago by name, kept nudging him.

He felt totally out of place in the shop, among genteel, immaculate women clerks and genteel, immaculate customers who regularly frequented such a place. Eichord stood looking at humorous greeting cards in the midst of the L.A. work day, such as it was; a homicide cop feeling the proverbial bull-in-china-shop as he sweated through his short-sleeved shirt, handgun harness, and stylish polyester.

The weight of the heavy revolver in the shoulder rig, the incongruity of the surroundings, the knowledge he was looking at cutesy cards with all that bad steel under his arm, made him feel ludicrous, out of place, quite uncomfortable. A trickle of perspiration trailed down his spine as a small and perfectly coiffed woman with a slightly rodentlike face asked him pleasantly, "Can I help you with something?"

He smiled automatically as he shook his head. "Just looking. Thanks." Brilliant. She would never have guessed you were looking. He was standing there trying to figure out which of the crazy cards a little girl would like. He was trying to recall what her age was now. He had her birthdate written down somewhere, but he'd forgotten where. He looked at another card and it made even less sense than the last one.

What would a little girl like to get in the mail? He'd tuck a twenty in there. Kids that age (what age?) would like money better than anything else. But would she be uncomfortable getting money? Would she remember him?

And what would her mother say when Lee Anne asked her who this man was?

"Oh, you remember Jack, Uncle Jack the cop?

What kind of a favor would he be doing a little girl whom he never saw anymore. Somebody into whose life he'd insert himself once or twice a year with a phone call where neither party had anything to say. Somebody growing up so fast. She'd been what? Fifty inches tall when he'd seen her last. A year ago when he'd called she told him how big she was, and she seemed to have sprung up a couple of feet overnight. They'd be unrecognizable if they saw each other again. But he couldn't let go.

He pulled another card from the rack, a ridiculous-looking caricature saying "You know there's nothing I wouldn't do for you. So this year, when your birthday rolls around again . . ." And you opened the accordion fold and the caricature assured the recipient, ". . . that's what I'm going to do for you: NOTH-

ING.'' He sighed and pulled the card and its envelope off the rack and went over to pay the lady.

Eichord thanked her and put his change in his pocket and walked out into the sunlight. He opened his car door and pitched the sport coat onto the back of the seat next to him. He was already drenched. Why was he so hot? It was just a card.

He wondered what Edie would say or what she would think when she saw a letter from him to her daughter. He thought about how she'd react to the twenty and he decided against sending any money. He'd write a note instead.

He was going to lose them, he knew. He was losing that sweet little girl too. The distance and time would do it, if nothing else. Life can be a bitch, he thought, wondering what would happen to him next. Would the fault crack open swallowing the shopping mall, the cars, him, the rat lady—all of us? Would the whole fucking thing fall into the ocean?

Eichord took the transmission lever out of Park and drove out of the expansive and posh shopping center, and as he drove by a metal trash barrel, he lowered the window and threw the card, envelope, and the sack into the trash and drove slowly out into the traffic, shaking his head as he shivered in the icy blast of AC.

What he ought to do was, he should go back and pluck that card out of the trash. But in that half-second he felt the chill of the eyes of the man at the airport. The man looking at him over the top of a greeting card. A wise guy's eyes. And Eichord shivered again, sweat chilling on him like the foreboding of death frightening the soul of some fey visionary. And the case intruded on the flash of imagery, as he realized he was leaving L.A. knowing less than when he'd started.

Somebody once asked Eichord, "What do you *do?* I mean, you know, what does a detective *do?*"

And Eichord said, "You look for footprints in the

cottage cheese." It got a laugh at the time, but hell, who's kidding who? There it was.

The "Eyeball Murders" were anybody's guess. Unrelated kills except for the assassin's trademark. The victims had their eyes shot out. It could be the old mob-style punishment hit. Or one of those and a couple of copycat kills. Or any damn thing. Whatever it was, Jack hadn't even a glimmer of a clue. It was, by the looks of it, another fine fucking mess and he couldn't wait to be away from Lala Land, and back to Buckhead, where NOBODY knew who the fuck John Frankenheimer was.

She had inherited her mother's skin, the kind of pigment that tanned to a golden coppery lustrousness, skin so smooth and pliant as to bedazzle and cause grown men to get a little catch in the throat at the sight of it when it appeared in any degree of expanse, such as displayed in a string bikini or a tiny halter top and short shorts. And that was Greg's next move, to get as much of that lovely skin showing as possible.

She had her father's eyes of many colors. Slate-gray to blue-green depending on the light. Greg gave her eyes his biggest smile and a wide sparkle of Hollywood white gleamed in his dark, beautiful face.

"Ummmm." He nuzzled her, roughly licking at her like a big puppy, leaving little love marks on her neck and moving down the side of her throat as he gently eased the little top off. "I could eat you up, you know that?" he said.

She made a contented murmur as he ran the tip of his tongue across her chest and down toward the still-rather-flat breasts and small nipples. He said something softly to her, but it was muffled in her chest and she said, "What?"

"I said you know where I want to take you?" he repeated, looking up at her as his tongue flicked out

at her in little darting moves like a bullfrog after June
bugs.

"Where? To bed again?"

"Of course. For sure. But I want to take you to one
of those great ski places like Vail or Aspen. You
know—get a little cabin of some kind all alone up there
where the powder is really bitchin'. Like on the ad-
vanced slope and like, uh, you know, just kick back."

"Oh, Greg," she purred, "it's just like I thought it
would be between us." He nuzzled her again and she
gazed down at him with her wide-set cat's eyes and let
her hand tangle in his curly hair.

"Do you know I love you?"

"Yes," she breathed. "And I love you, too."

"Ummm." He nuzzled and kept talking into her
body and she laughed softly. God, how she adored
him. It was working out, after all. It was so good, and
he was gentle and considerate, and she knew it was
going to be wonderful between them now.

"What?" She laughed.

"Can't you understand English, girl?"

"No. Not when you're talking into my belly button,
I can't."

"Hello," he said. "Anybody home?" he said to her
navel.

"Yeah, I'm home."

"Uh huh. Me too." He kissed her stomach tenderly
and along her tanned rib cage.

"Ah! That tickles."

"Hah," he said, licking her side and making her
laugh. She couldn't believe how beautiful he was.

"You're my movie-star hunk, you know that."

"I've got a hunk for you, all right."

"Now be a good boy and don't talk dirty," she said
as he started working his way up her chest again. Nuzzling, chewing, licking, taking her in his teeth very
gently. Blowing his hot Hollywood breath over her,
bewitching her with his soap-opera eyes and his magic

tongue. Working her. Playing her the way you tire a
fish before you net it, keeping his rod stiff and high,
taking his time, playing it out, never losing his patience, making the act a little art form all its own.

"Ummmm." He kissed her hard on the mouth and
said softly in his supercon voice, "Oh, baby, we could
like be skiing the advanced slope and then we go back
to our little ski chalet, our cabin on the mountaintop,
a Swiss lodge like in the movies, and like we get
snowbound and just make love for weeks on end. Lay
in a nice supply of goodies and get in a big old fur
coat or somethin' and snuggle down in front of the
fire"—and she kissed him on the mouth as he
spoke"—get logs once in a while, and sip some brandy
and toot a little stuff and, um, you know, just watch
the snow fall."

"Watch the snow fall," she said, a twinkle in her
eye.

"Does that sound good?"

"It sounds wonderful, Greg."

"Yeah. It sounds good to me, too." He kissed her
very gently, kissing the corners of her mouth and then
below her nose, then in the hollow of her chin, then
in her dimples, and then boxing the compass around
her lips and then letting his long, Harry Hollywood
tongue dart between those lips, and even her mouth
tasted wet and hot like a warm honeypot.

"Oh, Greg—I want you now." She was breathing
her hot breath against his throat and cheek and her
eyes were closed.

"Oh, yeah? Let's just see about that." And he
touched her. "Baby. Ouch. You burned my hand."
And she said something he couldn't catch and he let
his hand go back in again and said, "Hey, you're all
wet down here. Did I tell you to get all wet like that?"

"I couldn't help it. You make me that way."

"Do you really want me, Tiff?" He was watching
himself now as he always liked to do, chumping some

little bitch off with his slick-stud number, not looking in a mirror but going off somewhere in his head and watching his performance. Pimping a girl off. Getting her off with his Charlie Charm shit. Smooth as stuff and double tough as Memphis Garrett Snuff. Run that game right *down* her throat, understand? Oh, he liked it when it was like this, when he could play the girl like a musical instrument, make her hum and sing. Make her jump and shout and knock herself out. It was making him so hard to watch himself inside his good-looking head and he held himself on his elbows right over her. "You really want me, baby?"

"Yes. Yes. YES."

"Ask me nice, then. Beg me for it if you want it."

"Please."

"What?" He let the head go in, it was already slick. and it seared him with her cherry-red fire.

"YES, YES, YEEEESSSSSS."

Don't ever doubt there are some boss players out there who *know* how to take a little girl and make her a love slave. Just 'cause a few of 'em are thirteen, fourteen, don't think they don't got the ole diamond-cutter's touch for the big O. Cold got to be. Down, Jim. He could see himself getting her off now and hanging in there where a lesser stud would let 'er buck and kick loose. Hanging in and gritting his pearly whites in concentration, Stayhard Incorporated, and if you think I'm sexy, if you really, truly *DO* want my body, come *on,* girl, and tell me about it. Tell me more. Work with me, Annie.

"Nnnnnnnn," she responded to Dr. Feelgood's teen romance.

"Yes," he said, twenty-four hours a day and we're up all night.

"Uh." Slick as seals.

"Yeah." Fall in love with some of this. And Fourth of Julysville.

Oh, my. This is what they were talking about at

school. Oh. No wonder. God. Oh. Oh, yes. Greg. Oh, you sweet, you perfect . . . oh . . . OH GOD . . . OOOOOOOOOOOOHHHHHHHHHHH!

It's all he can do to make himself stay in her and keep the kisses going, a little soft reggae posturepedic boom-chickaboom-chickaboom-and TCOB, the doctor is still on the job, a few little gentle nuzzlings into the sweaty shadows, an endearment or two. Nice J.O.B., he thinks, and he's up and away and off chopping up some Hollywood high on the Formica.

"Let's do some lines, angel." Superstud.

Spain's first nightmares are gentle and deceptively lacking portent.

Even though it was only a nightmare, he saw it clearly, brightly, transcribed lucidly on the dream screen of his mind, a vivid and incredible scenario that was remarkably detailed and agonizingly real. And because of the absence of threat, it was all the more frightening to him. Unlike a dream where you're pursued by bad guys through a temple, jump into a waiting car, and just as you speed off down the hill, you run out of gas, and the nightmare comprises those seconds of fear as you hope the car's momentum from the downhill slope will carry it over the top of the hill to safety, but as it reaches the last few inches, the car begins to inch to a stop then starts rolling backward and the dream is your struggle to get out of the car as it rolls back toward them . . . unlike that sort of a dream, the nightmare he sees carried no overt threat. And later, when the violent dreams begin to assail him, he will remember this dream as benign and harmless, but when he has this dream, one of his first bad nightmares, it shakes him to the quick.

Here is the dream: it is afternoon. He is the sportscaster on a local radio station. No, he doesn't know why either, he was never on the air in his life and has little interest in sports. He is the color man, half of a famous color-and-play-by-play team, and the radio station is in the basement of a large metropolitan bank. The walls of the studio are lime green. He is quite successful and popular, and he enjoys a reputation for being adept at baseball, excellent at basketball, and the number-one color man for football games. These are all well-delineated details.

He is on the air. It is halftime at a big game. Saturday afternoon, and he can smell the smoke there in the hot, sweaty pressbox of the ball club.

The roar of the crowd.

"Unitas drops back," his play-by-play man says, "he's going to throw the bomb! Three seconds to halftime on the clock, Frank."

He responds without a trace of a lisp or hint of a stammer as he says, "That's right, Gil, three seconds and Unitas is in trouble, he's got to let it go now or— WOW! There it goes! What a cannon! Johnny Unitas gets off a perfect, textbook-classic spiral, what a gorgeous ball, and . . . unbelievable, Raymond Berry's got it in the end zone! A ninety-five-yard bullet out of the Unitas rifle and the Baltimore Colts end the half with a six-point lead over the Green Bay Packers as the gun sounds, twenty to fourteen."

"Into the spot, and you guys are sounding good in the truck," the voice says over the nightmare intercom. Dream logic confuses television and radio, but Spain is unaware of this and dreams on.

"Telegram, Frank," an engineer says, handing him the yellow Western Union envelope. He opens it and reads:

FRANK YOU ARE A WORTHLESS PIECE OF SHIT. I WISH YOU WERE DEAD. And it is signed Sylvester P. Landis III, and there is an address.

"Gil," he asks his phantom colleague, "who is Sylvester P. Landis the third?"

"Never heard of him. What's the matter, Frank?"

"Here," he says, "read this."

"Damn," the man says. "And you don't know this guy?"

"Never saw the name before. What ya think? Think this might be a prank?"

"Oh, hell, yes. Just some whacko out there listening to us. Throw it in the trash. Come on—forget it, man. Let's get the stats and go to work. You take care of the halftime and I'll pick up at the end of the color, okay?"

"Fine," Spain says, and he does a flawless halftime job. The baton twirlers, the marching bands, the Sousa music, he makes it all flow like fine wine. The rest of the game goes beautifully. At the end of the game he goes back to the station and there is a big fuss made by someone out in the parking lot. The men all go outside and find that the police have apprehended a weird-looking crazy who has defaced Frank's new BMW with a spray can of red paint. He has printed "piece of shit" on the trunk and "Frank sucks" on the passenger door in neatly sprayed aerosol Day-Glo.

"Do you know this man, Frank?" one of the uniformed cops says to him.

"No. Who the hell is he?"

"Claims he knows you. He says his name is Sylvester P. Landis."

"Some whacko. Look." He shows the cop the telegram.

"Did you send this?" The cops are looking at the weird crazy. He is a goofy-looking guy with a crazed, spaced-out expression. Thick, Coke-bottle glasses, horrible acne, bad teeth, a total loser.

"Sure, pig, so what? I wish Frank was dead."

"Uh huh. Mr. Landis . . . you are under arrest." And they drag the weirdo off reading him his rights, handcuffed, and ease into the back of a waiting squad car.

Time passes. Frank (Spain) learns the guy is a harmless crank who likes to send sportscasters hate mail.

Spain seems to realize he is dreaming at this point and wonders what the hell all of this has to do with anything. But the dream plays on. The spray painting of the BMW is the first act of vandalism the crazy has ever engaged in, and he is released. There are calls and mail, but Frank ignores it all. Then, one night he returns home and finds his apartment trashed. Across the wall in red Day-Glo is the legend I WISH FRANK WAS DEAD. The police arrest Landis. He confesses. There is a trial. He is found guilty and sentenced to two years in jail for Defacing A Sportscaster's Property, but before he can serve time, he commits suicide in his cell. He has left a suicide note. Spray-painted in red on the cell wall it says: FRANK IS A PIECE OF SHIT.

The radio management sense that Frank is on the verge of a nervous breakdown, but now this horrible crazy is gone and perhaps he will be able to lead a normal life again without someone bothering him constantly. They insist Frank take a week off. He does so. A few days later, back from a relaxing few days in the Bahamas, tanned and refreshed, he drops by the station.

"Er, uh, hullo, Frank," one of the newsmen says sheepishly. "What a, uh, nice surprise." He acts nervous and evasive.

"Frank! Oh! How nice," another of the employees says. "Did you enjoy your vacation?" Everyone is so uptight to see him. Down in the newsroom he is standing there idly, relaxing, just grooving around, reading the wire copy, when he notices part of a mailing tube there in the trash. As he sees the crude printing on the torn cardboard tube, the dream sort of shifts into high gear and begins to take on a glow, as if a light had just come on saying IMPORTANT PART OF DREAM . . . BEWARE! The bogeyman part is coming.

It is the unmistakable handwriting of the one called Sylvester P. Landis. And suddenly, even before

Spain/Frank knows what is in the tube, his legs and arms are covered in icy, fear-inspired pinpricks of apprehension and paranoia.

"Hey," he collars a newsman, "what came in this tube?"

"Huh?" The newsman shifts his gaze uneasily, refusing to look him in the eye. "I dunno."

"Come on, Bill. What the hell is going on?"

"See Schmertz." So realistic. Another station employee named Sid Mertz. They call him Schmertz. All the details crystal clear. Right down to the mundane trivia and who-cares minutiae.

"Okay, Sid," Frank confronts the man, "what's the deal here?"

"We weren't going to show you, Frank. You know. It's probably a prank." He's sweating now. "Go down in the boiler room."

"The boiler room?" Schmertz nods affirmative and Frank races down the stairs. The boiler room looks just like the basement of the school he went to when he was a kid. And there in the trash, waiting to be burned, is the rest of the mailing tube filled with papers. He retrieves the package from the trash bin and reads the address on the torn tube. It says, in part, FRANK—THE PIECE OF SHIT c/o the radio station. And the printing is unmistakably that of the dead man Landis.

The first piece of paper inside the tube is an ugly, primitive, crayon sketch of a crudely drawn clown. He remembers he drew it back in the second grade and they laughed at him. Now it is so bizarre and frightening to see there in the tube addressed by the crazy. Landis has penciled all kinds of filth around the clown drawing saying things like THIS IS YOU, SHIT FACE, I WISH YOU WERE DEAD. All the usual. Then the rest of the package is what really scares him. It frightens him so badly he wakes up, shivering, wide awake from the folds of the nightmare. Because inside the remnants of the tube are photos of his mother and father that were burned up when their home burned to the ground back in Agency, Missouri, over thirty years ago, at least five years before Sylvester P. Landis III was born.

The radio station with its busy teletype machines, and the offices he conjures up in the basement of a bank, actually were those of a finance company. They were places the boy, now the man who calls himself Spain, had run in terror to hide. Places that had spawned oppressive fears and memories of painfully vivid horrors.

Halftime at a football game had been another moment of heart-stopping fright for the child. Names and places of the past meant to conjure up stinging humiliation as he remembered the rankling cachinnation of his tormentors. Unforgivable wrongs once experienced in a boiler room just like the one in his dream. Fears, terrors, embarrassments, and cruelties that had led him down that alley toward his first kills.

Even the name—Sylvester P. Landis III, in truth a freely associated amalgam of humiliating and dread memories from his childhood past. A past shaped of events that had pointed him, like a gun, whenever his masters had directed him toward another target. A past that had rebound like a freak ricochet blasting apart his own family.

And Spain shook the dream off instantly upon awakening, with at first only the vaguest eidolons lingering in his mind. But he wouldn't let it alone and he was haunted by the evanescent image of that obscene clown, and he worried it in his mind the way your tongue keeps darting into the hollows of a newly broken tooth. You know better, but some things you just can't leave alone.

For over five weeks he'd wooed her, played her, bedded her repeatedly, romanced her, dazzled her with his fancy tonguework, done his whole repertoire of rap dances, all the while this gentle, handsome, soft-spoken, intelligent youngster is introducing her to cocaine and progressively kinkier sex and the fast lane. And he is getting her primed, ready, willing. Waiting for the right moment when he can turn her just so, take her out onto the dangerous shoulder of the road outside the fast lane, where only the special players run.

For more than five weeks he'd worked her like a twelve-pound outlaw cat precariously attached to a #303 Zebco, the monofilament stretched to the breaking point, and no net in hand, working her over into the shallows by the bank, sinking that hook in deeper and deeper, that cruelly barbed hook that only the hardiest fish could ever work loose, careful to keep that rod pointing skyward, taking up all the slack, but never too much, never forcing it. Watching himself play his new fish. All pro and totally up for it every time. Enslaving her with drugs and sex and romantic desire and promise. Letting the jism of his healthy, horny, Hollywood hotshots lubricate their one-way love affair, greasing her body for the long, hot slide down the dope banister.

"Greg, I love you so much," she purred to him.

"You're one sweet pussycat. You know that?"

"Do you love me as much as I love you?"

"You know I do, angel." He only needed to touch her around the throat and chin and mouth a few times and those full movie-star lips had her rarin' to go. He was an expert at measuring the response time and he was proud of how quickly she opened her petals to him now, a few seconds and she was hot to trot. He'd brought her a long way in just a few weeks. But he was already beginning to bore of the game, and the more he tired of her treasures, the more difficult it would be for him to sustain the illusion.

"Have you loved these weeks together as much as I have, Tiff?"

"Oh, God. You know I have. I've almost forgotten what it was like before. I want you for my husband, Greg. I want us to settle down and raise a family together," she said, her cat's eyes blinking. Her maternal instincts were very strong.

"That's what I want too. Look, I can just see us in that little snowbound log cabin up in the mountains, and the snow is falling, and we put another log on the fire, cuddle close together under the blankets, and make our first child together. Wouldn't that be wonderful?"

"Ummmm."

They kiss. First soft, little tender smooches that he knows will light her fire, and then he's going to work with his hands and the hard, probing, wet kisses begin, and just as she starts lighting up, he pulls back a little and looks at her with his sexy California blues and says, "If you help me, doll baby, we can have all that right away."

"What do you mean? Of course I'll help you." She smiles.

He kisses her and goes over and gets something out of his pocket and brings it back to the bed and shows it to her.

"What's that?"

"*That* is our ticket outta here, Tiff. That's our nest egg. That's what's going to let us be together and raise a family."

She looks at the little vial with her wide cat's eyes. "Yeah?"

"Dynamite White," he tells her. "Serpico, White Cloud Nine, Supersnow! I've got a way for us to get it all, baby doll, and I mean now. Me and Roger have this guy who can get us enough of this shit that one big sale will set us up and you and I can cut. We'll be out of this forever."

"Wow."

"Yeah. Thing is it is going to take one shitload of bucks to get us together. And we are stoney, man."

"I thought we had lots of money. I gave you all I had and the jewelry and you had the—"

"Yeah. Right. But we been in the Deuville for thirty-eight days. Double occupancy is a bitch. Just our motel bill alone has tapped us out. And we've *got* to get a score while we can or we'll lose our man here, and I'll end up a bag boy somewhere and you'll be waiting tables in a greasy spoon."

"I don't mind waiting tables, Greg. At least you can't get arrested waiting tables, ya know?"

"Yeah, well just forget that. We've got to move some shit, and I need bucks."

"I gave you everything I had, except for maybe fifteen dollars or so. You can have that." She starts to get up and get her purse.

"Hey, Tiff. Forget the fifteen bucks. Come on, man. Be serious with me. This is our future we're talking about."

"I was being serious. I thought you needed money."

"Yeah. Well, I need money. Not fifteen fucking dollars. I need three thousand bucks."

"Honey, I don't have three thousand bucks."

"Listen to me." He comes back over on her with the curls and the beautiful eyes right in her face, talking very fast, almost in a whisper. "You told me you wanted us to be a family. Look. Both of us are gonna have to make a big sacrifice if we're going to be together always and take care of each other. I got you. You're my only resource, Tiff. You gotta help me, baby. I'm going to ask you to do something that you're not going to want to do, but when I explain it all to you, you'll see it is the best way for us. I don't want you doing what I'm going to ask of you, but, baby, it's the only way, believe me. We've got to have enough to get our nest egg together, right? And I've got to be able to protect you—to keep you out of that prison you were in—and I'm the only one who can do that for you. Just like you're the only one who can do this for me.''

"What do you want me to do?" she whispered.

"We've got to get some good bucks together fast. You're all I've got. Listen, I need you to pull a couple of dates with guys. Now don't hit the ceiling. I—"

"You WHAT?" She starts laughing. "You want me to *what*?"

"I don't *want* it any more than you do. I don't particularly get off on the idea of my future wife having sex with other guys. But if you just—"

"Come on. Don't talk like this. You're nutsy."

"Like it's not such a big deal, anyway. Roger has this guy, nice-looking older dude with lots of money always wanting to get some young stuff. All you got to do is let him do it for a few minutes and we can—"

"GREG! Stop it."

"Everybody hustles. Couple, three minutes with a guy. It's not like it was a big deal, and you'll come back to me and we'll do lines and fuckin' forget it. And pretty soon we'd have enough I can make our score."

"Fuckin' forget it, all right. You got that part right." She's still laughing at the absurdity of it. "You crazy nut."

"I'm not kidding you. You've got to do it to help us. I don't like the idea either, but we've got a big chance here. I love you, doll. I want to get a home for us. A new start. But it's never going to work if you keep telling me to forget it. How would you like it if, uh, when you told me you wanted me to take you away from that old man of yours, I'd said, Bullshit—forget about it. You wouldn't have liked it much, am I right?"

She looked over at him. He was serious about this. "I want us to be together but I want it to be right. This wouldn't make it right. If you're really serious, just put it out of your mind. I couldn't do it if I wanted to, which I don't. I'm not that kind of girl.''

"I know that, angel. I *know* you're not that kind of girl.'' He began backing off it as he always did. He'd accomplished all he'd set out to do—put the germ of the idea in there for her to play with. He gave her a big smile. "We'll find a way. Don't worry about it.'' He lit the rock and took a lungful of the wonderful Dynamite White. A little piece of the rock.

"Ooof. Awesome,'' he said.

"Bastard,'' she chided him with a smile as he offered her the little glass pipe. "You really had me going.'' Greg looked as handsome as a movie star to her, she thought.

"Ummm.'' He smiled noncommittally.

She let out a big hit of it and they sat there on the edge of the bed together, listening to it crack as it cooked away, blowing both their minds with its magic, and they sat there quietly smoking, awed by the instant transformation. And the smoke made them both supremely intelligent, brilliantly wise, and impervious to the slings and arrows that wound lesser mortals.

As long as we're together we're never going to die, she thought, by chance quite correctly.

"How good is his shit?'' Greg asked Roger.

"This is Cocaine MacNugget, my man.''

"Do what?''

"Superpure and superpotent. Guaran-fuckin'-teed to kick your brain in the ass, and it's our shot.''

"How cool is this guy?''

"Hey. He's fucking golden, man. He's never burned any damn body with this good shit of his. We can come out on top with this one. He's got the most unstoppable, unstepped-on Dynamite White you can buy. Shit we can cook up into the best crack on the street. Two ounces will make enough pellets for five hundred fucking vials, Greg, and that's not even counting our own smoke. It's a beautiful deal, man. But we gotta move on it.

"Fuck it. Let's do it."

"Turn the bitch out, champ. We need it soon as you get it."

"No sweat," he said, grinning. "She'll be a fuckin' gold mine down here."

The new junk disease was endemic to neither ghetto, barrio, locale, region, country, nor people. It was ubiquitous, nondiscriminatory, and omnipotent. It could be found everywhere from East Forty-second Street to East L.A., and it was available to everyone from street animals to Granny. It would write some beautiful stuff on the slate of your mind for a heavenly quarter-hour and then take you back down on a roller-coaster rush ninety floors down to the basement.

The problem is that your brain loves the shit, and when you come down almost as fast as you went up, your brain says, WHOA! Wait a minute now. Do some MORE of that. That was *good*. You want that rush again, and right away. And you don't stop to be logical. You just want the rush. And that's the place the kid was taking her, the first pit stop on the race to hell. And he was loving every minute of it. His friend was nudging him.

"So?" Roger said with his sly grin.

"Yeah?"

"Let's move on it."

"Yeah," Greg said impatiently. "I just said fine. No sweat. You say he's golden, he's golden. Do it."

"Shit, man, I DONE my part. I mean, you got to get the bitch cunt pullin' the train. I mean he ain't gonna wait forever."

"What the fuck you want a goddamn instant fucking *miracle*. You just told me about the deal and like I'm supposed to snap my fingers and produce the money in TWO FUCKIN' SECONDS?"

"Yeah." He laughed. "I'm the candy man, you're

the dandy man. You got to get your fuckin' end earnin', champ.''

"You tellin' me how to turn a bitch out, are ya?''

"Hey, take it easy asshole.''

"YOU take it easy, ASSHOLE.''

"I put up MY fuckin' end, champ. I got you down here, in *whose* fuckin' ride, right? I'm the one got us prime to score, nifty. YOU got the bitch. YOU got to get her ass off the dime.''

"Whyncha' FUCKIN' *RUSH* ME a little more f'r crissakes.'' When Greg lost his cool he sounded like he was about ten years old, Roger thought. "She's OFF it awready.''

"Calm down, Wonder Warthog. I just fuckin' with your head. But seriously, man, I know you realize if we want the double ounce we got to get up and POUNCE.'' He held out his hand and Greg didn't slap it for him. He was still pissed but Roger knew he'd get the message. The bitch was going onto the set.

It was celebration time after her decision last night and they were smoking, letting it take them right on out there and she was sailing and soaring, flying higher than she'd ever flown before, working without a net, smart and tough enough to do it, and the rush was so wonderful that all she could do was just sit there and look at it happening and go, "Ohhhhh.''

And he said, "Ummm.''

And she giggled and toked, holding it in as he took a hit and they went, "Mmmm. . .'' at the same time, and smiled, laughing on the inside as they let all that white smoke out thinking how awesome it was.

And Greg thought three things, oh, yes—it is good, and flat little-boy tits, and let this awesome shit turn you out, darlin'—all three thoughts simultaneously. And with crack, thought is deed.

"Umm,'' she said softly as he pulled up her shirt and ran his fingers softly over the boyish chest feeling the nipples harden as his fingertips lightly brushed over them, looking at her breasts.

"Ummmmmm." She was flying way, way out there, and it was all so good and so right for the moment and so magical.

"Oh, yeah," he whispered to her, absentmindedly taking the nipple gently and just holding it between thumb and finger, holding it tenderly and knowing that he could squeeze, not squeeze pull touch kiss suck lick do any fucking thing he wanted they were all his and his power surged through his fingertips and she felt and sensed the heat as it penetrated the smoke and she winced a little as the hotness of it surprised her, and he let the magic flow from his touch and through her breast, a suffusive warmth spreading instantly up her chest and throat and into her face, and he saw it and leaned forward to kiss the hot places, expertly, laughing his cracked laughter and thrilled by the enormity of his power.

Last night there had been a candlelight-and-wine dinner, but that would soon be only white wine under the bridge, because she was going "on the set" for the first time. Even now she sat there in what he called her "ho outfit," a ridiculously short mini hiked all the way up to her treasures, and high stiletto-heel boots. The hooker wet-look. She hadn't stopped to question where he got the money for the clothes, or the wine, or the candles, or the smoke. The commitment had been made.

It wasn't the con that had worn her resistance down so much as the crack. Her whole being loved and craved it. She had to have it again and again. It made things so beautiful and right and warm and wonderfully manageable. It made order out of disorder and gave life a new meaning; it was the master plan of the addict religion. The purpose and joy of life in two words: get more.

It was what made her a princess again, and safe,

and in the arms of a lover who was going to protect her and hold her and give her all the love in the world and never leave her. And for that kind of a lover you have to make a few sacrifices.

"Easy money, doll." That's what he'd said to Tiff. It was one of his key phrases, constantly repeated, that would keep echoing. He used it to describe the prostitution and the dope deal, interchangeably. It was like his "highest form of love" con, used as a mini-argument in itself, reinforced by repetition, and later she'd have time to realize the heavy irony as easy money's resonance rang in her ears.

"Movie-star money," was the phrase the john had used. She'd remember what these men said later. Her men, she thinks. The men who helped her earn that easy, movie-star money.

But bathed in the cracking, white smoke screen of a new love, the prospects of her frightening new career had lost a lot of the former onerousness. It was now merely oppressive as opposed to unthinkable. Crack was self-propelling. It generated serious money. All it took was that initial nest-egg score. She needed to make some fast money. Easy money. And she was fourteen, and what had been ludicrous was now reality, and she looked at the curls and heard him say, "Pretty pussy," and her cat's eyes blinked, and she looked up at the magic mirror on the wall. And the mirror was clouded with smoke and did not reply to her stare.

And Greg watched her, looking over at her in her work clothes, looking at her with his West Coast eyes with the improbable lashes and smiling his white, Beverly Hills grin, thinking how boring little girls always became. He already had his eye on someone else. He'd cut Tiff loose just as soon as he got some fuck-you money.

"Stand up a minute," he commanded. Obediently she stood. "C'mere. Walk over here and let me look."

She stood right in front of him, standing between his spread legs. Her eyes closed and she tilted her head from side to side as he nuzzled her, moving her head the way you do when you have a stiff neck. Her fingers tangled in his long, curly hair.

"Ummmf." She couldn't hear what he said as he held her up close against him, running his smooth, hot hands up and down her tanned legs, cupping her cheeks and running his hand down her thighs and the back of her legs and feeling the tops of the slick, high-heeled boots, saying something to her, and the words muffled and lost as he pressed his mouth against her. Thinking to himself, What a guy.

Disconsolate, and for the first time in his adult life in fear of losing the only thing he has ever valued, Spain dedicates himself to finding her and bringing her back. Even he has no idea as to the vast amounts of time and energy, or the staggering sum of money that such an exhaustive search entails. He only knows he wants Tiff back. His daughter has disappeared like a puff of smoke. And he must use what tools he has at hand: the hunter's eye, enormous financial resources, and a web of contacts in the dark places.

When Spain did a piece of work he generally did not have to track an individual down to—as the jargon has it—"access" them. However, the few exceptions involved his subcontracting that aspect of the job to some ancillary worker or agency. He could not remember a time when he worked otherwise, even early in his career. There were so-called bounty-hunters around the country working for or as bail bondsmen. A number of these were notoriously willing to travel less-legal avenues if the fees were righteous enough. He had a couple of former cops working in other fields whom he'd also farmed subordinate action out to, and he considered the options confronting him.

He knew what he had to do. He'd stay legal with it.

There was too much open here. He was too vulnerable already because of all the notoriety involved. Too many people had come into this no-longer-private matter. There would be a paper trail. Questions. Police intervention, perhaps. He would have to go the legit route. Find a top private-detective firm and put them on some outrageous retainer. Let them reach out for her. The trail was already cold and the clock was ticking.

He knew the sort of private sleuth he was wanting. Spain called an attorney who was connected and who owed him, and added a few names to the list of possibilities he'd already worked on. He narrowed it down to a list of five firms who had big reps in child-custody work, deprogrammings, kidnapping cases, and the like, and then he got on the phone and started touching base.

Within a few hours he'd eliminated two of the names, one of whom was into big security work now, and the other an agency run by someone who struck Spain as too stupid. There were three left. He eliminated one of those in the course of conversation; the manager appeared to be too enamored of electronic gadgetry and Spain always went with his vibes in these matters. He ended up flying two guys in.

Each of them had a substantial national rep. He sent each man a down payment consisting of five crisp hundreds, just to get their attention, with ticket for a round-trip turnaround, and he was picking up the whole first-class tab: hotel, food, all expenses. Two thousand easy bucks, cash, for a twenty-four-hour consultancy and back home. No strings. An easy deuce.

His first interview was with "Beechie" Meeks, a Detroit private op who'd been with Wells and Pinkerton, two of the big four, and then gone out on his own with good success. He'd become famous for rescuing the fifteen-year-old son of a senior executive who'd been lured out to the West Coast by a religious cult, and whom Meeks had also subsequently managed to get deprogrammed from his former zombielike state. The kid proved to be actively, vocally antizealot and was sufficiently articulate and newsworthy that media gave it lots of ink and the odd name "Beechie" Meeks got a week of heavy press.

Beechie Meeks made a great first impression. He looked like a private eye in the movies. Good-looking guy with a tough, intelligent appearance and demeanor. Dressed to the nines in a beautifully tailored three-piece banker's charcoal-gray and a conservative Countess Mara under a snowy-white shirt collar, he looked like he might be a successful young attorney who was a former rodeo cowboy, now specializing in corporate mergers—the Marlboro man dressed up for church.

And then he had to spoil the initial impression by opening his mouth. Isn't that always the way? Superficially at least, Beechie Meeks was overly assertive, offensively venal, and absurdly hyper. A kind of megalomaniacal, Napoleonic little dude who sat there pontificating to Spain in his toy-store suit and diminutive wing tips, letting him hear the unabridged, complete Beechie Meeks Story, chapter and verse.

Still, he could probably get the job done. He didn't rule the little man out just because he was a self-promoter or because he acted like Jiminy Cricket wired on speed. Sometimes these cocky little guys were good. And that was the main thing here, getting it done. The problem was Beechie didn't strike Spain as trustworthy. Number one, he'd be a money funnel, no question. That was acceptable, but the serious problem would be later. What guarantee would he have that Meeks wouldn't tell all ex post facto? He was too fond of media. Too much the entrepreneurial hype man. And Spain didn't want publicity. Pass.

He brought in a private investigator from Cleveland whose name was Mel Troxell. The lawyer had told him, "Troxell is damn good but he's gonna be hog-high."

Spain said, "Mr. Troxell, you come highly recommended. But to give us a place to start, what can you do for me that I can't do myself?"

"First I'd like to know who recommended me," the man replied, somewhat crisply.

"I have to protect my sources just as I'm sure you do. But let's just say it was someone I trust."

"Well"—he shrugged—"fair enough. I always like to know who makes a recommendation. That's valuable information."

Spain was already making his judgment call. He clocked the guy as practiced, very experienced, touchy maybe, a hard case, not too smooth. Spain thought he'd use him. He smiled a little and said, "Can we just say it was someone I have faith in—somebody in the law-enforcement community."

That seemed to placate him and he tilted his head a bit, shrugging again with a little imperceptible movement of the upper torso and saying, "Sure. Yeah. Okay. Answer your question. I can do a hell of a lot of things you can't do."

"Such as?"

"Such as ask questions. I can put operatives on the girl's friends. You can't approach them yourself and hope to get much. Obviously the girl . . . What's your daughter's name?"

"Tiff. T-I-F-F."

"Obviously Tiff ran away from home. For whatever reason. You've told me a little about the situation here at home with your wife leaving. That may play a part in it. Whatever. Point is, her friends are not going to open up to you the way they will to my people. So the first thing I would do is try to build up a background of information from her friends and acquaintances. I have ways we can do that that you would find impractical if not impossible. The boys she apparently went with, they're going to have talked to somebody. Kids like to brag about where they're going. It just takes work, but that's the kind of thing we're able to do."

"What else do you plan to do to locate her?"

"Oh, I don't know offhand particularly." He was right, the guy was touchy and defensive. "I have a lot of standard places I look for clues, but every case is so different. Every case is totally unique. I'd go through her room, examine everything she left behind. We go through her papers, scrapbooks, just a lot of things that take time and work. Anything that gives us a starting place." He was brusque, somewhat hurried. He was telling Spain with body language, Come on, quit the bullshit, let's go.

"I notice you said clues. What kind of clues is a kid going to leave?"

"Oh . . . Hell, I dunno. The phone bill, for example. I take a look at the phone bill. You'd be surprised at how often we can find somebody just by looking at the unusual long-distance calls. It's all right there in black and white for you if you know how to look for the clues. You don't. I do. My operatives do."

"I'm sorry to want to know all this stuff," Spain said. "It probably is a little Mickey Mouse to be asking you how you're going to find Tiff, but all I know about private detectives is what I've seen on TV"—he let himself smile a little—"you know, the old skip-tracer image."

"Well, I don't even use the phrase *skip-tracing*. I mean, that went out in the 1940s, I think. We leave the bounty-hunting and the divorce frames and all that shit to the little mom-and-pop shops all over the country. Guy calls the one in the Yellow Pages with the ad that has a big eye emblem or something. He thinks he's gonna get Sam Spade."

"What kinds of jobs are you mostly involved with?"

"We work for big corporations, as you probably already know. I do a lot of security stuff, video surveillance, industrial stuff.''

"Homicides?''

"Jesus!" Troxell chuckled. "You know how many homicide cases I've been on in thirteen years? One. That's the television bullshit. That crap is all bullshit. The police do homicides. PI firms don't touch 'em. Oh, once in a blue moon some aspect of a murder might, uh, have to do with insurance liability, but I . . .''

As he spoke, Spain concentrated on the man, not the words, as he had been doing as he asked the first random questions that had occurred to him. This was what Spain had learned to do. He could read you as you responded, and he did it visually and intuitively. And suddenly he got the clear picture on this man. He could see this man was extremely intelligent. He was having to work not to use larger words in his responses. He was having to alter his vocabulary as he spoke, and the bluff, touchy exterior was role-playing. He used this, Spain figured, to create a slightly false impression. To help you drop your guard while he assessed you himself. At that instant Spain decided he'd use him for sure.

"Well, the only reason I asked, I noticed you were wearing a firearm there." He glanced toward the gun and the man slightly pulled his sport coat over the piece. "And I didn't know private individuals could still get gun permits.''

Spain noticed he looked rough, but in the facial features. The clothes said smooth. He knew the shoes must have gone for about a hundred and a half. The guy was making money or dressing like it.

"Yeah. We can carry in Cleveland. Got a thing there called the Private Police Commission, licensed by the City of Cleveland. You take these firearms courses 'n' that, and when you graduate, they let you apply to carry. And you can get a permit, and you can operate in that fashion . . ." He trailed off.

"These boys that took her. I have no idea if they are dangerous or what problems your people might encounter in getting her back safely. Is it legal, then, for you to"—he glanced toward where the man carried the gun—"protect yourself or someone else in that kind of situation?"

"The same laws apply toward us as anyone else. We're private citizens who in this case have the ordinary misdemeanor arrest powers or powers to ensure the reasonable safety or well-being of another person. If an individual threatens that safety openly, uh, or is exhibiting hostile or aggressive actions, naturally we got to act in defense. Just as you would if somebody menaced you at the supermarket. You would protect yourself or your daughter. We have the right to act in that same manner. You have to use your head, you know."

"I've heard about some of these cults and how the deprogrammers have to use force and I wondered—"

"We're empowered to utilize a reasonable degree of force in protecting ourselves or our clients."

"How difficult do you think it will be to get my daughter back?"

"The degree of difficulty depends on luck. How much hard work we have to do. The breaks. Sometimes you get lucky. Sometimes you have to pour the man-hours in. It's all how fast the clues develop. Did they have a car? On the phone you said, Yes, they did. That might make it harder, it might make it easier. Usually kids that age go down to the bus station or whatever and they're easy to trace. If they hitch rides, if they do this, or that—see, it's always different. But eventually we find them."

"It just seems so hopeless to me," Spain said truthfully. "I just don't see how you can find a fourteen-year-old girl when we don't even have an idea which direction she went.''

''All I can tell you is that it depends on you more than me. I always make my clients a guarantee. If you bankroll me—and by that I mean, if you are willing to keep shoveling the buckets of money in to me, and I warn you it does take buckets of money—if you bankroll me to that extent, I can find anybody. Anywhere on earth. I guarantee it.''

''I can't imagine how,'' Spain said rather quietly.

''Money. Like I just told you. That's how I find 'em. The same way you got me here. You give me enough money to do the job, and you got her back. I mean, if you're willing to give me an open bankroll. No problem. We'll find her and bring her back.''

Spain just looked at him, his face a cold, blank, and immobile stare.

''Money talks.''

The experienced hooker would have wondered about the john whose first act on entering a motel room was to turn up the volume on the bolted-down television set.

''We gonna watch soaps?'' She'd asked him the question semiseriously, the kid inside her hoping they could kick back and watch the latest *As the World Turns* or some nitwit game show, anything instead of the thing she was having to do to get Greg his easy money.

An experienced whore would have been on her guard. But this was no forty-five-year-old bimbo with ten years' pros experience at dodging freaks, vice cops, and the whips and scorns of time. We're taking about a fourteen-year-old girl. She hadn't even looked up at the guy's face she was so scared and nervous.

It hadn't been so bad so far. Roger and Greg had set her up on the first one. He came on like Mr. Suave. They'd made a deal with him—a freebie if he'd take it supereasy. Yeah, sure, he said. No problem. He loved fourteen-year-olds. He could damn near get off on just the idea. A good-lookin' little piece of tail like that for free? Hell's bells, boys, he promised, I'll be gentle as a lamb.

The second dude had been a married guy she'd picked up outside the bar of a hotel downtown. He couldn't believe his luck. She was so young and innocent-looking. And it was such a refreshing change from all the aging broads and uglies that he shot like a skyrocket. All of two minutes on top of her banging away and that's all she wrote. If they were all as fast as the first two, it was going to be easy money, she decided. If she could just keep herself from thinking about it. A little girl dressed in Mommy's clothes and four pounds of eye shadow.

She'd picked the next one, or rather he'd hit on her when she was back on the street a few minutes after leaving the second john's hotel. Just walking around like a little kid. Not thinking about the fact her clothes were selling the product and surprised when this old dude goes, "How much for a party?" And she almost told him to fuck off but caught herself in time.

Greg would be so happy. She already had a wallet filled with money and it was easy money just like that man of hers promised it would be.

"Movie-star money," the john told her in the room. But she could not foresee what was in store. She could not read the signs that a woman of experience might have seen and understood. She was Spain's mixed-up child of a fourteen-year-old daughter. Pure cherry and the third horse out of the chute is a bad one.

It is a business of numbers pure and simple. Hooking is all math. Bucks. Numbers. Sex numbers. Minutes in the saddle. Speed. Fast service and turnover, like a fast burger franchise. All by the old numbers. And the probabilities of problems are numbers again. It becomes a percentage thing. So much chance of getting ripped off. So much chance of a vice bust. So much chance of being hurt. So much of a percent you'll be crippled or offed by a psycho. Numbers.

Rip-offs. Johns. Whackos. Vice collars. Pimps. The life of a street ho is obviously marvelous. One reason why they do it. The bucks. Numbers again. Hers could have would have should have been number three hundred and seventeen or something. That was the john she might have been street-wise enough to protect herself against. But he was number three.

He moved in front of her and inserted the key in the lock and turned the knob and held the door open for her as she moved in, thinking in her mind how much she'd be bringing Greg tonight and wondering how many times she'd have to do this before she could go to him. Idly she speculated on the time of day it would be, hoping he'd take her out to a fancy dinner like last night. She would want to put all of this out of her mind.

It wasn't too bad if you thought about something else. She thought guys would take an hour or something like the kids did when they balled each other in their folks' cars. She didn't know that screwing and lovemaking were two separate things. The john would seldom need more than three or four minutes of a pro's expertise, and that would be it.

The main thing was she had to remember what Greg had taught her, the saying they'd rehearsed over and over, and his clever words kept playing back to her as she popped her gum and entered the strange room.

"Get money first, clean him off, get him off, get out fast. Get the money first, clean him off, get him off, get out fast. . . . Get the—" Saying it over and over to herself like a speed litany, chewing her sugar-free and feeling her palms get sticky, and then getting the saying mixed up in her head already in the nervous excitement of the moment, fear smearing it. "Get out fast, get the money—"

"Um. Hey, uh, could I like have the money now,

please?'' she said sweetly, not liking to ask like that but saying it so it wouldn't be just a question either, a tricky moment she thought, a tricky moment with a trick; she still hadn't looked at him.

"Sure, baby." He reached in for a huge roll and peeled a hundred off the outside, but she couldn't see what was in the roll. For all she knew or cared it could be newspaper in there. All she wanted was the hundred to put in Greg's trap money. "But now I gotta li'l favor to ask in return. No offense, but lose the gum, okay?"

"Huh?" she said, thinking he'd said lose the gun.

"The gum in your mouth, sweetheart. Get rid of the gum, please. It's like a little turnoff, okay, dear?"

"Oh. Yeah. The gum. Oh, sure." She plucked it out with her teenybopper fingernails and threw it into the wastebasket next to the bed.

"Excuse me. I have to go in the bathroom a minute, please," she said, and he smiled and nodded as he gestured expansively at the door. Get the money first, clean him off . . .

"While I'm getting undressed, would you please take your pants off? Thanks." She blurted it out as she closed the door behind her. What embarrassment. She'd never get used to asking a stranger to undress, but she knew what she had to do. Get the money clean him off get him off. One thing at a time. She wished that her case of nerves would ease up before she did something dumb. She tried to think calm, and then, as she was running water, she realized she had some Libriums in her purse. Mother's Librium. She came out of the bathroom with the hot washcloth, lightly soaped, the cloth dripping as she walked, still repeating her litany over and over to herself, and the guy hasn't budged. He's standing just where she left him like he's in shock.

"Come on now. Please let Tiff wash you off nice, huh?"

He pulled her over to him and took the cloth from her. "I'll sure do that in a second, hon, and I'll skin it back and clean that big ole devil real good for ya, but before we git to that, I jes' gotta have a little kiss from my sweet ole sugarbuns." He pulled her in close and she pushed away a little involuntarily as he relaxed his death grip on her arms. He was muscled like a weight lifter.

"Hey, easy, chief," she said, trying to remember what Greg had told her was the best way to handle this. He stunk of booze.

"C'mon. One kiss. One little kiss, whatcher name? Tiff? Tiff?" She nodded. "Tiff. Short for Tiffany." He laughed into her cat's eyes. "Oh, Christ almighty, that's great. I really like that one." He started kissing her on the mouth. "Yeah. That's real original. I only ever met one other working girl with the name Tiffany. Marvy."

"That's my real name," she said, slightly angry. "I use Tiff mostly."

"Tiff the Quiff. Hell, I like it. I might get you and my other Tiff the quiff together and we'd like get into something. A little double-Tiff ménage à trois?"

"Menagerie what?" she said, trying to pull free a little.

"It means whore sandwich in French, love." He was kissing her now on the mouth, but more and more he was taking her whole mouth in his when he kissed, big sloppy wet smackings suckings as he sucked her lips into his boozy mouth. He was as strong as an ox and she was starting to get angry. He took two powerful fingers and pinched her lips together in an exaggerated pucker, saying, "Ummm. Not menagerie what. Ménage à twaaaah." Saying it pedantically and drawing it out, speaking almost into her mouth, his sour tequila breath about making her gag. "Now you repeat after me, Tiff-quiff, say it. Muh-naaaaahhh-hhhj . . ."

"RRRRmmmmmgg."

This broke him up and he breathed more sour breath and tequila in her face and he squeezed the lips together more. "Oh, puss. You're so damn cute. I just gotta bite that little ole saucy mouth of yours, okay?"

"Rrrrr," she tried to pull back, unsuccessfully. It reminded her of an old aunt on her mom's side who always was going gitchee-goo to her when she was little and pinching her cheeks real hard. And even when she got older, the aunt would try to pinch her like that. But it only hurt a little bit and Tiff always tried to smile because her aunt was nice except for that. And suddenly his big, hard, yellow teeth are sinking into her lips and biting her mouth practically off and she is trying to scream but she can't get anything out except "AAAAAAMMMMMMMMMMM-MMMMMMMMMMMMMMMMMMMMMMMGGGG-GGGGGGGGGGG" as he bites into her and she can't stand the pain and her mouth is caught in that awful vise and it is like pushing against a brick wall and by reflex she has enough presence of mind to lash out with one of her pointy-toed high-hell boots, kicking him with all her might right in the leg and he yelps and she manages to tear free from his grasp as he makes a little noise like "Waaaauuuugggg."

And she is crying and screaming and almost hyperventilating, screaming in pain as she runs into the bathroom to see if her mouth is in tattered shreds or what. Oh my God oh Jeez it hurts so bad, she cries. It feels like her lips are bit clear through, and she's sobbing almost out of control and trying to get her breath and he's saying something this maniac is mubling some garbage and she isn't listening she's holding a cold, wet towel gently against her bruised mouth and crying and looking at the deep teeth marks in her face there in the motel bathroom mirror, but the john is in the next room and he doesn't care.

He's in the room where he bit her and he has his
penis out now and he's standing there grinning and
whacking off and squinting his eyes shut, grunting,
making a strained, groaning noise as he climaxes almost within thirty seconds shooting a hot arc of milky
white sperm to die amid the filth of the worn, burned,
stained, sleazebag carpet.

"Waaaaaaaauuuuuggg," again as he shoots his wad,
immediately rubbing his leg again where the bitch
kicked him. She'll pay dearly for this oh sweet Mary
and Joseph yes she'll pay.

He smiles darkly and in a mock-conciliatory tone
says through the door, "GOD dammit! Oh, I'm *SO*
sorry, little Tiffy." He can hear her still bawling her
lungs out in there. He knows he shouldn't bite them
but by the blessed Virgin it's hard. And you lose control sometimes when the real young stuff has a nice
sexy mouth like that one. Oh God he could cum right
now, cum again just thinking about it, and he touches
himself all smeared and wet with his orgasm and keeps
apologizing through the door to the young hooker.

In the bathroom she is still sobbing, but between
sobs and blowing her nose she is trying to tell him off
and he is asking her to forgive him in the next room
and the madder it's making her. And she's getting as
mad as fury as she feels the pain and looks at the ugly
teeth marks burning red around the sides of her mouth,
and all she can think of is how mad Greg is going to
be and she runs out of the bathroom trying to catch
her breath as she sobs and yells at the crazy john,
"LOOKWHATYOUDIDTA ME YOU, UH, YOU-
UHUHUH, MY BOYFRIEND'S GONNA KILL—"

"*HERE!*" He scares her yelling back at her as he
holds up a handful of money and she swings at his
hand, but he's fast and he jerks his hand back before
she can knock the money out of his hand and he
screams again, "WAIT. JESUS. DAMMIT. *WAIT.*

LOOK HERE, WILLYA!'' He fans out all the hundreds. A handful of hundred-dollar bills again right here in her face. It looked like over a thousand dollars all spread out like that. ''Oh, I'm so very sorry, honey,'' he says, very sincere and contrite-looking as he sells it to her. ''This is to make up for that. I don't know what came over me. This is yours, dear; take it, please.'' The fan of money again. It was the only thing that would have worked for him and somehow he knew to push the right button. The money stopped her dead-cold. ''It's a grand, Tiff. A thousand bucks. Plus the hundred I was about to pay you.''

She reaches out, still angry and hurting, and snatches the money from his grip, snapping, ''You should have to pay that and more. Look at me. Are you nuts or what? I'm not going to be able to work for days looking like this.'' She fingers the tooth marks.

And he keeps talking, conning her, lulling her with a big, dopey, apologetic look on his face. '' . . . so very, very sorry for losing control of myself, I don't know what came over me to—''

And she's thinking to herself, One hundred and one hundred is two hundred dollars. . . .

''Don't expect you to forgive me but let me make up for the amount of time you can't work. It's only fair that I pay for—''

And she thinks, And two hundred and eleven hundred is thirteen hundred, that's one THOUSAND, three hundred dollars!

''Know how much that must have hurt,'' and he keeps gentling her down, but she's not listening, and then she sees his hand come back out of that pants pocket and it is just loaded with money and she hears him rattling on, ''Want to give you some more to make up for it, okay?''

And all she can do is examine the math in her mind and suddenly the pain is totally gone. This is a fourteen-year-old child sitting here in her goofy whore outfit with some maniac who reeks of booze, trying to press more money on her. And all she can do is think about Greg and what he would say, how he sent her out today saying, Don't come back without at least six hundred bucks for me, six tricks. And she's got it all for today AND tomorrow, she thinks as he sits there begging her, but she only hears his apologies with half an ear as she continues her computations.

No way would she have done ten more hundred-dollar "dates." She knows this full well. With the two bills she already has, thirteen hundred, Greg could put over a thousand dollars into their nest egg. And she might not even have to go back out tomorrow.

That would still leave plenty of money to party with, and the thought of escaping from the pain and memories of this became very strong. A desire to smoke suddenly engulfed her from out of nowhere and she realized she could buy a dozen crack vials on the way back to the motel and *still* hand her man twelve hundred dollars. She ran into the bathroom again, idly wondering if makeup would hide the deep bite marks, and she took a little plastic bottle out of her purse and did a couple of lines right there. Sniffing and running her tongue over her sore, reddened lips. The angry red bruises looked so ugly and scary.

"Could make it up to you," his harsh, slurred voice intruded on her thoughts as she came back in the room, "and I was thinking . . . Hey, come over here a second." She stopped where she was. "I have a way to make it up to you right now." He had his big roll of money back out again.

"Party with me for just fifteen minutes more so I can get off—I'll be gentle as a lamb, I *swear*—and I'll give you fifteen hundred dollars more. How's that sound?"

"You kidding me or what?" She was almost speechless.

"Hey, Tiff. Does it look like I'm kidding? I'll pay

ya up front. And here's the whole thing right now, in advance. Jes' so you know I'm not kidding you." He had fifteen one-hundred-dollar bills counted out and was extending his arm toward her. She still didn't move.

"You mean including the eleven hundred—you'll pay me four hundred more if I let you ball me?" It hadn't quite sunk in.

"Hell, no, Tiffany girl. I will give you ONE THOUSAND FIVE hundred dollars *MORE* jes' so Ah can git off. That's a hundred bucks a minute, kid. Plus the eleven I gave ya by way of showin' how sorry I am for biting like that. You get what that means? That equals twenty-six hundred for a li'l ole fifteen-minute party— that'd make your pussy the most valuable twat in history. That's movie-star money."

"I don't know," she said, looking at his outstretched hand suspiciously. He dropped the money hand down in front of him and she went over and started to take the money from him. Looking at him real hard. Feeling how sore her mouth was.

"And you won't touch my mouth again. No kissing, no touching, *no biting* me *anywhere.*" The lines had bolstered her courage.

"I swear." He was shaking his head like it was about to fall off his body. "I jus' wanna git off and go home. Fifteen minutes. Straight ball. Nothin' else. *No kissing.* Nothing. Jes' let me put it in."

"You guarantee me no kissing or anything?" Very suspicious.

"Absolutely. I promise. And you got my money up front." He wore his best contrite look. "Look, Tiff, I can see I bruised y'r mouth. This will make up for you not being able to work awhile. A paid vacation. Just fifteen minutes inna saddle and you've got twenty-six hundred." This time she reached over and took the money and he knew he had her.

"And no more of this goddamn *biting*," she repri-
manded, cat's eyes asparkle

"And no more biting. I'll be a gentle pussycat, I
swear."

"Well, okay," she said, taking the money and starting to strip. "Clean that thing off first." The money
looked real.

He had the washcloth even as he was shaking his
head in compliance, and was dropping his pants and
skivvies and cleaning himself there in front of her. He
hobbled into the motel bathroom dragging his pants
around his ankles to wash off the warm soapsuds. She
had to smile through her bruised mouth as she rubbed
her sore face and thought about the money. God. Greg
would be so proud of her. Scoring like this her first
day out on the set. Um. Wow. *$2,800!* Get the money
first . . . clean him off . . . get him off . . .

"Now. Daddy's all clean," he said as he came back
out of the bathroom, wearing only a T-shirt and his
socks. Carrying his pants and shirt and shoes in his
hand like a clod.

"And NO MORE KISSING!" Just stand it for three
or four more minutes!

"You got it, sugar. No smoochin' and no bitin'.
Promise. Just in and out and easy money for Tiff."

"Okay," she said as they crawled into bed, and he
dropped his socks by the bedside and reached for her
gently, moving forward against her and beginning a
soft rocking motion as she felt him stiffen against her
body. She was deciding whether or not to moisten him
like Greg had said or to let him wet it himself for
insertion as he rocked back and forth, and she didn't
see him bring the thing out and put it behind them,
sliding the metal thing behind and under the pillow
beside them, then making the transfer to his other
hand, then easing out the other one out and having it
all set to go.

"*OOOOHHHH!* Baby." He was good. He knew

how to make a real loud noise just as he moved the cuffs. The one was in a little rinky-dink washcloth he'd got when he went in the bathroom, and as he snicked one cuff to the bed, he made a loud groaning noise that halfway covered up the metallic noise and before she had a chance to wonder what was that she'd just heard *SNNNNIKKKK!* Cold steel catching her around the wrist and his body weight pressing down on her with her struggling against him as he captured the other wrist easily, snikking the cuff up tight and then moving off her to fasten the other cuff and spread-eagle her out there, and that was her chance and she kicked out at him but with no shoe and he only suffered a toenail scratch and he was stoked *way* beyond that and still it torqued him off and he pounded her twice with a big, hard, mean right fist and shoved the little washcloth down in her mouth.

"That's the one I washed my little thing with, TIF-FANY or whatever the fuck your whorehouse name is, cunt. And here's a couple socks to go in there too." He stuffed a filthy sock into her mouth. She could feel bile rising in her throat and she was afraid she'd gag. Gag on the gag. Get the gag, she thought inanely as she struggled against the cuffs and tried to kick out again. He pounded her another hard right. This time catching her squarely in the solar plexus and taking all the rest of the fight right out of her. He pulled the gag out of her mouth and let her choke for a little, then wiped off her face and shoved the sock back in. Then changed his mind and pulled the sock out and took her sore face in his hand and made her pucker up for another special kiss.

She was scared now. Real scared for the first time in a long while. She remembered thinking to herself, Well, I guess this is it. And being so scared as he gently took her mouth in his, in those big yellow teeth of his, and then released her mouth and with the greatest tenderness kissed her unyielding lips and forced the rag and sock back in, pushing off her and going over to the television set and turning up the volume quite loud.

"You know how these motel walls are, Tiff. Paper-thin. We don't want all our neighbors eavesdropping on our fun now, do we?" He approached the bed cautiously and grabbed the leg nearest to him and held it against the bed as he caught hold of the other leg and started working his way back to her, easing up her body. He seemed to weigh a ton and she prayed she wouldn't start gagging again and choke to death.

"Tiffany is a nice name, very very pretty. Pretty puss," he purred in his there-there-now tones. She had a scream all ready but before he even pulled the gag out he let one go across her head and suddenly all she felt was blinding pain and shock and she was seeing a black velvet sky full of blue and red and yellow exploding stars, but she stayed conscious and as she opened her eyes again she felt the gag come out and he took her mouth in his again and this time it was as if she'd bent over a workbench vise and cranked the vise shut on her lips and tongue and had somebody jump up and down on the vise handle to crank it down as far as it would go and in the fierce and screaming unendurable agony she blacked out before he started to work on her with his hands.

An experienced soldier would have taken a look at the battleground and he would have should have could have recognized the thing curled up in the blood-soaked sheets. An experienced soldier would have recognized Spain's daughter perhaps, but from some sixth sense, some intuition, not from the physical appearance because there was no similarity between the swollen, blood-encrusted, battered thing there in the streaked and splattered bed sheets and the lively, lithe young girl who'd walked into this motel room only a few hours earlier, all full of her own nervous energy and undamaged youth.

She awoke in the darkened, strange surroundings, wrapped in a stinking sheet that seemed to be stuck to her, and there was a roaring so loud that she couldn't hear the noise of the traffic right outside the ground-floor motel room barely a stone's throw from the highway. And she was filled with terror as she tried to open her eyes and she couldn't get them open, and in her disorientation and panic she opened her mouth to scream and heard nothing and the child who was the daughter of the one who called himself Spain lay in a bloody sheet soaking herself in her own urine and fear sweat and sobbing soundlessly—tears welling up inside bruised lids so puffy they could not should not would not open.

He has gone two days without sleep and he is very tired when he looks up and sees a police car pull into the cul-de-sac that leads to his driveway, and as always he prays, this man who never prays, he prays to God it will not be bad news. And there is also that little catch in the gut and in the chest that he instinctively feels when he sees the law. And for the moment his prayers are answered and it is not bad news, only an officer coming with more of the endless questions and paperwork.

They sit in the spotless, unused living room that Pat kept covered in transparent plastic for some reason he could never fathom, a beautifully designed, interior decorator's "concept" room, kept pristine and untouched by the inhabitants of 10 Ruffstone Terrace in Ladue. Now they sit there and he answers more routine questions, keeping his concentration because although his work was always compartmentalized, his private life sanitized, these are the police.

The cop sits on plastic, writing with a plastic pen, asking about plastic. They write numbers and more numbers. Expiration dates. Request copies of things. Examine old records. Every question is asked twelve

different ways like a movie where the same take is shot
in reverse angle, then from above, below, up through
the ashtray, in the reflection of somebody's glasses, in
the hubcaps of a car. Enough already. The cops hope
to unearth a plastic trail. Spain suffers through it and
the officer finally leaves, temporarily content with his
newly acquired wealth of credit-card numbers. Some
other cop is getting the same identical data from the
credit-card companies. Why did they bother coming
out, then? Because they are cops. Why didn't they just
phone? Because they are cops. Why is the sky blue?

"When did you first think your daughter had run
away, Mr. Spain?" the officer asked, writing. He had
one of those flat, redneck voices that show boredom
easily. Spain told him. He wondered when it was she
had run away. She had run away from him a long, long
time ago, he suspected.

"And you didn't report it until . . ." Another question in a list of by-the-numbers rhetoricals that would
be asked from a clipboard full of numbers. Everything
came down to numbers. That's what he called the shots
he'd taken for Ciprioni and the family, his OTHER
family. Numbers. Funny how they liked to call things
by other names, these Sicilians and Italianos he worked
for. You didn't plan a robbery, you "made a move."
You didn't hit some guy or whack him out, you "did
a number." You "clipped" him. They didn't want
their hands dirtied by it. Didn't want to connect themselves to the "numbers." Somebody else could watch
those people bleed. Someone else could get that last
breath blown into their face as the number became a
cipher.

"Mr. Spain, who did you speak with at the Bank
Card Center?"

"Just some woman. I didn't write her name down."
This cop was calling him mister, a cold, bored tone
in his redneck voice. Just a little suspicious, automatically, as they all are. The last one had called him

Frank and been fake-hearty-hail-fellow with a phony, automatic rictus of a smile that would wink on and off as he spoke. Fucking cops.

"Had your daughter ever threatened to run away from home before?"

"No," he said quietly, his heavy-lidded eyes drooping. Christ almighty, he thought, get it done and get the hell out of here.

The questions continued. He was going over every fucking credit card. Plastic Man. Hey, cop, why don't you get a job with Visa? He sat there yessing and noing with the surface of his mind, stifling a yawn, and let himself think about what had put him here. Ciprioni had used him. These people who assured him he was like a son to them, they took his life and twisted it out of shape so that he could have nothing. He could not keep his own wife. Worse, he couldn't even keep his child. His own goddamn kid. They had done this to him with their fucking NUMBERS. He thought of all the chances he'd taken for them, all the bullshit he'd had to swallow—and here was the bottom line. Here is what he had to show for his years of dedication. A black hole of nothing.

The cop finally left and Spain got up and went to the door with him. He told Spain, "[something] find her soon," and Spain nodded and they shook hands, Spain looking down as they touched, and the car pulled away. The cop had middle-aged hands like his own, but they were worn from manual labor and the backs of the hands had freckles that looked like liver spots. Spain looked at his large, hairy hands, at the pattern of pores and wrinkles and scars on the backs of the hands. They were large, powerful hands but they didn't look as if they ever tilled soil or barked knuckles trying to work with a wrench in tight places or sweated pipe together or used a welder or ran a metal lathe. He thought of the things he'd done with those hands. It made his eyes sting, as if from smoke.

He had not smoked since the 70s. One pack he'd puffed on. It was on a job. He'd taken this weird contract the details of which were no longer fresh, but he'd found himself in a situation where he had to make some sort of crude, homemade time bomb. It was something he had to throw together quickly, jury-rigged from available materials at hand. He was nothing if not field-expedient. The fuse had been a cigarette from a pack of Winstons he'd found. He'd pocketed the pack automatically and later, driving through the night, he'd allowed himself the indulgence of smoking the rest of the pack. He had not found a single moment of pleasure from inhaling the hot, throat-parching smoke. He'd faced some kind of a mini-demon and prevailed. One always assumed time would bring a remission, even for the four-pack-a-day gang. Not a minor victory.

He tried to imagine a cigarette in his fingers and couldn't, so he picked up a fountain pen like a cigarette and just as he did a pang of terrible fear stabbed at him. Something was wrong. It was that kind of awful and consuming paranoia that cannot be denied or ignored. He could feel his heart thumping and perspiration trickling down his sides and back and covering his forehead like a fever.

It was not read as a foreshadowing omen, but as a presence. Something was there. Pinpricks dotted his back. It was a strong aura, not foreboding so much as it was just . . . there. He clenched his teeth. Something or someone in back of him . . . A presence. Somebody there in the empty house with him.

He walked very quietly, carefully, moving through the big rooms. He was suddenly aware of all the mirrors and glass, and he used this and was methodical as he let his hunter's eyes scan across all the glittering expanse of back bar, chandelier, breakfront, bookcase, mirror, picture tube, window, cabinet, picture-frame glass, anything that reflected, as he moved through the large rooms soundlessly, looking for a hint of shadow or movement as his mind quickly sorted out the random possibilities. Who would be a most likely candidate to want him hurt? The relative of a victim? A cop, coming in the back while the two of them talked up in the front of the house? Somebody high up in the family who would now view him as a threat in some way? Buddy Blackburn? He choked back a laugh as he realized what he was doing, looking up at the tired image in the reflection of the empty dining room.

He knew how the mind works under stress. He was very tired. He would take a couple of aspirin, drink a cup of coffee—caffeine perversely made him sleepy— and take the phone off the hook. And he knew he would sleep. And in that sleep. Yes. Dreams would come.

That was the nice thing about being back home, Eichord thought. You didn't have to produce any results. Just sit here in the grungy squad room smelling used smoke and listening to Lee and Tuny, the two-man uncomedy team who had been his friends since before the dawn of recorded time. These long-time partners who were so close they could piss in the same beer can.

He realized he'd been staring at the same page in the homicide report for about ten minutes. Reading it over and over again and still not seeing the words. Nothing registering. Out to lunch.

"I'm out to lunch," he told the room.

"What else is new?" his friend James Lee muttered.

"Hey, Jimmie," he said, tilting his head in the direction of fat Dana, "your girlfriend's startin' to look pretty good to me, man."

"Yeah? Well, she's allllllll mine."

"That's right, I'm already spoken for, so eatcher heart out, ya fuckin' wino."

Eichord was an alcoholic, and his friends handled it—as they did all things—with taste and diplomacy, and by calling Eichord a fucking wino. If you couldn't take a joke you didn't hang around.

So good to be back home, Eichord thought with a sigh. Back here where I belong with the rest of the rocket scientists.

Back in his safe and smelly cubbyhole in the bowels of Buckhead Station, Eichord felt far removed from a world where a mob assassin shoots his/her victims' eyes out. Had each unrelated decedent seen something they should not? Is this what the killer was saying with those two awful pulls of the trigger, You've seen too much? One thing was clear: when you take aim and shoot someone's eyes out, you are not just committing murder. You are making one helluva statement.

She was unconscious and she stayed out for a long time, awakening to a sense of being drugged but with a pain of such throbbing intensity the dope couldn't cancel it out. Imagine an impacted wisdom tooth, broken off in the extrication process by an inept oral surgeon, and raw nerve ends screaming for whatever solace waits beyond codeine, Demerol, Dilaudid. What high is next? The righteous heroin stone? Freebasing? A leaded baseball bat? You don't care. You just want the lights out.

The next time she came to, she could identify some of the sounds. Roger Nunnaly's voice, an older woman. The voices took shapes in the discrete colors within the variegated darkness and she saw through a camera lens layered thick with Vaseline. Then she went away again to sleep.

Greg had found her and debated whether to take her to the emergency ward of the nearest hospital but he knew the police would become involved. What a bother this girl had become. Such a hassle. One of Nunnaly's street friends knew a woman nurse who didn't ask questions, and the problem was temporarily solved. Private care. Of sorts.

Tiff was young and strong and healthy. She was a fast healer. But without proper medical treatment the bones did not set properly. She would have problems. The spine is also a funny thing. A blow to the back had impaired the motor nerves controlling lateral movement of the right foot. She would not walk as well as she had. The facial scars would recede to some extent. All in all, not so bad. Better a crippled dog than a dead lioness.

The RN the boys had hired cost money. The dope she was hitting Tiff with also wasn't free. And there was the problem of the impending score. Greg and Roger did what they had to do. There was a couple who needed a young girl for "a live-in domestic," as they put it, and Greg sold them Tiffany for sixteen hundred dollars cash. It was touch and go for a while. The Freunds almost backed out on the deal when they saw the extent of damage to their merch, but they gave her a thorough examination, slept on it, and finally reached a decision. What the hell. They had plenty of disposable income and it might be worth a shot.

Tiff was not consulted in the matter, needless to say. She had not only lost the $2,800 gold mine, she'd cost them a bundle to boot, and jeopardized an important score. There was nothing to talk about. If she could generate some income it was her place to do so. She'd be expected to do whatever the Freunds told her to do. Light maid work, probably, and sex anyway they wanted it. Anytime. With whoever they said. In return, the Freunds were picking up her "medical expenses." Fair is fair.

Charlie Freund had been into stags there in Hollywood, Florida, way back when it was dirty little loops of cellulite queens and skinny dudes in black socks. Broads corralled off street corners. Bimbos scouted at poolside. "Dirty Feet flicks," named after the hall-mark of the old-time porn quickie.

But the burgeoning market exploded and stag loops went the way of the sex shops and mail catalogs as production values accelerated, the new video technology bringing with it the mainstream money. And the cheapie porno film was obsolete almost overnight in a world where the next-door neighbors were taping their own action. Consumer need was reassessed.

The video boom signified megabucks, and soon the adult-movie market was the biggest enterprise going in America. When stag films dried up, he and his partner went their own ways, his partner going the massage-parlor route, Charlie concentrating on direct-mail specialties. He knew there'd always be a living just on the two hundred names he had. Pedophiles, people wanting circus shit, fans of heavy duty S&M. They had nowhere else to go for it but the small, kitchen-table porn merchants.

Charlie had cultivated a small stable of ladies who were into tit torture, spankings, humiliation, and the lighter forms of bondage and discipline. The rest of it was faked, and sometimes rather inexpertly. But the market was there just as he said. And since he was into it himself, he could see that the potential was astounding for quality stuff.

Porno entrepreneurs go under for the same reasons any other small business fails: undercapitalization, lack of management knowledge, unwillingness to change with the marketplace, failing to maintain a fair share of the active business, refusing to work hard enough. Charlie went to some people who had money and management knowledge, and offered his willing-ness to shoot at a new bull's-eye, work hard, and carve out a virgin mini-market for them. He convinced them he knew his specialty, which was pain, and Charlie Freund was on his way.

Charlie was married—well, not married exactly—

but he lived with a mean, vicious malcontent of a diesel dyke named Bobbie. They made a good team. They liked hurting women, but not exclusively. They had Catholic tastes in these areas. They had a surprisingly capacious repertoire and an insatiable appetite for punishing and hurting and dominating.

It began on the level of the barbed invective and the punishing insult, which they both cultivated as an art form. They had poisonous and deadly verbal skills. Caustic, biting, unforgiving tongues—both of them—capable of the most acrimonious linguistic surgery. Nonanesthetized probes homing in on the soft spots. Critiques of dripping, acidulous harshness. Scorn of the most withering and unforgettable acerbity. The problem is, they needed recipients for the abuse. Someone, preferably, who wouldn't fight back.

They went for prepubescent targets who could be dressed up as foxy little cheerleaders, virginal 4H girls, rosy-cheeked homecoming-queen fantasies from either sex. But they usually had to make do with tired hookers playacting, divorcees on the third bounce, doltish hash-slingers. They lusted for the animation and thrills of a yet-to-be-vanquished but vulnerable recipient for their gifts.

They were spoilers. It began with words, always. Scathing sarcasm that could puncture and deflate with surgical precision or pummel the target with crude bludgeons; devastating onslaughts of mockery and derision. Mercilessly savage rancor designed to cripple and main. And Tiff wore the designation VICTIM like a banner.

They used Tiff in some of the lower-budget affairs. Customized specialty orders where the camera might need to see the angry, red welts appear, or even a little blood dotting the skin in a "pincushion" movie. But the mainstream stuff called for pros. They used models for the tormented tit titillation, the fantasies catering to the clothespin-and-rubber-band crowd, the teen stewardess spanking sessions (See Patty paddled by Tara in this steaming bestseller featuring the stars of *Teddy Torture*). Tiff was okay for the untitled junk. The hardcore work went to a grossly overweight dominatrix in Pennsylvania, who regularly sent them Polaroids of her guilt-ridden hubby, a weight hanging dumbly from his flaccid cock-ringed dong. Custom jobs for the whackaroonies.

One physical act held unique appeal for Charlie and Bobbie. DBC was a subcategory of discipline and punishment that rivaled even the boundless thrills of creating an emotional basket case. It was a bizarre tangential tributary of S & M called Disfigurement by Consent. A young and soft victim would be drawn into this with sufficient drugs and time and the proper increments of humiliation and force. But the fun was in getting the child to want it herself.

"Do you know what we keep in here, slave?" Bobbie asked Tiff in her sexiest, most dangerous contralto.

"Hmm-mmm." Tiff shook her head in the negative.

"Get those eyes off of me, you freak," Bobbie hissed, and Tiff cast her eyes to the floor obediently. "There, you cunt. That's much better. Now. In this little rosewood box your mistress keeps her silver branding iron. If you want us to keep feeding you all that dope, you greedy little bitch, you'd better show us you want to become one of the family. Soon you'll be begging your mistress for the privilege of wearing our brand on your ass." Tiff appeared to be nodding off and Bobbie slapped her somewhat absentmindedly. "If you could only learn to behave more like Ginger. Junkie cunt."

They were always talking to her about Ginger. She should try to act more like Ginger. Ginger Deaton had learned to really like it, they assured her. She had been extremely plain, with a personality still embryonic, but Charlie and Bobbie had brought her along with all the artifice their collective perversion could muster, gentling this quiet, passive creature further into their nightmare swamp because they smelled the strong scent of victim on her. She became a favorite protégée in time.

One cannot be hypnotized against one's will. But Ginger's own needs were such that a notoriously unscrupulous hypnotist was able to further enslave her on the Freunds' behalf. Once Bobbie heard a noise in their bedroom closet, to illustrate the extent of their dark proclivities, and jumped out of bed in alarm. It was Ginger, unable to control a sneeze, for which she was later whipped to the edge of her pain threshold, the girl's head visible from hair down to upper lip. The rest of Ginger Deaton mummified in four and a half feet of tightly wrapped bandages.

Charlie remembered then that Ginger had requested discipline "a few days ago," and he'd forgotten about the quiet little slave who was silently dehydrating to death in their closet. Devoted Ginger bore cruel Freund brands on both legs, the inner thighs, the cheeks of her ass, her armpits, tits—the rest of her a living dart board of disfigurement from cigarette burns, pin and needle holes, God knows what. Why can't you learn to be more like Ginger? they'd taunt Tiff. Learn to serve us.

But Denise was their piece of least resistance. Their masterwork of depravity. They had spent over two years working their magic on a gay, twenty-year-old boy named Dennis Majors. They were ardent, persuasive, and very cunning. Their love affair with Dennis would survive the test of time only if he would be willing to meet them halfway. By which they meant if he would allow the woman within him-her to finally, fully emerge from the cruel joke that life had played on him-her-it.

It required the greatest concentration, effort, and planning on their part, not to mention personal risk, while they scammed their victim for the eighteen months Dennis spent under the observation of a reputable psychiatrist and a physician. But Dennis-Denise, who had been living as a woman for years, now with the benefit of a year and a half of hormone injections et al, was allowed to go under the scalpel.

Several weeks later, to the Freunds' great amusement, the youth committed suicide after they unceremoniously dumped her in a scathing, derisive, blistering attack by telephone. They had informed her, with never a second's hesitation or moment's remorse, that his-her gender reassignment surgery had been the punch line of a hilarious practical joke. They had reached a level of vituperation and scorn that surprised even them, and Denise's self-immolation was an exciting payoff.

These were the hands into which Spain's daughter had been placed for care and feeding.

Later, with seldom if ever a tender moment, Spain's daughter, branded and fully hooked, was working "love shows," the euphemism for live sex acts, having celebrated a birthday by performing in a particularly nasty S & M show in which she was listed as "golden shower-receiving."

But the quality of mercy droppeth as the gentle rains. Tiff's addiction and crippled body they could accept. Her stubborn streak was a continual irritant to the Freunds. Her owners now regarded Tiff as worthless chattel, fast becoming a tiresome liability. When the Freunds are approached by some mob-connected people who need an untraceable live target for a snuff movie being shot out of the country, she is sold for what will be the last time.

Maybe it was around the time his daughter disappeared that the bad dreams began, he thinks. Or was it earlier—when he came home from the trip to the coast and discovered Pat and Buddy Blackburn were sharing his bed? Spain cannot recall the precise instant the nightmares began. Only the dreams themselves, which are bloody real and etch themselves into his memory banks.

The large picture window framed a vista of falling autumn leaves that dropped from the tall oak, maple, and sycamore across his landscaped lawn. The leaves and grass appeared to have lost all chlorophyll content overnight, the lush look becoming sparse as the dead, brittle leaves floated down to turn to mulch. The *Archilochus colubris* had long disappeared, and it was just as well, since there was no longer anyone to tend the feeders.

All the losses were building deep within Spain, and about the time he thinks the awful, aching hurts have become a dull, throbbing pain, some new shock wave of recognition hits his core. Ever the realist, he senses that his child is gone for good.

One day she'd been buying Cabbage Patch dolls and Care Bears and the next day she's hitchhiking and getting birth-control pills. Why couldn't he have spotted all of this coming and done something to ward it off? Over and over he makes himself look at things that had happened between himself and Pat, between father and daughter, the harshness and coldness that had alienated a wife and then a daughter.

He could sense now that there would be no reunion or eventual reconciliation. No firm but fair fatherly attentions to put his wayward child back on the track. There would be no reprieves for them. No second chance to become a family again.

He'd been in the family room, staring out the window at the falling leaves, when he'd seen the shadow again or a sense of some movement there in back of him and he'd whirled, instinctively, his right hand going for the small automatic he carried and then catching himself all in the same moment.

That feeling again. The eerie feeling that someone was there in the big, empty house with him. Watching him. Jesus. He felt the skin on his arms and shoulders prickle with what his dear mother had called "goose bumps." And this man who feared nothing shrugged it off. He knew the tricks that stress and lack of sleep could play.

He tried to mentally add up how many hours of sleep he'd actually had so far that week. It was Thursday morning, he thought, and since Sunday night he didn't think he'd had sixteen hours' sleep, and much of that furtive. Still, he told himself, Edison invented the light bulb on less. He was very tired.

His eyes stung and he decided he'd take something and hit the sack. Good night, his mom would say tucking him in, sleep tight. Don't let the bedbugs bite. Now I lay me down to sleep. I pray the Lord my soul to keep. If I should die before I wake . . . CHRIST, he saw it again, a movement of some kind behind him as he headed up the richly carpeted stairs. He had to catch himself to keep from saying something out loud. Get a grip on yourself, man, he told himself and headed for bed.

He had begun to dream the moment he put his head on the pillow, sleeping on his face with his arms under him, the blood cut off. And the dream was very bad this time. One of the worst, in fact.

It is the kind of day that makes you glad to be alive. He is driving down a black-topped service road somewhere in the country. The road runs parallel to a set of railroad tracks not far from a busy interstate. A crop duster periodically dives low over the road to spray the adjacent fields of milo and soybeans, and Spain admires the grace of the small, yellow biplane.

A train is approaching in the distance and the appearance of the countryside, the flat farmland, the old-time plane, the train approaching, it all combines to give the atmosphere a kind of quaint, old-fashioned feel, as if it should be photographed in a freeze frame and made into a calendar scene for a drug company.

The crop duster zooms down across the road again, leaving another trail of white spray through the azure of the crystal-clear sky, and Spain and his companion drive through the falling, dissipating chemicals where the blacktop bisects two halves of a field.

The monstrosity beside Spain says, "What a beautiful day, eh?"

"Yes. It's nice."

"The kind of day you really feel glad to be alive."

"Sure do."

"Just beautiful." The monstrosity leans back expansively, the car seat creaking under his massive weight. "Really pretty."

"Yep."

"Hey," the thing asks Spain, "d'ya know what a kris is?"

"Chris?"

"Yeah. A kris. A Malaysian dagger. Ever seen one?"

"No, I don't bel—" And before he can answer, the monstrosity reaches over and prizes one of Spain's fingers—his right thumb, actually,—loose from the wheel and slices something across it, squirting a gush of blood like the end of a garden hose squirting bright red over the dashboard and the wheel as Spain cries out in agony. The thing has sliced his right thumb off with a ridged, serpentine dagger and the pain is just unbearable now as Spain fights to stanch the flow of blood and the monstrosity laughs.

"Oh, wow. I wouldn't worry about that too much if I were you. You ain't gonna have time to bleed to death," it says, and the kris bites into his neck, the thing slashing the sharp, wavy edge across Spain's jugular, then tossing the blade down and picking up a club as the bloodspurt bathes the interior of the car, and saying, "Adiós, motherfucker," as he slams a home run using Spain's head for a ball, and just as the club slams into his screaming face, the car coming in

the opposite direction hits them head-on and they are
spun around and back-ended by an eighteen-wheeler
loaded with steel and in the crushing impact they are
smacked out on to the railroad tracks and the train
grinds down on them just as the crop duster crashes
down out of the sky on the deadly tableau and Spain
sits up in the grinding, crushing, pulverizing meat
grinder shaking and bathed in nightmare terror, and
the thing in the shadows there with him in the empty
house speaks for the first time as he jerks out of the
dream, and Spain feels his whole body cover in chill
bumps as the ancient and horrible voice says, "Hello
there."

"Who, uh, how did you get in here?" Spain dreams.

"Who how did I get in here? You sure have a way
with words."

"You're the one who's been watching me."

"Bingo."

"Why don't you come out of the shadows? You
scared?"

"Uh-huh."

"What are you scared of?"

"What are I scared of? Not you, big fella."

"Are you a demon of some kind?"

"Will you just listen to yourself? You're getting all
worked up over nothing."

"Motherfucker."

"Oh, no. I'd never fuck her. My mother is sin and
you never fuck sin. Sin fucks you. Sin and madness."

"Go to hell."

"From your lips to God's ear."

"Horseshit."

"Sin, madness, hell, and horseshit. The four horse-
shits of the apocalypse."

"*Fuck you!*" Spain screams, lurching out of the
dream in the empty darkness of his bedroom, waking
as the abrasive echo of his curse resonates in his mind.
The shadows are very near now and soon they will

find him and enclose him, enveloping him in a shroud of insanity and death.

"Come on, man," Morales said to the slim, dark-haired man as he adjusted one of the large, heavy-duty lights for the third time.

"An' wash whe' jew put dose feet, baby, jew knock this motherfucking light over jew *buy* it, man." He was fussy about his expensive lights.

Big fucking deal, Belmonte thought. It looked like a "real" movie set with all the lights and cameras and shit around. Cables running everywhere.

"Hey, these fuckers burn *out* I leave 'em on too long, man. Come on, *'mano,* jew look real pretty. Let's get this motherfucking chit over with, eh?"

"Yaaaa," Jon Belmonte grunted noncommittally as he carefully brushed his dark hair. Even if he was being shot from the back, he wanted to look good. He'd watch this shit later with the new bitch. When he was satisfied he slipped his shirt off and pulled on an old shirt that he could burn afterward. This bitch wasn't going to splatter a new sixty-eight-dollar shirt.

"Jew ready now, Marlon."

"Here we are man, Spic and Span." They laughed. "Le's do it."

"Hey, li'l mama," Belmonte said as they walked into the room where the girl was resting on the bed. "It's star time," he said with a giggle as he spread his arms out expansively. "Right?"

"Nnn." She nodded dumbly, eyes heavy-lidded, features slack.

"Hey?" Nothing. "HEY, bitch. Talk to me."

"What?" she said.

"You ain't gon' fuck this up now, are ya?" He smiled. She shook her head slowly, nodding. "Wake up now, li'l mama. You remember your big line, now, doncha?"

"Mmmm," she grunted.

"Say?"

"Yeah. Umm. Yeah, I remember."

"Say it." She gazed off into space, a smile fixed on her face. "SAY IT, damn you. . . . You stupid li'l bitch." Nothing.

"Ay, chihuahua, jew hit her with too much. She ain't gonna even look like she's alive."

"Fuck it, man, let's get it done." They started kicking on the rest of the lights. A powerful bounce-light and a light that looked like it was surrounded by a silver umbrella, and a bank of small lights on a portable stand.

Tiff, blinded momentarily, put her hand over her face and said, "Shit. Hey, the light hurts my eyes," and both of the men broke up laughing.

The photographer, Morales, said, "Hey, li'l *puta*, jew ain't going to have to worry about having nothing hurt jew eyes for much longer, so don't worry about it."

"Cool it, goddammit," Belmont said as they laughed, jiving around as they set up for the payoff shot.

"Make sure we got film in the motherfucker and that nothin's fucked up 'cause you ain't got a second take on this one, C.B."

"Yeah. I hear dat chit all right." He double-checked the monitor. He was shooting a video master with a rinky-dink portable generator, but the picture looked to be all right and the cats bought this shit they weren't too choosy about Panaflex cams and Scope. Just let 'em see it nice 'n' clear, you know. See the little *chiquita* get fucked up in a nice color close-up. No big fucking deal just as long as everything showed good.

"Jew miked?" Morales asked Belmonte.

"Unnn," he said, making sure the cord from the lavaliere was tucked down on the side the camera wouldn't see. Cheap shit wouldn't even have a fuckin' boom on it.

"How's this look?"

"Looking good," Morales said. He made a last-minute adjustment as he squinted through the camera apparatus. "Yeah. Okay."

"Yeah."

"I'm ready. You got your chit together?"

"Nnnn. Tape rollin'?"

"Yo. Mark it."

"Teenage Snuff, fucking TAKE *ONE*!" He was in the lower right of the shot. A two-shot of Tiff in close-up, back to a medium shot where you could see Belmonte's back, and the long metal thing in his left hand.

"I told you that you'd pay for displeasing me, you cunt," he emoted into the mike clipped to his shirt. Nothing. The dumb cunt had forgotten her line. "DON'T STOP THE TAPE. KEEP THE FUCKER ROLLING," he shouted and stepped close.

"No sweat," Morales said. He slapped her with the free hand but she just held her head a little differently, the same dumb smile on her face. He could see she was out of it. Fuck it.

"Teenage Snuff, *TAKE TWO!*" he said his line again. "I told you that you'd pay for displeasing me, you cunt," and he started plunging the metal thing into her and she screamed.

Morales thought to himself the blood was looking damn good. Best damn blood squibs you ever wanna see. The good part was just starting. He couldn't wait. He was anxious to see Jon put her eyes out with the thing. He loved to see a little white honey get all fucked up like this.

Jon Belmonte, a.k.a. Juan La Bellamonde, was seldom in the wet vid they cranked out at Rhapsody Video. He'd do a little off-cam thing now and then, but this was a special exception. It would take some expertise. You didn't want to go too far. It would be easy to lose your head, get carried away, and off the bitch before you get to the good stuff. Expendables

were expensive. He also couldn't see laying out good
coin for some dude with a big cock just for something
they could shoot over the shoulder in a little back-lit
quickie two-shot. And he knew he could keep her alive
at least till he got to her eyes.

He knew just how far to stick her in the tits to look
good on cam. Get the freaks up for it. Stick her plenty
of times but nice little shallow jabs. He knew he could
trust himself not to go crazy and blow it. He'd done
plenty of this kind of shit himself. He just hadn't filmed
all of it. No problem.

He was a packager. He had the whole production
thing, the last stop on the pain line. Rhapsody, ironi-
cally titled by the former owner, was just one of the
indies feeding the Blue Kriegal operation, which was
tied to St. Louis people. He didn't know who was
involved and didn't want to know, It was bad enough
having to deal with a freak like Kriegal. Kriegal's thing
was run by St. Louis, who was under Chicago, and
them fuckers—the less you know about them, the
longer you live.

Porn was a family operation as far as he was concerned. And his level of the family, the remora sucking up to the big fish that could get you through the
heavy surface scum, really was a family. A freak family but still a family. A small circle of people all involved in the same shit. The people he bought the girl
from, the Fruends—shit, they sold to Blue Kriegal.
There were indies all over the country. The production
end wasn't shit on the little cheapie stuff like this. All
that bogus bullshit about how the mob controlled pornography, that was just newspaper jive.

Pervs controlled that shit. Kinks like Jon Belmonte,
who got off on little kids, or torture, or whatever circus love you were into. What the mob controlled was
the distribution end, which was where the bucks came
from, the guys who pulled the exhibitor's strings. The
one way you always knew where the mob was, you

follow the money. The little stuff, the nickel-and-dime skin house, nobody cared. But get into some serious money and it was the family.

Blue Kriegal was always braggin' about how well-connected he was in the St. Louis operation, but Jesus Christ, anybody with half a brain would have sense enough to know that was about 90 percent bullshit. Who in their right fucking mind would have anything to do with a stone whackadoo like Blue Kriegal if they didn't have to? He was a fucking maniac. Little tiny kids 'n' shit. Damn. It was enough to make you sick.

Belmonte had to deal with him a couple times a year when Kriegal would come down through McAllen and want Belmonte to get him some Mexican stuff. And he'd have to take the weird son of a bitch over and get him straight with some poor little baby. Crazy fucker. That was the kind of maniac you had to deal with sometimes.

Personally Belmonte got off on young chicks. Even a good-looking young boy once in a while. Take 'em down real good. He could dig that. But not no little *babies* 'n' shit. He was a little kinky sure. Plenty twisted and whatnot. But he wasn't fucking *CRAZY*.

The loud voices echoed through the Homicide squad room at Buckhead Station.

"It's your turn, that's why," the fat detective snarled at his friend as he produced a couple of withered ones from a disreputable-looking billfold. He leaned over with some effort and tossed the folded bills onto his partner's desk. "Large coffee-with and one of them big long things looks like a schvatza's pecker."

"Say ya want a big long thing that looks like Arnold Schwartzenegger?"

"Missing out on life?" fat Dana Tuny announced to the room, cupping his ear like a radio broadcaster and pushing his voice down an octave. "Why go another day without the revolutionary new hearing aid from Say What Incorporated. It's the exciting hearing aid made for assholes! That's right! You heard me correctly. It's the new miracle hearing aid shaped like a suppository. You stick it in your ass instead of your ear—"

"What's a five-letter word beginning with *S* that means Athenian lawgiver?" Jack Eichord interrupted from across the squad room where he was engrossed in a crossword puzzle.

"Schmuck," James Lee said helpfully.

"Schmuck is *six* letters, you schmuck. Hey, Eichord, Lee's goin' across the street. You wanna banana daiquiri or anything? Or is the sun over the yardarm yet? I mean, it's eight-forty-five in the morning, hey?" The partners began to giggle like little girls.

"Sorry, I didn't hear that, I have a banana daiquiri in my ear," Eichord muttered.

"You ain't supposed to be diddlin' around anywhichway," Lee told him. "I heard you were on some big-mob thing."

"Yeah. Tryin' to find out who wasted Dutch Schultz."

"I'm workin' on it right now," Eichord mumbled. "SOLON—that's the mother." He filled the word in.

"What'd he say?" Lee said to his partner.

"Say what?"

"Say WHAT? What do I look like anyway, a hearing aid for assholes?"

"I said Solon," Eichord told them.

"Okay," Lee said, getting up and heading for the door, "so long."

"Yeah," Tuny called to him, "write if you get work and hang by your balls."

Long ago Jack had learned to tune them out. If you worked out of Buckhead it was a thing you developed early on. A hearing aid for assholes, he thought as he doodled the word *Solon* with a black pen. He shook his head.

He had learned a trick about detective work from a writer. A nice old gent by the name of Carlton E. Morse. Guy used to write *I Love a Mystery* and *One Man's Family* on radio. Morse had taught him the secret of opening your mind to the flow of ideas. Another dude who was in the intelligence racket had shown him a trick or two to make the flow come easier. Eichord appeared to be doodling aimlessly but his spongelike mind was soaking up whatever trickled over the top of the dam.

He had drawn a huge S O L O N and made the two *O*s into old-time pie-cut eyes. Given them eyebrows. And as he blacked in the eyes pushing hard with the felt-tip pen over and over, the paper tore and his pen plunged through one of the eyes and he saw the eyes of the first cadaver, the bloody sockets, the headline EYEBALL MURDERS, the eyes of a little monkey holding its hands over its eyes, SEE NO EVIL printed on a greeting card, and a man looking up from a card, casually, but with a flicker of recognition in the wiseguy eyes, and it all merged in Eichord's mental storehouse as he picked up the phone to call the Major Crimes Task Force, his employer of record.

Eichord had looked into many unusual mob assassinations because they had drawn lots of ink in a given jurisdictional area. Jack was just one of the people the feds would pull in on crimes of homicide that would draw what might be termed "undue notoriety." Potential scandals, in other words. Sensitive homicides. Most of these were not technically serial killings. A serial kill, at least the way MCTF played it, was when there were four or more related murders. That was the official Quantico definition. Who ever decided three weren't but four were—that nobody could ever quite pin down, but the definition stuck.

Three men down. Eyes blasted out. Payback, West

Coast Mafioso-style. Wise-guy eyes. SEE NO EVIL.
A too-casual glance away after the flash of visual recognition.

"Hey, homeboy, what's to it?" he says into the
phone. "Yeah. I got a biggie." Pause. "Don't say can
do until I lay it on you." Polite chuckle. "What I need
is—I need to know the name of every male passenger
who left for St. Louis from LAX between five-thirty
and six A.M. on—" He glances at a calendar and gives
the man a date.

"Huh uh. No, I'm not sure what gate either." But
then in that open sponge a metallic voice resonates:
PASSENGERS NOW BOARDING FLIGHT TWA
BLAH BLAH FOR ST. LOUIS GATE 41. He can see
SEE NO EVIL looking up from the greeting card at
the voice over the speakers, leaving, moving out a
boarding gate. "It might be forty-one. Forty-four. I
don't recall. I think it was a TWA flight. But check
'em all please. Yeah, I know. I want whatever the air-
line has on all those males. There couldn't have been
that many planes leaving L.A. for St. Louis at that
time of the morning. Be surprised if there's more than
one. Thanks, babe. Yeah—I need it day before yesterday."

Eichord flashes on the eyes, trying to put a face with
it, but nothing comes. Just hooded eyes looking up.
Cop awareness. Savvy showing. Cops and wise guys
are habitual watchers, and old-cop habits die hard.
Could be anything. Could be nothing. But after so
many years in the arena Jack Eichord had finally
learned to trust hunches.

Under the S O L O N artwork with the penetrated
eyeball he printed SEE NO EVIL, and the words laid
a shiver against his spine.

Belmonte had a nice, tight little operation, and a
secretary with a nice, tight little pussy, and this shit
with the snuff movie got him so hot he couldn't wait

to get back to her. Cathy was always complaining about her big work load and he'd got her a secretary of her very own. She was good-looking, but dumber than a fucking lox. And he was already starting to work the new girl over too.

He liked to go up and rub his package right in those big fawn eyes and be talking some movie bullshit to her but stiffening right in her face. Let that hard cock tent the fly of his slacks and show her what he had while she squirmed around and tried to act like she wasn't looking. A nice two-handed pat on the shoulders. Welcome to the team and whatever. And rub that nice hard cock against her cheek just a little. Get Cathy over and start some serious touching right in front of her.

He liked her in old-time hooker clothes. Today she'd had on that out-of-style 60s green mini-skirt. Fish-net crocheted, green, wool job you could see right through. He'd fool with his new cherry a little, then take Cathy in and make her clean his office. Have her do it the way he liked, keep those legs real straight and bend from the waist while she dusted so the little short skirt would hike way up there on those silky thighs. Damn. She had a beautiful butt on her, and those legs. Nice stuff on the bitch.

And he'd go over and slip her little bikini pants down and thrust himself right on in there dry. Make her cry out a little. Pinch those beautiful things for love handles and hold on to her while he banged her up against the wall, then pull out and shoot his load in her face the way he enjoyed. Watch that hot, milky juice splatter across the gorgeous sheen of daytime makeup under those eyes like big black spiders. Shoot his hot wad into those pink, wet lips and watch her lick it all off him.

And just as he'd climax he'd be thinking about how the little doped-up slut screamed when he put her eyes out.

Part Two

SPAIN

Who was this man who sat alone in his well-appointed prison of a home waiting? Waiting when under a different set of circumstances he would have gone after her himself. This was, in truth, no man. On the outside you saw what appeared to be this creature of his own design: one Frank Spain by name. A pair of cold, emotionless, hooded eyes that had long ago mastered the trick of staring, unblinking, into space.

His was a face used to showing nothing. Reflecting nothing out of the ordinary. Visage, bearing, demeanor, composure, all icy cold. Placid. Calm and unruffled. But what you saw had in fact become what he was. Empty. Over the years the slaughterer's trade had taken his humanity from him. Spain was a hollow man.

Mr. Cipher. Blank stare. Distorted, flat vision. Bulletproof sensibility, scarred soul, Wizard of Off. Deathman. This was the shell who answered the phone to hear the voice of Mel Troxell, flying in from Cleveland with bad news.

Spain made him tell it on the phone, of course, and listened to the entire report without interrupting. When Troxell was through, he simply thanked him and told him that he would see him when he got to St. Louis tomorrow.

At least Mel Troxell had the balls to bring the report and hand over his bill in person. For Spain's exorbitant bill from the P.I. firm he got a list of names and a small canister of film that he could not bring himself to watch. The list had cost Troxell a bundle. The report was as good as anything Spain had ever attempted himself. Maybe better. Beyond thorough. Meticulously double-referenced. Triple-checked. This guy's people were damn good. It was worth the money.

The man who called himself Spain answered a few questions, asked many, many more. He surprised Troxell with his coldness and lack of tears. He took the news like a man with a heart of stone. Clearly he felt something, but he must be one of those who chose to keep their grief a private matter. He would do his crying alone. Mel Troxell had broken his share of bad news to people, and his impression was that Spain would be able to deal with it. The only part he had any reservations about was the final payoff.

Then it became Spain's turn to talk. He knew instinctively that Troxell would have to be convinced, and he dredged up reserves of inner strength and managed a consummate piece of playacting. He knew the degree of conviction he would have to show to convince a pro like Troxell that he was incapable as a father of following through on the case. He would use the tools of the Method actor and let the report itself trigger his scene. It wouldn't be that tough. As soon as he heard who was involved he could feel the floodgates starting to burst inside.

His own people. HIS OWN FUCKING PEOPLE had killed her. Oh, not directly. Those were punks. Nobody types on the outer rim of the mob. But they were working for his own fucking family. Ciprioni. The old man Sally Dago's people. Those sons of bitches. He could feel himself reddening with the madness of it. It was all he could do to think he wanted to taste the revenge so badly. He fought to stay cool as Troxell took him through the report of his daughter's murder.

It was critical that Troxell bought the scene so he

took it by the numbers, drawing him out on details as
he imagined a "normal father" would in such circumstances. It was easy to do. His emotions were those of
any father. Grief. Bitter sadness. Disbelief. Violent
rage. Then crushing heartbreak. He feigned confusion
at the chain of command, trying his best to muddy the
waters with Mel Troxell wherever he could with regard
to who was guilty.

"Do you mean those boys—those *children*—they
sold her?" He wiped tears.

"Yes, that's exactly what they did." Troxell began
explaining the sticky, red trail of abuse, torture, and
death that began with the boys Dawkins and Nunnaly,
and led into the sordid milieu of the most depraved
porn merchants, and Spain winced as he heard names
he knew so well. Punks who worked for the family.
He had to fight from snarling at the name "Blue Kriegal." That piece of shit. He was *NOTHING*. Some
trash who sold kiddie porn. Tied to Dagatina in only
the most remote way, but of course Troxell had no way
of knowing that. The family *used* trash like that for
mules and mokes. Garbage to stand up and insulate
the people who were of some consequence. Porn—in
fact, the whole skin racket in general—played virtually
no part in the scheme of family business. To think his
own people . . .

"—understand what I'm telling you, here." Troxell's tone jolted him and he said, shaking his head in
confusion, "All these *names* . . . Who *are* these people? Why didn't the police do something? Who's responsible?"

"In a general sense we all are. Anybody who buys
a videocassette that contains pornography is feeding
that business. But this was a special subbranch of that
particular world. Child porn is a bigger industry than
most of us think. It has a relatively small but intensely
active production and distribution chain. It is obviously aimed at the underground. The home market and

the illegal subculture—and it's within that distribution and manufacture that the industry is tied to organized crime. The men who killed your daughter—Morales the cameraman, and Belmonte the packager, and, if you want to call him that, the producer—were making a snuff film for an outfit that is run by a man named Kriegal. He controls production for much of the midwestern and southern states.''

"If his identity is known, why don't the police arrest him?''

"It's not that easy. He's like most of the smart mob people now. He stays sufficiently insulated from the actual criminal acts that he remains just out of reach so far as the law goes.''

"I just don't see how that can be. I mean, pornography and—torture—and murder—''

"It is the same as the narcotics business. It is protected. Protected not just by dirty cops or politicians but by the green curtain of money that gets pulled across the face of any business with a semilegitimate facade. The crime families are enormous now.''

"This man—does he control the porn business for the Mafià here?''

"Yes, but he's just a soldier in an army of mob people, and the snuff movies and all of that are at the extreme outside of the circle of syndicate production. What is now sometimes called The Syrian Mafia, just a newspaper name, but it refers to the top men in the crime family here, two men named Rikla and Measure who control mixed ethnic factions of what is left of the old crime organizations.''

"And they specialize in porn with children?''

"I doubt if those men even realize the extent of Kriegal's kiddie-porn operation. They are older men—both in their seventies, and technically they are called 'crew bosses' for the top capos. A man named Salvatore Dagatina, now elderly and in prison. A man named Tony Cypriot, his real name is Ciprioni, who more or less controls the underworld in the Midwest, but their so-called 'underbosses' "—he glanced at a piece of paper—"this James Russo and Lyle Venable, they take a part of Kriegal's profits, so presumably they, at least from a structural standpoint, oversee the operation for their higher-ups. It plays only the smallest part in the overall crime cartel."

"How do you get justice for something like this? The real murderers are as much these men you've just been talking about as they are the ones who actually did it."

Troxell saw what he thought might be the hint of total breakdown in the face of the man. His body suddenly had that brittle look a person sometimes gets before they come unglued. Spain let himself shake in an uncontrollable spasm. It didn't take much playacting on his part. Ever since he'd heard Ciprioni's name he'd been shaking visibly. That cocksucking scum. All the times he'd kissed that guinea ass. Yes sir, MISTER Ciprioni. The times he'd killed for him. Jesus CHRIST, it was too much.

He could hear himself telling the PI, "I just can't . . . I can't go through it. No more. I've lost my wife and now my KID!" His body felt like it was going to self-destruct right then and there. Additionally, there was the curious sensation of watching himself putting it on for Troxell. He wondered for just a fleeting instant as he tried to manifest the signs of a nervous breakdown if indeed he *was* having one. "The endless questions. Tiff's name smeared in filth." Going on as he shook apart, letting the words freeze his heart. Something about the legal system being what it is. Turnstile justice. The incompetence of the doo-dah and the law's doo-dah, and so forth and so on and vamp to the coda. "Years of agony and notoriety for my dead daughter and WHAT THE FUCK FOR? They'd never do a week in jail for it—" on and on.

Troxell just looked across at his client and mentally

shrugged. He couldn't put this guy through it. Here was a man on the brink of total collapse. One look and you could see he was unwrapping.

Now he could see he'd read Spain all wrong. The facade he'd thought was icy strength was just a persona—the frozen mask of a man wound tight, a mainspring about to break under pressure, a bereaved father strung out to his limits and beyond. Frank Spain was somebody balanced on the lip of a deep nervous breakdown.

Still, Mel Troxell tried to argue for the prosecution of the guilty as much as the system would allow. He gently tried to convince Spain that he was too far gone to handle this properly, which brought out all the stops. Spain went into a screaming rage about how he was the client paying the bills, he was the father who had lost a daughter, and he did such a job of portraying a mind about to snap that Troxell finally just shrugged one last time and left. The irony was that it was only an act in Spain's mind. The reason he'd been so convincing with Troxell was that he was in fact going insane. And this beckoning insanity was what the PI saw and what allowed that door to be closed.

The moment the man left, Spain shut off the flow of emotion the way you'd close a faucet. He sat very quietly reading the report again, although he didn't need to do so. Every name, every phrase, every comma, every sentence, was burned into his forebrain, blasted into the cortex forever. Yet he read the report again. And yet a third time. Reading between the lines with the years of insider knowledge that led him down new streets not covered on the pages. He made new, more informed assumptions. Conjecture and theory gave way to the beginnings of his plan. Again, a fourth rereading, this time making notes on a yellow legal pad as he reread the story of his daughter's seduction, abuse, addiction, torture, and degradation. And then, her horror-filled death.

Once again he reads of the fourteen-year-old stranger—this child of his—and the utter and absolute monstrousness of the crimes and inhuman acts committed against her. And once again he follows her trail down to Florida and to Texas, and across the border and into Mexico for her last, screaming, blood-flecked moment/ of "stardom" in the blinding, white-hot lights. And as he reads the hand of death touches a burning match to a slow fuse.

He begins his own list. It begins
GAETANO CIPRIONI and then
SALVATORE DAGATINA.

And the list has many, many names. The list becomes sacred to him. It is his holy quest. Names. An endless list of what he now thinks of as numbers. Numbers he will do. All of them, each as responsible as the next for the death and horrors of his beloved Tiff as surely as if they were the physical perpetrator.

He makes a little shrine of the film canister and it sits on a shelf there in the study, resting like an urn of ashes from the crematorium, tugging at him and spearing his heart and tearing at his mind until he feels himself burst inside.

And Spain sits there feeling himself disintegrate and the pieces going off the deep end, and he carefully draws a line through the name second from the bottom,
ROGER NUNNALY

He will study the thick dossier until his reddened eyes sting with exhaustion. There are other names he will want to add to his holy list, his private shit list of numbers. Others who will now have to pay with the dearest possible currency, as he has. All of them connected into the network of terror and degradation that conspired to take his family from him, and then to make his daughter's dying a hellish nightmare.

He sees an immediate twist to his plan that will make the joy of what he is about to do all the more rich and delicious. How he savors his taste for the names. And this, the way he will play them against one another, knowing their great weaknesses as he does, this is frosting on the poisonous cake. He must pull himself together, he thinks.

The tears have long dried. But as he reads and makes his notes, his body continues to shake with fury and despair. And he prays for madness to take him now.

"So there I am in my red Santa Claus suit and I got the fake beard on and, shit, an' this little girl comes up with this fox of a mother and I go, Climb up on Santa's lap an' tell him what you want for Christmas. An' when you're done, MOMMY can climb up on Santa's face an' tell him what she wants."

"Bullshit," Eichord could hear James Lee telling his partner. "You ain't got a fuckin' lap. You got a couple of lower fat rolls you might push together— that'd be about it." Eichord held the phone closer to his ear but then he heard the recorded music again and pulled it away again as he heard Tuny say, "Might push YOU together and make a fuckin' gook accordion," and he changed ears with the receiver just as a voice came back on the telephone and gave him the answer to his question.

" 'Preciate it. Thanks. Yep," he told the phone, "I will. Thanks again." So that was it. The last dead end on the paper trail of one Floyd Streicher. Somebody jetting out of LAX just plain didn't exist. He'd run the whole nine yards through MCTF. Everything from motor vehicles to telephone records. He'd run it out for a hundred-mile radius around Metro St. Louis. No such animal. Floyd, he of the hooded eyes—Eichord felt sure—did not exist. So Floyd boarded the TWA flight, but some other wise guy deplaned in St. Louis. So what? Now what?

* * *

The killing came from mysterious and dark energies stockpiled during the long weeks of hybernation and doldrum, at first an expulsion of high-energy flow resulting from a prolonged gestation period and then a shaking of the carbonation in its vacuum-sealed, hermetic skin sack of bubbling, exploding pressures.

At first he could never fully wake up and he slept fourteen sometimes sixteen hours a day. A deep, drugged sleep-coma that hammered him senseless over and over, and he'd crawl back into his nest of dirty bed linens scarcely rumpled from the last sleepathon and with eyes already stinging seek the dark, forgetting comfort of slumber. He slept hard. Mind on hold. His subconscious floating along in the black, timeless oblivion of perpetual night.

Sometimes his bladder would poke him awake and he'd lurch out of his mummy wrappings to pee, eyes half-closed in his prune face as he splashed carelessly over the sides of the commode, staggering back to his unknowing stupor, sound asleep even as his sheet-scarred, wrinkled countenance slammed back down into his beloved, warm nest of covers and unclean bedclothes. Soreness was his alarm clock and discomfort was all that kept him on his feet for seven or eight hours a day.

He never fully awoke. Minimal activity, meals, the mandatory rituals of existence, a sedentary period of staring off into space, then the great weight of it all returning to settle over him like a wet and heavy cloak, weighing him down and forcing him back into his snug, fetal curl within the womb of darkness and collapse.

He sat very still for nearly two days and a night staring with intense concentration at the small can of film as he watched the disaster of his life unfold again and again on the instant replay of his merciless memory. He got up from the chair a few times when his body ached from the motionlessness or from a need

to relieve itself, and back in the same seated position
to stare some more.

He forgot to drink water for a time and after nearly
twenty-four hours his throat had become so raw it was
all he could do to swallow.

By the next day he had begun to hear strange things.
The noises of the house had become unbearably loud
and annoying. He could hear the blood coursing
through his veins, and he imagined he could detect
arteries beginning to clot and harden. Cells beginning
to die. Synapses misfiring. Relays failing. He imagined the machine of his body beginning to self-
destruct.

He imagined that the cauliflower of his cerebellum
was rotting. His olfactory sense detected the smell of
rotting vegetable, and neurons, millions of nerve cells
in the hippocampus, attempted to feed the atrophied
terminals of the brain's computer. The computer, red-
lining on dangerous overload, short-circuited, back-
fired, and blew the lights out in his mind.

He fell into a deep, brain-dead sleep. Inert. Torpid.
Comatose. Spain no longer dreamed.

When I awake, he thinks, I awaken all atingle. The
plan has asserted itself. He awakens remembering all
the words to ''Lonely Teardrops'' as sung by Jackie
Wilson. He is fairly certain he could bench-press 350
pounds. He knows his brain has been totally rewired,
and he smells burning leaves, toast with ham and eggs,
chocolate cupcakes and cold milk, steak tartare with
blood running on the platter, freshly baked bread, Tu-
borg, a German wine he cannot pronounce, Chanel,
newly mown spring bermuda, all of these disparate
smells sensed simultaneously as his brain screws its
olfactory bulb back into the socket.

He knows he could mentally run the hundred in 9.9,
memorize the A-through-C section of Webster's unabridged (AARDVARK: of its genus, *Orycteropus*, it is

sole representative of an order, Tubulidentata), climb
tirelessly and never fall, fully understand the impli-
cations of the theory of noctivating flora, remember a
joke about a man named Wolfshlegelsteinhausenber-
gerdorf, knows he could now play "Willow Weep for
Me" on a B-flat alto, and awash in the diluvial sea of
information flooding into his brain, he showers, shits,
shaves, brushes, flosses, medicates, deodorizes, and
begins to pack.

As he packs for the trip south he is amazed to have
Finley Wren, which his eyes read when he was seventeen, repeated back to him by his brain. He has broken through some neural barrier. His memory is trying
to tell him something and he senses it now, fully up-
right after his long, inverted, and perverse couvade,
and the enormity of the possibilities sheathes him in
yet another layer of invulnerability and resolve.

In his mind he has already completed the journey
for which he is packing, and now prepares for the main
event, picking up the phone and calling a realtor. He
puts his home on the market, having concocted an appropriate scenario, and, using another identity, tele-
phones another real-estate agent to look for something
more suitable to his needs. He smiles at the prospects.
Finishes packing. Slides behind the wheel, glancing in
the rearview mirror and smiling into the slate-gray eyes
of a madman.

For over fifteen years he has worked as the top enforcer for the National Narcotics Council, called the
Commission within the families. It was the governing
body that presided over the eight primary drug families comprising the largest unit within what is wryly
called "Organized Crime." It's a difficult concept for
the layman. We know of the Mafia and little else. That
element, the old-timers within certain sectors of the
primarily Italian and Sicilian communities, represents
only a minor aspect of the huge drug monolith.

The purpose of the National Council or Commission

was to attempt to control an uncontrollable thing that fed on human greed: a billion-dollar business whose continuation required the lowest possible profile. Years of loyalty and success, and the hand of fate reaching out to destroy or incapacitate his superiors, had contrived to elevate Gaetano Ciprioni to the throne of that secret organization. As their enforcement chief it was Spain's function to finalize those solutions that could not be achieved by discussion or threat. He was empowered to act in the Commission's behalf, which meant he was a hiring agent as much as he was a worker.

Working totally outside the families, accessible only by toll-free long lines linked to a special radio-telephone system, he had been for over a decade the busiest professional working outside the military-intel-law-enforcement umbrella. He was the best that drug money could buy, and that means he was the best there was.

Frank Spain's twisted plan of revenge would lead him back, ultimately, to St. Louis and the dark heart of Salvatore Dagatina, titular don of the St. Louis crime family, and to the man who had made this nightmare happen: his traitorous mentor Gaetano Ciprioni. An insane father hungry for vengeance against the mob, that would be one thing. But this is *SPAIN*, the killer. And in the crushing of his ego he no longer views the hideous death of his daughter as the act of individuals, but rather as the collective responsibility of many. He has devoted himself to a bloodbath of retaliation against all of those he sees as directly culpable.

It would be bad enough to attack him personally. His response to a nociceptive stimulus would be predictably awesome, lightning fast, and devastating. But this goes far beyond protective reflexes. They have created an all-kill bomb, set it in their midst, and started it ticking. Let's see how they like a wet red

path of torture and death when it's run back down
their throats. Over the edge and on a rampage of revenge, Spain begins.

As Spain drove he chewed over a piece of annoying
news. The punk Roger Nunnaly had been killed in an
automobile accident. Too bad, he thought. What a
shame—eh? But no use crying over spilt blood.

For mental exercise he tries to alphabetize the doz-
ens of names as he drives toward the Freunds:

Alba.

Annelo.

Belmonte. No. That should be under the L's, for
La Bellamonde.

Casagrande. Ciprioni. Oh, yes. Then young Mr.
Dawkins. Shit. Dagatina twice, then Dawkins, then
DeVintro.

Dudzik.

Eggleston.

Freunds. Um-hmm. The Freunds twice.

He finds the punk Dawkins without any effort,
thanks to the detailed Troxell report. The punk is in
a kid's arcade and pool hall, and Spain waits. He
follows him. When the kid parks, Spain is on top of
him and he is very deft with a blackjack. He carries
a leaded sap that can kill but he uses it now with
surgical skill. A quick tap. The Dawkins punk crumples in the street and in a few seconds his trunk is
popped and Spain is loading the boy, handling him
like a sack of potatoes with the adrenaline charge of
action and the hypo of mad, vengeful hatred giving
him all the strength he needs to do the job effort-
lessly.

"Ohhhhhhh," the Dawkins kid says, blinking,
Spain pulling him from the trunk of the suffocating
vehicle. He has lost all sense of time. A moment ago
he was getting out of his ride and wham—the lights
went out and there was an exploding pain. And when

he woke up he couldn't breathe and it was hot and he couldn't move.

"Hello, Greg."

"Mr. Spain." His hands are fastened behind him and he can't feel anything in his arms. No pain. Nothing.

"Bumpy ride?" He can't make out where they are.

"Listen. It wasn't my fault Tiff ran away. Don't blame ME for—"

Spain backhands him rather gently. "Shut up, Greg. Don't try to use that slick con shit on me. It's too late now. Dig?" Tiff's father is speaking calmly, but Greg can see the look of icy hatred in his face.

"Please, Mr. Spain. Please don't hurt me. I didn't— AAAAAAHHH! AAAAAAAAAAAAHHHHHHH-HHHHHH OOOOOHHHHHHHHHH CHRIST DON'T DONNNNNNNN'T!"

Jesus, Greg thinks, this crazy fucker is stabbing me. It doesn't really hurt that much. But it scares him to death to see her dad suddenly pull out what looks like a small kitchen knife and slice a line across his chest.

"AAAAAAAAAAAAAAAAAAAAAAAAHHHHHHHH-HHH!" he screams again as Spain quickly cuts another line downward across Greg's chest, cutting right through the shirt, cloth, and skin, slicing with great precision. Then making a third long cut. Then, as lines of red begin to bleed through, Spain rips the boy's shirt off. It is only then that Greg Dawkins realizes his feet are already hobbled as he vainly tries to run and pitches forward in another scream of agony.

"These cuts aren't that deep, Greg. Please. Relax," the man tells him soothingly as he rolls him over on his back. "You see what I've done here is carve a nice upside-down U shape on your chest. What was the old joke about the guy who dated a cheerleader from Michigan and he had a W on his chest. Or was it a girl dates a guy and her roommate sees a W on her from his letter sweater and some shit about, Was he from Wisconsin? and she says, No—Michigan. Something like that—I forget how it went. Well, your girl can be from Utah, I guess, eh?'' And the knife went into the top of the inverted U and started making a little series of carving motions and then the Dawkins boy started screaming as loud as he could.

He woke up in awful, intense pain, and the fear of Spain's presence was as bad as the physical burning. And as he came around again he looked into the eyes of Tiff's father who said, "Greg. Please. Don't pass out like that, son. You've got to learn to be a MAN now. Otherwise, you little piece of shit, how am I ever going to get you *PEELED?*'' And the hot, biting steel began to carve again.

He took a long time with the Dawkins kid. And when the boy was dead Spain buried him there in the remote gravesite he'd prepared, and got into the car and drove away. He drove for as long as he could keep his eyes open. It occurred to him that he'd felt nothing as he inflicted the pain on the punk. He had taken no pleasure whatsoever in the act. He wanted the family. He wanted to take it to them.

It was all he thought about as he drove through the long night, and the anticipation of the sweet revenge plastered a frightening smile across his face.

Stoked to the boiling point on speed, hatred, adrenaline, and insanity, he came for the Freunds wired to the max. They were such pathetic garbage to him that he didn't even bother with a professional approach. No special, carefully concocted penetration plan. No elaborate presurveillance. Jeezus. They were NOTHING. Pure shit.

Driving past a dumpster in an alley in back of the

McAllen telephone company, he stopped almost as an afterthought, grabbed a few papers out of a box, some manifests and carbons and crap, shoved them into a cheap clipboard, and headed for the Freunds' residence.

It is amazing what you can get away with by using nothing more than a businesslike tone of bored officialese and a clipboard. There's something vaguely but instantaneously intimidating about somebody standing at your front door writing on a clipboard. What could it be? Nothing good. At the very least, it's the census people and God only knows what Uncle Sam does with those figures nowadays.

When the woman Bobbie answered the door, he made sure he had the right party by simply asking her, "Mrs. Freund?"

Spain's state of mind was such that she could have said, I'm Samantha the baby-sitter, and he would probably have been right upside her head anyway, just on general principles, but the woman said,

"Yes?"

"National Express package. I need you to sign please, ma'am," and he's thrusting that official-looking clipboard in front of her, holding something under her face to sign with the pen right there for her.

"Sign here?"

"Right there where the checkmark is," pointing vaguely. But that's enough to keep her looking down and she is midway through the phrase "I don't" when she feels something take out her coordination. What it is—she has the door braced with one arm, and she's trying to see where to sign her name—where is the damn checkmark? When he lets her have a nice hard one from the spring-loaded sap and pushes right in with her, talking to her as she falls, timing a very ordinary-sounding fake conversation to muffle her impact as she crumples to the floor, and doing all of this in a split second. Doing this with professionalism and

care, now, on dangerous footing at this stage, moving
back through the house hoping he'll find Charlie alone.
Hoping he won't have to kill anybody else. No next-
door neighbors or passing strangers. Because anyone
he sees now will go down. People. Children. Dogs.
Cats. Parakeets. Gerbils. Cockroaches. Any fucking
thing that moves or breathes dies.

He was still running his mouth about where he was
supposed to go with the package and he was glad to
bring it in for them it was so heavy and he was glad
to do it or some such jive nonsense as he rushed
through the rooms when he spotted a long, lanky dude
getting off a sofa where a television set was blasting,
and Spain didn't even bother to use a real weapon on
him, he just threw the sap at him when he raised his
arms going, "Heeeyyyyyy," and that's when Spain
kicked him real viciously in the nuts and put Charles
Freund in a world of sudden hurt.

"AAAAAaaaaaaaaaaaaaaaa," the man moaned.

"Huh?" Spain said, taking hold of him.

"Awwwwwwwwwww," Charlie repeated on cue.

"You like pain so fucking well," Spain muttered as
he dragged Charlie across the rug, "what's the big
deal?"

"Ohhhhhhh, aaaaaaaaaaaaaaaahhhhh," and Spain
tore his hands away and kicked him again. A real
bruising sixty-yard drop kick in the balls, and Freund
screamed at the top of his lungs, "AAAAAAAAAAA-
AAAAAAAAAAAAAAAAAAAAAAAHHHHHHHHHH-
HHHHHHHHHHHHHH!" and it was music to Spain's
ears as he thought about Tiff.

He wondered how long Bobbie would stay under,
and he wondered if anybody else was in the house,
thinking these things automatically as he sized up
Charles Freund moaning as Spain pulled him across the
rug. Moaning and groaning like he really meant it.

"How's that feel, pops? You like that shit?"

"UUUUUHHHHHHHHHHHHHHHH, awwwwww-
wwwwwwwwwwwwww!"

"No shit? I'm surprised to hear that," he said con-
versationally, "the way you love that pain and all. I
mean," he said, dragging Charlie Freund over to a
straight-back chair, "let's see if we can get you into
some. How's that sound, fuck-face?"

You can forget all that karate shit. Some guy rushes
into your living room when you're kicked back watching the tube and he throws a lead-weighted blackjack
at your head, and as you raise your arms to ward off
the thrown object coming at your head, he kicks you
expertly in the testicles, you can kiss all that kung fu
bullshit *adiós*. You're in the big, green, hurt locker.
End of story. Good-bye.

Freund was crying and pissing and moaning, his
balls swelling up like grapefruit, and Spain got him
nice and snug, then went and wired Bobbie, who he
figured would be the tougher of the two by far, came
back, and went at Charlie for serious.

Charlie Freund gave up the Morales punk, Jon Belmonte, and nine more names while he was waiting to
die. Some of them were new names and Spain's list
was growing. Charlie and Bobbie were glad to have
the other names for him.

He got elaborate, voluminous descriptions screamed,
slobbered, begged at him in the closing minutes of
their lives. They were imploring, wheedling, whining,
praying him to stop please stop anything we'll tell you
everything do anything you want just don't hurt us
don'tpleasedon'tdoooooooooon't.

For people who liked pain as well as they did, they
sure couldn't get behind any of it. At the last there
they would like to have had forty or fifty more names
for him. Good stories to tell him. Anything to prolong
the time they had, anything to postpone the agony and
hurting they knew was in their immediate future.

They were giving him bankbooks, dope caches, coke

stashes, secret money boxes, hollow books, closet
safes, account numbers, cookie jars, film masters,
mailing lists, and when they ran out, they started making things up the way people always do. They would
have given him Lucky Luciano, Willie Sutton, and the
Vienna Boys Choir if Spain would have just kept listening.

Big, flowery descriptions. Addresses. Hangouts,
hobbies, habits. Moles and scars. Christ ohnoooo-
oooooo dontpleasedon't ANYTHING. We'll tell you
what you want to hear.

He had all the real stuff down cold two different
ways when Bobbie went under for the last time. Charlie had been more resilient than he looked. He looked
like a fag, Spain thought. But of course a person's pain
threshold is just a fact of life, like their blood type.
You can't do a whole lot about it when trauma paints
it all black for you.

Charlie hung in there pretty good, all in all. Spain
had his chest almost half-skinned when he finally went
out for good and wouldn't come around again. Spain
was really sorry to see them go. He had lots of time
but they just couldn't keep up with it all. And he hadn't
even branded Bobbie on the inside yet.

He took no real pleasure from torturing them. It
made him sort of tired. But then, when he walked
around their place later, looking at the spots where
Tiff had suffered at their hands, his rage returned, and
he found a very sharp kitchen knife and really did a
jay-oh-bee on the Fruends. It was good to get rid of
some of the hostile energies, he thought to himself.

He looked down at what was left of the Freund ca-
davers finally and said, "Are we having fun yet?" and
laughed at the sound of the words.

His long-time colleague in Homicide, Detective Sergeant James Lee, the "Chink" of the legendary cop
duo Chink and Chunk, was trying to explain the finer

points of the Oriental Basket Boff when the loud voice
of his partner, fat Dana Tuny, came bellowing down
the stairs as "Chunk" descended into the bowels of
the squad room at Buckhead Station. He was singing
a well-known song to which filthy lyrics had been ap-
pended. " 'Neath a twilight canopy, you're so mel-
low—" was being loudly sung as " 'Neath a toilet can
of pee, urine so yellow."

"Jeezus," Lee said to Eichord, "it stinks like a taco
fart but it looks like a blimp. What the hell izzit?"

"Good morning, ladies," Chunk said, *"Kee-rist,* it
always stinks down here. Smells like shrimp sub-gum
farts."

"Good morning, Mr. Goodyear," his long-suffering
partner said.

"Morning," Eichord greeted him. "Honcho in
yet?"

"Fucked if I know. What do I look like, my fucking
brother's keeper?"

"You look like a sperm whale with a double hernia,
but I still need to know if the honcho's in yet."

"You look like five guys wearing the same clothes,"
Lee suggested.

"I didn't see his smiling face, dear," Tuny told Eichord, turning to his skinny partner saying, "and you
look like the dildo float in a fucking Chinatown pa-
rade, you little moo-shoo porkpecker."

The phone on Lee's desk rang and he snarled, "Hill
Street Eaters, Lieutenant Hunter," before snatching
the receiver up and saying, "Homicide. . . . Okay."
He signaled for Eichord to pick it up as he hit the hold
button.

Today they would be Hill St. Blues television cops.
Eichord was partially to blame for their style. Ever
since he'd told them about the guys in Chicago who
were Cisco and Pancho one day, Hawaii 5-0 the next,
they'd started doing their own version of wacko cop
theater. Every day Chink and Chunk "played" some-

body. Like little boys. If you didn't like them it could drive you bats. Fat Dana the Kingfish one day, with his partner Andy of Amos 'n' Andy.

"Well, er, uh, abba dabba, looky heeyuh, now, Brother Andy, those are serious allegations," and the other one saying on cue, "Well, I is de alligatee. And you is de alligator, dere." Just a way to make the time pass between them. TV shows, radio shows, movie scenes—they were a team and they'd been together so long that they literally knew what the other one was thinking. It made for so-so comedy relief, and on occasion some fair-to-middling cop work.

Eichord liked them. Especially Jimmie Lee, with whom he'd been close friends for as long as he'd been a cop. He could hear them banter back and forth as the woman was droning on about the plastic scam in his right ear. One of them saying to the other, "She only lets you go down on her 'cause you got a face like a douche bag." They'd lasted together for so many years. Longer than most marriages.

". . . is not the same story we got at all . . ." His brain kicked back in for a second as the woman's voice grated in his ear. An employee from one of the credit-card outfits hassling him about something that was tied to a junkie-related homicide. He glanced up at the wall clock. Smack dab in the middle of the clock face was the tiny printed message "Eatin' Ain't Cheatin'." He managed to get off the phone and they started in on him.

"Hey, the captain's in now," fat Dana said as soon as he hung up the phone.

"Uh-huh." He waited.

"The captain? Did someone ask about the captain?" Lee said with great excitement. "Captain Furillo?"

"Sorry," Tuny said. "Furillo's out with AIDS today, Mick. I'm in charge."

"You, Lieutenant Butt?"

"It's *Buntz!* You dork-brained little peterface." He straightened his tie like the guy on TV did.

"Grrrrrrrrrrrrrr," Lee snarled menacingly.

"Get hold of yourself, Rinty."

"Watch it, Puke Breath."

"Hey. No way to talk in front of Mizzzzzzz Davenport here."

"Good morning, Detectives," Lee chirped in his best falsetto.

"That's good morning, Detective Lootenant, you titless tramp. That no-dick, cold-fish husband of yours ain't here ta proteck ya."

"Listen, Craterface, or Inspector General Zitz, or whatever your freaking name is," Lee squeaked, "when my husband Furillo gets back he'll have your ugly ass up on charges for this gross insubordination."

"Yeah? I'll have you up on ole Pork Mountain in a minute, Mizzzzzzzzzzzzz Daybed, now haul your skinny ass outta here."

"Sounds good to me," Eichord said, getting up with an audible sigh.

"Oh, don't go away mad," Lee screeched, still in falsetto.

"Two minutes to nine and you maniacs have got me tired already. You wear a person down with that shit."

"You know, Jack," Tuny said, "I wasn't going to say this. But you have a right to know."

"Mmmm?" Eichord said, turning as he started out the door and arching an eyebrow.

"Yeah. We weren't going to tell you. Some of the guys are saying you might be a latent heterosexual."

"Absolutely," he said, turning back. "I guess I can come out of the closet now." He started upstairs.

"Coming in the closet is how they caught on to you in the first place," Tuny told his back.

The pretty girl sitting beside the first-floor dispatcher looked up at him as he mouthed a Hi and she pantomimed a kiss at him as she spoke into a headset contraption. He gestured with a thumb in the general direction of their fearless leader and she nodded. He winked goodbye.

He knocked on the open door as he went in. " 'Morning, Captain," he said to the huge, red-faced man behind the desk, who grunted at him without looking up and said,

"YOU look like shit on a stick this morning."

Eichord thought of one or two rejoinders as he eyed the bulging girth threatening to pop the buttons on the man's shirtfront, but he smiled and said, "I need a vacation."

"You just had a fucking vacation."

"You call that circle jerk in California a vacation? I call it a sentence."

"Well, you invincible crime-crushers have a tough time."

"Gimmee a break, Cap."

"You wanna break? You need another vacation? You got it." He slid a Task Force envelope across the desk. "Forthwith."

Eichord went through the motions of opening it and chatting briefly about the summons to St. Louis, even though in fact he had initiated it himself. He was going up there to see if he could fit SEE NO EVIL into the recent St. Louis mob hits. Different MOs than the L.A. EYEBALL work, but the elusive Mr. Streicher was a burr under the saddle.

As soon as he could do so he extricated himself from the captain's presence. In the entire time he'd been in the office the captain had never looked up at him. There was no love lost between them. Eichord didn't respect the man much, and he supposed that it showed. The honcho made no bones about the way he felt about Eichord. Jack was a drunken bum of a prima donna who would have been booted off the force years ago but for the intervention of the McTuff people and the efforts of his rowdy friends Lee and Tuny who had so often rebuilt the bridges he'd tried so hard to burn.

Eichord wasn't disturbed by their relationship. He figured he would have probably felt the same way had their positions been reversed. Everybody from Jack's "rabbi" down knew that the captain was Eichord's superior only in the most nominal sense. Jack served only one master: the Major Crimes Task Force.

Jack Eichord at least knew he was no invincible crime-crusher. He was just another plodding, sweating, paper-shuffling, workmanlike flatfoot. One more booze-battered copper whose butt was growing larger by the day and who had a gray hair for every city he'd ever been in. Somebody whose true cop value fell right in between the extremes of "Éminence Grise of Serial Murder Experts" (*Criminology Magazine*) and "shit on a stick."

When he finished cleaning up after the things in Florida, Frank Spain headed cross-country for Texas, and days of long driving later, he was crossing over into May-hee-co, passing a billboard advertising a TV show or a beverage or something that said, VIVIR UN POCO. It was the first time he'd smiled in a long time, and he muttered out loud, "Abso-goddamn-lutely," when he saw it.

He'd had all that boring, flatlands driving to plan. To churn all the names and the people together and blend the mix in his head. He understood the organization better than most. Ciprioni, his treacherous mentor, had seen to that.

When Spain was a kid, first working as a mob gofer, still a youngster who they looked on as somebody to cultivate, Ciprioni had pulled his coat to the inevitability of the Dago family's rise and fall. "You won't have to worry about nothin'. I'm going straight up. The Man—he's going to the very top. But these people here"—he meant the other St. Louis family, the ones down the ladder from the big Chicago mob, not to mention Kansas City—"they gonna fall apart when the old man goes."

The Man, a name he always spoke with reverent emphasis, was his—not just patriarchal godfather but everyone's—*spiritual* leader. More than the bosses' boss. He was the force that held it together. As far removed from the Dagatina family as America was from the old country. With Tony Gee gone, Sally Dago would be just one more insignificant hood trying to run a crumbling empire.

So much had happened over the years. Sally finally went away behind a racketeering/extortion thing and was still inside. But Spain would figure a way to bring him down too. And that fucking Ciprioni as well. No one was invulnerable—history had proved that enough times.

Sally Dago's people had been a mixed lot, Italians, Sicilians, and mostly Syrians. The two main factions could be played against each other. As Spain drove, he formulated his plan. The way he would take the small fry off first. He'd whack one on either side— figure it out just right—the people would have to be strategically placed *just so* to make it look like the people "across the street" were making a move of some kind. If he did it right, worked carefully, kept his emotions in check, he could start a fucking gang war.

He stopped and used a telephone, calling someone whose name had appeared in a sidebar of the main dossier.

"Hello."

"Yeah?"

"I'm calling from L.A., can you hear me awright?"

"Yeah. Who's dis?"

"I'm a friend of a certain mutual friend of ours. He tol' me you might be able to put me onto a dude that don't ask too many questions about takin' pictures of pretty girls . . . You know what I'm talking' about?''

"Naw. I dunno what chew talking about.''

"Dat's awright. Listen. He said to mention Juan's name,'' he gave it the heavy H-sound, "and like if you could put me in touch wit' the Morales dude or somebody, there'd be a taste innit for you, comprende?''

"Oh.'' The interest went out of the other voice. "You talkin' about Morales. Which Morales you talkin' about?''

"Paco, man. Who you tink? Hey, how can I get in touch with him, I runnit by him.''

"I don't know fer sure. Who'd jew say dis was?''

"A friend of a friend of Juan's—a good friend, you know? He said jew was cool, man. So what's the big deal? Paco still over in the trailer court?''

"Yeah. I don't got his number, tho.''

"Well, how, uh, where can I leave word for him? He's gonna get *well* on dis' shit, man.''

"Hell, I dunno. You might try d'Bacardi.''

"Huh?''

"Yeah. You could leave word at d'Bacardi. He hangs out dere sometime.'' Pause. "Shit—I dunno, man. I don' see him dat much.''

"What's the Bacardi?''

"A BAR, baby, d'Bacardi Bar's d' name of it, okay?''

"Hey, *gracias,* if you see him tell him Bob Long called. Okay?''

"Yeah. *De nada.*'' The line clicked.

Spain asked around a little very quietly. It took him about five minutes to locate the Bacardi Bar, which was a nameless cantina that took its local nickname from a big, neon B A C A R D I up on the roof of the building.

He spotted the mobile-home park across the road and cracked the door on the stolen van he'd picked up back on the Tex-ee-co side and waited for a few minutes. He didn't see much street activity. He got out and scouted around a little, looked at a couple of mailboxes and saw Morales, walked up, and knocked on the door. Spain had very carefully tried the knob as he knocked. He'd learned many years ago that to his surprise half the doors you try are unlocked in the first place. This wasn't, but it had given easily. He wouldn't even need plastic. He turned around and walked away as if he was going back to the van, and when he didn't see any eyes, he made a little stutter-step like a double take, a bit of I-forgot-something pantomime with the hands, and walked back to the trailer.

It was an ordinary if rather long, used, singlewide. Spain figured it to be maybe a fourteen-by-seventy. Morales could be asleep in there back in a bedroom. He stuck the little piece of metal in and the door gave with a loud popping noise. No inside chain. Spain went in fast, closing it behind him and blinking in the semidarkness of the interior. He waited a second listening. Heard nothing and started back into the long rectangular home, his weight shaking the flimsy particle board floor as he walked.

It was a pigsty. Nobody home. Stuff strewn everywhere. No dog. No caged bird. Nothing. Good. He went to work on the door immediately with some pocket tools, fixing the cheap frame so that when the owner came up to unlock his door, it wouldn't push in with the first touch and alert him. He superglued a metal strip in place to hold the latch plate, the plate he'd forced loose, and then darkened it with a fast-drying marker to make the metallic shine less conspicuous.

He waited and tried to keep from breathing any more than necessary. This punk must never bathe. What a hole, he thought. Just a punk who worked the camera on the stuff Jon Belmonte did locally. Rhapsody Video. What a name. Connected to the distribution arm of the kiddie-porn biz through the St. Louis people. The Freunds, Belmonte, all just punks. Pervert scum on the fringes of the sex industry. Spain shivered. Disgusted that the families would tolerate freaks like this. But then they used street hypes for dope salesmen, so what's the difference? The families would pay for their lack of discernment. He would make all these scum pay with their dust.

Almost two hours. A little car pulls up and two beaners get out, talking their fucking greaser talk, chattering away and laughing, and Spain moves back into the hallway as they come in, his piece out in one hand, a sap in the other, piece with a suppressor on, then that whole thing wrapped. A dipshit .22.

The door closes. They start to say something and he steps out of the darkened hall with the piece pointed. Tells them to freeze *en español*.

"Turn around, punks." He motions.

"Whachew wan'?"

"SHUT THE FUCK UP," he hisses. "Morales, listen to me, punk. I need some information and I'll leave you be. You first—put your hands behind you." One of them does, and that's cool. He didn't give a *cucaracha* which was which but he had to know who was who. He quickly sapped the other one lightly. Wired Morales' hands with a twist-em, stepped on the back of one of his knees, taking him down to the floor. Did a half-frisk. Slipped a billfold out and nodded. Gagged Morales, now that he'd seen the name on a card in the man's wallet and knew they weren't jiving with him, and quickly leaned over and fired a .22 Long Rifle round into the head of the man he'd sapped, placing the shot behind the left eye about one and a half inches from the ear and firing in an upward trajectory. The wrapped, suppressed .22 sounding like a loud, metallic fart.

"Fucked up that towel, didn't we?" He took the coat hanger he'd laid on top of the TV, all nicely

straightened, and his pliers, and wired Morales hands
nice and tight. The punk's eyes were as big as silver
dollars.

"Sí, sí, señor. You're in a bit of trouble here, *chinga
chinga*. What do you think?"

"Mmmmmmffffffff." Morales struggled.

"Wass yo' name, *amigo?* Paco? Listen, douchebag,
you really like taking pictures of the little kids, eh?
You and your pal Juan," he exaggerated the name,
"get off on the kiddie stuff. So I'm going to fix you
up good." A straight razor flashed open from nowhere
and Spain showed it to the man. Then he pocketed it
and wired Morales' ankles, pulled the razor out, slit
the man's fly of his trousers, and picked up his pliers.
The eyes were like golf balls now.

"Hey, I'm not going to hurt your pecker with this,"
he said gently to the bound man. "This is jus' so I
don't have to TOUCH your filthy excuse for a cocko,
Paco." He carefully pulled the limp brown penis from
the man's pants and undershorts using the pliers. "No,
see, I'm not goin' to hurt you with this." The razor
flicked open again. "I'm going to hurt you with
THISSSSSSSSS," he said, making the final cut on the
last Morales scene.

"This is a little something my daughter wants you
to have as a going away present, you spic greaseball
garbage." Smiling real big, he stuffs the thing in the
man's mouth. "You like the little kids so much, you
motherfucker," he says in his tight, fierce whisper,
"now you got yourself a little kid's pecker." And he
started wiping off prints, careful not to step in the
blood.

He took a last look at the two on the floor and walked
out to the stolen van, parked right there in broad damn
daylight across the road from the Bacardi Bar. Fucking
Reynosa.

Adiós, Taco, or Paco, or whatever your fucking
slimebag name was." Spain drove back the way he'd

come. Driving calmly now. Driving past the back of the VIVIR UN POCO billboard and heading toward Jon Belmonte's.

Five names were now lined through at the bottom of his long list:

Greg Dawkins
Roger Nunnaly
Charles Freund
Bobbie Freund
Paco Morales

He picked up a sixth name back across the Mex-Tex border. The only one of the first six that was the least little bit tricky. Of course the Nunnaly punk had been a gift from God. But he couldn't just go up to La Bellamonde and gun his ass down in the street. He needed more names and corroboration of the way the Blue Kriegal thing worked. He didn't want to miss anybody because of an itchy trigger finger. Turned out he had to shoot him anyway.

The Mel Troxell people had been achingly explicit about the part Belmonte/La Bellamonde played in his daughter's torture and demise. Another insult on top of insult was the way nobody had even bothered to be very secretive about the snuff movie. Like it was so protected who'd bother them? The cops in Mexico are in with the beaner wise guys anyway, but you'd think Belmonte would at least have been a bit circumspect.

Spain knew he'd have to exercise the greatest degree of self-discipline to keep from whacking Belmonte out immediately.

He found him in back of his house, beating two little tables with a chain. He had the tables out in the hot sun of his courtyard working them over to age them. He hit the captain's desk about a dozen times, not hard shots, but just enough to bite a little wood out each time, and he was going to start on the honey pine chest when he heard Spain walking across the courtyard toward him.

Spain could tell his reflexes were good the way he turned with a graceful, balanced half-spin still holding the chain down by his right leg, and nodding to Spain as Spain said, "Excuse me, sir. I was wondering if you could tell me how to get to this address," as he pulled a folded up piece of paper from his shirt pocket.

Spain looked at the paper as he got closer and shook his head as if perplexed. But he could see Belmonte shift his weight a little. He was moving back as Spain moved forward. Spain read off a fake address and held the note in an outstretched hand but J.B. wasn't having any of it.

He shook his head politely and said, "Sorry, bud, but I haven't lived around here long myself," moving a little as he spoke, wary and experienced, keeping the piece of chain beside him as he stayed a chain-length away from the stranger with the outstretched arm.

Spain read the situation and clocked the guy for a pro, shrugging as he folded the note back up and smiled, saying, "No problem, pal, I'll ask back at the gas station," turning as if to leave as he dropped his sport coat around the .25 Browning and turned firing low. The shot made a loud *SSPPPAAAKK* as it blew a hole in the coat and hit Belmonte in the hip. He dropped the chain as he fell in a shout of pain, and Spain got to him fast, kicking the chain away and clipped him lightly, then dragging him into the nearby garage.

He had the man bound and gagged and the blood flow stopped within a couple of minutes, and was backing into the garage and loading him into the trunk. He went in the back door of the house and checked it fast, racing through the house with the gun ready, but it was empty. He got in the car and drove out of town

until he found some country roads that didn't look like
they had much traffic on them.

Juan La Bellamonde came to with his hands wired
behind him, bound to a tree. Spain reached down on
the grass beside where he'd been sitting and got a
straight razor and a small bottle of smoky-looking liq-
uid. Dr. Spain pulled on his rubber gloves, which he'd
picked up at the hardware store, and bent to his task.
Spain's rubber-covered fingers ever so gently blotted
the watering eyes and removed the glass stopper from
the acid.

"Do you believe in an eye for an eye?" he asked
the man, rhetorically.

The man's eyes teared again, lidless, as he soaked
the front of his trousers with urine.

"You've got one chance. And goodness gracious,
stop pissing all over yourself—you've got to learn to
control your emotions a little." He picked up the wad-
ded tissue and held it in front of the screaming man.
"Know what these are?" La Bellamonde knew before
he looked into the bloody tissue. "These are your *eye-
lids,* freak," he said through gritted teeth.

"And this"—showing him the smoking stuff—"is
your acid, you see." The man tried to bite through the
gag and began to choke. Spain pulled the gag out for
a moment, and when his choking had subsided he told
him, "One chance. I want everything about the Kriegal operation. Every name in the mob you can think
of. Every address. Every method of contact. Take me
through the whole thing by the numbers, from what
Blue does with the little boys and girls to who he buys
'em from to what brand of rat poison you put on your
cornflakes in the morning. All the dirt. You miss a
comma in there. You even ACT like you're getting
tired. You leave out one fact and I catch you . . ." He
holds up the acid.

La Bellamonde was voluble and forthcoming. He
told him all the nitty 'n' every bit of the gritty, but in

the end it didn't help. Spain was getting bored with him and he sighed, picked up the acid, and removed the stopper, smiling, holding it real close and saying liltingly, "Murine time . . ." as the man fainted.

Spain was in a great mood by the time he'd taken up temporary residence in a motel a week later. He was doing several things at once, constructing his cover, cultivating a cutout, building a mail-drop legend, all the things he'd done a score of times before, but doing it with a difference now. For the first time he wasn't working for pay. He was working for revenge and it filled him with something akin to glee. The singer was wrong. Living well wasn't the best revenge. RE-VENGE was the best bloody, fucking revenge there was, and anything less was just kidding yourself.

When a worker wants to insulate himself—or for that matter, when a dealer wants to protect himself—an innocent party is used. Mules, mokes, they're called different things. Square johns who can be spotted, iso-lated, cut from the pack, cultivated, and put into play without their knowing it. Spain had newspaper ads set to hit the next day at a motel he was using only for fake screening of job applicants. A girl-Friday execu-tive assistant for a mail entrepreneur. He would set some turkey up with a cheap storefront office first. Have her depositing real checks, opening a mail drawer, all that shit. Then he'd use her to take care of details like dealing with realtors—all the things he'd be needing where he didn't want personal contact.

Meanwhile, he did something very tricky. He care-fully scripted a meticulously worded scenario and when he had it just right he phoned the cop who'd been out to his house that last time to see "what they'd heard" if anything. They had an odd, linear conver-sation that had been laid out like a script so that later—if necessary—Spain could always say he had called the police like the concerned father he was to ask if the cops had learned anything about who was responsible for the death of his daughter. In tandem with the Troxell report it wouldn't fly too far but the conversation had been sufficiently ambiguous that it would be something. A card to play just in case. It might be enough to buy him some time when he needed it.

The good part was that it told him Mel Troxell hadn't talked. That was what he had to know. He took the first steps of his plan through the painful motions of calling Pat. He wanted to talk to her like he wanted to chew on broken glass but he was going to lay down whatever cover he could. It was cheap at this price—a few telephone calls.

"Pat," he heard himself saying, "Have you heard anything from Tiff?" wanting to tell his child's mother, his murdered baby's mother, wanting to tell her that he hoped she was happy now. Wanting to rub it in. Wanting to ask her if Buddy's big cock was worth losing her little girl. But number one, he had to play this one straight as an arrow, and number two . . . Shit, that bitch, it probably wouldn't get to her that badly. The cold cunt.

He got through the phone call on automatic and prepared to go into action. He felt the excitement inside him. The knowledge that he was going to bring those sons of bitches down. He was going to start a fucking war.

Part Three

EICHORD

The fact that Eichord had detected a wise guy or an ex-con or whatever breed of felonious monk the non-existent Mr. Streicher might or might not prove to be, would have been insufficient to pull Jack to St. Louis. The gangland type action might not have reached out for him. It was a thing of one too many coincidences. Bad vibes. Rankling hunches. The St. Louis kills were firebombings. Some shootings. But no EYEBALL M. O. No ballistics, forensics, or any other hard information linked the California assassinations and the St. Louis murders.

The randomness of the kills were, however, a factor in themselves. The St. Louis homicide reports told of brutal and what appeared to be unconnected slayings. They could be strictly gangland stuff. But like the L.A. area murders the media attention was noteworthy. When you add to this factoring the coincidental sighting of a definite wise guy leaving the Coast for St. Louis, Eichord thought it might be worth a look.

He was coming in superficially just as he had in L.A., at a summons from the Task Force. But this time he would not be a cherry to be picked, chewed, pitted, and spit out. He'd not be manipulated again by "liaison" smoothies. He'd come in quietly. Unannounced to all but the local honcho. No VIP stuff. He'd ease on in and look around. Check it out his own way.

Jack had fond memories of the St. Louis he could recall from the couple of good years he'd lived there a

159

quarter-century ago. But from the second the cab left Lambert he might as well have been on Mars.

Similarly he found himself unprepared for the Special Division, a compact unit working out of the Homicide Bureau at Twelfth and Clark downtown, now Twelfth and Tucker Boulevard. He found the burg largely unrecognizable, this town he'd called home in the 60s, in Plaza Square, not two blocks from the Division HQ.

Homicide occupied the fourth floor of the six-story building where Chief Adler ran his command post for the Metropolitan Saint Louis area. This was the headquarters for the detectives assigned to the nine St. Louis Police divisions.

The city was a completely different ball game than he remembered. Gone was the old, infamous Pruett-Igo, where two-man cars eventually became open game for snipers. But there were still low-income housing projects in heavily black areas north of the city. Still pockets of unrest and crime. It would take some time to get used to the absence of Gaslight Square, and the wide open Strip. De Baliviere Strip had been notorious back in the druggy 60s, a hot tenderloin of street-corner smack dealers and hookers flagrantly offering their wares. Now De Baliviere, the Seventh Police District—was all rehabs and pricey condos. And the only dope was being sold by $200,000-a-year professional men.

He thought the Bureau looked like a city room of a very-laid-back metro newspaper, or the offices of a prestigious yuppie insurance agency. The cops looked like schoolteachers or ad men for an ultra-conservative house account. Anything but coppers. Only the eyes and the holstered Smiths said different.

"Good morning, Jack, glad to have you aboard," his new temporary boss said with a half-smile in an exchange of the initial pleasantries.

The district commander, under whom Eichord would

nominally be working, was out of the city taking an FBI-agent-taught course sanctioned by the University of Virginia, and the acting shop head was Lieutenant Victor Springer, whom Eichord found distant and routinely polite, as if meeting Jack was 361 on a list of 362 things he had to do that day, which it probably was.

"Come on in. You settled yet?"

"No," Eichord said, "I just came in this morning."

There was the ritual of getting coffee. The usual exchange of amenities. The obligatory comments about Eichord's track record and the expected questions about his fame and the Chicago case. The comments about lodging, the bread-and-butter basics of payroll stuff, where he'd sit, his temporary place in the scheme of things. Then Springer laid it out for him.

"As you know, we have what appears to be the beginning of a full scale gang war on our hands."

"Yeah."

"These mob killings have up until recently been just that—within the crime factions. Wise guys taking down other wise guys. So we thought. But then there was the shooting at Laclede Landing." Springer shoved a newspaper across the desk. "I saved that one." The headline said TWO INJURED IN SAINT LOUIS MOB SHOOT-OUT. Replete with front-page crime-scene photo.

"Mayor Carrol Donovan told St. Louis Police Commissioner Powell, 'Instruct the police department it either cleans this mess up or their replacements will. This city will no longer tolerate an atmosphere of violence,' " Eichord read aloud.

"Well, Jack, you know how it is. You got gang homicides." He shook his head sadly. "Most of the time you're not going to be able to do much. Hell. When they keep it in the family you tend to just go with the flow. The paper's headlines or the position of the *Ten*

O'Clock News' 11 pretty much dictate how many man hours we have to waste on looking into something like that." Eichord nodded. "I mean, you got a pro job, well . . . " He shrugged and the thought trailed off into space.

"But you got guys going for a whack-out in Laclede Landing, Jesus. It's a helluva mess."

"All these firebombings," Eichord said. "These all related?"

"Yep. Here's what you got." He got up and uncovered a standup easel with a family-tree genealogy plotted out on it. "St. Louis family is really several different factions. You got your basic made wise guys, the old LCN, which was under the legendary Tony Gee, who I know you've heard about. He was the fucking *man*. He ran the whole schmear. His main man was another Tony, Tony Cypriot, and that's where they got the old name the papers used to use: the Two Tonys Mob. But it wasn't that at all. Gee ran everything for Chicago. This is back when I guess"—he glanced at some papers—"you were living here, if I remember my notes correctly."

"I was here in sixty-two and sixty-three," he said. He was looking into the lieutenant's eyes as he spoke and Jack doubted if there were too many notes Springer would remember incorrectly.

"Well, Tony Gee pulled the pin in the seventies. And what he left was Sally Dago—Salvatore Dagatina—who's still alive, by the way, and in the can. And a half-assed dope empire. The old-line Italian and Sicilian factions that had one time controlled all the gambling and narcotics and prostitution, which were under the splinter groups of Syrian, and Chink, and Latin wise guys—and the bikers—now these guys are getting long in the tooth too. And they can't control the ethnic groups 'n' that. So you got the whole thing breaking into factions.

"Now you got your two Tonys gone. One dead, one

kicked upstairs—Cypriot a big shot sitting on the national council, and Sally Dago takes a fall and goes in the slams. So all the people capable of running anything are out of pocket. Gee dead. Cypriot gone. Dago behind bars.

"See . . . Tony Gee was the last peacekeeper. He was like a, uh, orchestra leader, ya know? He pulled the whole thing together. And with the other Tony and Sally out of the game there was nobody left with the brains, balls, and experience to keep the family unified. No godfather, like the papers are always saying. No safety valve for the territorial disputes and the faction arguments. No more clearinghouse. If you had the balls to make a move, you made a move. Never mind whose country you were in. Forget that turf shit—you went for it. So you had a mess.

"Tony Gee's lifelong confidant and counselor, Paul Rikla, and his bodyguard, James Measure, who had always hated each other's guts but coexisted out of necessity, had been elevated to underbosses with Sally Dago. Now Sally goes and you got these two Syrian dudes each running a faction of the family. The classic power struggle."

"These guys—Measure and Rikla—they're the two heads of the family now?" Jack asked. All the names were beginning to swirl. He'd just learned a whole set of California name. Now here comes another set.

"Right." Springer nodded.

"Where's Cypriot all this time? How come he's not back here taking over?"

"Aw, this is nothing. St. Louis is nickles and dimes to the big boys. Organized crime here isn't shit, and I'm not saying this to, you know, go, Oh, what a clean town we run. I just mean it isn't a big-crime town, as I'm sure you're aware. Kansas City has a little action but there isn't that much here. You got a couple things in East St. Louis, couple things north of town and whatnot, but it's small potatoes. Cypriot's on the national council. He's working in the Big Five New York families, working with the Chicago and Vegas and Miami people. He's a high roller now. St. Louis is like East Dipshit, Nowhere, to the big boys.''

"Okay." Eichord couldn't seem to get his mind to kick into gear. His mouth had that familiar cottony taste that neither toothpaste nor mouthwash could stay from its appointed rounds.

"So you got the old-time *consigliere*, Rikla, and the bodyguard, Measure, running the family. Okay, now Rikla and Measure are both in their seventies. Old-time warlords. Rikla's enforcer, Jimmie the Hook, Jimmy Russo, he gets killed in a car bombing. So Rikla, he firebombs Lyle Venable, who was the underboss for Measure—and you got a very volatile situation.''

"So it's a purely gang-related thing, you think."

"Umm." The lieutenant's face collapsed a little. "That's hard to say at this point. Some of the kills are so . . . random. They don't seem to fit the pattern of payback or vengeance hits but it's hard to nail it down. Like this Laclede Landing thing''—he shook his head and rubbed hard at his eyes as if he'd walked into cobwebs—"it just isn't the way you do things. You don't draw that kind of attention, that kind of heat. You don't let something get out of control like that.''

The first briefing finally got interrupted by the pressures of the day's activities, and Springer passed Jack along to other hands. Eichord spent the rest of the day trying to absorb the odd structure of the Special Division, a subunit within the dozen main circles of responsibility. This was the central cog of a wheel with spokes that disected the city jurisdictionally, and it was typically complex, labyrinthine, and geographically (not to mention philosophically) puzzling to him.

As always he felt his way along carefully, shutting nothing out, the sensors purring quietly; listening, watching, feeling as much as understanding. Tactile,

impassive, questioning softly, absorbent, nonjudg-
mental, open to possibilities. Learning, sensing,
spongelike.

The cops in SD looked like teachers for sure. At
least more State than street copper. No narky-looking
dudes. No gold chains. Businessmen or schoolteachers
in their short sleeves and ties. No gunfighter mus-
taches. No long hair. No fat guys. Lean and clean.
State roddish. Feds maybe. Very unstreet.

Loose, but not giving him much. All business. Welcome to St. Louis. Nice meeting you. Here's your
desk. This is a telephone. Here's how you get outside.
This is how you dial on the Intercom system. Here's a
directory. This is a map. Very rank conscious. Cool
smiles and paperwork. Guys who wanted good pay-
checks for their good policework. Young career cops
on the make.

Eichord wasn't sure what he'd been expecting, but
whatever it was, this wasn't quite it. The last place he'd
done any temporary duty they'd been worse flakes than
the maniacs who were his beloved brethren at Buckhead. Sort of an orderly lunatic asylum. Before that
he'd been working out of a metro force so corruption-
ridden that it had acquired a national rep. The force
was generally conceded to be one of the big three cen-
ters for crooked cops on the take. It was a thing that
went back sixty, seventy years, back through two and
three generations of cop families sometimes—an or-
ganic part of The Job. It was so bad there that straight
cops could hardly function within the "pad."

The pad went all the way to the top, dizzying heights
if you were street heat feeding the maw of a machine
that reached far beyond the PC and the mayor and
right into the black bag that got passed around the
state house every week. When a pad is that thick, with
tentacles that far-reaching, going right through the
judges and prosecutors and county officials and into
the legislator's pockets—then you can forget about it.

It was part of a way of life. The pad went way beyond being on the arm for the odd goody-gumdrop. This was going on the take as a CAREER DIRECTION and there were those who went for it the same way street-smart old-timers angled for a certain beat before Knapp hit the NYPD. Eichord knew his share of cops who saw the street as a free lunch for the entrepreneur with savvy. He didn't share their rationale about the payola perquisites, but he'd managed the minor miracle of staying relatively straight in one of the two or three most corruption-ridden shops in the country, without earning any of the pejorative nicknames like Mr. Clean or St. Eichord that would stick to you and haunt your career.

Vic Springer had been cordial in a cold kind of way, but Jack had a solid first impression of the man and he liked him. That was vital. At least that the ostensible cat in charge be somebody who wouldn't bury Eichord in bullshit. He thought Springer looked like a good, hard-nosed straight shooter. A good cop.

What Springer looked like was in fact a caricature of a hound dog. A plug-ugly version of Lyndon Johnson. A sad-eyed basset but photographed by Karsh. A woebegone hound who had one of those faces that wore a perpetual expression of dolorousness. Eichord would soon learn that this was his happy face. In normal repose his countenance registered abject misery. When he was upset, angry, or dejected, his face caved in like a wrecked building. But Eichord knew that faces are only masks.

Jack shook the necessary hands and left to seek appropriate lodging. On the minus side, the cop shop looked like it could be a problem. He'd put on his best PR hat and try to shake it out. The killings seemed so unrelated and, for want of a better word, random he hadn't even begun to comprehend it all. A tough case for Mr. Keen, and impossible for Mr. Eichord. Where the hell was the Falcon when you needed him?

Also on the minus side, he didn't remember a damn thing about the St. Louis of today. Where had Gaslight Square gone to when he wasn't looking? Where would he go to drink his single light beer as he sat at a friendly sidewalk café talking with amiable strangers? How would Mr. Crime Crusher find his way around town? What was he doing here? Why me, Lord? he thought.

On the plus side . . . . he liked the arch.

Forewarned about the St. Louis apartment scene, he'd headed for a motel that advertised you could SLEEP CHEAP under their hospitable roof, and the room smelled like a chemical pine forest where the trees smoked, but the bed looked good. He didn't. He glanced at himself in the mirror as he was hanging up his clothing, trying to see what kind of canine he resembled, and he finally decided a street mongrel. The dark-eyed pound hound glared back in silent reproof.

It had been weeks since Spain had woken bathed in nightmare sweat. The killings in Texas and Florida and across the border had left him serene and calm. He'd been sleeping like a baby of late, sleeping the kind of sleep you get from hard work, good health, peace of mind, and an untroubled conscience. But this time something had been off-key. He'd worked a bit too hard. Gone to bed exhausted. Vulnerable.

He'd fallen asleep fully clothed, bone-weary, and for the first time in many nights a bad dream came and got him again. It was the worst one of all. It began in absolute black with him dreaming he was dreaming, listening to his own loud snores, then seeing something moving in the corner of the darkened bedroom and jerking awake in fear. Did he forget to throw the bolts he'd just installed on the doors? Had someone entered the house while he was sleeping?

A horrible, undefined presence fills him with fear. It moves again. Just a suggestion of an outline moving there in the deep blackness, and he almost screams at the eyes that blink open. Huge yellow eyes glowing brightly as a cat's eyes will appear to reflect light in darkness, but these are electric yellow, piercingly bright, a couple of feet apart. Whatever this thing is, it is huge.

In his heart he knows what has come to get him. This dark, millenarian force that sleeps the sleep of death. Spain's mind feeds him a word he does not know: chilead. He shivers. This evil thing he sees has chosen to wake up in the midst of Spain's dream. And although he cannot see in the darkness he knows its mighty razor claws are clutching a single, amaranthine *fleur du mal*. He can imagine its reptilian dragon skin, this ultraxerothermic thing that thrives on blast furnace heat, and he knows of the dread monster's power. And he is so afraid that before he can catch himself the scream escapes.

The monstrous thing roars to life in an explosion of wind rain light fiber optics rainbows oil slicks fire ice fog hurricane typhoon monsoon tornado tidal wave blizzard intense heat invisible cobwebs catching in the hair and eyelashes a sense of foreign substances being injected down through subdermal layers as the thing's feeders extend out like shoots of lightning stabbing him with surgical precision in his orifices like blinding catheters of death and . . . He shudders with the first deft feeding touch that drains his lifeblood in a violent, spasmodic suck. The thing opens its reptile jaws and articulates, "Well, hello dere." And it laughs raucously as he feels the thing begin shooting the alien microorganisms back down through the catheters, filling him up with the foul scavengers' anal drippings taken from the bottom of the deepest trench of the blackest vomitorium of hell, fucking him with the devil's sperm scorching him as the thing forces it back down inside him.

The enormous thing moves closer and Spain can see

that it is encased in a gelatinous membrane that houses its food and waste sacs. The reptile's skin is pale, dead-looking like a freshly powdered corpse, stretched tightly across a misshapen skull, but brightly colored, with unnatural highlights that suggest an opalescent mutation. Eyes are the color of pus afire.

The long silver tongue appears sanguine, as if a large, garlike fish had been dipped in coagulating blood, and it is forked, barbed, ridged, and extensile, still coated with a recent regurgitation.

Bright wet red on rubidium silver that inflames when the air hits it as the thing articulates, "Come on now, give us a big kiss," and roars again in a massive par-oxysm of uncontrollable hilarity and vomits up his blood. Spain is drenched in a boiling hot shower of exudate, leukocytes, offal, bloody tissue, and feces. And he wakes up dreaming he is drowning in a Ni-agara of scalding filth hearing the ancient monster's laughter in the distance, muffled as if underwater as Spain dies hearing the thing's voice say faintly, "You *kill* me," as he is drained, burnt, shocked, drowned, suffocated, asphyxiated, exsanguinted, and fright-ened—to death.

And Spain dreams he dies, transfused through vas-cular nasties by Demogorgon's putrid, poisonous, scorching, deadly coital ejaculate, and boiled in killer fuck.

Eichord was no big whodunit sleuth. Not in his mind. No white knight or blue crime crusher. He saw himself as no better or worse than most of the co-workers. The attitude made for good vibes. So Jack would get along with even the worst and the stupidest and the most corrupt among them if the case de-manded it. He was totally into getting The Job done. And he loved the action of Homicide.

MCTF, originally funded to handle unusual major crimes of violence, had been restructured shortly after the Doctor Demented thing, and Eichord found himself playing a new role—that of a key agent with an elite special unit.

McTuff was more than just another tax-dollared, tunnel vision committee-run hand job. It was federally funded, to be sure, but there similarities ended.

When an agency, local or otherwise, plugged into MCTF it accessed a vast network offering some of the richest data product ever provided law enforcement. COMSEC at Ft. Meade, the counterterrorism think tanks here and in Europe, the Academy at Quantico, DEA, the military, you had it all a fingertip away.

You could cross-reference crime-scene reports on a possible serial killing in Mississippi or plumb the incredible resources of some of NCIC's best-kept secrets, all in the push-button miracle of high tech.

For the last few years the paralyzing rivalries that had torn through certain areas of law enforcement had begun to disintegrate. A new director had revamped the FBI to the point where it was now dealing with both the locals and the gents in Langley, and there was some actual sharing of important collars, as well as information and evidence. It was truly without precedent, codifying computerized group-think and launching the new, emergent criminologist, which boded ill for criminals. The new spirit of liaison was especially important in narcotics-related cases, but it also meant that certain types of homicides had a much better chance of being cleared.

McTuff produced crime-profile printouts that reflected an unbelievable degree of sophistication. It structured threat-assessment work-ups that had enormously beneficial capability on many levels. And best of all to police, it was user-friendly. Jack was a believer. He thought that the Task Force's greatest strength was its subtle, implicit reliance on the human being. It seemed to understand there was only one way to really find out what somebody else was thinking or

what they were going to do—and to find that out, you
had to use people. Other cops. Informants. This was
the area where McTuff worked its most fertile and pro-
ductive soil. It could build you a snitch machine.

Life is a series of trade-offs. The art of compromise.
The understanding of quid pro quo. One hand washing
another. And in the strange, murky, quirky world of
law and the lawbreaker, justice demanded the oily,
slippery lubricant of the deal to continue functioning.
If you accepted this you would make the system work
for you. If you didn't your life on The Job could be a
nightmare.

The complexities of the maddening legal system itself could hamstring a law officer to the point of pa-
ralysis. The jurisdictional intricacies, the opaqueness
of the codes, the double-think of the statutes, the sheer
insanity of the procedures, rules, postulates, and dis-
ciplines, could nail you through your shield; leave you
rigid, desk-bound, static, immobilized by the bone-
crushing weight of the paperwork, skewered by the
uncompromisingly doctrinaire methodology of the
frustratingly inadequate system that had failed the society it promised to protect and serve.

MCTF had been devised, implemented, pro-
grammed, and calibrated by people who had worked
their whole lives within the system and they had used
their hard-won knowledge. The computer knew how
to search for potential information keys, and it gave a
user the proper leverage with which to put a machine
into motion. A lowly copper in Buchanan County—
miles, histories, quantum leaps away from a powerful
DA in Suffolk County, just as one example—could
patch right into a heavyweight plea-bargain deal that
would accomplish what only the best negotiators could
pull off: make all the parties happy simultaneously.
McTuff knew how to make a jam disappear, and crime
is solved by snitches, never doubt it. It was the ultimate snitch machine.

The Task Force had no centuries-old tradition of policework as a heritage. Fathered by high tech, its mother of invention had been the bestial serial murders that had seemed to spring out of the poisonous karma of the 60s, like some mutation from Agent Orange. Zodiac, Manson, Gacey, a blood-soaked trail of bodies sweeping across the country, leaving a wake of grisly legend.

The Task Force, obviously, was a child of the times. So Jack Eichord, people-oriented copper, had become Jack Eichord, task-oriented organization man. These were not your run-of-the-mill bad guys, these serial kills. They were a new breed of evil mutant and they had to be found and stopped—at any cost.

It was to McTuff that Eichord turned first, with a fat dossier full of fact and conjecture and a dozen thankless tasks that could not be accomplished by computers and think tanks alone. PEOPLE would have to go interrogate all those TWA flight attendants and stewardii and gift-shop employees. Somebody had to ask all those questions and hear all those answers, and as always—in the end—it all came down to shoe leather.

And Big Mac failed him this time. SEE NO EVIL had, for all intents and purposes, vanished.

The one called Spain sat perusing his St. Louis dossier, now more of a scrapbook actually, and his gaze fell upon a small two-column clipping razored out of a recent *Post-Dispatch*. Its headlines read MISSOURI APPEALS COURT REVERSES CONVICTION, and he saw the name Andrew Dudzik and something clicked in place in his mind. He remembered the connection now and he scanned the article again.

The Missouri Court of Appeals at St. Louis has reversed the conviction of a St. Louis man on a charge of dealing in narcotics and controlled substances. Andrew Dudzik, 28, of the 800 block of

Bancroft Avenue, was accused of selling heroin and various stolen pharmaceuticals to an undercover officer posing as a Cairo, Illinois, drug dealer, according to Lawrence V. Goetz, assistant St. Louis circuit court attorney.

Goetz identified the accused man as Andrew "Candy" Dudzik, owner of American Industrial Laundry, Inc., of Washington Park, and St. Louis organized-crime figure, with alleged ties to the Dagatina crime family, which authorities believe controls the narcotics and child-pornography rackets in St. Louis.

The Appeals Court ruled Tuesday that the crime had occurred in the state of Illinois, not Missouri, and writing for the court Presiding Judge Richard B. Brewer said he "regretted that such a conviction must be reversed, particularly in light of the complex interstate transactions of our present day." But that "any change from existing law must be addressed by our legislature."

"A written accusation submitted in the case was defective, it was also learned, because it failed to charge all of the elements of the crime," Goetz added.

Noted criminal defense attorney Jacob Rozitsky, Jr., denied that the ruling was "unduly restrictive" and "highly suspect," in the words of an unidentified source in the circuit attorney's office. "This reversal of an unjust conviction showed great fairness and courage by the court," Rozitsky said.

Concurring with Presiding Judge Brewer were judges Quentin R. Ide and James DeMournier.

He closed the scrapbook and underlined the name Dudzik, Andrew, on a loose sheet of yellow, lined paper and then added the names Rozitsky, Jacob, Junior, and Brewer, Richard B., printing in tiny, meticulously precise letters.

He opened the St. Louis telephone directory and searched through the Brewers until he found a Brewer, Richard B., and he made a note of both the office and home addresses by the side of the name Dudzik, next to his address at 827 Bancroft Avenue, connecting the two listings with a tiny double-pointed arrow.

He started to draw a tiny question mark beside the Brewer entry, but then he pursed his lips in thought for a moment and said softly, "Fuck it." And then he began to laugh.

Everything was working beautifully. He grinned with delight each time media headlined another mob-war story. He'd touched it all off himself with the two fire-bombings. The rest of it had been the two sides retaliating for imagined assaults by the opposition. He loved it. Perfect justice.

The laugh dies. His face tightens again into a frown of hatred.

Candy Dudzik. Candy fucking Dudzik wasn't even a maggot crawling on a piece of shit. And he could buy protection and claim to be tied to the Dagatina crime family. That was the precise reason even a greaseball like Gaetano Ciprioni had sense enough not to fool with scum like Jimmie the Hook and Blue Kriegal. Jesus. What had the family come down to? He couldn't believe it. He thought about the scum and what he was going to do when he took the big ones down—how he'd make their suffering long and hard. But it was making him sick to think about them, and he couldn't get the images of Tiff out of his mind and finally he forced himself to think of something else.

He looked back on the mob the way it had been when he had been elevated along with Ciprioni to the level of the top enforcer for the national organization. These so-called mob leaders had been the lowest rungs of the ladder back then. This Rikla and this Measure were nothing. He remembered Measure, who he figured had to be seventy-four now if he was a day. Nothing but some muscle who'd had his eyes on the twat industry. His big deal was he came to the family twenty-five years back and they'd brought him in as a bodyguard. Then later they gave him a heavy sports book for his initial livelihood. But he was nothing but a glorified button man.

He'd been given some massage parlors, outcall houses, a couple of the sex shops, and an X-house—the porn thing. He'd brought William "Blue" Kriegal in from Detroit to help him put it all together. A couple of ancient faggots. He'd whack them out in the most painful ways he could invent—and this fucking Rikla was the original town pervert. All garbage. He'd make them suffer the way Tiff had.

He found the Brewer address that evening. Clayton. Medium swank. Semishabby but huge home that stunk of old money. A woman in the yard watering something. He pulled on past the house and down the block, up a back alley. Dogs barking everyfuckingwhere as he slowly cruised the alley, parking behind the Brewer home. He got out purposefully and walked up to the back-door steps and knocked on the door. In about twenty seconds a man answered the door, not opening it but saying "Yes?" through the screen.

"Hi," Spain said with a big smile. "Man, I'm sorry to trouble you folks but I need to get at a phone for just one second. I'm Ron Ryan with KMOX, and I've got to call in a traffic accident." He gestured down toward the nearest main thoroughfare. "It's a local call, but I'm not in the unit and they need to get some cops and an ambulance out there." His face taking on a serious, worried, responsible mask now, the heavy-lidded eyes open as wide as he could get them.

"All right," the older man says with an irritated sigh that he didn't try to conceal, "if you won't be long."

"Oh," Spain says, "that's so good of you folks. I sure do appreciate it."

The man points at the phone and Spain nods and picks up the receiver and begins dialing. The older man may or may not be Brewer. The house is nicely furnished but not opulent. Could be a judge's home. "Hello? This is Ryan. Could I have the newsroom please? Thanks." He covers the phone like there's someone on the other end. "You're not Judge Brewer, are you?" Friendly smile. The man nods and smiles slightly. "I THOUGHT I recognized you." And he lays the phone down as the .25 comes out of his pocket. "You be a good boy now, and Mrs. Brewer won't be bothered. You don't want her hurt, do you?"

The judge shakes his head.

"I just want you to come with me to talk with some people. If you cause a commotion I'll just whack you out and come back here and waste Mrs. B. You don't want that. So don't give me trouble. The vehicle is in the alley out back. When you walk straight out the back, if your wife sees you just smile and tell her you'll be back in a couple of minutes. If she asks you where you're going, just say you'll explain to her when you come back, you want to see something this man has. Just mumble something vague and get in. Don't stop or say anything suspicious to her. Understand?"

"Yes."

"Move." Spain motions with the gun. "Don't do anything dumb." He notices all the paintings. "Tell her somebody has a watercolor for sale or something. Be convincing unless you want to get shot."

They get in the car, which Spain starts, and when he sees no one is watching them he tells the judge to put his head down. As he starts to bend down Spain clips him lightly with the gun and the man crumples forward as they drive off. They are still driving as the man makes a groaning noise and Spain tells him, "Stay down. Just keep your mouth shut."

"If I'm harmed I want to warn you of the se-vere—"

Spain kicks him in the teeth and he begins crying. "Shut the fuck up," he hisses.

Soon they pull up in front of a huge cornfield. Spain turns off onto a gravel road, then turns again into a path made by a tractor where mud ruts have solidified to the consistency of cement. The narrow path is between the outer row of stalks and a thick and massive hedgerow beside the road. They stop.

"Get out." The man obeys. He is a pleasant-looking man in his late fifties to mid-sixties. One of those faces you can't peg. Deeply creased face. Portly, but only fat in the belly. So probably went to fat late in life. Dark tan. A golfer or a yardwork fanatic. Expensive diamond ring. Gold watch. Good shoes. He sees all this in the half-second or so it takes to register an opinion. Sizing up people is part of the worker's trade.

"Stand there," Spain says. Getting out. They walk in between two of the huge rows. The corn is as high as an elephant's eye, or something. Spain pulls out a small awl. Awl or nothing at awl, he thinks. This is what he likes.

"Listen to me with the greatest concentration. If you lie to me. If you whine. If you claim you didn't take any money. I will hurt you. I only want to know this. How much were you paid to reverse the Candy Dudzik conviction and who paid you?"

"I don't have a clue as to what you . . . AAAAAA-AAAAAAAAAAAAAAAAAAHHHHHHHHH," he screams into the row of corn that towers over them. "Ohhh-hhhhh. Please. I didn't take any money. Honestly. Please don't hurt—"

"SHUTTUP, YOU FUCK!"

"OOOOOOHHHHHHHHHHHHHHHHHHHHH, JE-SUS, DON'T," he cries again.

"How much? And take your time—we have hours."

"Two thousand dollars."

"Who gave you the money?"

"A lawyer." He's whimpering like a little child.

"WHAT lawyer, asshole?"

"Rozitsky."

Spain stabs down into the man's shoulder, down through shirt, skin, tendons, dignity.

"AAAAAAAAAAAAAAHAHHHHHHHHHHH-HHHHHHHHHHHHHHHHHHH!"

"You've got a point," Spain tells him, in a good mood as he thrusts the needle-pointed awl into the man's ear. "YOU PIECE OF *TRASH*!" He thrusts the awl in again and again. When there is no sound or movement he pulls the man by his ankles, pulling the body out of the corn and toward the trunk of the vehicle. "You fat shit," he mutters.

The judge is deceptively heavy. His face is dotted like a cartoon of someone with measles.

A bird soars over them, diving down between the rows of corn, making a noise that sounds to Spain like "Kill-deer, kill-deer."

"Fucking right," Frank Spain says aloud. Still in a very good mood as the trunk opens. "Here come de judge," he says.

Eichord's second day in town he met a vision. A vision that squeezed his heart with both hands until he begged for mercy. A vision that knocked on his forehead with a small, finely boned hand and whispered, "Anybody home in there?" A vision of the most eyeball-popping, totally captivating beauty and prodigious sex appeal he'd seen in, oh, several days at least.

The problem is Eichord was at the point that many single, busy men sometimes reach in midlife; they begin to suffer from the old and feared exotic disorder Lack-a-nookie, and so you must understand that a vision squeezed his heart with both hands until he begged for mercy once, maybe twice a day. But this vision was different. This was one Gang Busters of a lady named Rita Haubrich.

He hadn't scheduled himself to talk to anybody for a couple of days. The plan had been to start wading through the mountain of paperwork but he just couldn't get into it. The smallest thing, finding the drawer where such and such a folder was kept, presented a major challenge to his disoriented mind that morning. The strangeness of the city had bothered him since he hit town, and he decided to bite right into that first, so he went to talk to the two people who'd been hurt in the Laclede Landing gunplay. The two civilians.

The survivors, so to speak, were a couple of innocent passersby walking in opposite directions, a man and woman. The man on the outside of the sidewalk, a carpet salesman named Sorga, had taken a .38 slug in his left wrist, the impact flying him into the Haubrich woman, whom fate had placed next to him. She had taken a severe injury to her neck when she was smashed up against a stone wall. Neither had claimed to have seen much, but one never knew. He'd hike over the told trail again.

He intended to catch Sorga, then go by the towing business that was Paul Rikla's semilegit front, on his way back from University City, where the carpet guy was recuperating at home. On the map at least it was more or less on his way to Forest Park. He'd have to talk with Measure and Rikla sooner or later, although the odds of him getting anything were not worth considering. The morning was a disaster.

He spent the whole morning spinning his wheels. Mr. Sorga was a grumpy, reticent, ill-humored character who spent forty-five minutes jerking Eichord's chain about one thing or another, mostly the fact that you couldn't go about your business anymore because the police were too busy writing traffic tickets to blah blah and on and on. After this had gone on awhile he started wishing Sorga was one of those taciturn types with a natural disinclination to gab with strangers. In his case he was only reluctant to give Eichord any useful information about the shooting. He hadn't seen anything, anyone, anytime. It all happened too fast. And so on.

It looked like six streets over and down the block on a little gas-station map, but Rikla's Towing Service was a world of traffic away and Eichord nearly got accordioned in his borrowed wheels between a plateless truck and a tailgating maniac. St. Louis traffic was ridiculous. It looked like the San Diego Freeway at ten-thirty in the morning. The slowest traffic seemed to be the middle lane, with the faster vehicles passing on both sides. He made it to the Rikla operation and was told Rikla was out. Where? Don't know. Any idea when he'd be back? Nope. He left a "special agent" card with his temporary phone number and extension inked in, asked Mr. Rikla to give him a call. Wonderful.

It was amazing when you'd lived in a town so many years back and you thought you'd forgotten all the names. But you get out there trying to find your way around in the drive-time kamikaze traffic and the names and locales start flooding back over your memory. The older you are, the more cities you've lived in, the more it all blends together into a kind of Great American Vista of Gravois and Grady and Natural Bridge and Northwest Parkway and Kings Highway and Turtle Creek. He was beginning to get some of it back now, the memories of Florissant and ... DAMN! Look where you're going, you idiot. He hadn't seen traffic like this since he left Orange County.

The day was already half over and he hadn't had lunch yet. He hated everything about this case. The people at headquarters were cold and suspicious, he didn't think he liked St. Louis anymore, the traffic was abominable, he was getting a killer headache, it looked like it might rain, he hadn't a notión what he was doing here, and to paraphrase the late Mr. Lewis, "This was as good as he was going to feel the rest of the day.''

It wasn't the times he'd got into the dark, salty-smelling bars to chat with the guys over a Strohs or Oly Light that tested him. He could easily sip one or two cold ones and catch just enough of the buzz to enjoy himself and not feel like he was deprived of all the fun in life, go home, have a nice cup of instant or a cup of tea, and call it a night. He did it all the time. Had for years. There was no demon there at all. Or so he always hoped.

Long ago he'd made himself drink a beer against his better judgment. Like a normal person. He had business in bars. The Job took him where booze was. He had to handle it. There was never a problem. A couple, even three beers led him nowhere. The john maybe. That was it.

It was the hard stuff that beckoned with that middle finger. Times like now, when he was bouncing around in same strange burg and not able to find his kiester with both hands, a nice headache coming to get him, dreading going into work every morning, going out and accomplishing nothing, coming in and accomplishing less, feeling around on the outsides of a seamless, complex case, no input, no information network, nothing but his cop sense and luck to work for him, times like now—he could taste it a little.

The fear of it kept him from falling off. He could never get used to the ease with which it could sneak up on him. Eleven-forty A.M. and driving into Forest Park. How easy it would be right now to hang a left there, pull up beside that little ma-and-pa tavern, and be raising a triple before you could say, Katie, bar the door. He was always that close to going over the edge, so when he sensed it creeping up on him he'd block it out. Fear works, he thought. At least so far.

Later, when he thought about it, he could never remember much about the first time they met again. The

whole day receded into a nice blur. He'd gone into the
Acquisitions Office with temples pounding and a fairly
colossal-looking receptionist smiled a hello and raised
her eye brows and he'd asked for Rita Haubrich and
did the lady happen to have any aspirin?

And she said, when he told her his name, "Don't
you I'm-Jack-Eichord *me*." With that look and smile
and tone people get when they want you to know you
should recognize them.

"My goodness," he said, looking again. "Is it Rita
Paul? From a million years ago?"

"You remembered." She smiled a sunny smile.
"And it's Rita Paul Haubrich now, and that's a hundred years ago, please. Let's not make it any worse
than it is. You look just the same." He was starting to
tell her how great SHE looked, but she said, "And
I've got some Tylenols right here if that will do? Let's
see . . ." She began to rummage and he spoke while
he looked at her.

"Rita. What a nice surprise. I just never expected
to see you here."

"I'm not the receptionist. I usually work back
there," she said, gesturing vaguely toward another
area, "but Terry had to take her child to the doctor so
I'm filling in. When you called I started to say something but it took a minute to sink in that it was you.
I've had so many of the local police and reporters talk
to me that . . . And what are you doing back in St.
*Lou*is anyway?"

"I'm working on some gang homicides."

"I saw your name in the papers once. Some investigation where you were in the headlines, and I wasn't
surprised. I knew you were going to be famous. You
were so dedicated."

"Remember the DA's office?" They both laughed.
"That was a fun place," he said, and she sneered and
puckered her lovely mouth.

"Yeah. Real fun. I got out of there not long after you left St. Louis."

"You married the big lawyer. That guy you were dating when we knew each other. Haubrich."

"Yep," she admitted. "Good memory."

"His name's something like Don?"

"Winslow. Winslow Haubrich."

"God. That's right. Winslow. Good ole Winslow," he said without conviction. "How is old Winslow?"

"I haven't seen old Winslow for a while, I'm pleased to report. We're divorced."

"Oh. Sorry," he said with even less conviction. "You still married?"

"Not for a long time," he said, shaking his head. "Well," he sighed, having to force his mind back on the case at hand, "this is great to see you. What a nice surprise." He meant it.

"It's nice to see you too. You really haven't changed a bit." She smiled and he loved it.

"You either." He thought she was a lot better-looking since the last time he'd seen her—but that was years ago. Maybe he hadn't been quite as horny back then. He would never have recognized her in a crowd and he realized immediately it was her hairdo and clothing and not her face. She'd aged beautifully. "Excuse me—just a second." He walked across to a water fountain.

"Sure." He took the Tylenol and walked back to the desk.

"We might get interrupted," she told him, "but we can go ahead and talk if you want to."

"Sure, okay. Let me just get my notes here. What can you tell me about the Laclede Landing shooting?"

"It's just like I said to the other guys, which I know you have in your files and all. I wish I could help but I really didn't get more than just a glance at them. It all happened so quickly. I heard the noise and the man hit me almost at the same time. I just saw a car. It was

a car with either two or three men in it. I know I saw
a gun out the right-side window in the front seat and
I just have an impression of a—a shotgun, I think it
was—and I can't be sure if somebody was in the back-
seat or not. It was all so fast.''

"You got a look at the car?"

"Not really. I just have that impression. Of a gun
out of a window and the firing. I couldn't even say it
was a dark color car for sure. I just . . . Well, the shots
hit that man and he hit me as he fell and I went into
the wall and it was all over in just a second. I was
getting up, trying to get up. It was kind of like if you
had real bad whiplash in a car accident or something.
I heard all the screaming and there was a lot of blood.
I saw the men who had been shot then. And people
were all crouched down and it was so frightening—I
don't know—"

"That's fine. I just thought perhaps we could talk.
Sometimes if you think back you can remember some
little detail you might have overlooked. The appearance of the man with the gun, for example. You don't
remember anything about his face?''

"I couldn't tell you if he had a beard, what nation-
ality, nothing. I just didn't retain anything about him.
Just that short shotgun sticking out the window as he
fired again and how loud it was. It was enough to scare
you to death. I'd never been through anything like it
in my life.''

"You said shotgun the first time, then short shotgun. What kind of a short shotgun? What do you
mean?''

"Oh, like you see in the movies. Sawed off, I guess.
It was a short gun. Not a pistol. It had one barrel, not
two like some of my dad's guns. I remember this gun,
oh, I do recall seeing a hand move on the gun like it
was cocking it or whatever you call it. That's when I
got hit, as the second shot was fired and the man got
hit next to me on the sidewalk.''

"Rita, I noticed in the reports you had a severe injury. Obviously you seem to be fine now." So fine, in fact.

"Yes." She smiled. "I was pretty lucky. It was weird. I thought for a day or two I was going to be in some trouble. The doctor was talking about the possibility of surgery on a disc, and I was getting kind of worried. It was very painful, like a pinched-nerve thing back here." She gestured toward the back of her neck, a move that rearranged her clothing in a most attractive way, and Eichord fought to look impassive and official as she continued telling him about X rays, and how it was better the next day, and how she was okay now.

She was warm, outgoing, genuine, sunny, affectionate-appearing, and yes, very sexy. And she was someone pleasant in a day of unpleasantness and he just stood there drinking her in. God. Rita Paul. Who'd a-thunk it. Her cheerfulness and warmth, and yes, her sexiness chipped away at his official reserve. She finally broke his icy police professionalism down but it hadn't been easy. It had taken her a good twenty or thirty seconds of conversation. He felt like silly putty.

It wasn't only the fact that she was dynamite-looking. It was also the fact that the day was half over and he hadn't had lunch. It was the fact that this was as good as he was going to feel the rest of the day. And, too, let's be fair. It was the fact that she was DYNAMITE-LOOKING! All right. Wow! Ummm. Yes. He could no more walk away from Rita than the man in the moon could turn into cheese.

"Let's get to the bottom of this," he said in his most Sherlockian tones, saying it just to be saying something funny, then as the words came out he winced at the hidden double entendre, and she laughed sweetly, and . . . oh, shucks. The rest of the day just faded into a hazy memory, when he looked back at it. The fact that he'd walked into the office of someone who was a witness to a crime scene and ended up asking her out for coffee was merely—oh, what would you call it?—a social courtesy. Public relations. Just being friendly. Let's have a cup and talk about it. That kind of thing. A good with-it police representative wants to have cordial relations with the public as much as he possibly can, right? And Jack DESPERATELY wanted to have relations with Rita Haubrich.

What's the matter with me? he remembered thinking to himself, knowing full well the answer as a time-less Hawaiian malady coursed through his veins. Look-ing back on the fuzzy day all he could really recollect was that he'd had a marvelous time with this colossal-looking lady from out of their mutual past and that it hadn't turned out to be such a bad day, after all.

By the time he ended up back at Twelfth and Clark it was late midday and time to do serious policework. This is why there was a federally funded Task Force sitting there throbbing, humming, purring away with its network of interfaced computer linkages. This is why the most sophisticated forensic scientists and ad-vanced criminologists in the world called McTuff the "greatest contemporary aid to law enforcement." This is why the combined brainpower of a great metropol-itan law-enforcement agency would reach out for help. It all came down to one man. The finest detective of the century.

Genius is an abused word, he thought, but perhaps it does apply in this case. The genius crime crusher of all time. Thank GOD that these people had the wis-dom and the courage to reach out for Jack Eichord to help them solve these puzzling homicides.

Here is what they got that afternoon for their money. Okay, first off—unless you really have a comprehen-sive understanding of vector analysis, the calculus of complex mechanistic variables, the ellipsoidal har-monics of heterogeneous configurations, hypergeo-metric functions and orthogonal paranomials—in other

words, just your basic genius stuff—this won't seem
like much to you.

First, Jack drew an enormous letter *A* that filled a
sheet of white paper with its symmetry, and with a
felt-tipped pen made it look as if it had been carved
from wood, complete with knot holes and dents and
gouges, and then he gave it dimension and then he
shadowed in the perspective.

Next—and this was the brilliant part—he carefully
printed out the names of everyone he'd come in contact with today whose first or last named ended in a
letter *A*. Sorg*A*, Rikla he hadn't met but he'd thought
a lot about so he printed Rikl*A*, Rita he printed with
an especially neat *A*: Rit*A*, printing the names so they'd
sit next to each other beside the giant *A* which would
then be the last letter of their names, you see. This is
his "Big A Doodle," which took up a good ten to
fifteen minutes. Meanwhile, genius that he was, he
was able to listen intently to the whispered conversation around him.

He learned that the Cards were three and oh on the
season, Dr. Watson, and had dropped thirteen of their
last fifteen games counting regular season play. That
everybody on the Cardinal bench hates Dallas. That
two detectives named T. J. Monahan and Pat Skully
had either a friend or colleague named Art Castor who
told disgustingly gross jokes. That it was going to rain
tonight. That the tomatoes were all gone.

This so inspired Eichord that he took his felt-tipped
pen and began an "Art Castor Doodle." He was
pleased with the intricacy of it: an ornate series of
interconnected squigglies that surrounded a twenty-
word transposition of the name "Art Castor," and—
here's the wonderful part—made contextual sense. The
sentence that comprised the doodle read "Art Castor
cast a rat to act as Castro," and "to cast Coast actors
to co-star as Croats to roast Astro Astor." He felt a
surge of unbridled excitement as it occurred to him he

might add a phrase "to tar or rot a Tarot tart, to start to trot," which would add a dozen more words that could give him another fifteen minutes of doodling, when a voice behind him said. "I'm certainly glad we got McTuff's heavy hitter on this bitch. Now that I see the caliber of brilliant detective work we can expect," followed by maniacal laughter.

Eichord turned and a huge man towering behind him was laughing.

"Bud Leech, Intelligence." He laughed. "Gladaseeya."

"God, I hope so," Jack said, laughing with him. Two friendly faces in one day, it was almost too much luck for one afternoon. Leech was more like the cops Eichord was used to, and they went downstairs and had coffee, Eichord beginning to slosh when he walked, and talked some about the case and the peculiarities of the city.

Jack learned what it was. The unit had been burned recently in a citywide scandal involving the mob and two of the coppers who had been caught on the take. Everybody had figured him for a natural shoe-fly. They assumed the McTuff thing was a setup by the sneaky assholes in Internal Affairs Division.

And Bud Leech told him a lot more as the day wore on. He learned about how the mob had penetrated the highest levels of the force here, how their tentacles stretched out into the court system and into the senior strata of government. Facts to reaffirm Eichord's feeling that St. Louis was more than it appeared. He was beginning to at least see some of the pieces of the puzzle, but the problem was what names to ascribe to them.

Law-abiding or lawless, victims or victimizers, as always in what laughingly gets called real life, nothing much is pure black or white. Reality appears in shades. Degrees. And there was an added layer of complexity here. Eichord suspected they were dealing with something more than warring mob factions.

He played Las Vegas style. When you're cold, you fold; when you're hot, you shoot your shot. He phoned Rita Haubrich, getting her voice on the first ring, and wondered if she'd help a newcomer find his way around the town a little this weekend and he could remember later thinking about all the red hair and those long legs and that mouth and getting in the car and he's singing softly about how the pale moon didn't excite him and trying not to move his lips, thinking about this great-looking redhead when the first October raindrops started splashing down on his windshield.

In Spain's motel room he had a small box with the printed legend GRETA GRISWOLD. The box contained a man's brown hairpiece, a pair of ordinary rectangular-framed glasses with clear lenses, a pipe and pipe tobacco, and other small items that he used to pull a certain persona together. This was the persona who, under yet another alias, owned the fictitious company Direct Import Enterprises. And it was behind this mask and assumed character that Spain went whenever he had personal contact with one Greta Griswold, who was his cutout gofer, hence the name on the box.

Thanks to her efforts he'd be in the house soon. He was already working on plans for the Interrogation Room, which would add a necessary dimension of security to what he was about to do. The higher up in the organization his revenge took him, the greater the hazards would be to him personally, and this was one of the reasons for a safe, sanitized, soundproofed place where he could linger with his targets, take his time with them, take as long as he liked, where their screams would not draw unwanted attention. Where the blood could flow.

A woman named Greta Griswold was helping him in this regard. He'd hired her through his girl-friday ad. She was fifty-two. Plain. Timid. Obedient. Reasonably efficient. Not excessively bright or curious. He paid her just enough that she was grateful for the good wage, yet not enough she'd be suspicious. Spain did most of his business with her on the phone, but to avoid appearing too bizarre he had to have some contact with her. As it was, he had her convinced that he was simply a very busy, preoccupied, and eccentric employer who paid well and was willing to delegate a lot of unusual responsibility.

He put on his entrepreneurial hairpiece and glasses and pipe in place headed for their storefront office nearby. The disguise was not enough to fool anyone who knew him, but for someone who only saw him for a few minutes at a time, it might be enough to render him faceless in a police report. Glasses and a pipe and other certain mannerisms and affectations would be what she'd remember about the man himself.

"Good morning," he said, in a clenched voice that he used with her.

"Good morning, sir," she said, immediately starting in on the hundred things she'd saved up to tell him. "I've got your mail from the box there on the desk, and I cashed that check and put it in the deposit with your money from before, and this is the picture of the house," all over him with her little duties fulfilled, handing him a key, while he went, "Ummmm—fine."

"And this is for four-three-one. There's the Xerox of the multiple listings. You can't tell much from it but it has that, uh, unusual roofline and ceiling combination you said, uh, and you can take a look whenever you want. That's five-fifty a month. And this is how I entered that sale in the new ledger for accounts receivable . . ." And as she went on with phony business, he tuned out, looking at the grainy picture of the house. He'd seen the rental property from the outside and it looked perfect. The lay of the land was an unexpected bonus.

He let her go on about fake-business stuff until she'd run out of things to tell him. She'd been "running his traps" for him. He had her take care of anything where there was personal contact with others, where a surveillance camera at the bank would retain an image of a depositor, where they'd retain a likeness of the individual who rented a postal drawer, anything like that. Rental properties seemed easier to negotiate than an outright purchase, so he'd had her deal extensively with the realtors. He would be a subject of much discussion there for his idiosyncratic way of having a secretary do his house hunting, but it wouldn't be the first time a busy executive delegated that to another party.

Once he got in the house he'd have no real reason for contact with either a real-estate agent or the home owner, as long as all his checks paid the rent well in advance. He would keep Greta busy with make-work, preparing mailings for his nonexistent business and responding to monies he would funnel into Direct Import Enterprises through another of his mail-drop covers. Keep her available for those unexpected times when a cutout was required.

"I'm going to go look at the house today. Nobody's in there doing repainting or anything, right?"

"No, sir. I was given to understand it would be empty."

"Okay. I'll let you know. I'll call and if I like it you can go ahead and wrap it up for me. Lock up here and just work on that, and when the house deal is settled you can go home early. All right?"

"Yes, sir. Thank you." She brightened at the idea of quitting early.

As he drove toward the home he let himself roar with laughter at the joy of what he'd already accomplished. Setting the mob factions against each other had been a beautiful touch, and accomplishing it, thanks to his assessment of the Troxell report and his own intimacy with the family's weaknesses, had been child's play. He relished the phrase. Child's play.

What made him laugh the hardest was the fact that he'd finessed those dumb shitbrains into whacking Lyle Venable for him. He had his eye on a target for each side that would really set this thing into motion. Blue Kriegal's long-time bodyguard, Johny Picciotti. And his counterpart within the other side of the family, another legbreaker named Tripotra. Their respective deaths, if handled right, would appear to be more gangland retaliation, if only to the cops and media.

He looked at the house and it was ideal. It had been made for his purposes. Both the isolation and the rooms themselves. He'd wanted "an unusual roofline with angles going every which way," he'd told Greta, even given her some sketches. "I like houses with unusual-shaped rooms, cathedral ceilings, sunken living rooms . . ." And he'd gone on about his likes. But what he really wanted was a house where a secret room could be built and the walls wouldn't give it away.

Spain thought it was perfect. He stood there in the quiet house imagining what it would be like to hear the tortured screams of filth like Blue Kriegal and he laughed out loud. Most of all, to bring Ciprioni here . . . Oh, what a pleasure it would be to cut him open and slowly pull his guts out, make him watch as he was slowly, gently disemboweled and fed his own poisonous, shit-eating guts.

He went back to the motel and removed his Greta Griswold hairpiece and picked up the phone.

"Direct Import Enterprises," the woman said with enthusiasm, in one of her two or three contacts with the outside world each day.

"It's me," he told her unnecessarily. "I love it. It's nice. So go ahead and pay them the two months and get all the keys. Sign for me if you can."

"Okay. What if they have to have you come in and sign?"

"Explain to them I'm too busy. That I'm involved in a very delicate business deal with many meetings where I have to be available all the time—and just get anything that needs a signature and I'll sign it and have it returned to them." They hung up and Spain went out to the car and took a large sack of heavy items from the trunk.

He worked on hardware the rest of the day. By late afternoon he was parked down the street from the apartment house where Tripotra lived. He could see the man's fancy car in its parking stall. He'd be real tough to tail with a black Mercedes and the sophomoric vanity plates BADTRIP.

Spain felt his head falling to the side and he woke up. It was night. Shit. He'd dozed off. The Mercedes was still there. Forty-five minutes later and getting very uncomfortable, somebody comes out and gets into the black car. Spain follows him from a distance when he pulls out. Fifteen more minutes and he stops and talks to somebody Spain doesn't recognize. They get in their cars and he follows them out to the boonies.

The other car is a dark-colored Caddy, and it passes the Tripotra car, so Spain stays back with BADTRIP.

It was getting dark now and more difficult to tail. The lights of the traffic were starting to hurt Spain's eyes. He'd been in the car for hours and he was getting sore. His neck and back hurt and his butt was getting numb and he had a slight headache. He rolled down the window a bit and rubbed his eyes.

He had lost the black Mercedes momentarily with some idiot trucker darting in front of him, and then he saw it again and moved a little closer. He'd lost sight of the dark Caddy completely.

Suddenly they're both going up an off-ramp and Spain has no choice but to stay with them. It's a three-car convoy now. He can make the Caddy out. He's wide awake now and his mind is working very fast. Trying to figure what they'll do. If they stop at the top of the off-ramp, will they go left or right. Right. He has no choice. He'll have to go around them. No telling.

They don't stop, they keep moving to the right. Spain hangs in there.

The traffic up on the highway sung along in the nighttime symphony of semis and fast cars. The black Mercedes swung sharply around a curve and over a concrete-and-steel bridge, coming down off the blacktop a little too fast and fishtailing a little as it hit the gravel.

The driver braked behind a parked vehicle and killed the lights, getting out and looking up and down the road. He gets in the other car. Spain, who has been following the Mercedes, sees the man get into the parked car and he pulls over just on the other side of the curve. It looks deceptively close but he knows what it will be like trying to move through the wooded area there beside the highway; the grass looks fairly short but he has no idea what he'll be getting into. It's worth the effort, because if they'll stay in the parked car awhile it's a perfect grenade shot from the woods.

Even as he starts stomping through the high grass as he goes down the steep berm he thinks he might go back and just drive down past them, turn around as if he was lost, and pitch it in at them as he goes back. No, he decides, he'll use the tube and thump a round or two in on them with that. It's a perfect piece of terrain for the tube. He can turn right around, come back up the hill, get in his car, and he won't appear to have been anywhere near the other vehicles. The traffic and the insect noises are covering his sounds as he nears the edge of the trees.

Condensation from the driver's breath has formed a little frosty *O* on the inside of the windshield and he sits there listening to the other man talk, seemingly mesmerized by the spreading windshield fog from their hot breath.

"I gotta crank down the fucking window here," he says, and lowers his window, inhaling the night air with its wet redolence of tree fogs and crickets and mosquitoes. "Motherfucker stinks."

"Why doncha turn the goddamn motor back on and run your fuckin' air-conditioning, then."

"I could put the defrost on," the driver says, but he makes no move to do so.

"Yeah. You could do that. Then we wouldn't sit here be havin' the fucking mosquitoes eating on us and shit. Why doncha turn the fucker back on and get som'p'n goin' in here. Or just leave it alone and let the fucking thing fog up. One r'the other."

"Fucking weird time a' d' year, you freeze to death if you run the air-conditioning and you goddamn melt from the heat if you don't or—"

"Yeah, okay, well, look, I got to drive way the fuck out in the county yet tonight. Let's get it done, can we?"

"Hey, no shit, I ain't got all fucking night either. Do it." The man behind the wheel turns and with some effort lifts a heavy sack from the floorboard in back of him, lifting it over the seat.

"Whatcha got?"

"Eight and a half each I gotta get on these. Thirty-four cents."

"Jesus. That's fuckin' *LUGERS*. I don't want fuckin' Lugers."

"Hey. Dem's fucking P-Thirty-eights. Dey ain't fucking Lugers."

"Whatever the fuck dey are I don't wannum. Dey look like fuckin' *LUGERS*. I want Thirty-eights. Fucking REVOLVERS, for Chrissakes."

"These are not fuckin' LUGERS, goddammit. This is my business here. We're talking genuine fucking Walther Parabellum P-Thirty-eights."

"I don't care if it's a paregoric model don't wave the motherfucker around f'crissakes."

"Yeah. The fuckin' chipmunks might see it out here. Look: you fire this bitch in a Holiday Inn and the round goes through your lady's head and through the wall and the headboard of the next-door-neighbor's room, *his* ole lady's head, the round comes outta her skull and goes *bop* onto a tit, bounces off the tit and lands on the fucking bedspread. You can send room service over to get the lead for you. We're training *penetration* here. A Luger isn't jack shit."

"I don't need no Holiday Inn gun, man. I wanna go through the wall of a Holiday Inn and clip somebody's ole lady I'll fucking *drive* through the sonofabitch. I need a revolver."

"You don't know guns, man. No offense. I coulda got you garbage here. The sears that crystallize and shit. When the hammer is down you turn the thumb safety it locks the sear. But you turn this with the bitch cocked, a little steel arm trips the sear and the hammer falls on the safety not on the fucking pin like some of that postwar shit. You can jack a round in and BA-BOOM it fires the fucker. Suicide guns. Thirty-four is *stealing* these fuckers. These are *rare*. You say no I can do another thing and have nine hundred fifty apiece by *domani*, you understand?"

"Hey, all fucking due respect to you an' that shit, ya know, but you don't know guns any better'n me. You just a fucking thief same as me, ya know? All dis shit about how you got to go to Sears an' get a hammer an' that shit. But that's awright. I'll take the paregoric Lugers or whatever and I'll give you twenty-five for the sack, and I'll take the merch an' live with it even if they ain't fucking revolvers. So what'll it be? We gotta deal or what?"

"Hey, tell ya what, *paisan*, you give me twenty-five hundred, I give you a great piece. I got a brand-new Colt Government Model in forty-five ACP, fucker's customized, gunsmith blueprinted, tight as ten-year-old snatch and clean as Mary Green. Got checkered grips, got the ejector port'n' feed ramp ground down, got the wide spur hammer on it, speed-shooter safety, Pachmayr mainspring housing, adjustable trigger, speed-load lever, adjustable rear and combat blade sights, and I throw in a couple mags with special springs and cutaway feed lips. Twenty-five bills and you got it.''

"I give you twenty-five for the four Luger deals here.''

"Pasadena.''

"Say what?''

"El Paso, baby. I need thirty-four beans. Cash American or I take my merch elsewhere. That's the deal.''

"I'll go twenty-seven-fifty absolute tops. An' you throw in a couple hundred rounds of ammo.''

Laughter.

"Listen, I really enjoyed it, hey. But I got to go do some things. Seriously. You want 'em at 3400 or no? Say the truth, now. I got to book.''

"What about the ammo? I don't gotta buy the fuckin' ammo too, do I?''

" 'Course you do, baby. I don't get that shit free either, dig?''

"Hey. Fuck it. I'll shop around, ya know. The car door.

"Listen. Gimme thirty-four hundred, I'll toss in four boxes of parabellum.''

"Four what?''

"Four boxes of nine-mm. That's it. Thirty-four beans cash now.''

"Awright. Fuck it.'' Pause.

"One, two, three, four, five, six, seven, eight, nine, ten. One, two, three, four, five, six, seven, eight, nine, ten . . .''

Spain had started to squeeze the trigger and the light popped on in the car as the door opened and his man got out. He had an M-31 loaded in the tube. He'd built

it himself from a practice rifle grenade, one of the
demilled jobs with the fuse and explosives out and with
the copper cone where the shaped charge goes intact.
Fins in real good shape. He squeezed as the man
ducked back in the window and the man was leaning
in and counting, "Eight, nine, ten, two thousand, and
one, two, three, four," peeling off hundreds when the
shaped charge exploded against the side of the car. He
heard the coughing plop when the charge exploded out
toward him, but by the time his mind had registered
the sound and he'd paused long enough to look over
toward the trees his head and upper torso had turned
to red, disintegrating Alpo; the driver and the car and
the sack of "Lugers" and the rest of him were all
blown to scarlet shit in a flaming orange ball of fiery,
explosive death.

Spain turned and began moving back through the
trees, climbing back up through the tall grass toward
the highway. He glanced back once at the inferno
burning down on the road, the billowing, black, oily
smoke a strong chemical smell. The Mercedes was
still intact but the flame should ignite the tank soon,
and he spat once and turned back breathing deeply of
the fumes and the mixture of gasoline aromas wafting
from the wake of the passing traffic. He got in and
started the engine, listening for the blast as he pulled
out onto the highway.

Bud Leech and Eichord were on their way to knock
on a couple of late doors when Leech rogered a call
on the two-way.

"Eighty-one-eleven," he told the dispatcher, which
was the numerical designation for the Intel unit.

The radio voice gave him the word and they were
on the way to the crime scene in a hail of static and
incomprehensible copspeak. Eichord recognized
"forty-three-oh-four," a number of the Homicide Bureau, and "Castle Road," and that was about it. They

were northbound, moving fast in a marked scout unit,
Eichord having to concentrate to follow the twists and
turns and then giving up and relaxing as they sped
through the nighttime traffic.

"I have no idea where we are."

"Know which district you're in?"

"I'm not even sure what state I'm in."

Leech smiled and said, "Just remember the high
numbers are the districts north of St. Louis, north of
town that is, and—" The radio interrupted. He ex-
changed another brief bit of cryptic copspeak and told
Eichord, "It's a car bombing." Another homicide or
two in the growing file that was called "Russo" after
the hood whose murder had precipitated the gang war.

Bud Leech worked the field. He was technically an
intelligence supervisor but he'd come from a smalltown
background where you did it all; you secured a crime
scene all by your lonesome, took the pictures, gathered
the evidence, came back and wrote it up, investigated,
you were a one-man team. Now he was a watcher. He
watched the religious cultists, the dudes with the para-
military club who got off on merc fantasies, all kinds
of things beside what feel under the usual "organized
crime" provinces of gambling, pros, extortion, loan-
sharking, porn, and of course, the biggie narcotics.

"What is your procedure as to who rolls on a homicide call," Eichord asked as the scout car shot
through the cars in the fast lane.

"How do you mean?"

"In terms of whether or not you hear about it?"

"Oh, I'm gonna hear about it all right. But you mean
if the dispatcher calls us."

"Yeah."

"Anytime a call comes in to the dispatcher for homicide to respond—let's say to a fatal shooting—the
first individual on the crime scene automatically calls
for an ambulance, and if the victim appears to be dead
four people automatically get the call. Five now with

you. You got homicide, you got the medical examiner, you got the ET unit, and us.''

"ET unit?''

"That's the mobile van. Evidence technician. So we've got a fairly well-preserved and -documented crime scene in many instances. The ET guys are right there with all the tools ready to have at it.''

"Would there be exceptions in fatalities? Like where you'd never get called in?''

"Oh, sure. Like a traffic fatality. Something of that nature, sure.''

"No. I mean, say they find some dude hanging from a rope in a fleabag hotel. Suicide note pinned to his chest and he's swinging from the light fixture. You gonna be there on the scene?''

"No. Probably not in that case. No.''

"No.''

The perpetrator or perps unknown had been very lucky, Leech and Eichord learned upon arriving at the crime scene. The lieutenant was already there and Springer told them, "At least two dead. Bodies absolutely blown to shit. May be a third one dead. One in that vehicle''—he points in the direction of some charred and smoking rubble, and then at the wreckage of a car on its side in the nearby field—"and there's some human remains over by that one.'' He glances at some notes. "Eighty-eight Mercedes registered to one Anthony Tripotra, a.k.a Tony Trip. Muscle in the Dagatina family. No way to tell on this other one.''

"The guys that did this got lucky as hell. There's nobody home in any of the farmhouses and homes on down this way. And all the good citizens that heard the explosion goin' by up on the highway, all the smoke'n' shit, nobody called it in to us. We wouldn't be here if Fire hadn't caught a call on it.''

"Hey! Lieutenant''—a uniformed officer and two detectives were over by the edge of the road poking around in the bushes and trees—"over here.'' One of the homicide cops, a detective named Richard Glass, was holding up a shell casing of some kind in an evidence bag. The smell was offensive beyond belief as the smoke wafted toward them.

"All the earmarks of a pro whack-out."

"Right." Eichord looked at the contents of the bag. A technician was walking down the road with a weapon he'd found somewhere. It looked like what was left of a Walther P-38.

After several minutes of poking around, Leech and Eichord looked at each other and shrugged simultaneously, heading back to the scout unit.

"You've seen enough?" Leech asked.

"Yep."

"You didn't say much back there," Leech said as they got in the car. "I figured we'd see some real criminology goin' down but you just kinda poked around and stuff. I was pretty disappointed." He was grinning.

"Yeah. Well, it was an off day." They drove back toward the city. "You didn't say much either there, by the way. Real quiet."

"That's my thing, Jack. I don't do much. I just lay back in the weeds real cool."

"Um hmm."

"Check it out."

"See who the bad players are."

"Gotcha." Traditionally cars that roll on a homicide call the findings back to a district supervisor who would arrive and take charge of securing the scene. He would be maybe a detective sergeant but he would remain in charge no matter what kind of rank showed up subsequently. If the criteria met the right guidelines, then Eichord would eventually get a call. He wanted to make sure it was going to happen.

"What are the rulebook criteria for who gets called on a firebombing or any homicide of this nature?"

"Well. First . . . somebody's gotta be fairly dead."

"Good. I agree, of corpse."

"Jesus. All right, I quit. Okay. It would like depend on case saturation. The call depends on that day's work load more than anything. But you can stop worrying. It happens now. Everybody knows. Jack Eichord gets in on the act first thing.

Bud Leech was the first cop he'd met in St. Louis other than Springer who'd been willing to give him shit all about anything. He looked over at the man. He had a hypognathous jaw and a large, broken beak that gave him almost a Dick Tracy look. All it would take was a less towering physique, and Leech could put on a snap-brim and a yellow trench coat and pass for the Gould comic strip hero. Eichord said:

"Give me a crime stopper."

"Huh?"

"You know, a Dick Tracy crime stopper. Something I can use in the investigation."

"Okay. If you want to take notes, it's fine. You ready?" Eichord grunted he was. "Don't step on your dick. That's a crime stopper!"

"Hell. There's *no* chance of that."

On the way back in, Leech told him about the special Intel unit. The functions had ranged from dignitary protection to maintaining an active watch file on the organized-crime dudes. Sometimes it worked as an independent unit. At other times it coordinated with state, county, or federal agencies, task forces like McTuff, DEA; it was big with the narcs. Their byword was informants. IRS, Leech called it: Informants, Research, and Surveillance.

Eichord knew all about informants. They became friends. Even though you never wanted to "go to bed" with them figuratively or any other way, you ended up doing it. There was a strong, undeniable bonding pattern that develops over the years between a cop and a snitch. Even the worst degenerate junkie is a human being just like you are. And if that person gives you important information and helps you make cases of any consequence, it is difficult not to look for their redeeming qualities.

They talked about it and Leech said, "I've got people I've been close to for nine, ten, eleven years. They don't owe me and I certainly don't owe them but they still give me good shit. Maybe nine, ten years back they got jammed up some way. Arrested, waiting trial, or trying to get clear of something, and that was how we got hold originally, but now there's nothing hanging over them and still they give. Same with you?"

"Yeah. Absolutely. And they do become friends."

"Right. Somebody helps you and it's just the nature of the relationship. If you're human, pretty soon you feel very friendly for them. It's weird."

"Love is strange."

"I remember that one, too. Mickey and Sylvia?"

"Chee-rist. You're even older than you look."

"I'm bigger than I look, too. So watch it, pal."

"You can't be bigger than you look, Godzilla. You look big enough to hunt geese with a rake." That broke him up.

"That's the second time I heard that one," he said, shaking his head.

"Only the second time?"

"Yeah. The first time I was nine years old."

Every crime scene Eichord remembered you'd get hit with a little shot from the sudden-death thing. It didn't matter how many times you saw it, even the most crusty, hardened ME felt something at the bad ones, some sense of waste, some flicker of remorse at the loss, or perhaps it would come on them slowly, layering its cumulative effect in a tiredness, manifesting itself in world-weary humor or black, low comedy. Anything to get you through it.

Eichord had seen the bad ones. The kids. The pets. The old folks. Whole families. Mass graves. Torture scenes that made paintings of hell look like Wyeth landscapes. There were some he'd never completely shake loose from.

Rolling through the night traffic they passed a place where the highway had been blasted through some boulders and on a rock about the size of Providence, Rhode Island, some moron had left a bit of late-twentieth-century wit and wisdom. There across the huge boulder, fading in the sunny passage of time, crudely spray-painted in shaky letters is the legend,

D E B B I E   S U X

The lost generation. The beat generation. The me generation. The high-tech generation. And now, the Debbie Sux generation. Fucking words to live by.

Some future archeologists from the planet Garbanza X will have a time trying to decode some of *our* more primitive hieroglyphics. Jack Eichord thought to himself that he'd like to be there when the Exalted Chief Expositor of the Eleusinian Mysteries is called in to translate the profound meaning of "Debbie Sux."

John-boy was not so easy. He didn't drive a bright-yellow Volkswagen with vanity plates reading SOLDIER. But professional or not, Johnny Picciotti would go down like a stone. Easy and greasy.

He lived in an apartment hotel—didn't any of these assholes own a fucking home?—But, no problem. Spain used a man he'd farmed a couple of jobs out to in the past. Told him to be in front of the place at a certain time. To wait. A woman would tell him when he could go up.

Spain was across the street in another vehicle watching his worker as he talked to Greta about some mythical duties she would be fulfilling in the future, but both watching his watcher and waiting for Picciotti, whom he'd nailed to a fairly regular schedule. Johnny usually left for Blue Kriegal's place about a quarter to ten every morning. He was on time this morning.

"We'll be bringing in about five thousand boxes at a time. They'll be flats, and what you'll do is hire a couple of kids to put these together and stack them up when we start . . . Uh, say listen, do me a favor, I've got to go meet someone. See that man in the blue car there?"

"Yes, sir?"

"Do me a favor." Spain pulled a money clip out of his pocket and peeled off a twenty. "Walk over there and tap on his window and just say, Go on up. He'll know what you mean."

"Go on up?"

"Right. It'll save me a couple minutes 'cause he always wants to talk to me and I just don't have the time to waste and, you know, I just don't like to be rude but he's one of those guys who never shuts up." They both smiled.

She said, "Sure. Just say, go on up. I don't need to tell him anything else?" "No." He put the twenty-dollar bill in her hand. "Then just walk back across the street and . . ." He turned around. "See that cab-stand over there?" She nodded. "Just take a cab on back to the office." He had to check himself from telling her to keep the change. He knew she would account for the fare the next time he saw her and probably agonize over what percent tip to give the driver. He thanked her and she got out and started across the street as he pulled away from the curb.

He drove around the block. Waited a sixty-second count. Slowly eased up into a parking area next to a business down the block from the cabstand. He waited until he saw the woman walking across the street, going over to the first taxi. Driver gets out. Opens a door. She gets in. They seem to sit there forever. Finally the cab pulls out. Spain starts the engine, pulls his car up in front of the apartment hotel. Goes straight on in and takes the elevator up to Picciotti's floor. The door is unlocked, which is what he has just paid a man he's never allowed to see him over a thousand dollars for.

Spain goes in and starts brewing coffee, making himself right at home. He's locked the door. Now all he has to do is settle down, relax and wait for Mr. Picciotti to return home. The maid's laundry cart from the fourth floor has mysteriously disappeared. It's in Picciotti's bedroom. Johnny won't be leaving here on his feet, I'm afraid, Spain thinks with a smile.

It is three-thirty in the afternoon when Spain, relaxed, reading on Johnny's satin bedspread, hears the key in the door and he quickly gets to his feet and waits behind the bedroom door. No noise for a minute, then a blaring television set is turned on and Spain reaches for his .25 automatic and eases into the room.

"Don't," he says, pointing at Johnny Soldier's surprised face. "Don't even think about it, Johnny. If this was a hit you'd already be greased, right?"

"Wha' the fuck ya wan'?"

"Attaboy," Spain says, pulling a piece out of the man's holster. He can barely get it loose. "Some fast-draw rig you got there. A PPK." Spain laughs. "What are you, James fucking Bond?"

"Who d' fuck are ya?"

"This is who I am, asshole." He kneecaps him and Picciotti drops to the carpet in pain.

"You're *dead*, you piece a' shit," Picciotti grunts.

"Yes, eventually we all end up that way. Well," He goes over and snicks cuffs on the man, but Johnny pulls away before Spain can get them both on properly so he kicks Johnny in the head, catching him with a pointed toe in the side of the neck, and finishes getting the cuffs on.

"How d'ya like working for Blue, Johnny? Good job, is it?" He kicks the man again, in the face this time, then goes into the bathroom and gets a couple of hand towels and a washcloth for a gag.

"You're going to tell me all about Blue and the boys.

All about the operation, you wop peckerhead, but first we'll take a little ride. Okay?'' He wheels the maid's cart in. Johnny is bleeding out of his mouth and Spain soaks one of the towels in it and puts the towel in a plastic bag.

After Picciotti is off-loaded, his next chore is to take Johnny's car keys and unlock the man's vehicle and wipe the bloody towel across the headrest. Just a bit of theater. This done—they leave.

The spur had been a busy linkage shunt at one point but the tracks had long since been torn up for scrap. Everything was gone now except the deep scar through the woods where the railroad trains had once run parallel to the water's edge and several hundred meters inland. It was all gone now. The railroad had literally vanished. The county had even hauled away the gravel in the roadbed, every pebble, every scrap, right down to the dusty spikes, dumping the detritus and junk over various backroads throughout the Missouri boonies. And for a long time to come, farmers would remember the railroad when their pickups rolled rubber over the odd errant spike.

Spain pulled his vehicle well off the roadbed and into a light, declivitous place adjacent to where the county had blocked off the roadway with a stout barricade of treated cross ties. There was a big oak nearby and the vehicle fit nicely between two of the huge root systems that had come reaching out of the low spot like gigantic, gnarled fingers. He started carrying tools and material over toward the water's edge.

It was a tiny spot that was secluded and totally invisible from virtually every angle but one, a natural cove made by erosion from the bank forming a small *O* with a pie slice eaten out of it by the river. The sign back on the road identified it as a Headwater Diversion Channel. As he looked down into the moving waters it looked deep and muddy even inside the little cove,

and he wondered idly how many rivers fed this body
of water he was looking at. He supposed the Mississippi, the Ohio, maybe even the muddy Mo, and he
spat down into it and walked back for more.

His load broke a sweat on him in no time and the
cool breeze felt good as it dried him. He unloaded
three feed sacks partially filled with small rocks he'd
shoveled off a county road—maybe one of them had
come from here in the first place—and a few broken
bricks he'd found near a construction site. He had a
half-dozen bags which he began filling with loose dirt
and closing with twist-'em wire-closures. He had a
razor-sharp sickle, a spade, a posthole digger, gloves
and an abandoned wooden door which he'd sawed off
to six feet by roughly two and a half.

He sickled his way into a likely spot and began
carving out a two-foot-wide, six-foot-long trench with
the sharp digger. He was very strong and the blades
bit into the soft surface soil easily. His goal was to go
down three feet and he put a lot into it, not particularly
pacing himself or holding back, but working with grim
determination. In a few minutes he'd pulled out so
much dirt that he had to start filling bags or move into
the hole. He liked the leverage he had at the trench's
edge, so he took time to fill the plastic bags and when
the hole was accessible he started again.

The sun was falling now and it was setting spectac-
ularly across the river along the horizon, and it shot
dappled orange and peach and crimson highlights
through the willows bent gracefully out along the water's edge and along the banks choked with dog fennel
and foxtail, thorn and thistle, creeper vine and cockle-
bur, ragweed and chigger-weed, poke and poison ivy.
But Spain saw none of it, standing there on the edge
of Mother Nature's leafy wonderment, digging a shallow grave as the jarflies and mosquitoes and frogs sang
relentlessly.

Something cracked through the wall of insane concentration and for that moment the one called Spain realized where he was and his surroundings permeated the dense death haze that he carried with him now. He had impressive banks of information stored away. Trivial and important knowledge. Minutiae he'd accumulated in his half a lifetime such as the fact that the Indians had once made a tobaccolike mixture called kinnikinnick. It came back to him in that moment when his eyes observed sumac and dogwood bark, relaying the message to his brain cells, and in that flush of cognition he realized that all the rain had kept much of the green here. Ladue had been barren-looking when he left for the South. The thought, lonesome amid the rest of the screaming abnormality, fled, and he was pleased at the way the recent rains had left the earth easy to dig in.

When he had the grave he wanted, neatly rectilinear and ready for its occupant, he went back to get Johnny Picciotti, Blue Kriegal's bodyguard. He was lighter than he looked, Spain noticed as he dropped the man's mummied form into the shallow grave and began filling it carefully, tamping the pieces of broken brick in and then starting on the dirt. From time to time a muffled scream would be audible, but when the first layers of bricks and rock and dirt covered it, you couldn't hear much. Just frogs, mosquitoes, and the incessant buzz of the jarflies.

"Glad we could have this little chat," he tells the silent earth.

The phone by the bedside table rang and the man picked it up, having to reach over the sleeping body of an inert young boy to lift it from the cradle.

"Eh?" he grunted into the phone, glancing over at the clock that had some kind of fancy numbers some decorator thought looked good and he could never tell what the fuck time it was.

"Boss?"

"Who d' fuck is this?"

"Boss, this is Blue."

"What d' fuck ya doin' calling me dis time a' da fuckin' night?"

"*BOSS*! Walk up, f' shit sake it's important."

"What?"

"Can I talk?"

"Fuck, I dunno. No. Whatd'ya want, goddammit?"

"I gotta talk to ya."

"Fuck it. What?" He rubbed at the sleep in his eyes.

"Dey got Johnny."

"Whadya fuckin' mean dey got Johnny."

"Johnny. He's fuckin' disappeared. We got his car."

"No fuckin' way, He's prob'ly wit' a broad. Fuck it. Go back ta sleep."

". . . f' shit sake, wake up, goddammit. They got him."

"Who got him? Whatd' fuck ya talkin' bout f' the ten't damn time?"

"Rikla dat piece'a shit got him. We got d' car. Deres blood innit."

"Blood?"

"Blood, gaddammit, on d' headrest thing dere. *RIKLA* he hit Johnny d' no good piece of SHIT his fuckin' children should *DIE*! Hadda be fuckin' *RIKLA*!"

"When?"

"Huh?"

"Whenja fina car?"

"Jus' now. Me'n' Gino found it."

"How long has Johnny been gone?"

"Since las' night. I mean, we figured like you, ya know, it hadda be a broad or a fuckin' game or sum'pin', but we finally go up dere to dat place where he lives an' look inna gargage and we checked inside d' car an der's the goddamn bloodstains'n' shit."

"He could be hurt. Inside. Not answerin' d'
phone."

"Naw. We got the super guy to let us in. Nobody
up der. RIKLA NAILED HIM, de fuckin' cock-
sucker."

"How do you know so fuckin' sure?"

"Who d' fuck else gonna be wit' de balls to hit
Johnny Soldier, f' shit sake? Hit him where he lives
like dat. You know it hadda be some fuckin' som'bitch
wit' no respec' for where a man lives. Dat fuckin'
Rikla garbage go inside an' clip a man where he lives.
An one of US ain't gon' clip a guy where d' guy
fuckin' LIVES, goddammit."

"Yeah. Well." The man sat up and yawned, rubbed
his eyes again, looking at the thin boy asleep beside
him or pretending to be asleep. "Get Buck n' Lowenstein. You and Gino meet me at d' other place in
about . . ." He glanced at the clock again. "Fuckin'
goddamn shit clock it don' even tell the fuckin' time.
Fuck it. Meet me over dere in half an hour. Bring ya
tools 'n' shit. I don't guess we got to take dat fuckin'
shit."

One of the main reasons he couldn't concentrate was
he had Ritafication on the brain. Tonight's the night,
he kept thinking. It was amazing to him the way he
could always revert to a sixteen-year-old kid mentally
at the mere cross of a leg in a high-heeled shoe. I
mean, healthy is one thing, but Holy Moly, Captain
Marvel, gimme a break here.

So Rita Paul now Haubrich of the legs and the red
hair was the way he rationalized it. Whatever the real
reason, this case was still a jellied blur.

The whole day had been spent first with Springer
and a couple of homicide and organized-crime guys
trying to do a chalk talk which had him so confused
he erased it from his slate and tried his own simplistic
version on a legal pad. It began like so:

THE TWO TONYS GANG
Cypriot (gone/NY?)   Dago (slams)
Rikla . . . Measure
Russo . . . Venable

He said to a detective nearby. "Hey, Glass?"

"Yeah?"

"Who is Johnny Picciotti?"

"Johnny Soldier. Punk worked for Measure's people. Blue Kriegal's bodyguard but it looks like the job's open. Appears he got himself snuffed."

"But no body, right?"

"Yeah. He's in the foundation of some new condo out in Lake St. Louis."

"Uh-huh," T. J. Monahan said, "or he's got compacted in the trunk of an old junker out at Used Car City."

"Right. He's now the rear bumper of a Dodge Omni."

"And Tony Tripotra. Was he with Rikla or Measure?"

"He WAS with Rikla. He's with the angels now. Dead muscle. A thief. Had a package behind ADW and an armed-robbery thing that he beat. I doubt if he ever made his bones even. Just a guinea moke for Rikla."

"How did Blue Kriegal get the name Blue?"

"Blue movies," somebody suggested.

"Naw," Pat Skully said. "It was because he *blue* so many little boys." Eichord thought it had warmed up a little or maybe it was just that he'd become punchy with the information overload.

"EEEhhhhh," Leech called out to him as he clomped through the squad room in his size-fourteen wides, "How's the Capo di Tutti Frutti today?" He said to Eichord.

"Sweet as ever and never been kissed." But fixing to remedy that situation, he hoped.

He shaved again for the date. Cut himself nicely, which was always a good sign, and looked at himself in a favorite sport coat and decided, No way. Ung. Not a shot in the *world*. He could feel his Right Guard going even as he pulled up in front of her place. She looked. What's the word? Gorgeous doesn't cover it. She looked like . . . Oh, let's be calm. Precise. We're a trained observer, he thought. She looks *YIPPPP- EEEEEEE*!

She was nice. Everything about her was nice. She looked very nice. Smelled nice. Smiled nice. Talked nice. Thought nice. This is going to be a nice, breathlessly boring date. Niceing each other to death.

She suggested a place at his request and it was— right—nice. A quiet, dark but not too dark, nice little place with good service and probably good food and wine. He didn't taste anything because he had Rita Haubrich to look at and taste. Pitiful and nobody's proud of being a slobbering, drooling sex maniac, but these are the facts, ma'am.

Rita drank a chilled white wine which she had to order as he had been struck numb, dumb, and pantingly goofy by the tactile senses that her presence had assaulted. He ordered something and it sat there untouched in front of him while they talked.

Yes, dammit to blazes, it was NICE talking with her about all kinds of things. He liked her a bunch and she seemed to be able to somehow tolerate Eichord, even laughing at his attempts at good humor. But then who wouldn't be charmed by the sophisticated, rapier wit and hilariously piercing *bon mots* such as the following:

"Well, how time flies," she had said to him with her big smile lighting up the dark corners of the restaurant. "We've been talking, or I should say I have been talking on and on. Did you want to do something else this evening?" And Jack Eichord replied—and get this now for some of that repartee, he didn't hesitate a moment—he replied brilliantly, "Hammma, hammma, hammma," which she had the taste to think was sublimely funny. She had probably seen various folk struck numb, dumb, and pantingly goofy before. She was what they used to call a looker. She had always been pretty. But now she was nothing less than SENSATIONAL.

They had fun talking and they sat there for hours making fools out of themselves not in the least. Rita kidded him that he was the first adult male she'd ever known who wasn't a lawyer.

"Are you sure you didn't become a lawyer in all that time?"

"I assure you I—"

"Promise." She made a pretty face. "Cops sometimes study for the bar."

"Cross my heart. Defense rests." He knew when to let a straight line go by untouched.

"Are you WANTING to be a lawyer?"

" 'Fraid not. Is that good or bad?"

"Yes, probably one or the other but irrelevant. It's just so very wonderfully different. You are the only adult of the male persuasion I've ever met in the last twenty years who wasn't a lawyer."

"Still just a plain old cop."

"Cop, maybe. Old, ehhhh. Plain. Huh-uh." She laughed. She looked at his dark black hair flecked with gray, and dark eyes that bored into her soulfully, and that was when it happened.

"Oh, shucks," he said, summoning up a hidden wellspring of conversational brilliance. Thrilled to his sex-mad core. He *LOVED* St. Louis.

"You know," he began, some lame crap just to say something and he just couldn't finish the stupid sentence. He was absolutely bowled over by her and he let it hang there unfinished, just looking at her in admiration.

"Yeah?" is what another woman might have said to

his unfinished dialogue. She thought it and he understood. And he thought that she could read the sincerity in his eyes. It was ridiculous, of course, but it was so damned biochemical and metaphysical and dad-gummed blue-eyed fun that he just nodded at her as if to say, Yes, I agree it was nice to be able to have a conversation without speaking. And then suddenly both of them got very self-conscious about it and at the exact moment Rita started to say, "It's interesting how a person can—" he started to say, "Have you ever considered the fact—" and they said them in unison and both broke up laughing and then they said, "Go ahead."

"I wasn't going to say anything."

"You go ahead, I wasn't going to say anything either."

"Would you believe I'm having lots of fun sitting here having the dumbest conversation that has ever been held?"

"Me too." And he wanted to ask her if he took an ink pen and connected all the little tiny dots on her body would it be some kind of far-out beautiful Picasso-like Cubistic artwork? And could he try that later, maybe? He could use something water-soluable. He had other thoughts, too.

They talked about old times. The St. Louis they both loved back in the delightful, SoHoish Gaslight Square days that made the town seem like an oasis of hip in the hopeless desert of the Midwest. They laughed about a district attorney, a preposterous guy who both of them still remembered. She told him all about her dad, a former judge and lawyer turned pol and long since retired. Her brother was a well-known criminal lawyer in Kansas City, and her former husband, Winslow Haubrich, was an upwardly mobile trust lawyer with North, Haubrich and Dechter, a firm solidly plugged into the St. Louis banking system.

Pretty soon they found themselves flirting with each other uncontrollably, and then they started laughing at themselves and that was fun too. It was as if the intervening years had never happened. And Jack didn't know for certain but he thought if she'd just let him kiss her once he could go home and compose a 300,000-word essay about that face with its special collection of perfections. Delicate bones that stopped just on the comfortable side of being cover-girl, traffic-stopper looks. Yippee.

Ex-husband notwithstanding he sensed a kind of virginal, fresh, and tender thing about her. Rita looked like one of those girls whom you take back to their apartment and it's all chintz and lace and four-poster-bed room and plants out the kazoo, Lautrec on the wall or a bullfight poster, or worse—horses or velvet children with the eyes—but she wasn't. She was one great, fan-damn-tastic, ummmmmmm-good, super surprise.

"God!" he said again. "Rita *PAUL*! From out of nowhere." And that broke both of them up again.

On the way to her place he started making a list of the things that were phenomenal about this lady. He'd start just with her face. Just the purely physical stuff:

1. The red hair
2. The lips (a: smile) (b: corners) (c: fullness) (d: coloration)
3. The nose
4. The chin
5. The eyes
6. The eyelashes
7. The eyebrows (he'd *never* looked at eyebrows before)
8. The cheeks (a: cheekbones) (b: flawless skin)
9. The ears
10. The forehead.

She was the first woman he could ever remember seeing about whom he could actually say there were ten beautiful things just above the neck alone and that's not counting the back of her head, her teeth, her tongue, et cetera.

But even before he got to the wonderful sloping upper chest and that long and lovely throat and the other 469 things he thought were terrific about Rita, there was the apartment. One more surprise.

She'd met him at the door, so he hadn't seen inside her apartment. He was surprise to find it sparse, white, and functional. Not that high-tech crap with all the chrome things and everything all self-consciously spherical and slick, but a great pad. Even the greenery looked good. He liked everything about this lady.

She was another one of those rather pretty women who age like wine. The ones who suddenly wake up one day in their late twenties to find out they've done something miraculous. Or rather that God has. He's let them turn sensational-looking while they were asleep. Because those women sometimes seem to get that way overnight. It's not a slow, evolutionary thing, but a fast, breathtaking process that comes on them while asleep. And plain Jane wakes up one morning in Knockout City. Reasonably pretty Rita wakes up beautiful.

It doesn't happen a lot. But when it does, it can be heady stuff and not every woman or man can deal with it. A woman like that sometimes can get a real crush on her mirror if she isn't careful. Not Rita. She handled it by not believing she was sensational-looking at all. She laughed at Eichord's compliments. He told her how pretty she was and it really put her away and she laughed hard and the laughter was genuine. What a comic he was. And that knocked him out too.

Mr. Haubrich had helped her ignore the striking reflection in the mirror. She told Jack he still helped her. Anytime she thought she was pretty neat stuff all she had to do was remember the day she'd come home and made dinner and waited for him to come home as usual and the burning humiliation of the phone call from his MOTHER. *HIS MOTHER*, for God's sake. He didn't even have the style to tell her himself. Even a note taped to the pillow. Anything but his goofy mother calling to explain that Winslow wouldn't be home that night . . . Oh my God, the embarrassment! She still couldn't take the thought of that phone call and everything it represented to her.

Finally the shock wore off a little and Rita realized that crazy Win and his secretary could go right up in smoke for all she cared and that getting on with her life was the immediate priority item. As more time passed she began to look on it as the blessing that it was. Her husband had been a weak, self-centered kiss-ass heading up the corporate trust ladder with Daddy's contacts and a doting Mommy who still kept him tied to her by the apron umbilical.

Eichord's impression of Rita was that she looked like a sticker who didn't run from problems. She would have been willing to keep trying.

She said, "My marriage vows were serious stuff to me. It really was what I'd committed myself to forever."

"Once I said the same thing, but I let a demon get hold of me."

"For me his leaving was a positive thing in the end. I may have taken a pretty good shot to the old self-esteem but it let a lot of fresh air back into my life."

"My ex-wife probably could say the very same thing. I wasn't marriage material for anybody. I doubt if I would be for anybody. It takes a lot to keep a marriage going in my line of work. You give so much of your time to it. It isn't fair, truly, to subject a spouse to that kind of second place in a partnership."

"Maybe not. Maybe so. But there are cops with great marriages, no?"

"Some. Sure. But I think as many cop marriages go

sour. You've got a lot of strikes against you right off the bat." He suddenly switched metaphor because suddenly every sentence that went through his mind had the word "balls" in it.

They dimmed the lights and talked more and soon they kissed and it was so soft and tender a beginning that he nearly laughed out loud at the marvel and sheer pleasure of it and rightness and oh, baby, yes, the niceness of it. The unexpected reunion had created a hothouse atmosphere for both of them.

She wore a white, long-sleeved blouse and no jewelry. She had a beautiful body. Breasts that were almost too good to be real. The kind of classic, luscious melons that look so soft and white but spring firm to the touch, perfectly proportioned, neither small nor overly large. A tight, flat belly and smallish rib cage that suddenly curved out in a pair of gorgeous globes.

She turned and lowered the lights completely, turning on a single light behind her, the rest of the apartment in darkness. Her legs. My God. She was showgirl, pony, absolute yippee all the way. What a pair of lovely legs she had.

He had the odd and awesome sensation of having something deliciously sweet in his mouth, and he breathed deeply of her body's uniquely feminine fragrance. She still had on her glasses and as she turned on those legs that he couldn't quit staring at she pulled her glasses off and it was like a striptease. Just that alone was. And that long, giraffe neck and the model's chin, the long neck and throat curving out like a Modigliani, and the throat and beautiful upper chest minutely freckled in kissable texture he would have to investigate closely, and those killer legs in the little scanty panties and up very close he could see almost invisible veins in her long, alabaster legs that just kept going and going.

Against the light her hot and lovely body was silhouetted in the sheerness of the silky, wispy thing that covered her breasts, falling away in an inverted *V* in front and the perfection of her dazzled him with desire and inflamed him.

The long flame of hair curved and caressed her as it dropped long and straight then following the lovely lines of her throat down through the soft shadows.

Her eyes blazed at him wanting him back and he imagined tasting that full, hot mouth soon burning himself on their lust. He watched her and she watched him and they took their time tasting the anticipation of it. He let his eyes travel up and down that gorgeous body standing there profiled for him. High, firm breasts pushing through the wispiness, nipples thrusting and pointing at him, erect and ready to explode with the heat of a touch, a flat and beautiful stomach—a teenager's tummy, so smooth and supple—and then the classic curves as the body flared out into a woman's sexy hips and the shadowy triangle of her little, soft bush in the tiny diaphanous bikini panties, and the long, long loooonnnnnngggg perfection of legs, down to high heels. A sultry picture of pure sex.

She stood there unmoving. Absolutely rigid. Lancing him with her heat and beauty. Telling him that this—all of this—was his to take and use, and his brain overdosed on the fire that had spread through his body and he pulled her down.

Neither of them quite believed it. It was over so quickly for both of them and exploding out of them together in the thing that started as tenderness but crushing, demanding, consuming came together in a molten release that was so fast they just lay there together, Eichord still in her, she still clinging to him, both of them wet, soaked, sledgehammered, steamrollered, hung out to dry. And she said softly to him, "I want romance and I want it now," and he understood.

Later he sat on the edge of the bed beside her, with all the lights on, both of them nude, and he stared at all of her an inch or so at a time, just drinking her in

and so obviously stoned on it she laughed and asked
him, "Hey, buddy. Watcha starin' at?"

"Modigliani," he said, enraptured by the long
curving throat and flawless upper chest.

"Never mind that Bo Diddley stuff," she said.
"Let's screw." And he fell off the bed and laughed
until he cried. And when he'd calmed down she got
down on the floor with him and they did it on her
bedroom rug. A first, she told him. And they agreed
that America was a phenomenal place.

Eichord had been still for a long time. Listening to
her deep breathing, and it startled him when she asked
him, "You asleep?" in a quiet voice.

"No," he said softly.

"What were you thinking about?"

"Nothin'," he lied. Shaking his head and turning
the corners of his mouth down. "Absolutely zero."
Vowing that he would see no evil, hear no evil, speak
no evil.

The old man sat quietly eating his dinner. It was not
the standard prison fare. There was fresh fruit. Excellent fish. He tasted nothing. The frustration of it all
was enough to make you go mad. He had to summon
up all his willpower, which was considerable, to keep
his patience. He was too old for all of this. What garbage the thing of theirs had become. He shook his
head slightly and took another small bite of fruit.

He fumbled with his reading bifocals trying to get
them out of the case which he dropped and ignored,
not even watching as the large, frightening-looking
man who stood behind him quickly and silently re-
trieved the case and placed it beside him, returning to
his position to the old man's rear.

What had these boys become? Fucking Paulie and
Jimmie. His goddamn brothers in the thing. Fighting
each other and killing and breaking the oath right and
left. You didn't kill someone where he lived. Not even

if there was a contract. It just wasn't done. If you caught him with your daughter, maybe then you clip him near his home, but never like this. He tried to read about it in the summary.

He could do nothing. It hurt him to piss, it hurt him to shit, it hurt him not to shit. His old fingers were painfully arthritic and the first words he read set him off again. Jimmie the Hook. Crazy Lyle. Fucking maniacs shot at Toot Smith down in the middle of Laclede fucking Landing with people all over the fucking place. Jesus, Mary, and Joseph, blessed Virgin, Holy Mother of God, what an I gonna do?

The Commission couldn't give less of a shit about the family's problems out in St. Louis. He was expected to run this thing from *JAIL?*

He took a series of shallow breaths, his little bird chest wheezing, huffing, and puffing, ancient, abused lungs sucking air as best they could. Fucking prison air on top of everything else. Just more than a human being could stand. And the brotherhood expects me to pull this shit back together for them. He raised the first finger of his right hand a couple of inches from the table and felt the presence behind him moving and a looming shadow draw near at his command.

"Where's, uh—" Oh, Christ in His Heaven, now I can't think of his name. Finally it came to him. "Where's Duke? Is he in population?" His voice was thin and raspy.

"No, sir," the voice rumbled like gravel loose in a metal pan. "I 'tink Duke's down in Ad Seg."

The old man nodded. "Get him." And the large shadow moved.

A few minutes later there were footsteps and two men entered his room.

"Siddown," he said to the man after they gave each other the formal greeting of respect.

"Duke"—he slid the paper across the table—"I want the word out. Enough is enough. The next one

who violates this thing of ours, the next—outlaw—
that's it. He goes under. Give it to Big Mike Stricoti
and Jack Nails. Tell them to get their own crew. Whoever it is. I want that shit clipped.''

Spain sleeps. And in a sleep of death this man to
whom control is so all important dreams that all control is lost.

A cloaked finger approaches from the shadows of
the dream and a skeletal, clawed hand emerges from
the folds of the dark cloak, tossing ancient bones from
a skull cup.

The secret oracle gazes at the bones and foretells of
sudden and violent occurrence.

Somewhere in the Orient a sage writes of myriad
straw dogs, and high on a mountaintop an aged holy
man pierces a veil of understanding.

A secret society prepares a virgin for ritual slaughter. Spain sees that it is his daughter.

A once-sentient mind now begins to recede into a
dark, inner chamber where sense, impression, and response cannot penetrate. A bioelectrical circuit brea-
ker is thrown. The chamber goes to black.

The dreamer lifts a hammered goblet that once held
the blood of Christ, and drinks deeply of serpent
venom. He sees the fissures of his brain transubstan-
tiated into a nest of writhing eels.

The cold, inky force of the nightmare pulls him
down, and two hundred fathoms below the surface he
is held in a powerful, swirling whirlpool.

He dreams of giant sea snakes and mutant water
scorpions and eyeless, slithering things that come to
transfuse him again with devil-filth, and the oracle tells
him he will return to the surface world to do murder
by skill and magic. And he spirals up through the
black, rushing helix at the command

''Expunge!''

* * *

The following day Spain rested. And the following night he made a totally random kill. Parking a stolen car out in front of the Robert Schindler Building across from the Press Club, a few blocks from police headquarters, walking in and looking at some names on a rubber name-plate thing by the elevator. And when the elevator man came over to him and asked him if he could help him, something in the man's tone, his pigmentation, sent Spain into a fury and without warning or a hint of premeditation (yet he had stolen a car), he pulled Mary Pat from her sheath taped to his left forearm and stabbed the diminutive elevator operator/doorman to death there in the lobby of the Schindler Building.

Back home and safely ensconced in the rental house he was busily remodeling to suit his bizarre and terrifying needs, he played with Pat, tossing the nine-inch stiletto into the soft wood of the table where it stuck again and again. He had read Leslie Charteris as a boy and remembered the dagger that The Saint had named after a woman—Anna, was it? And he named this deadly bitch after his wife and gave her blood to drink.

The stiletto stuck in the soft pine again, the cruciform silhouette casting its shadow along the tabletop. The appearance was exactly that of a crucifix, the shaft and guard making the sign of the cross, the grooves and relief work of the turned metal grip suggesting the crucified body of the Savior.

He took the thing and flung it with a vengeance across the room from him, hurling it by the point, throwing it with that practiced movement of the arm that he had developed over two decades throwing every type of knife—dagger, dirk, screwdriver, sharpened pencil, all manner of pointed and edged objects—and Pat bit into the wall with a comforting thwocking sound as the shadow of the cruciform fell against the wall, suggesting someone who had been crucified upside down and Spain set there staring at the stiletto in his wall, feeling a chill touch him there in the very warm, empty house. And Spain was now mad as a hatter. And he sat there quietly gritting his teeth, thinking about how good it was to stab the elevator operator whose tone of voice and coloration evoked the image of Gaetano Ciprioni. But he knew he would retain the professional control necessary to achieve his ultimate goal. That degree of controlled resolve would not desert him in his madness. Killing, after all, was what he did.

For three days Jack Eichord had been tied up with the flood of violence and then he had time to breathe and he called Rita.

"I've missed you desperately," she told him, and all he could do was breathe into the phone.

"I know, you've missed me too. I can tell by the way you're panting."

"Yeah," he told her very seriously.

"What is happening here?" she asked him.

"What?"

"What's happening to us?"

"What do you mean?"

"You know what I mean, you rascal you."

"Oh, you mean *that?*"

"Yes. That."

"It's a biological phenom that I've read about in books. It's quite natural."

"Oh, that's good, then."

"It's very good, in fact."

"Does it have a name?"

"Yes, it thurtently doth," he said, sounding for some inane reason like a cat in the cartoons. "It means we're falling in sex."

"How romantic."

"Would you like a little romance tonight?"

"I could probably squeeze you into my busy schedule."

"Squeeze me about seven, say?"

"Consider yourself squeezed."

"I've missed you too. A lot."

Even better the second time? he asked himself afterward. No way. But it had been. So wonderful. They lay there laughing like fools, so pleased with each other and the nice discoveries. She fingered his second belly button, a puckered navel where an old wound had eventually smoothed over.

"You've led an interesting life, I see."

"Unquestionably, my dear Watson."

"What made this? Did someone bite you here?" She touched its indentation.

"Probably." He said as he felt the small groove that was a long, forgotten souvenir from a blocked Fairbairn thrust. "Ancient history."

"I feel sure it must be from a woman. A bite."

They sought each other's mouths and her tongue zapped him like the touch of a high-voltage line and he was copper winding down to a long, coiled grounding shaft that took the power hungrily and fed on it and he reached deeply to take as much of her hot, sweet lightning as he could, letting the energy of the electricity charge them in a crackling surge of current.

"Who is it?" Eichord said to Bud Leech, who was already on the crime scene.

"Little joker named Betters. They really played Hurt You with this boy. Hope you've had dinner already."

"Hey, Bud," one of the Homicide people said to Leech, nodding to Eichord.

"Yo."

"Can they take him?"

"Uh, hold it. Not yet, babe. Tell 'em hold it a few minutes."

"Okay."

"Small time jive-ass little punk named Vinnie Betters. Some gofer in with Measure." He shook his head. "I don't know what this is about," he said, jerking his thumb toward the kitchen on the word "this."

"You get done dusting yet?"

"Naw."

"Smells great in here."

"Jesus." Eichord put a handkerchief up to his face. "Herrrrrrrre's Vinnie."

Eichord looked and turned away after a bit.

"Obviously whoever did this—"

"Yeah." He laughed without humor. "You could say that, all right."

"Seriously. Whatever the reason why he was killed, whoever did it was trying to get something out of their system. Nothing professional about that."

"I figure two, three, maybe four guys taking turns. Really getting themselves worked up. Nothing professional about it, as you say. Unless they were pros trying to tell somebody something—that your point?"

"Right."

"Really did a J.-O.-B. on the little mother."

Vinnie was upside down, with maybe nine hundred puncture wounds in him, turning into maggot food under the kitchen counter there in his ex-wife's house.

"Who called it in?"

"His wife, er, uh, HEY!" He motioned to a detective. "Yo." He motioned for him to come over to the kitchen area.

"Tell him how you caught the call."

"Yeah. Well, it was his ex-wife. She said she'd just come in and found him. Claims she was shacked up with her latest old man in Atlantic City. We're checking it out. Vinnie's got a little yellow sheet. Little half-assed rat package."

"Maybe he ratted out the wrong dudes."

"Could be Rikla's people. I admit it don't look like no hit. Anyway, he was always trying to get made and

didn't have the eggs for it, and—far as I ever heard—
he just never had his shit together.''

''He's got his shit together now.'' They laughed.

''F'r sure.''

''Lynch Street people got here first. They called us.
I came. You came. That's about the whole shot.''

''Think they'll have anything on the street on this?''

''Naaaaaa. I doubt it.''

''A payback thing. Somebody's gonna say somethin' otherwise it's all wasted. You know how the wise
guys are.''

''Nobody gives a shit about Vinnie. Nobody's gonna
miss him. He was a schmuck. Even his ex–old lady
pegged it. She said when she came home and found
him gathering little white wormies and smellin', in her
words ''—the cop looked at a notebook—'like ten bags
of dead skunks.' '' They chuckled. ''It was no big
surprise. She told the Lynch Street guys, 'Hell, he was
lucky he lived THIS long.' ''

''Quite an epitaph.''

''Leech.''

''Yo.''

''Can we take this fucker yet?''

''NO, GODDAMMMIT YOU CAN'T TAKE THIS
FUCKER YET, I done tol' y'all fourteen times.
Whatsa big hurry, fi'r shit sake?''

''No hurry at all. We LIKE standing here smellin'
this puke 'n' shit.''

''Right. I know it's a revolutionary theory but what
if we would bring latent in here and dust this scene
and, you know, find the FINGERPRINTS of the dudes
what did the crime. You know, like on TV?''

''Sure. Wonderful.''

And that was what happened. Jackie Nails, a.k.a
Jack Annelo, and Big Mike Stricoti of the Dagatina
family—''alleged gunmen,'' as the papers worded it—
had left their big guinea paw prints all over the house.

It was enough to make a couple of tentative arrests and within twenty-four hours media was running neat little sidebars about the "big break in the mob slayings."

The entire unit was on hand by chance when the next "big break" took place. A lab finding nailing Annelo to one of the earlier shootings. In the best spirit of *omertá* he'd clammed up, and that made him look even better for the wise-guy killings. Except to Eichord.

He was prepared to believe almost anything, on one hand, and on the other his healthy skepticism had been replaced by a monumental paranoia about the case. For one thing, ever since the Ventura Boulevard hit in Studio City, there had been no more EYEBALL murders. He kept thinking one of these gangland kills in St. Louis would tie to California, but it wasn't happening.

All the facts and the serious conjecture indicated solutions involving more than one perpetrator.

A: The street rumors floating back to Homicide at LAPD pointed to a couple of local punks for the Studio City job.

B: The Laclede Landing shooting had been a shooter and a wheel man at the least.

C: The two Dagatina hoods were tied solid to the Betters killing. Jackie Nails to at least one other hit.

But for all that, Floyd Streicher of the hooded eyes would not get out of his head. And Jack rubbed his eyes, sighed, and looked down at the phrase he'd been doodling:

DID I LIVE? EVIL I DID.

And in a long expulsion of air he emptied his lungs and read the sentence backward. Realizing as he did so that he had no idea what the fuck he was involved in here. And against his better judgment he took in more air and kept going.

* * *

At precisely 1430 the following Monday all hell broke loose. The CP was screaming on the phone to Victor Springer that the notorious mob lawyer Jake Rozitsky and another individual believed to be an innocent bystander had just been blown up in a gangland bombing downtown. An unprecedented number of units responded, as well as the fire department, and Eichord.

Brass balls to the walls. Media going insane. A circus of mobile units, flashing lights, roiling smoke, sirens, you name it. Two television news choppers almost got into a midair chickie fight trying to jockey for position for best shots of the burning building and the obligatory scene of cops and paramedics and firemen taking Rozitsky and the other man, thought to be a building worker, out to a waiting ambulance in body bags.

Glass came running up to Eichord hollering something at him and it was so noisy he couldn't hear.

"What?"

("MUMBLE MUMBLE")

"WHAT? I CAN'T HEAR YOU!"

("SOMETHING") He looked like he was saying metro something. Then he made the universal sign for telephone and Eichord got it and grabbed his two-way, switching it over to the metro freq and taking the call from McTuff. It was one of the things he'd put into play on his own, and the Task Force had reached out just in time. He went over and told Springer, "Lieutenant?"

"What?"

"Come inside the car here." He motioned.

"Huh," Springer screamed.

"In HERE."

"Jesus," Vic Springer said, falling into the car. "Sounds like World War Three goin' on out here. Shit, un-fuckin'-real, I can't hear any—"

"We got something, maybe," Eichord told him.

"Yeah?"

"I got a court order for a wiretap. I put it in through McTuff. Roundabout through the DA's office."

"How come you didn't ask me about it, Jack?" He looked so dyspeptic Eichord wondered if he was going to be all right and then he remembered it was just a face. "What tap? Whose phone?" He kept caving in.

"Rozitsky's." He nodded toward the smoking building where firemen were still at work putting the last of the blaze out.

"You tapped Jake Rozitsky? When was this? How come you didn't talk to me?" A basset is all Eichord kept thinking as sad eyes looked at him.

"Just a few days ago. I didn't have a chance, Lieutenant. Always somebody around or I wasn't near a telephone I could trust. Taps go two ways. I got a bad feeling about this Russo case."

"Yeah." Springer sat quietly for a second. "You're saying somebody in the unit is dirty."

"No. Not at all. Just saying—well, you have to consider all the options. The bottom line is. I had his private line tapped when he was killed."

"Umm. And?"

"I think I've got the killer's voice on tape."

Back at Twelfth and Clark everybody in Chief Adler's Special Division gathered on the fourth floor as if for a wake or a quiet riot. It took a long, l-o-n-n-n-g forty-five minutes for the agent to show up with the dupe of the original.

"Go ahead," Springer told him, and the special agent threaded the tape into a playback unit.

"Okay. Uh"—he cleared his throat—"this is not going to be real great quality so we'll have to concentrate and make as little noise as possible, please, so everybody can hear this clearly. This is a dupe of the original and we lost a lot of the sound quality dubbing it but we knew you wanted to hear the content as soon as possible. We should have the real thing for you all remastered and quite audible by tomorrow afternoon. Meanwhile this is all we can give you.''

''All right. What it is—this is a tap made from an office bug in the law office of the decedent, but this was patched into a mobile phone which transmits through high-frequency radio waves. It's a cellular unit, like your two-ways, or paging services, things like that, but this is not off the open tap that addresses the device by harmonics, this—''

''Uh, excuse me,'' Eichord interrupted. ''Sorry but we need to hear this, so if you will hold off on the technical stuff for later.'' Somebody said showtime as the agent nodded and hit Play. For five minutes all they heard was a lot of crap about the Dolphins game, and the line on the game, and the point spread. Then there was a new conversation.

Eichord listened to the somewhat poor-quality tape as the lawyer's secretary spoke with someone else's secretary, and there was a pause while the other party came on the line. One of the cops in the room said, ''This is James Measure he's talkin' to.''

''Yeah,'' a gruff voice barked.

''Mr. Measure, please stay on the line for Mr. Rozitsky.''

''Yeah, awright.''

''Jim-baby,'' a rich voice enthused.

''Jake. What's up?''

''How are ya, booby?''

''I'm awright. Not too bad.''

''Listen, Jim . . . I gotta talk to ya about a couple of things later, ya know?''

''Yeah.''

''I had that meeting with our friend over there, and it's just what I told you. He's holding us up, but he's gonna' swing with it, so that's all there is to it we just gotta push his buttons.''

''He's holding us up awright, the cocksuck.''

"Yeah. That's going to have to be taken care of. We gonna get banged for some sweetener, ya' know?"

"Oh, I figured that out awready."

"He's gonna have to have some sweetener but he'll pop for us I promise ya, no problem at all. We gotta waltz him around a little first, and then he's gonna waltz us around a little, and then we're all gonna dance a little more, and finally we gonna get a bottom line, and that's the way it'll work. I mean, we'll get there it's just gonna take a dance or two."

"I don't give a fuck he gotta go with me on this thing, that's all there is to it."

"I talked to him. Look, Jim, he knows that's your country here and he's gotta go through you to do this thing, and some dues get paid both ways, he's aware of this."

"Fuckin' right it's our country here, the mother-fucker."

"So it's just getting banged for a little sweetener and dance a couple dances with the sonofabitch and that's that, emmis, but it's like a bullshit thing with him, ya know? He's gotta put you through the numbers, see, so it looks like it's all kosher, and Mr. Big Business-man, but at the end he's got his hand out. He just don't ask for the sweetener like a man, he gotta waltz us around all over the place first. But that's what you got me for. I'll dance with the cocksuck for a while and then we'll do something."

"So what's he gonna nail us on it?"

"I figure another ten dollars on it."

"Je-sus *CHRIST!* Whattya' fuckin' MEAN ten shit. That sonofabitch thinks we're made outta fuckin' money, fer Chrissakes? Fuck him."

"So we'll get banged for a little sweetener and that's the name of that tune. But you know, what pisses me off he can't be a man and just come out wit' it he's gotta' waltz around all over the place first and act like Honest John, see, and the slimy sonofabitch is puttin' his hand down in your pocket and telling you this and that and the other thing like he can't do this and he can't do that.''

"This is bullshit. Ten large. Christ, the fuck, gonna bang me for another ten large I better see something happen pretty fuckin' fast is all I can tell ya. I ain't payin' ten dollars more for a hand job.''

"I'll let you know what finally gets decided on that. But meanwhile on the other thing you had me reach out for—?''

"Yeah?''

"No problem. He's very understanding to our situation. I can absolutely fuckin' guarantee you we reach him when we want him. The only thing is it has to be handled with kid gloves. I don't want to do it myself.''

"Just take care of it whatever ya' think.''

"Yeah. I'll have somebody here in the office drop around and give him the envelope. That's no problem. And he's quite understanding and sympathetic. The thing is you know he says there has to be something for show. My feeling is we can expect a very smooth thing there, though.''

"When we come up? What is it—three weeks?''

"Yeah, right. Jim, another thing good for us there is that he's got his friend wants that political thing. That appointment is like a fucking lifetime annuity, ya know?''

"Ya better fucking believe it. Those cocksucks don't do shit and the fucking thing pays seventy large while they sit on their asses, and they don't gotta run every couple years like them other assholes. Shit. They gotta fuckin' bird's nest on the ground.''

"Abso-fuckin'-lutely. Shit, I'd take a fuckin' judge-ship over there. And of course he knows you got the fix in with the Committee too, so we got no problem there whatsoever. So his friend has done all that work for the ticket, see, and we just ease him into that, we got two out of three bases covered over there.''

"Goddamn right."

"Well, I'm sorry about the other but I wanted to let you know about our friend over there. I think he'll bang us for ten dollars and that'll be that, so hang tough, and I'll get back to ya when I have something concrete."

"I got something concrete for the cocksuck."

(They laugh.)

"Take care—talk to ya later."

"Awright, Jake, lemme know."

"Will do, my friend. Talk to ya soon."

"Okay. Now listen," as the voice-activated Norelco kicked back on again and Eichord heard a soft, extremely precise voice ask the secretary if Mr. Rozitsky was in.

"Who shall I say is calling, please?"

"Tell him it's Roy Cohn," the man said.

"Yes, sir, Mr. Cohen, one moment please," the woman said, missing the man's joke.

A few seconds later a laughing voice came on the line: "Jake Rozitsky."

"Hello, Mr. Rozitsky. You don't know me and my name won't be important to you, but I have some information that you're going to find very valuable with respect to a criminal case you're going to be involved in within a couple of weeks."

"Who am I talking with, please?"

"Oh, just think of me as a friend of the court. Listen, I don't want money. I just want justice. And I happen to be in a position to tell you something about a certain person that will be of great help to you in the upcoming situation."

"If you're talking about the hearing, I really can't discuss something like this over the phone and I—"

"Cut the bullshit," the voice said quietly. "I'm a friend. All you have to do is listen and judge for yourself. I don't trust this line of yours at all, for starters, and if you have half a brain you'll know what I'm talking about. If you want to hear the information I have for you, no strings attached, go downstairs to the pay telephone in your lobby. Do you know the phone I'm talking about?''

"Yeah, but that—''

"This is important. I don't have time to bullshit with you. I'm phoning that pay telephone in three minutes. If you're there to answer it, fine. If the doorman or somebody answers it, I hang up and you won't hear from me again. If I get a busy I'll dial it again in three minutes, but that's it. You've got three minutes to get downstairs.'' The line clicked dead before the lawyer had a chance to argue about it.

"He told his secretary he'd be back in a few minutes," the cop said to Eichord, "and that was the last thing he ever said to anybody as far as we know.

"There was about a half a pound of plastique under the pay phone. It went off approximately three minutes following this last call. Blew him right in half, took out the front windows, glass fucking everywhere, killed an innocent man—''

"*Adiós*, Jake.'' another cop said.

Eichord thought about the line in Shakespeare's *Henry VI*. The one about "Kill all the lawyers." He rewound the tape back a little ways, listening to the cool, well-modulated, soft tones say, "Tell him it's Roy Cohn." It was a distinctive voice. The man speaking barely above a whisper, enunciating with the greatest precision, accentless and bland like an announcer but without the professional smoothness, each syllable distinct from the next. Overprecise. Confident.

"You don't know me and my name won't be important to you," the soft voice said, pronouncing each vowel so precisely.

Jack Eichord reached over and rewound it back again and tried to imagine the man's mouth as it formed the *o* sounds, "You don't know me and my name won't be important to you—"

"Wrong," said Eichord to the tape.

"Hey, I can tell ya one thing about that voice for sure."

"Yeah?" They looked at the cop who had spoken.

"Jackie Nails it ain't."

The thing about Rita was. Yes, you dirty old man. That *WAS* the thing about her. And there were other things he liked too. He *liked* her. He liked—hell, he *LOVED* the idea of liking a woman. One woman. He was nuts about liking.

It was good to be, as the previous generation had put it, "of an age." He guessed they were of an age, okay. It was an interesting age, too. No doubt about it. Even with the anxieties and the doldrums and the infrequent paranoia, there was that wonderful feeling of being comfortable in your skin that so rarely is gifted on the young. They have other things going for them, sure. But he wouldn't trade places.

Take Rita, and he certainly would. Every chance he got, thanks. She had that class you can't acquire by any shortcut. Money will definitely not buy it. It's more than style, or flair, or good breeding. It's class. Even in her wildest, hottest moments of abandon, he thought her touchingly decorous.

He knew he could talk to her of *Casablanca*, Sibelius' *Valse Triste*, Dostoyevski and Diaghilev and Della Street and Vivian Della Chiesa, and she might know and remember. He could whisper to her of Madame de Beauvoir and Ted de Corsia and Vaughn de Leath and Demosthenes and she'd not lose her marbles. But would she remember Les Damon and Les Tremayne, Brad Runyon and Margot Lane, Olan Soule and Omar the Mystic, Jack Packard and Michael Axford, George W. Trendle and Phillips H. Lord? Would she recall the pussycat on Kilimanjaro, Moxie and Chox,

Chickory-Chick, Stan Getz' Stella? Stella Dallas? Or
only Dallas . . . ? He knew, and the flood of knowing
engulfed the hard consonants in a stream-of-
consciousness distant sharing.

She was his salvation, first of all. The one thing that
could elevate him out of the dour, drab, sordid milieu
that held him in its more or less permanent grip. Rita
could take him out of there in an eye blink. Just the
thought of being with her, that long, flashy, red mane
of silky-soft hair that framed her pale and angelic
beauty, the look of her striding across a room on those
killer legs of hers, it was enough to turn him completely around in a New York second. The lady made
him crazy. What a fox. He especially liked her mouth
and told her so as they moved forward in the moder-
ately long line waiting to see *Asphalt Jungle.*

"You've got some mouth on you," he whispered to
her, "you know that?"

"Yes. A lot of people I know say I've got a real
mouth on me."

"Well, that too. But even that turns me on."

"Laundry lists turn you on, Binaca breath, so what
else is new?"

"Waiting in lines doesn't turn me on. But I'll do
anything to see Marilyn again. You two had something
in common, ya know?"

"Oh, sure. I want to list all the things that Marilyn
Monroe and I have in common. I'll list them in alpha-
betical order, okay? We're both women. She spoke
English and I speak English. When she was still alive
her body temperature was about ninety-eight point six
and by coincidence so is mine. Well, that's pretty much
the end of the list. We do have a world in common,
don't we?"

"I could work on the body-temperature part if
you've got a minute."

"You want me to call a cop, mister?"

"The worst thing about being close to you is that

you don't get to look at you from a distance. I wish you could be with me and across the street at the same time, so I could watch you walk. If I could see you walking down the street right now on those lovely, long legs of yours . . ." His black eyes were sparkling at her and he was speaking very softly in her ear.

"Well, kindly try to NOT jump on my bones here in the line. Dad is retired, and I'm not at all certain we can count on Winston bailing us out if we were arrested," she whispered, "for creating a public spectacle. After all, this is St. Louis, almost the Bible Belt."

"Is that right?" he whispered back, hotly.

"Also," she said, the tip of her tongue touching his ear for emphasis as she whispered, "if you keep nuzzling me like this we may not get to watch *The Asphalt Jungle* again, which you've probably only seen roughly twenty-seven times. I don't think I could stand something like this on my conscience."

"If you really don't want to see Marilyn and the gang we can bop on over to East St. Louis right now. There's a little neighborhood art house showing Dick Powell in *Cry Danger.*"

"Oh, my God! Really? Can this be true?" He nodded affirmatively. "Be still, my beating heart. This is too exciting. And who is the leading lady in that one, Lillian Gish? No. Don't tell me. Just say this much. Is it a talkie?"

"Yes. Of course. It's the ultimate trailer-court movie. Seedy and sleazy just the way you like 'em."

"Good." She shook her red mane as if in pain at the thought. "Do we know each other well enough I could ask one small favor?"

"You got it, shweetheart," Bogie said. "Just whish-tle."

"After we've been together for a few more months— you know, when we really start to know each other— there's something I'd like to ask you to do for me. It's kind of wild and crazy. And perhaps it isn't something you'd want to do on your own, it's so kinky. But please, keep an open mind about this. Sometime—if I'm good—could we go see a NEW movie? You know, one that's in color? With *living* actors?''

A long pause while Eichord considered this.

"No. Sorry." He shook his head. "You ask too much."

"Sorry! Oh, my!" She mock-winced to herself. "Bite my tongue."

"I'll take care of that," he said as the line inched forward in the direction of the stale-popcorn smell.

Hell, you never know where you'll find a clue, right?

Spain tried to remember when he'd gone to a doctor for any kind of a checkup. He was getting a feeling that he didn't like. Not every day but quite frequently he'd get this sort of dizzy sensation, this feeling like he was falling. Just the way he felt when he was about to come down with a bad cold. His sinuses were killing him for some reason. The new bed he'd bought for the house didn't feel right. Something was wrong with the mattress. He had a painful ingrown toenail he couldn't seem to do anything about. He went to the bathroom and was reluctant to look at his stool.

It was when he was in back of the small funeral home that he had that odd feeling again. The desire to kill the next person he came in contact with. He correctly analyzed it for the insanity that it was and pushed it back. He wanted a large cardboard box like coffins and refrigerators and things come in, and that is why he was there. It was for the soundproof room he'd built.

Frank Spain had experimented with convex polygons, rhomboidal parallelograms, every imaginable shape. A trapezoidal quadrilateral of two short, matching sides and a slightly longer back seemed ideal. The front of the roof would be for interrogation.

The trapezoidal shape played off the weird roofline, allowing him to create a set of plausible fake walls that appeared to butt against one another. He built them as double walls, eight walls, not four, the hidden inner room—not much more than a walk-in closet—being a double-walled soundproof chamber.

The back of each wall in the office, his L-shaped storage room, and master bedroom were covered in acoustical soundpoofing tiles, which he'd cleared with the landlord long before he made a deal to rent the place.

The small space between each pair of walls was filled with egg crates, or would be as soon as he found his large sheets of cardboard to hold them just so. Then the inner walls were covered in carpet remnants. There are few more effective sound baffles.

There was no cardboard in back of Lane-Freeman's, a small, middle-class funeral establishment. He walked up and tried the back door. Unlocked. He walked in. It was an empty anteroom of some kind. He walked in, turned to the left, and went through a door marked PRIVATE. It was a preparation room. Spain smiled. The feeling was very strong. What if someone who looked a little like Gaetano Ciprioni would suddenly show his ugly face in the door.

Spain quickly went over to a metal table next to a sink and picked up a sharp instrument which he held by his side as he walked out of the building. No one had seen him. The feeling passed and he went on to another establishment and found his sheets of cardboard, which he could barely squeeze into the back seat of the large vehicle.

Back in his special home he finished the egg-crate sound block and walled off the make-do baffles with the cardboard, creating both a double dead-chamber and an effective sound-stopper. The center of the small, concealed room was over a deep, drainage ditch that had been the deciding factor in the choice of ren-

tals. What the landlord didn't know was that his new
tenant had enclosed a small section of this ditch, now
a pit of lye, and sawed through the floor of the home,
making the pit accessible from inside the house.

In the past weeks Spain had been collecting make-
shift torture tools as the spirit moved him. And in a
corner of the small "interrogation room" was a box
of shackles, pliers, knives, razors, hooks, picks, pin-
cers, things made to pierce and rip and torment and
mutilate and eviscerate. On the back wall there was a
shelf of deadly chemicals and in the corner some saws
and an oxyacetylene torch.

It was just a very nice, middle-to-upper-middle-class
brick three bedroom from the front. Unusual only for
the isolated location and the busy roofline. And now
Spain's custom interior work. He left the house, flip-
ping on his security system—can't have burglars
breaking in—and got in the car.

He dialed his cutout from a pay phone and heard
some good news. "Glad you called," she told him.
"A Mr. Hitter called twice for you. He said he'd be
at this number at the designated time. Just touch base
as soon as you could. He wanted me to say it just like
that. At the designated time. Just touch base as soon
as you could."

"Okay." Spain chuckled warmly. "You make that
sound like a code." They both laughed. "He's a character."

"Well, he was explicit about the message. He
wanted it just like that, so . . ."

"Fine. You did good. He's just an oddball. Thinks
his way is the only way, you know." She mmmmed
and he ended the call but with the nagging feeling of
paranoia he was starting to get careless. The idiot
didn't have to make a big production about the fucking
time. All that had been prearranged to avoid just that
sort of suspicious-sounding bullshit. He'd have to cut
his secretary loose soon, or better yet give her more

routine, normal work. These weird calls, sending her across to say things to a stranger in a car . . . these were things she might remember. Five thousand dollars cash and the son of a bitch couldn't handle a simple phone message. He dialed a pay telephone impatiently.

"Yeah."

"Is this Mr. Hitter?"

"Okay. I found him. This heeb he uses posted for him and he's hidin' out in a place the family owns out at the lake." He gave Spain an address and directions. "He's got one guy inside, one guy outside. Outside guy is in car. I think the guy inside's a fag." He giggled. "Anyway, that's it. Anything else I can do for ya."

"That's got it. Nice work."

"Call me anytime."

"Will do." Fucking idiot. They broke off.

Spain went back to the house and put on a leather coat, got a hat, some other things. Drove out to Lake St. Charles.

The Park Avenue was sitting about a hundred and fifty yards from the front door. Visible from the house and to passing traffic. It was't ideal but he'd handle it.

He walked up in plain sight, noticing the guy move slightly. Probably had his hand around a piece.

"Yeah," the man in the car grunted, putting a question mark on the end of it.

"Sir, please place both your hands on the steering wheel," he said, letting the leather ID case flop open. A hunk of fancy enamelwork and gold and a well-done laminated photo card flashed into view. "You have the right—"

"Ay, what the fuck is this shit?" the guy said, but bringing his other hand up empty on the wheel. "Who'd—"

"—to remain silent. You have the right to an attorney." He brought the silenced pistol up and shot the man in the temple. A bright fountain of hot, red blood gushed out of the head as he fell to the right. "You have the right to a mortician." Spain kept talking into the car as he slid the piece back in a pocket. "If you wish a mortician but cannot afford one . . ." He stopped and got back in the car and drove up to the front door. He got out and rang the buzzer.

A thin, pale man with dirty blond hair answered the door. "Yes?"

"Your name?" The shield blinked out again.

"MY name?"

"Yes, sir. State your name please."

"My name is Dorn."

"Sir, we have a search warrant to inspect these premises in relation to a federal investigation." He was moving past the man as he spoke, "Well, just one minute here . . . And he shot the man in the face moving quickly into the room even before the man dropped, holding the piece on Kriegal, a nice firm double-handed hold like in the movies.

"Blue," he said, "you're under arrest, asswipe. And here come d' judge." He laughed, feeling good for the first time all day.

And then he saw the pictures on the walls.

He thought for a moment it was a hallucination. Those weren't really pictures of little kids in each other's arms and in the embraces and oh my God in the embraces of adults and in the positions and in the savage postures and in the bound and screaming punishments and in the awful, ah, the vileness of it, in the commission of obscene acts frozen by a camera, professionally mounted and matted and framed under glass.

He whispered to the stocky, balding man seated on the long sofa, "I'd like to slice that filthy head off and shit down your neck hole, you—" He really couldn't think of anything foul enough to call him. He'd run out of words. He moved forward and kicked the man in the stomach, being very careful, kicking him as precisely as he could so as not to allow his emotions to run unchecked. He knew if he let loose now it'd all be over in thirty seconds, and that would be a shame. That would defeat everything he'd been working for. The whole point was to make the scum crawl. To drag their tortures out and turn some of the suffering back around in their direction.

The one picture of the two little girls kept nagging at him, and against his judgment he let himself steal another glance at it. One little child about nine, ten years old, doing something to another one. The one on the receiving end reminded him of Tiff in a favorite scrapbook shot, and just for a few seconds his rage bubbled over beyond the rim of control and he kicked Blue Kriegal about twenty times as hard as he could. He had to get him out of there or he'd waste him. Spain didn't even bind his hands. He had such disdain for him he just went out and popped the trunk, came back and rolled the unconscious body onto a small throw rug and dragged Kriegal out past the body of his slain companion, and unceremoniously horsed the dead-weight into the car.

William Kriegal awoke in darkness and in intense pain and fright, but then the trauma took him under and he woke up much later with that choking sensation you get from smelling salts, but when he tried to pull his face away from the gagging spirits he could not move.

"Aaaaaaaaaa, pleeeeease," he begged the man snarling into his face.

"Good morning. Did you sleep well?" He capped the small bottle.

"Jesus, buddy, I'll give you anything please don't—"

"Blue, Blue, BLUE, shut your asshole a second. My name is Frank Spain. Did you ever hear of me?" he asked pleasantly.

"Uh—" The man's brain was going a mile a minute. Where the fuck was he and how was he going to get out of this one?

"You're not feeling so hot, right?"

"Huh uh." He felt like he was going to go under again.

The man said, "I'm going to give you something to make you feel better, okay? My name's Frank Spain. But you can call me Mr. Spanhower. Say, Hello, Mr. Spanhower."

" 'Lo, Mr. Spanhower."

"Good."

"Please, Mr. Span—"

"Now, Blue. See what I've got for you. Vitamins," he said brightly. "This'll put some lead in your pencil." Kriegal flinched when he saw the hypodermic needle.

"Oh, hey—Blue, don't sweat *this*. This is just something to get you feeling in the pink again." He shot a minute amount of fluid into the air, "Don't want to shoot an air bubble into your bloodstream and *kill* you, for heaven's sake." Spain deftly found a vein in Kriegal's meaty arm and plunged the spike in.

"Mmmm." The man made an involuntary fear noise as Spain depressed the syringe.

"Yes. I understand, Blue. Nothing is quite as potent as tetrodotoxin. Especially *this* little mix. Hot as the Orinoco Basin, baby. Quirky as a Shuar poultice. Heavy-duty as voooooooodoooooooooooooo," he said, playing with the man.

"Please, listen mister, I don't know how come you're doin this, but I got over two hundred thousand in a—"

Spain shut him up by simply shoving his palm over the man's mouth. "Hmm-ummm. No talking. Just take it easy. You're going to need all your strength. Don't guess you're hip to brugmansia? Datura? *Zombie's* cucumber? Jeez, Blue, what am I going to do with you? Ain't you gotcher ethnobotanical, ophiological shit together? Well? Speak up, man. Cat got your tongue?''

"Jesus. Please."

"Oh, relax. I was just jivin' witcha' about the zombie stuff. That's just plain old gasoline. But Blue, I didn't scrimp. It's *PREMIUM*. Does it smart a little, Blue?" Suddenly he lost the grip on his control and started screaming *"DIE DIE DIE YOU PIECE OF vile shit!"* He was screaming into the face of the man as he picked up the stolen trocar, which is a sharp thing embalmers use to insert a cannula into the torso of a cadaver to drain the body cavity, and drove it again and again into the living, screaming body of Blue Kriegal.

"I had all these plans for us, Blue," he sighed, calming down. "But I don't think we're going to be able to keep you around long enough to turn you into a zombie, darn it. I believe you're fucking dead, Blue. What do you say—eh?" His voice was loud in the small enclosure, as he watched the lye down in the drainage culvert take the dark, red whirlpool. He stood there for a long time, staring with cold eyes, transfixed, as if awaiting further word from the high oracle.

And that night in his sleep, Anubis, jackal-headed god of the ancients, Protector of Graveyards, presided over the Weighing of the Heart at the Last Judgment Rites.

The distinguished-looking man locked his study door and walked over and sat down behind the massive desk. He bent over and did something to one of the legs and the front of what appeared to be the desk leg came off in his hand. He reached in and took out an instrument with red and black telephone receivers on it. He pressed a button, a light came on, and he placed the red phone in the central cradle section and picked up the black phone and dialed.

"Yeah. . . . I wanna order a sit-down. The whole council. Emergency session." He barked a hard response back into the phone. "I know that, for fucking shit's sake. I'm not an idiot. Listen. All the dons. I don't care if it's fucking Apalachin all over again I want reps from ALL the fuckin' families. We got a war on our hands and it ain't what everybody thinks. I know who's behind all this shit. It could only be one man." He let air out in a sigh of anger and frustration.

"Now listen. Here's what I want. I want you to get a crew . . . No, a crew, shit, I want a fuckin' PLATOON of soldiers. I'm going to give you an address in Ladue, Missouri . . ."

ST. LOUIS MOB FIGURE CHARGED IN CHILD-ABUSE CASE MISSING St. Louis, Mo. Missouri News Service Wire, Eichord read, skipping M08-44-29173301 and reading,

A one-time foster parent for the Missouri Division of Family Services, recently targeted in a federal investigation of St. Louis area mob activities, was charged with abuse in two counties after police found what was described as "thousands of porno photos and films involving children." The evidence was confiscated at his home in Jefferson County.

William "Blue" Kriegal, 41, of the 12000 block of DeSoto, was charged Tuesday with six felony counts of child abuse in Warren County, and two counts in Jefferson County. He was released after posting $75,000 bond, authorities said, and is believed to have fled.

Police have been searching for Kriegal since Wednesday, and a warrant has been issued for unlawful flight to avoid prosecution. Kriegal's family declined all comment.

Kriegal was targeted as a "principal suspect" in a federal investigation centering on the alleged

"crime family" of Salvatore Dagatina and other un-
named individuals who are believed by authorities
to control the child-pornography and narcotics rackets in the Midwest, according to Assistant Jefferson
County Prosecutor Kenneth Wales.

"We're still developing pictures, and establishing
venue, in addition to statutes of limitations," Wales
said at the time of the child-abuse charges, "as Missouri has a three-year limit for prosecuting this type
of a case."

Kriegal was a certified foster parent for the Division of Family Services at one time, and was responsible for the care of several children ranging in
age from nine to thirteen in the Columbia, Missouri, area, according to Melinda Zook, the agency's deputy director. She refused to discuss Kriegal's
record as a foster parent.

Zook said that prospective foster parents were always investigated as thoroughly as possible but she
conceded to reporters that "picking good foster-
parent homes is an inexact science."

Authorities believe that Kriegal is involved in the
production and distribution of so-called "snuff"
films, pornographic films in which actual scenes of
beatings, torture, and murder are also seen. Kriegal
is believed by authorities to have been responsible
for films in which children were tortured and killed,
according to a source in the Jefferson County Prosecutor's office.

He read the words aloud to himself, and even though
they were words meant to be read silently, to speak
them gave them impact.

Eichord was on trail now. He had the voice. And
now he had a hint. Something nudging him. This was
what he lived for. His inviolable work ethic: the ele-
mental foundation, catharsis, curative, analeptic. The
restorative and stimulant to his soul as he hunted

through the sewers and putrefaction and corruption and evil. And reading the words chilled him as he felt the familiar vectors beginning to cross. *He* was out there somewhere. Waiting to kill again. A death master. And now there was a voice. And a pattern. And vectors crossing.

He knew his next move for once. He should have done it earlier when he picked up on the pattern of the kills. Eichord no longer knew or cared if the Floyd Streicher SEE NO EVIL wise guy was involved in this. He got Bud Leech and got him away from the Homicide Bureau.

Leech was sensitive to the maneuver and wanted to know, "How come you don't wanna talk up there?" gesturing to the cop shop.

"Come on," Eichord said. "Let's walk."

"You worried about a fucking bug?"

"Forget about that. I got something, Bud."

"Yeah?"

"I think so," he said. And he told him what he needed. About the surveillance he wanted.

"Hell, let's put the damn van on it."

"No way," he said. A decision he'd immediately regret. "I want this just you and me, podnah. Let's just you 'n' me handle it."

"Shit, okay," the big man said with a shrug, "you got it." Implicit in the shrug was a question. You think the Special Division is dirty.

Eichord just said, "I just want to be careful. VERY careful. This is . . . Well, hell, I don't know WHAT it is.. But it's something more than warring gang factions." He didn't say it to Leech but he thought, SUPERKILLER.

Two days later a "professionally made bomb containing a large quantity of high explosive" blew up the stretch limo in which one of the sons of "Jimmie the Hook" Russo, Phillie Russo, was riding with his chauffeur/bodyguard, Bugs DeVintro. Homicide, Intelligence, and Arson rolled on it, as did Eichord, and it gave him his first close look inside the St. Louis mob.

He was at the crime scene and a massive, Italian-looking man with swarthy features and a face that looked like the dark side of the moon came up to him and said, "You d' one from d' Tass Force?"

"Yep."

He handed him a note with a phone number on it. "Mrs. Russo wan' you to call her," he thought the man said.

"Mrs. Russo? Rosemarie Russo?"

"MISS Russo. Angelina. You call her?" Eichord nodded. "Soon as you can, please. T'anks."

He went to the nearest phone and dialed.

A woman answered it on the second ring. "Yeah."

"Hello, this is Jack Eichord calling for Angelina Russo, please."

"Yeah, I know. I'm her. I'm Angelina. C'n you come over here to d' house?"

"Sure can. Right now?"

"Yeah, awright. Soon as you can, okay?"

She told him where she lived, not realizing he'd been there first thing when he hit St. Louis and couldn't get an audience with the Russos, and he thanked her and headed across town.

He didn't have any trouble finding his way to the Russo house again. He parked and went up to the door and knocked. He rang the doorbell. Knocked again. Inside a baleful, huge bodyguard was saying to his charge, "Miss Russo, you makin' a mistake, please don't talk to no coppers."

"Let him in, Johnny."

"If Jimmie were here, he—"

She cut him off with a look. "Right. If Jimmie were here you wouldn't question what I asked you to do. Now let him in, please."

He turned and opened the door. Johnny had been with the family nearly as long as she'd been on earth. He was like family himself, but he still called her Miss Russo out of respect. She knew what was going through his mind for him to talk to her in that tone. She didn't care. Nothing mattered anymore. Just stop the killing.

"Jack Eichord, Miss Russo." He handed her one of the Special Homicide Division cards. "I got your note." The huge bodyguard eyed him like he'd like to string him up but he backed out of the large room and shut the door quietly behind him.

"Sit down please. And I appreciate you comin' here."

"I've been here before but I never got to speak with you."

"I had to talk to someone. The police."

"All right."

"I—" She took a very deep breath and her body sagged visibly, as if she was going to collapse. For a second he almost thought he should go over there across the room where she was sitting, be next to her if she fainted, and then she straightened up with another breath and said without preamble of any kind,

"I'm afraid for my mother."

"Oh?"

"And myself. Why not say the truth, right? I'm afraid whoever is doing this will want us, too. My brother and I were very close. I heard things." She looked at him with reddened eyes. "He thought it was somebody outside the family." Eichord didn't say anything, waiting. She coughed. "Somebody tryin' to make it look like there was a power struggle . . . inside the family. You understand what I'm saying?"

He nodded. "Did your brother have any idea who was behind the killings?"

"No. He didn't. Look—I'm even talkin' to you like this—I'm sayin' things I could be put under for. I would *never* rat out anybody in da family for any reason. You can do nothing with what I give you. If you say I told you this I'll deny it. If you try to use it I'll go down. You're gonna' be sentencing me if you tell someone else. You understand?"

He inclined his head and kept silent.

"I won't ask for your word because I don't know you. I don't know if you are a man who takes his word seriously. But if you tell *anybody* you put me under. They'll clip me for sure. Am I getting through to you?"

He nodded again. Angelina Russo had a voice that was used to issuing orders. "Go ahead," he encouraged her.

"There is a council, board, call it what you want, there is this council that meets in New York with the big families. These men govern the society. Their word is the absolute law. Not your law. *The* law. What we live by. You understand when we meet—as *amico nostro?* To be with us, with the thing of ours, is to imply honor that you can trust to the death. But it is a joke. The society, the friends of ours, this has no more meaning than a society of you coppers. Like you police, we are all the same. There is only a handful you can trust.

"So these men they must protect the family. Whenever there is power and money there are always others who want it all for themselves, and our family, like yours, exists because of greed. It is these men who have a few trusted workers within the most secret part of the society. Nobody knows who these men are who work for the *capos* of the families. Not even the lieutenants who run the top crews. They work in secret.

"Phillie knew that the killing was coming from outside. He was sure of it."

For a while Eichord thought she was going to say more but whatever she had been about to say she had changed her mind. He read it first in the eyes, which went absolutely blank, and next in the body language, and he felt it in the atmosphere as she metamorphosed in that heartbeat, changing back into the Mafia girl in front of him. Within that second she'd completely shut him out of it, come to the edge and almost *almost* opened the door for him and then, no, the years of habit and influence restored the adversarial climate in which such a woman existed. And he knew he was unwanted here and that any more conversation would be a waste of his time as well as hers, and he got up and left, letting himself out, hearing the solid door slam behind him, shut out of it by tough guinea anthropophagy.

As Eichord got in the car and left, a pair of eyes watched him from across the street through expensive surveillance equipment. They were sometimes greenish-blue in light, sometimes slate-gray, and cold as gunmetal. The eyes of a madman, a professional watcher, glad the girl was still inside.

These mad eyes did not see the girl as a grief-stricken sister and daughter. He, the silent watcher, was more interested in her living brother, Joe Russo. He was watching her because she was the sister of one Joseph Russo, eldest son of Jimmie the Hook, currently serving a fifteen-year sentence for second-degree murder. He was watching Angelina because she was his ticket to Joey Russo, a convicted murderer doing hard time in the same prison as the old man—Salvatore Dagatina.

But above, to the left, and behind him, there was another pair of eyes. Someone was watching the watcher. And when Frank Spain left the premises, Bud Leech of St. Louis Intelligence was tailing him.

Back inside the cop shop the word was that the mob had hit the streets in force. They were tearing up the city but in a way none of the coppers had seen before. Not faction in-fighting but a cooperative effort. As if all the brotherhoods had banded together and put out a contract on somebody. People who'd been feuding since the days of Tony Gee were suddenly spotted on the streets together. The mob was looking for somebody and the cops were asking each other, "What the fuck is going on?"

Which is precisely the question Eichord wanted to ask Bud Leech when he showed up with a shit-eating look on his face and the bad news that'd he'd LOST his surveillance target. Jack looked up at the huge man and said, "Tell me you're shitting me."

"Yeah, well, I wish I was. I'm sorry, man." Leech was so contrite Eichord would have laughed if he hadn't been so fucking pissed.

"How did it happen?"

"These fucking imbeciles . . ." He gestured out toward the traffic. "Ah, why make excuses? I just fucked the duck. I was playing it by the book. Changing lanes. Staying back real good 'n' that. This fucking semi comes barreling out of nowhere, I'm in the middle lane, old mom and pop on the left in the passing lane and the fuckin' truck was gonna hit the goddamn car if I didn't get over, I hadda tap the brakes. The motherfucker cuts in; by the time I can get around the dude on the right he's fuckin' gone."

"What'd he look like?" Eichord said quietly.

"Shit, Jack"—he shook his head—"I never got any kind of look at his face. Ordinary build. Our age, maybe a little younger. Dressed real plain."

"And of course you checked on the tags and it was on the hot sheet, right?"

Leech nodded. "I'm sorry, babe. What can I say?"

"It happens. Fuck it."

"Want me to put the van out there on the house?"

"No," Eichord said. Another decision he'd regret.

BeBop Rutledge was about to get into his wonderful phoneman swindle and he figured it had to be not a

penny less than four hundred dollars. He could get
DOWN with four bills you can take that shit to the
bank. BeBop snapped his fingers, jiving, gettin' it on
with his bad self, diddy-bopping down the street,
scattin' along and feelin' fine. BeBop Rutledge was
not a black jazz musician. He was a very white, Anglo-
Saxophonic person of your WASP-persuasion-type
race. He was twenty-three, and he liked to smoke a
little dope now and then, just some hash or whatever,
and maybe snort some blow once in a while but nothing serious.

He was coming up on a fucking totally bogus Possession with Intent to Distribute in a few weeks and
he had to come up with something. He thought about
taking the four hundred dollars he was going to scam
the phone operation for and head out West, but then
U.S. Magistrate Wilma Smith was such a hard-bark
old bitch she would definitely kick a hole in his ass
the size of a fucking headlight if he split. All he needed
was a federal fugitive warrant on top of that other Possession bullshit. BeBop wasn't going to let it bring him
down.

The Possession thing was a total circle jerk. A guy
he knew had come by BeBop's house with about two
pounds of white powder in a plastic bag, it coulda
been Comet or any damn thing in there, granulated
Domino sugar—shit, what did he know, right? And the
dude goes, Hey, BeBop, say hey, hold this for me an'
I'll give you a trey. Shit, why not? What's a friend
for? And then first thing you know Rabbit, which is
his name, Rabbit's Foot, he boogies and these cops
come pounding on the door 'n' shit, and they come in
and find his stash, and there's this bag and he didn't
know there was fucking two pounds of COCAINE in
there. Damn. What a surprise, right? And then he's
gotta draw Wilma Smith, her fucking ballbreaking
honor the judgeship, and she just loves to step on
BeBop's stones anyway, so first she sets a detention

hearing and he has to make the fucking national debt in bail, and now she's gonna' try to slam him down for hard time on this absolutely bogus Possession with Intent to Distrib.

But he refused to allow this gloomy horizon to bum him out. He might just take that four hundred and get straight. Do himself a thing, you know. And it all fell together so beautiful for him, see, there he is bopping down the street when he sees this dude put a move on this other dude.

He was just about to phone The Man with a kind of bullshit thing about some fags who were into some B & E that he'd heard about, just a nothing little thing to lay some groundwork for the Possession number until he could come up with something for real, and he sees this shit. BeBop goes, "Oh, WOW!" and "Check it OUT!" when he eyeballs this one dude grab this other dude and kind of like shove him into the EGA theater. The EGA has been closed since the Last Supper, but like he sees them bop right on in there and he figures he'll see what's goin' down. Who ever knows, right?

And he pushes on in there and he can see the dudes have taken a bolt cutter or something to the big, thick chain that holds padlocks on the doors on each side of the EGA box office. And it's darker than the inside of Bessie Mae's pussy but he eases on in real quiet. Where the fuck is everybody? And he hears this mumbling shit coming from inside, and he moves on ahead, just about pissing his britches he's so scared.

The EGA—which was called the REGAL but over a period of time it lost its *R* and its *L*, and so everybody just called it EGA—it was gonna be torn down to put in another fucking condo or whatever, and it had been just this little ma-and-pa theater about a hundred years ago, and it held tops maybe 150 dudes in there go in see a fucking cowboy double feature, *Lash Larue*

Whips It Out, one of them pictures, and BeBop eases
on around so he can see the haps.

Two dudes down front in the dark, like they got good
seats you know, right in the middle, and he can barely
see 'em from a little EXIT light thing over on the side,
and the one dude says something and this other guy
he goes, "I want you to meet Mary Pat Gardner"—I
think the name he said was, or maybe Mary Pat Garner. Something like that.

"Say hello Mary Pat," he tells this other dude.
And the other one goes, Yeah, cool, "Hello, Mary
Pat AAAAAAAAAGHHHHHHHHHHH!" And he
screams like he just got a tit in the wringer, you know.

And it's quiet then and the first dude says, "The
bitch was real thirsty," or some shit like that, and he
raises something that looked like a knife and sticks
the other one again but there's no sound and, man, I
just about shit my pants, BeBop tells The Man.

"That's when I phoned you, man. You better get out
here right away. And bring a fucking ambulance, man.
This ain't no wet dream either, my man. I'm givin' you
a fuckin' MURDER ONE here." And he was just starting in about the bogus Possession thing and how Her
Honor U.S. Magistrate Wilma Fucking Smith was planning to put his stones in her pliers again and send him
away to Springfield or somewhere and he'd come out in
a couple of years with an asshole like a cannonball when
the ungrateful fuckin' cop hangs up on him.

Which is how BeBop Rutledge of East Alton, Illinois, and parts unknown, got to make the acquaintance
of a cop named Jack Eichord. And which is how
BeBop had his day ruined, and his four-hundred-dollar
scam fucked over, but which is also how he got his
main man to promise he'd talk to Magistrate Smith,
which was worth four hundred except for the fact that
he probably wouldn't be able to sleep for a week.

Eichord played the tape and BeBop said, Yeah, that's
the dude that knifed the other one. Same voice for

sure. And he asked was this guy twenty-five, thirty years old? And BeBop told him, No, this is an *old* guy. About your age, he said. Endearing himself to Jack in the process.

And after the evidence crew and the ME and everybody cleared out and the inside of the EGA was back in the black, Eichord sat in one of the ratty seats (special this week, kids, free gum under every seat) and looked up at the darkened screen letting it all wash over him.

He sat there for along time, free-associating, thinking about the madman who was killing, trying to make it take a shape, his mind taking great leaps, suddenly refocusing without logical connectives, making wild ellipses, meaningless non sequiturs, random ramblings. And he began talking quietly to himself as he waited for Weyland the artist to finish with the snitch who might have seen enough to give them something, but he wasn't counting on it.

He mumbled to himself in a whisper, maundering like some nutbasket who'd lived alone too long, which in fact he probably had. Testing, theorizing, probing, bullshitting, trying to get some kind of a handle on all the sudden deaths.

Sitting there in the pitch black of the musty, crumbling dream factory where another innocent victim's blood had just stained one of the faded seats a sickening incarnadine. Another human being murdered by a madman, and he looked for the commonality that wasn't there, and chewed it all over again.

He'd go back and take a look at the backgrounds of the doorman in the Schindler Building and this latest victim, an agency art director who was getting a tag tied around his toe. Another innocent man dead. One more piece of a puzzle that wouldn't fit. But now, at least, he had a lone watcher at the Russo house, and a lone killer here.

It was one man. A madman. Acting alone.

* * *

He was still talking to himself the next morning in the squad room but soundlessly, running it all over in his head as he doodled aimlessly, letting the swirl of the cop-shop talk eddy and flow over him as he doodled and meditated and chewed his cud.

"No, ma'am," he could hear T. J. Monahan telling some woman on the phone. "You gotta go to the District of Occurrence on that. You need to call the LAPD or if that's in the county it might be like the East L.A. substation, okay?" L.A. Christ! He couldn't get away from the fucking place.

"—had 'em by six points but I wouldn't give you a nickel for that worthless, no good—"

"—know those projects out there and I guarantee there's a bunch of hypes living out there who don't do anything but steal credit cards for—"

"—just as soon go to Vegas and drop it all on Red and let 'er fly, if—"

"—fruit hustler working Tower Grove we think he killed the boy in Carondelet Park last—"

"Jack," Lt. Springer said, snapping Eichord out of his reverie, "can you come on in my office?" And they head toward the end of the hall, Springer picking up bodies as they went. He had Glass, Leech, Skully, Monahan, a couple of the others from the unit in there with them.

"Look," Springer said to him, "none of us can find our ass with both hands on this thing. We've got the lab report on the weapon that did Mr. Cooper yesterday. We got a dorky eyewitness jammed up on a dope bust. We got a half-assed Identikit sketch that could be my brother-in-law. Jack, you're the serial-murder expert here. What the hell are we lookin' at?"

"I wish I could tell you something." Eichord shrugged. "But I'm in the dark with this too. I can't make a connection between the two civilian stabbings and the gang murders—but you know how it is with hunches, I think they're connected.''

"You can't make a connection," Richard Glass said, "because there isn't any, Jack. Bet on it. Two different perps. Apples and oranges.''

"Maybe," he breathed deeply, "but I don't think so.''

"What's your intuition on the thing, Jack? You say you have a hunch. Hell. Let's hear it," Springer said.

"A hunch is all it is. Nothing more. Nothin' solid at all. I can tell you what I'm afraid it is and can't even give you one firm indication of why I feel this way.'' Nobody spoke so he went ahead. "I discount the Rutledge ID. Bud, you got a space cadet," he said, smiling. They laughed. "You got BeBop. A flaky snitch headed for the joint behind a coke bust. He wants to sing our song. So even with him ID-ing the voice on the Rozitsky tape I'm afraid we don't have anything.

"But"—he tilted his head as if it suddenly weighed too much—"on a visceral level I think it's the same perp, and if it is, we're looking at something pretty frightening. I've never come up against anything like it before.

"You got your psychopath, your assassin or hit man who will have an organized mind, and a psychotic: somebody who is disorganized in his kill pattern. The first guy—sometimes above average in smarts. Plans what he does. The second perp has psychoses that cause him to murder at random. The psychopath knows the difference between right and wrong and he has a motive for what he does. If he kills it may be emotionless and carefully planned in execution. The psychotic on the other hand, he or she kills according to mood, the traditional crime of passion, the unplotted and sometimes motiveless random kill.

"As you know, the main way we catch psychotics is by the murder weapon which they often will keep in their possession or leave at the scene of the homicide. The psychopath of course carefully destroys the murder weapon or he hides it. In a psychotic we have to look at what the perp does to the victim before he kills them. Does he tell them to say hello to Mary Garner or whatever? In other words if these killings are somehow interconnected, and I feel like they may be, we're looking at a perp who is BOTH a psychopathic killer and a psychotic looney. A professional assassin of some kind such as a trained mercenary or a hit man who is also, simultaneously, going out of control and killing people at random. We're looking at a hybrid killer, in my opinion.''

"Jeeezus," somebody said as the phone on Springer's desk rang.

"Lieutenant Springer."

"Right." He hung up and jumped to his feet, moving. "Let's go. He just firebombed Measure. Four dead." They all rushed for the door in a cop logjam, Leech and Eichord rode with Vic Springer and a detective sergeant named Thompson.

Homicide and Arson, Intelligence, ET, all screaming down Missouri Avenue in the River North area behind Fire. Redballs and light bars flashing, sirens screaming past the condos and rehabs, chic boutiques and galleries, plant-choked eateries and ferny bars on the way to the Measure house.

"What the fuck." People milling around. Guys getting pissed at one another. Some signals had got crossed and it hadn't been a firebombing, after all.

"Where's the fire?" somebody said.

"Fuck you," somebody replied.

There were four dead inside. And one they didn't know about yet. Spain had hit James Measure, Gino Sclaffani, Edward Sidenfadden a.k.a. Eddie Sides, and Tony Alba. All deader than last year's Christmas trees.

"Holy shit."

"Man, they look like they been used for targets at a firing range."

"Unreal."

"Whatya got?"

"It was a fire in the other room, is all. One of these things caught the drapes on fire. Little smoke. No problem."

It looked like some sort of a gas canister.

"Lieutenant, here's another one." He showed him another of the canisters.

"Must be how he took 'em down. If it was gas I don't smell any trace of it." He glanced at a man examining one of the bodies. "Any idea how long, Doc?"

"Not really." Wonderful. "An hour, two hours, maybe longer. I ain't whatsisname on TV f'r chrissakes."

"What'ya think? An Oozey?" he pronounced it. "Or an Ingram? Something?"

"Shit. Hadda be. Probably something like an Uzi. He gathered up the mags but he left all the brass. Why the fuck would he do that?"

"Because the son of a bitch is a whacko. Fucking looney tunes, that's why."

"Coulda been a belt-fed weapon," somebody offered. "That'd explain why there aren't any magazines, only brass shells, eh?"

"Wonderful," Springer said.

"He got in here somehow. Or got somebody else in here. Or two of 'em got in here somehow. And they put 'em under with the gas and then he and his partner made meat loaf out of them with submachine guns. No?"

"Why not?"

"Jack?"

"Vic?"

"It's a mess, huh?"

"Shit." A hybrid killer. Some kind of superfly mother.

What they didn't know yet was how the hit team or

hit man made his entrance. Measure's pad was supposed to be a fortress. But they got in somehow. Or *he* got in. They could scarcely believe one man could have brought about all this slaughter. It was a mess, all right.

They didn't know about Lowenstein yet.

Ben Lowenstein, a slickie from Narcross, Georgia—Spain used him for the door key. Got him alone and took him home to the interrogation room in his house and worked on him for a few minutes and he gave him a way in. Told him about a boy who would do anything for money. And Spain got a mule to take the gas bombs inside. It cost him five thousand but it was worth it to nail Measure. When Spain was through with Lowenstein he put him down in the culvert in Treflan cans. A right leg and torso here. An arm, head, and leg there. You could say Lowenstein was laid off permanently. He got the ax. With severance.

There was nothing at the crime scene but the gas cans and lots of spent brass. Brass and gas. And gangster blood. There was one hell of a lot of that. No fingerprints that didn't check out. Nobody saw anything, as usual. Nobody heard anything, until a neighbor saw the smoke from the drapes. Zero. And these were not the GSA, these were hard core, made Mafs. Experienced wise guys and he—or they—took 'em like they were asleep. If this was a single man, crazy or not he was very, very good.

Eichord drove around, wanting to call Rita and not wanting to wish himself on anyone that sweet in the condition he was in. The idea of a couple of beers sounding pretty marvelous. Jack was neither brilliantly deductive nor was he even extraordinarily ratiocinative. The process of exact thinking, the mastery of reasoned train of thought, the Holmesian modes of deduction, all eluded him.

What it was, instead, was his ability to distill and extract the essence of a thing that made him so relentless a bringer-forth of the coldest trail or the faintest clues. However dissimilar, he was a pro at educing the latent commonalities when there appeared to be none.

He could evoke the forgotten images, elicit carefully guarded responses, extract the buried nuggets of data, extort the best-kept secrets. Eichord was superb when it came to extrapolating the unknown, excavating the buried, exculpating the innocent, extricating, exonerating, extirpating, and eliminating, and don't mess with Mister In-between.

He called it by a simpler name. To Eichord it was—vibes. His was a critical mission in the holy war of Good vs. Evil and it was the mission that made his work autotelic and sancrosanct. He plodded down the center, absorbing, listening, soaking it all in, watching. And he never stopped working. Not completely. Except with Rita. That was his one time to let it all fall apart and cleanse his mind in the soft, clean, happy, and carefree music of their relationship.

He was drawn to a phone like a magnet and he called her and just the sound of her voice on the phone lifted the load from his shoulders and he couldn't wait to see her again. And that night his blue funk dissipated and for a short time he was able to forget the sick, violent world of murder and madness and lose himself in her.

She was his music and he soloed magnificently, blowing hot, unashamed jazz licks. Triple-tonguing the instrument. Playing riffs he never thought possible. His embouchure so flawless the mere touch of his lips made her come to life beneath him. Nice 'n' easy and then penthouse-wild and finally jailhouse jam. Kissing the delicate hollow of the throat, the edible declivity of the lower lip, the back of the knees, above her metatarsal arch, the delicate ligatures; tactile symphony of smokin' hot, mouth marmalade. And then easing out in a dreamy coda and back for a steaming, cookin' finish to blow minds, loving each other with the loose insouciant ease of soulmates.

And they loved it. It had never been better between them. And after a long time Rita turned and whispered, "Oh, boy? The memsahib would like to fool around with the natives again? Speak to me, gunbearer."

But he was gone.

The mob had hit Spain's home in Ladue and gone through it like a cyclone. Leveled it. Buddy Blackburn's live-in lady had come home from Walmart's and felt something clamp over her mouth and suddenly she was in an awful world of danger and pain.

"We want Frank . . . Spain . . . understand?" It was the softness of the voice. The mock gentleness of the swarthy, scarred man who held her face cupped in one of his huge hands. Other men were holding her arms behind her.

"I don't—" Her face was being crushed by a grip of steel.

"No. You . . . ain't . . . listening. You say I *don't* again I give you to Shake. He likes to hurt women. Where . . . is . . . Frank?"

She blinked back tears and thought carefully. These men were going to kill her. She tried to talk and remembered she hadn't breathed in a while and took in a big gulp of air and gasped as she sobbed, "Our little girl . . . he hired . . . this you know, this . . . detective and he. . . Frank said. . ." And she started crying and somebody had an arm twisting her hair the pain her shoulders elbows dislocating pulling hurting. "He was a private detective. Traskle or something like that, I swear . . . That's all I know. I don't know where Fr—"

"You did a no-no," the scarred man whispered. "You said I *DON'T*."

And she heard a raucous laugh as he made the lights go out.

* * *

Willie Ray Campbell was his name and he was about 379 million miles away from Jack Eichord ethnically, spiritually, mentally, anywhichway. Any honkie was galaxies and races apart from the North St. Louis ghetto that was home turf to Willie Ray. Yet Jack and Willie would touch, in a way, as strangers sometimes do, when destiny beckoned with her long and crooked middle finger.

Unblinking, hard, midnight-deadly. Outrageous and old-timey do-rag over his conk. Perfectly razored pussy-tickler drawn in a straight black slash over a cushiony pair of swollen-looking Naugahyde lips, Willie Ray looked the part. Big cokey nostrils. 110½-proof Jamaican straight gangster with a dangerous, sullen mood, a nose full of bad dream, the stale tuna taste of unwashed twat on his tongue; 229 pounds of snatch-licking, rum-sucking, coke-tooting, pipe-packing, mean motherfuck of a no-nonsense nigger.

Standing out there on the corner of Struggle and Die, out there with the bad bros and the fierce fros, out to scuffle up some geetus, out to COP, you understand, 'midst the chicken-shack, chump-change, no-dick, no-chance, bust-out shooters, street-dealing hustlers, bogus flimflammers, sugar pimpin' chile macks, hos, bros, and fros. Out there with the junkie hypes, black bloods and princes of the netherworld, with allllll them other assholes, waiting to hear on some fucking humbug sham charges The Man had trumped up the way that terrible, worthless, chuck white devil likes to do. Keep a man down. Shhhhhh-hhhhheeeeeeeeeeeeeeeeeeeeeeiiiiiiiiiiiiittttttttttttttttttt!

Hi five to a boy he knew.

"What it is."

"Yeah—down."

"Keepin' on."

"Same old same ole'."

"Work it on out. Later." They parted with the sign. Past Soul Food and HairQuarters and Barbee-Q, the

smell of hot home-boy cookin' comin' over and gettin'
into his blow.

"Doctor Good," he greeted the man behind the
counter.

"Say Hey, Willie Ray. Today's the day."

He finished his soul food, shot the shit with the
brother for a while, and walked back out and stood
around on the corner jivin' with the passersby.

A mean street subghetto called Sunset, the shacks
across the tracks from the projects. Willie Ray "married" to a pouty little mama who had started tricking
part-time. Bringing him a little trap money. He'd done
a little plundering outside the family. Moved up to
some gunwork. A little hit-and-miss action to cover
some mistakes he'd made in his stock portfolio, don't
you know? He'd been all right if he'd stayed with smack
and snort and shit, but he hadda go be a big goddamn
fucking GANGster. And now Willie Ray Campbell
was standing there waiting for the next load of deep
shit to get dumped on him.

Waiting for nighttime and the sound of sirens that
was the symphony of the subghetto after dark. Waiting
for the neon night and the smells of this open prison
that held him like a black, stinking armpit in the
shadow of the high-rises—Willie Ray could have taught
them about soul. Miles of that motherfucker. Taught
those whiteys how to talk that talk. Bunch of jive no-
good shit. And as if she'd heard the thought, Destiny's
bony fingers curled around her quill and she dipped it
in the darkest ink and added the name Willie Ray
Campbell to the shit list.

Many miles away, on the other side of St. Louis, a
man who called himself Carl Duncan at the moment,
a.k.a. Frank Spain, was printing Willie Ray's name
midway up a list of names. C-A-M-P-B-E-L-L. Prov-
ing that no matter what they say, it doesn't always pay
to get your name in the paper.

* * *

Jack "met" Willie Ray a couple of days later. He'd
been working on his revised, updated "family tree"
and crime chronology. On it the crime families were
the international automobile industry. It was a thing
he sometimes did as a learning trick—giving things a
metaphorical identity. He looked at the National
Council or Commission as the CEO and VPs from the
big automakers. The Colombians and Syrians and
other factions were the Japanese car market—hated
competition but in bed with the Americans. He gave
Sally Dago the rank of general as in General Motors.
Tony Cypriot, Gaetano Ciprioni, was the admiral in
charge of Ford. Rikla was Oldsmobile and Measure
was Buick, and so on.

Certain patterns in the kills had begun to emerge.
There was something else. A thread running through
all the gangland wet work. Drugs? An internal power
play by a rogue lieutenant? Who was left? The X factor. It was in the murders at the lower end of the spec-
trum. Jimmie the Hook Russo and Lyle Venable still
both appeared to Jack to be gang whack-outs. But the
way wise guys were turning up missing, and the civilian hits—something there. His mystery madman involved.

Eichord had not been watching his television or
hearing a radio that morning so he had no idea there'd
been another hit—a black dope dealer tied to the family, two cops and a bus driver had all been killed in
another bombing. So he was doubly amazed to learn
that Paul Rikla, his "Buick" competition also now
dead and gone, was waiting at Police Headquarters to
"turn state's evidence." Rikla wanted protection, as
he had told a bewildered cop.

Rikla had "given himself up," as he put it, because
of a black dope dealer by the name of Willie Ray
Campbell. They'd never met. Campbell, thirty-two,
coal-colored, with Son of Kong lips and smack-brown
eyes, was aboard a federal prison bus headed for ex-

tradition to Kansas, where he was wanted for bank robbery.

When the television newscaster had reported the story about Willie Ray being extradited he had accurately referred to him as an "alleged narcotics dealer in the family headed by Paul Rikla. Rikla, owner of the Rikla Towing Service, is believed by police sources to be tied to the sale of narcotics and child pornography in the St. Louis area. Rikla, allegedly an underboss in the Dagatina organization, could not be reached for comment."

Rikla was now as scared of the Dagatina people as he was of the Measure crew, what was left of it, but what happened to Willie Ray was the final straw.

At about eight-thirty that morning Campbell, head covered in an old-fashioned do-wrap over his straightened, styled "conk" that looked like something from a Negro documentary, was just sitting there on the bus minding his beeswax, sitting there in his jail clothes when the whole friggin' bus blew up.

A two-man guard detail and the driver were also killed. No fucking reason. All the police told media was there was evidence of electronically detonated high explosives. No known motive. No suspects. Another in the series of gangland-related homicides that had St. Louis terror-stricken. And now Measure gets taken down and his people are STILL goin' under. Suddenly Rikla felt like he had cross hairs painted on his forehead.

The bus bombing had occurred at approximately four-forty. The news had it on the early cast. Five minutes that included a three-and-a-half-minute sound bite at the crime scene and lots of gore. Rikla was home, watching it on a tummy TV, with a real bad case of the green-apple quick step. Two hours later, Paul Rikla and a pair of attorneys from Rozitsky, Karp and Nathan were waiting to see the DA and talking about RICO and the Federal Witness Security Program and trying to put some kind of a deal together for their very nervous client. Rikla figured, "I'd rather be a live rat than a damn dead man." Which pretty well summed up the situation. The consensus among all those close enough to hear the comment was that he'd described himself accurately, one way or the other.

Rightfully, Rikla had told his personal mouthpiece, "I don't know who's doin' da shit, if it's coppers, wise guys, or a crazy contract man that's doing the work. Whoever they are if they got the balls they can blow up a federal prison bus. I'm not waitin' around for 'em to come for me. That's it. Fuck it. I'm history."

So there he sat in his "surrender" clothes. The bottom half of an eighteen-hundred-dollar silk suit, and a Neiman's cardigan over a LaCoste golf shirt, gold chains, watch, ID bracelet, pinkie diamond big as a grape, pure twenty-four-karat wise guy, wanting to go public behind the "witless protection program," as Leech had called it.

They were joking about the four-hundred-pound hit man who had been given a new face with plastic surgery, a new identity, and flown from the Boston area to Seattle, where he was relocated under a new name. After a few months of boredom he went back to his old line of work and was promptly found and obliterated, being the only four-hundred-pound hit man on the West Coast with a South Baaahston accent you could cut with a knife. What they cut with a knife wasn't his accent.

Rikla, who had been Sally Dago's counselor, friend, confessor, confidant, and sounding board, knew where *all* the bodies were buried. He went back to the beginning of the Dagatina thing. He claimed he knew things that nobody else in the family knew and if the feds would take him into the program he'd testify. Give us an example, the big boys asked him, and he teased them with a tale of a chief enforcer trying to wage a one-man war against the families, and tantalized them with the promise of dirty cops.

"When I know I got full-time protection and d' coppers or the Dagos can't touch me, I'll give you the whole outfit. Right from the top down and you won't fuckin' believe it. I've got coppers runnin' my own scams right here in St. Louis. I ain't just talking about no bagman, I'm talking about swindles where you go in a certain place of business an' if we don' get five cents the coppers will come around and shut the house dis way," meaning they'll close the business down.

"Give us a for-instance—like what jurisdictional area?"

"I'll give ya a taste but dat's it until I see the thing come together for me. Awright, would you believe Metro East?"

And it went on like that for a while and the big boys took him away for bigger and better things, and Leech told Eichord about it. They were both tired. First thing they got off on "what's the worst thing you've ever seen" stories, and Leech told his, which was the old lady that committed suicide with an ax. Eichord said he didn't believe it and Leech told him,

"Emmis, my man, she was a stout old gal about eighty years old, big heavy old gal with arms like this, and she went nuts, got into it with her old man, and chopped his head off with an ax while he was dead-drunk. Doubt if he ever knew what hit him. Then she decided to kill herself."

"With the ax?"

"Exactly."

"Hey. Could I ax you a question?" a cop named Wunderlicht said, and they laughed. "How can you do it with an ax, slit your belly open?"

"Nope. She took hold of the handle with both hands like so, held it as far out as she could, and goes WWWWHHHHHHHAAAAAAAMMMMMPPPPP!

Right smack dead-center in her forehead. Right between the running lights.''

"Bullshit.''

"I got the fuckin' lab photos if you want to lay a ten on it, Jack. You can see it. She's still got a holt of it, and you can see the skull and that sucker is wedged in the brain real good, like a big ole ripe melon that busted open.''

"This conversation has made me hungry. Let's go get some melons.''

"Seriously, how can you—'' And for ten minutes they lost themselves in a discussion of the ax weight, and the best way to hold an ax to kill yourself with it, and on and on like that.

Eichord knew cops. He liked them, too. He knew what made them tick. Why they were there and what it took to keep you sane on The Job. This kind of talk was just blowing off steam. It was a way to say, This dirt I live in, this filth that I work in, it's not real. It doesn't really touch me. It doesn't exist. Just words. At least this was the way he looked at it.

He listened to another cop, Pat Skully, talking about the time back when he was a narc and they raided a house and dead babies were everywhere. It was the worst he'd ever seen and there was no joking during the story. Two dealers had beat the cops to the pad, which was a shooting gallery for hypes. The woman who ran the house had four little kids ranging from a newborn baby to about six or so in age. When the narcs found them the dealers had killed all of them in a rage. The babies were flattened. As Skully started telling how it had been done, Eichord got up quietly and unobtrusively left the room.

Bud Leech caught him down on the street.

"Let's catch a buzz,'' Eichord said.

"Why not?'' And they went in the nearest tavern and tilted a cold one each.

"The funniest thing about Rikla, you know, giving

himself up today. I know this pervert from way back.
I go back to when I was working in a little hick community and hearing horror stories about how Mr. G.
ran St. Louis, an' these St. Louis ad vice guys were
telling me all about this dude named Paul Rikla who
was a chickenfucker. And I told them, You mean he
liked little boys, like a chickenhawk. No, he liked
fucking chickens.

"He had priors going back to this time they answered a disturbance call about some perv waggin' his
wienie in this residential neighborhood. Man in a car
nude, they hear. They investigate and there's this
Coupe De Ville parked there, and the cops go up to it
and shine the light in, and out of the Caddy hops Rikla,
stone mother naked and carrying a butcher knife all
covered in blood. This is a true story, by the way. He
looked like he wanted to be shot real bad and he almost got his wish 'cause they damn near popped a cap
on him when they saw him like that.

"Inside the car was the rest of the story. He has this
beautiful young Syrian daughter, and she was with
him in the front seat of the car, and the vehicle is covered in blood and feathers. Rikla would slice the head
off of a chicken and daughter would ke and jam
the fowl's severed windpipe down on Daddy's cock-a-
doodle-doo, and the headless bird would flop and bop
him off."

"I—" Eichord started laughing before he could get
it out.

"I swear, man. If I'm lyin' I'm dyin'."

"Oi. It's been a long day. Let's go get somethin' to
eat and get outta here," he said, draining the last of
his Light.

"Okay. Where you wanna eat?"

"Colonel Sanders?"

Eichord liked Bud Leech a lot. He was good people.
Jack could imagine how much the incident of the lost
tail would goad Leech every time he thought about it.

He was a good cop and it could have happened to anybody. What Eichord didn't know was that very soon Bud Leech would acquit himself of his great sin.

But Jack's thoughts kept returning to that teaser from the very frightened Mr. Rikla. The "bullshit" story about a chief enforcer waging his own solitary vendetta. His SEE NO EVIL brainstorming and hunch-playing finally had the vestiges of a motive to chew on. One superkiller. What if they *were* dealing with a mad enforcer on a rampage?

They were on their way to chow and picked up the call on the two-way. Eichord knew what it was before he heard the word Russo in the clear. Multiple-shooting fatality. One male, two female Caucs down. Christ. The house had been under "loose surveillance," which meant that once an hour or so a scout car would slowly roll by, what they call a "boogie man." Wonderful.

Eichord knew he'd find Angelina and her mother dead. All the way out there he thought about the unpunished crimes. The crimes committed every day by land barons, police officials, network executives, union bosses, TV evangelists, petrochemical tycoons, political figureheads, automakers, commercial mavens—all the dirty, mendacious hypocrisy. The bushwacking, degenerate, back-shooting no-good bullshit that people get away with. It kept his head busy till they got to the crime scene.

The killer had massacred the bodyguard, the maid, and Rosemarie Russo. No sign of forced entry. No sign of Angelina Russo.

A news reporter had phoned the archdiocese to inquire about the state of health of Auxiliary Bishop O'Consky, and while he was on the phone and they were chatting he happened to comment about the terrible thing—how awful for the lovely Russo family—he was a personal friend, and with James and Phillip taken like that, sure 'n' it would be so hard on the rest of the family. And the newsman seemed so unusually solicitous, the man on the other end told him how there was a special service being planned, and one thing led to another, and in the course of the conversation the caller discovered that the bishop had never actually met any 'of the Russo family, and one thing and another.

So when the bishop himself called from the archdiocese to inquire if he might come 'round tomorrow just to pay his respects to the Russo family, and give them some mementos of the deceased, also to show them some material that had been donated to the Cardinal Glennon College Seminary School, of course he'd be welcomed in and greeted by the grieving survivors, Mother and Daughter Russo.

"Dominus vobiscum," the good bishop whispered, crossing himself in his own special way as he made his way up the steps.

"Et cum spiritu—"

A passing motorist might have observed the bishop himself helping the exhausted and grief-stricken Angelina Russo down the steps and into a waiting vehicle. Ominous vobiscum.

Angelina, now hog-tied, gagged, blindfolded, weeping silently on the floor of the back seat, would be the next visitor to learn of the peculiarities of Spain's house. They traveled down a long, winding gravel road. The house was located on four lonely wooden acres.

Following the road, rather indifferently maintained county gravel, one reaches the end of the county's responsibilities. Winding past a small family cemetery with its overgrown headstones and massive, horrifying ironies, an old graveyard beginning to push up remnants of the long dead. Past the weed-choked graves in dark, deep thickets, where old bones are working their way toward the surface.

The last hundred yards of this dirt road becomes a mudhole in heavy rain. You want to make certain you're never caught out on this road in a rainstorm because should your vehicle bog down and you go to the nearest house for help, your gracious host may prove unpredictable. He might be witty, urbane, even comforting. All the amenities of telephone, warm fire, even a libation, might be offered.

The next few minutes *might* be uneventful. Simply a pleasant, comforting respite from the elements while you waited for a taxi or a tow truck or a friend. And then again, there could be minutes that would drag like days. Minutes that would plunge you down into an unspeakable world of sudden and exquisite pain. Because your host is two, very different, wildly unpredictable men.

Both of the men who call themselves Spain kill. But the second Spain, the one whose madness has taken him far out over the edge and flung him screaming down into the bloody nightmare of his psychoses, this Spain kills without reason.

These split halves of the killer live in that ordinary-looking brick residence by the side of the lonely, gravel road. Spain the psychotic. The cold-blooded, trained assassin who is killing in a blood lust of revenge. The Spain who plots to take Ciprioni and Dagatina down. The one whose kills are premeditated. Carefully prepared.

Then the other half. Even more dangerous because he kills from some unknown, dark, and motiveless wellspring. Taking human lives at random. Lashing out without cause or fear of consequences, murdering blindly, spurred by some psychotic fountainhead that has burst within his soulless center.

Here, in the house that had heard the tortured screams of Blue Kriegal, the house of Ben Lowenstein's final agonies, in a murder laboratory less than two yards wide, this is where Angelina Russo's blindfold is removed. And the first thing she sees is the face of the smiling madman, and behind him the bloody wall of the charnel in which she now awaits his pleasure. And the split halves of Spain silence her scream in a steely-fingered grip telling her, "Now now now now now. There now," in his soft, measured speech, "there, there now. Calm down. You could wake the dead." And her tears flow and, angry now, she forces the crying to stop and spits in his face. And she knows she is dead and only hopes it will be quick and merciful as she says to herself, Yea, though I walk through the valley of the shadow of . . . And she sees him laughing as he carefully wipes her spittle from him and says to her, "You should meet my wife. You and Pat have a lot in common. Perhaps later. Yes, very soon, in fact, I'll let you say hello to Mary Pat. And you and the bitch can talk over your mutual interests. She has a great thirst . . . for companionship. And she's dying to meet you." And he chuckles again and asks her, "Do you believe in demons?" And her throat is very dry now and a faintness is coming over her like an ocean wave and he says, "Would you be surprised to learn that I am what you would call in your quaint underworld patois a worker? That I was your society's chief enforcer for many years? That I was the cutting edge of your Capo di Tutti Capi and never in all the contracts went shy? Never. Would you be surprised to know that succubi transfuse me while I sleep? Do you believe in magic?" And he touched her then and she fainted.

"Did you have a nice rest?"
"You crazy *face da borco*—"
He slapped her viciously and spoke in his soft tones. "You can make this hard, you know. Very hard. And your life will end for you in a soundless and tongueless scarlet sheet of awful, mind-mangling pain. Say hello to the missus."

"Hu—hello." The point of a knife was touching her throat. She imagined a trickle of blood.

"Say, Hello, Mary Pat."

"Hello, Mary Pat." She knew this was it. It didn't matter what he said to her. She could see the insanity and death in his hooded eyes.

"If you do as I say I will let you live. Otherwise, I will let her slake her thirst on you here—" He penetrated and she fought back a scream. "And here." Angelina cried out in pain.

"Now do as I ask or Mary Pat will SLICE AND CARVE AND TEAR UNTIL YOU ARE ANYTHING BUT RECOGNIZABLE, YOU GUINEA SLUT. DO YOU UNDERSTAND ME?"

"Yes."

"Good." He moved out of her vision for a moment and she heard a clicking noise and he held a piece of paper on it with a typed message. Read exactly what it says. If you fuck with me Mary Pat will rend the side of your face into pumping, dripping shreds of bloody meat." His icy calm was more frightening than the screaming. She read as he held the small microphone to her mouth: " 'I am alive and well. You must do as I say. Dagatina m-mus' die. Here is what you mus' do if you want me to live.' " She had read almost all of the message before it occurred to her what she was reading. She figured the lunatic would play this for Joey, her older brother, to convince him to whack out the old man. Even then, she kept reading. Angelina did not want to die. Not here. Not now. Not like this.

It actually began with the most unlikely of sources, the one and only BeBop Rutledge, and a conversation between Bud Leech and his snitch along the lines of, "You gotta help me, man, this ain't FAIR."

"Life's a trade, BeBop. You gotta give to get."

"I gave till it hurt, man. I come right to ya with it."

"You ain't give us shit."

"Murder fucking one."

"You're goin' down behind that righteous coke bust and we both know it. I can't go to MY boss and get somethin' for you with no better'n this. I mean, I can talk to Her Honor for ya, but you want some heavy-duty clout you got to gimme. You got to bring some to get some."

"I didn't SEE the fucker. Just that second or two in that funky light from the goddamn EXIT sign. I don't think I'd know the dude if I bumped into him."

"That's a shame, BeBop. Dig it, my man: the lieutenant's got him a SLIDE into Wilma Smith. I mean, if you could really think, put your shit down tight for it and give us a better sketch. Shit, The Man would start talkin' and you'd start walkin'."

"Aw, man. I guess I could sit down with the dude again. Whatsisname with the drawings."

"Weyland. Yeah. That's it, my man, you need to sit down with the dude again. Concentrate. Think real hard. Maybe he'll come back to ya." So it was that, fuliginous visibility notwithstanding, a refined Identikit got put together. Sort of. More or less. The more BeBop thought about Judge Smith stomping his grapes the better his retroactive vision became. He saw the light so to speak. And there is no vision with greater clarity than 20-20 hindsight.

With the exception of Eichord, perhaps held in check by the powerful fabric of SEE NO EVIL intuition, only the wise guys still worked to nail a lone assassin. The cops themselves appeared to no longer be interested or concerned with the mad enforcer—only that the thing, whatever it was, be contained from escalating into wide-open gang warfare throughout the inner families and ethnic fringe factions.

"The Two Tonys gang is a fuckin' memory," Eichord heard one cop tell another, "and that means you know what."

"Turf up for grabs."

"Fuckin' A." It was times like these when a couple of defecting gunmen could start all-out war by themselves—never mind the "lunatic chief enforcer" theory. But Jack did not share their preoccupation. He listened quietly as they talked.

"Russo torched the old man, right? So what have you got here? You got a power thing from the inside." Sally Dago! The madman had managed to reach inside the prison walls. Soak the old man with oiled gasoline and torch him in his cell. Joey Russo righteous for it.

To Eichord it was so clearcut now. The enforcer had kidnapped Angelina. Somehow got through to the brother in the slams: either hit the old man or your sister dies. Some scenario along those lines. She'd told him how close they were. The watcher had been watching. Had he also been listening? Anybody with this level of skills would find audio surveillance little more than child's play.

Jack pulled Leech aside. "How can I get to Tony Cypriot?"

"You tell me and we'll both know." Leech laughed. Jack just looked at him. "You're serious. Okay. I doubt if you can. Why?"

"I just want to get a message to him. On the telephone. How would I call him?"

"He'd never talk to you. You'd have to go through a million underlings. Shit. It'd take a week."

"I don't got a week. How can I reach the man? Think."

"If you had something he wanted. You could get one of his top people to get the word to him, I suppose. Maybe somebody in New York." Leech sounded very unsure about it. Like it was a total timewaster.

"Humor me," Jack said to the big man. "Who

would be somebody could reach Cypriot right now? Rikla?''

"Fuck, no.'' Leech laughed. He thought for a moment. The wheels turned. "Okay. There's a guy who's inside. Serving a twenty-to-life. If he thought it was in The Man's interest. You know.''

"Can you get a message to him quietly?''

"Does Oscar Peterson sweat.''

"Oscar Peterson? Oh, yeah, the guy plays basketball for Cincinnati?''

"He could play it if you'd hum a few bars.''

"Okay. Hum a few bars of this: tell him to get word to Tony Cypriot. Jack Eichord has something to sell the godfather. He can give 'em the man they want. Tell him that I want the scum dead and I'm afraid if we bust him he'll end up walking. Some high-priced legal talent will plead him fruitcake and he'll be back on the street. If Cypriot wants him handle it through me personally. Him to me. Tell him to call me. I'll do all the talking. He can listen and make up his mind. That—or the man he wants to nail so bad keeps waging war.''

Now it was Leech's turn to just stare. "He'll never buy it,'' he said finally. "No fuckin' way.''

And of course he didn't. Not for a second. But within twenty-four hours he was on a telephone in Eichord's ear.

"Don't waste my time. Whatd'ya REALLY want?''

"It's not what I want. It's what you're going to do. You're going to go pack a few things—don't take much because you don't have a whole lot of time. Get on a plane or your private jet or whatever, and fly back here. I'm going to put you in custody. For your protection.''

Cypriot began laughing uproariously. Roaring, hysterical guffaws. Eichord waited him out.

"Oh, shit,'' he said, catching his breath. "I haven't had a laugh like that in weeks. Christ. Oh. You're

all right. That's funny. Hey, listen. I got to go now
and—''

"HOLD IT! You put this monster on the street for
the Council or Committee or whatever you assholes
call it. Do you have any idea what the other families
will do if I get the word to them that YOU were responsible for all these kills within the organization?''
He didn't hear any more giggling. "Your ass will be
grass.'' When Jack Eichord wanted to seriously
threaten somebody his soft-spoken tone hardened into
a razor-blade edge, and when he opened the floodgates
and let all his poison pour out in a hot, acid gush,
you'd better not be downhill.

"Forget about it,'' Cypriot said disdainfully.

"Forget about it, huh? If you don't cooperate with
me and come under our protection . . . I go right to
the dons. I'll tell 'em what I know about your chief
enforcer and how you fucked this up.'' Eichord was
winging it now. "And by next week there won't be
enough of you left to fill a fucking shoe box. Now you
gonna cooperate or what?''

Any other time and Gaetano Ciprioni would probably have told this no-dick cop to go fuck his mother.
But he'd just had the sad and awful chore of canceling
out one of his great friends and one of the company's
most trusted vice presidents. The Russo kid had got
word to him about the hit. What should he do? he
wanted to know. Ciprioni knew that Spain knew—he
WAS the godfather, the REAL godfather, to Angelina
Russo. No way he'd let her be killed for the old man.
So he passed the word back for Russo to do it. He
hated to do it. Helluva thing. But sometimes you had
to cut your losses. "Go ahead,'' he said. "Tell him to
burn him.''

Then they'd finally run down Troxell, the two-bit,
whorehouse mouse of a shamus back in Cleveland or
Cincy or wherever the fuck he was. Found out about
Spain's daughter. Run that back to its origin points.

Ultimately this whole fucking grab-ass began to make some sense. Of all people to go over the edge. Spain. He shook his head as he thought about what he should do—and in those few extra seconds he listened to the cop he'd ordinarily have hung up on as he told him, "I know a way to set this guy up but I have to know all about him and how this happened. If you cooperate with me I can guarantee we can get Angelina Russo back, number one, I can guarantee your safety, and I guarantee you we'll take this lunatic down." The more the cop talked the more Ciprioni thought it might work, against all his instincts. Who'd ever believe THIS shit—he smiled humorlessly—the cops an' ME on the same fucking side!

Eichord cinched the deal with some clever tap dancing about the charges that could be brought to bear in re the ex-Mrs. Pat Spain, and a general amnesty number, and one thing and another that he thought he played by ear rather well. But long before Tony Cypriot could pack a bag Eichord had talked to the PI in Ohio about his client, and he was back on the phone to The Man.

"One thing I need day before yesterday," he told Cypriot, "is that film."

"What film?"

"What film? The film of Spain's kid. The snuff movie. I need it NOW."

"That's no problem," the man told him, and he called and had two prints on Eichord's desk before you could say "Anytime you're ready, C.B."

And not a minute too soon, either.

Jack Eichord was the official greeter when Cypriot arrived on his company's private Lear. Two bodyguards got off first and Eichord was surprised they didn't fit the usual defensive-left-tackle and nose-guard stereotype. Both were small men, extremely profes-

sional, and—like Tony Cypriot—looked like businessmen but with a hard edge.

The man himself was distinguished-looking. A natty
dresser in a two-thousand-dollar topcoat over quiet
Savile Row banker's gray.

"What's he for?" he said to Eichord as a police
photographer flashed a bulb at him.

"Publicity." Eichord told him about the setup he
was planning. At first Ciprioni balked but it was too
late to back out.

Jack said, "I give you the same guarantee as on the
phone. We'll take this maniac down and you'll skate
clear of your problem." He would be nice and safe in
his bulletproof long johns. "He won't hurt you. I
promise."

The snitch's Identikit composite had brought forth
nothing from the St. Louis area realtors. Cops had
been ringing the doorbells at motels, hotels, rooming
houses, trying everything from trailer parks to camp-
grounds, anywhere they thought there might be a possible trail. Nothing.

Ciprioni looked at the sketch in the car and nodded.
"That's him okay, but you can't tell shit from the likeness." He started talking about the hooded eyes and
the differently shaped forehead and nose and Eichord
promised a touch-up from Weyland, as he visualized
the SEE NO EVIL face in the airport gift shop in L.A.

As soon as Mel Troxell had run it all down for him
he knew the man Spain was the one. It all fit together,
and the killings of a couple of innocents along the way
proved Eichord's hybrid theory. Spain was a maniacal
schizoid assassin. One deadly and dangerous manhun-
ter who had gone insane.

Ciprioni said quietly, "If that crazy fuck has hurt
Angelina I wanna whack him myself," and Eichord
thought he'd never heard the transitive verb "whack"
as often as he had since he'd started on this investi-

gation. Back home when you got whacked out it was
on PCP.

"You know your attorneys have already okayed your
deal. You've got complete, unilateral amnesty. So I got
a question. The "Eyeball Murders" in L.A. . . . did
your, uh, council order them?"

"Nah." Cipriona exhaled. "That's their country out
there. Who knows from fucking California." He
wouldn't give him anything extra. "That's somebody
playing games with the eyes. Like sending the dolls
with the pins in the throat. That's all Mustache Pete
bullshit. We don't play that way."

"Was this Frank Spain's work?"

"Ehhh"—he shrugged—"who knows? He didn't always clip the numbers himself, ya know? He'd control
the job. Hire the workers himself. That's the way he
liked to work."

Jack fed the St. Louis area media a juicy photo story
on the infamous "Godfather" Tony Cipriot who'd been
placed under official police protection. He gave it to
some key media friends around the country such as
Letty Budge, who would give it lots of ink and mileage. He knew there was no guarantees that Spain read
papers or watched television or turned on radios. But
the word was also all over the street. Eichord had
Gaetano Ciprioni. The man who, more than any
other, could be considered ultimately responsible for the
kiddie-porn business and therefore the torture and
death of Tiff Spain.

Troxell the PI, who'd already been "debriefed" by
the mob, had taken Eichord back along the trail of the
Dawkins and Nunnaly plan to turn Tiff out as a pros.
Mel Troxell told him about the boy Nunnaly being
killed in a traffic accident. About the missing Dawkins
kid's probable fate, the disappearance of the daughter,
and the why and wherefore of her death.

Eichord had put Jeeter Oliver to work. Jeeter was
the cop shop's guy who handled anything related to

motion-picture film, surveillance videos, and similar
materials. Eichord was setting up his game in several
different locations. Just in case. A couple of extra face
cards in the deck, in case of . . . well, just in case.
He'd pick locations where he thought Spain might be
comfortable. Places he might trust again.

The Special Division had come alive with activity.
Realtors and land owners and renters and managers
all over the greater St. Louis area were being shown
the newly revised revision of the Frank Spain sketch,
which Eichord had presented to Bud Leech saying,
"What's his name—Rebop? Your snitch?"

"Yeah—BeBop. Yeah?"

"Flaky little fucker's *RIGHTEOUS*. And give yourself a raise, by the way."

Eichord patted the big fellow on the back and strode
briskly back to his temporary desk, leaving Leech
scratching his head and saying, "A raise—what the
hell is a RAISE?" But Jack hadn't seen that wide a
smile from him in a while.

Eichord was taking care of the million and one loose
ends that suddenly loomed large on his horizon.
Checking out final details of his trap with Chief Adler,
through the good offices of Victor Springer, playing it
by the book now as he tried to think of everything.
Stay one jump ahead. He had the last survivors of the
Dagatina family picked up. He had people surveil Pat
Spain's insurance hustler, the Dawkins and Nunnaly
houses, everybody that manpower would allow. Covering the bases.

No sooner than the pictorial coverage of Tony Cipriot splashed onto the front pages than the switchboard
plugged a call into the division and Springer was
screaming at Jack, "RUN!"

And Eichord came tearing down the hall and picked
up the phone on the lieutenant's desk, conscious of the
ubiquitous Realistic recorder plugged into a telephone

adapter jack, the machine taping every breath and utterance as he said, "Hello."

"This the cop in charge of the gang-related assassinations?" Eichord made the voice instantly and his flesh crawled the moment he heard the distinctively enunciated, oddly precise speech pattern.

"Yep. And you must be the one and only Frank Spain, right?"

"Very clever. So what?"

"I was hoping we could make some sort of a deal. You know we're not altogether unsympathetic to your situation. Who cares if some worthless vermin get wasted? We're on your side, believe it or not." He could hear his own voice selling too hard.

The very measured, precisely calm tones in his ear saying, "I have no idea how stupid you are personally so I can only offer what I feel is sound advice and hope you take it. What you do not want to do is to bullshit me, can you comprehend this?" The voice overly precise. Frighteningly cool.

"I meant it about the vermin," Eichord said in his quietest tone. "We've got Ciprioni. We'd consider a trade for the innocent woman if we had certain assurances."

"Will you take a fucking cab?" Spain snorted. "You're either an idiot or you think I am to fall for such silly shit. Either way you're about to lose. What's your name—Officer Oehlert?"

"Eichord. But no, I don't think you're an idiot. I just think we have something mutually—"

"Whoa. Save us both time. Let me cut through. You have some barren, pitiful scheme to entrap me. Okay," he sighed audibly, "I know you have people at the phone company matching pairs and so on. Tell them to forget all that. I've been doing this for a lot longer than they have. By the time you figure out where I'm calling from I'll be long gone. You'll offer to swap that garbage you have in custody for the little lady.

You have SWAT and tactical people ready and when I show up I get arrested. The music swells. You get the girl and ride off into the sunset, and the closing credits roll. I've SEEN those shows. No.

"Don't you think I know it is impossible for local fuzz to swap out live bodies?" Eichord started to answer but he said, "Put all that sophomoric DRECK out of your head. You with me?"

"Well, I don't know . . ."

"Give it a rest." Spain laughed coldly. "CIA, now maybe THOSE assholes swap people but you guys don't. Well. So why I called you is, I'm going to tell you why your plan won't work and why you *will* do precisely what you just claimed. Why you *WILL* give me the scum Ciprioni. Because if you don't several more innocent people will die, not the least of whom is the buxom Miss Russo. Who, by the way, is not doing well at all. If I don't get what I want I don't believe she's going to pull through." Laughing again. For the first time Eichord thought the caller sounded crazy.

"I just went into a grocery store and left a calling card. It's one of those old-time pineapple grenades from World War Two. People buy them for paper-weights. Only this one isn't inert. It has the powder and the goodies and a nice short fuse. It's behind a stack of canned peaches or something—I forget what. It's just an illustration of one of my larger, uh, ideas. It's the IGA store on Olive. Also, I've shoved a couple of pineapples down into the cushions at Bielerman's furniture."

And the cops listening to him give an address took off as Springer nodded and pantamimed, GO.

"See. I pull the pins, put the rings in my pocket, walk out nice 'n' easy. Somebody goes in and sits down on a sofa or pulls the wrong can of peaches off the shelf, or opens the wrong dresser drawer and—BA BOOM!"

"Where did—"

"I *WANT* you to find these, see. I mean, I know you guys are thick so I'm trying to teach you what it will be like. The same only different.

"Not pineapples next time. Something better. Not little shaped charges of explosives to take out one or two people but big surprises for lots of people. That's the sort of legacy I'll leave behind before I show up for any swap.

"I realize even I cannot predict the behavior of bureaucrats, not to mention imbeciles, so it's entirely possible you might attempt to sandbag me in spite of what you'll find at the grocery and furniture stores. The cop mentality being what it is. If that should be the case I will have left behind suitable payment. You will have deprived me of my vengeance, and I will have retaliated with commensurate force. Convey this to your superiors. If they try to outwit me by capturing me, all of us lose—and for what? For the life of that human garbage Ciprioni.

"Since you know me you also must know that in my field I am considered the best there is. As a professional you can appreciate what that means. So you understand that if I tell you I know demolition—let's say—inside out, you know I speak the truth."

"I understand."

"I hope so. You'll cost a lot of loss of life if you don't. I have considered how I would be treated after capture. I am a sophisticated and experienced man. I will have taken pains to . . . Well, what's the point of belaboring this. You'll either believe me or your actions will cause many, many persons to die unnecessarily. If I don't have Ciprioni handed over to me tonight, those deaths will be on the police's hands, and I have sent a brief summary of this situation to certain inquiring minds in the media. I think you'd be well advised to cooperate."

"Obviously," Eichord said, "I'm going to have to

talk to the people in charge. But I think I can say with
some certainty that we'll be reasonable. We want to
avoid any more bloodshed.''

"That's nice. But if it turns out to not be the case—
or if your superiors don't believe me—I'll be glad to
blow up a few dozen people just to show you I'm for
real.''

"Come on, Mr. Spain. You know you don't want to
do that. I'm sure we'll find a way to give you what you
want. Ciprioni is nothing to us—just one more hood-
lum.''

"Just stress that his life isn't worth the lives of hundreds of innocent civilians. That should do the trick.
But, if not—''

"I think it will.''

"Tell them if my instructions aren't carried out, if
you fail to bring that garbage to me tonight, I will
begin a series of executions that will turn this town
upside down and inside out. I'll begin taking lives in
the most terrible and spectacular ways. Remember—if
you need proof you'll get it, and lots of it.''

"When you say bring him to you tonight, what did
you have in mind?''

"What did I have in mind? I just told you—bring
me Ciprioni. Period.''

"I mean, where did you want him brought? We'll
gladly comply with whatever precautions you might
want to take to ensure your personal safety if we make
the trade you propose—''

"It's YOUR personal safety you'd better concern
yourself with, you understand?''

Leech signaled him no—meaning the tap had turned
out to be another phone which Eichord knew would
be the case.

"Absolutely.''

"We'll trade tonight. At midnight. You bring me
Ciprioni and I'll guarantee not to kill again if I'm not
threatened. Also I'll turn the Russo twat loose when

our deal is consummated. If you cross me or try to capture me or you don't have the scumwad with you—a lot of people will have the bad luck to become very fucking dead.''

"You won't be double-crossed. Where do you want to meet, assuming we can go the deal.''

"I don't give a shit. It can be in the damn police station for all I care. Remember—my legacy of death depends on your giving me what I want. You take me out and you've removed the key to keeping lots of people alive. The, uh, legacy is such that even if you had the locations you couldn't, let's say, disarm the items.''

"Where do I call you when I find out if we can do the trade?''

"Pathetic!'' Spain laughed again. His laugh was not a thing of humor but of madness and rage. "I'll call you, Mr. Eichord. And tell your bosses, don't forget, if you screw with me I'll also be forced to deal with Miss Russo in the harshest and most permanent manner—she'll be one more death you've caused.''

"I'm sure we'll go the trade. The bosses won't like it but you haven't left them much choice.''

"Whichever. I'll be phoning back soon so you don't have much time. Don't be stupid.'' He saw the auto-stop kick the tape off as the telephone receiver clicked.

"Well,'' Springer said, "how about them apples?''

"Yeah. Well. I read it as pure bullshit.''

"Jack, you think he's bluffing about the bombs?''

"I think we'll find the grenades. But no. It's bullshit. He's a sicko. And he's good. A pro. He thinks he's invulnerable now. He didn't even bother to lie convincingly. That was all bullshit about him writing letters to the papers.''

"Yeah? You think?''

"Sure. The implied contradictions. One second he shows he knows how we work, implies we respond to media pressure, then he runs the letter thing by us forgetting that if such letters were sent, they'd also tell the press we gave a mad killer a human sacrifice. He's just jerking himself off now. I think he knows we're going to take him down but the desire to smash out at Ciprioni, coupled with his guilt and mental illness, probably have brought him to this point."

"I hope you're right."

"He's crazy as a fucking loon, of course." Eichord wiped perspiration from his forehead. He moved his head from side to side and heard bones pop. "Hey, look at me—he's saying." Springer nodded glumly. " 'Course . . ." Jack added with a sly half-smile, "on the other hand I could be wrong."

"Wonderful. Fuckin' voon-der-bar."

Suddenly Eichord thought of eighteen things that could and probably would go wrong, ranging from the weather to Jeeter Oliver. He looked at a yellow legal pad in front of him and couldn't read anything he'd written. He wanted to take his notes and hand them to somebody and say, "Run these down to the lab."

He picked up the phone and put it down again. Went in and peed and sat back down at his desk. He thought of all the things that could go wrong that he HADN'T thought of before. He hoped the fault lines wouldn't crack apart and swallow him as the terra unfirma had threatened to do before. He hoped that it would rain on Spain and he'd fall mainly on the plain. He hoped that Jeeter would not get the jitters.

What could go wrong? EVERY fucking thing, that's all. Everything could go wrong. Eichord thought to himself, I can have a heart attack and bite it right now. That's what can go wrong. And he felt his palms turn damp, and he had a hot and unpleasant feeling inside his head, and out of nowhere he thought of Rita and realized that it was true what the sages wrote, that abstinence made the fond grow harder.

Time compressed like a drunk's afternoon and early evening, swirling fuzzily, and it was all gone and he could feel how cold he was and how hot his forehead felt as the time slogged on. The phone ringing stabbed like a knife wound. He had heard the phrase triple-take before but never seen one much less done one. He did a triple-take. He was starting to walk into the next office and his phone rang and his head came back then returned in the direction of the body movement, then corrected, then recorrected, then changed its mind—a little St. Vitus dance here on American Bandstand.

"Hello." His throat sounded like he'd been gargling Drano.

"Well?"

"Okay. They say you can have Ciprioni but they want assurances from you. What's to stop you from leaving time bombs anyway once you have what you want?"

"Nothing. If I was out to destroy the city. But if I was out to destroy the city the fucking city would be GONE, wouldn't it?"

"Uh, yeah."

"Brilliant. I've told you I won't kill anymore if you give me my dear friend for disposition. A deal's a deal. I can't bring my daughter back. I will have reached them all and dealt out the appropriate punishment." Eichord hoped that in the throes of his insanity he'd have forgotten that the police were holding Rikla under guard.

"Fine. I made a list of meeting places, do you want—"

"You want me to come there? I don't care. I've warned you what will happen if you try to take me down."

"Um. How about that theater where you were. The EGA they call it. I'll bring Tony Cypriot there at midnight if you'll assure me Angelina Russo will be there alive."

"Forget snipers and all that crap too, friend. Remember my precautions are no joke. I fall down go boom, EVERYBODY goes boom—'' He chuckled mirthlessly. ''You read me?''

''Right. I don't see a problem. Frankly, Mr. Ciprioni has no value to us. But Miss Russo is a civilian. She's no more tied to the family business than your daughter was tied to your work. We don't want to see another innocent hurt and I don't think you do either.'' He wondered if he'd gone too far. A pause and the voice had turned to stone. Cold and hard like a tombstone.

''You bring the scumbag. You personally.''

''Okay.''

''I see anybody else. First thing I do is I drop this Russo bitch like a real bad habit.''

''All right. I'll be alone and I will have Mr. Ciprioni. See you inside the theater at midnight.'' The line went dead. First question he could decipher from the legal pad was, what if he's waiting outside? What if I can't get him inside? Hey, no fair, these are too tough for this late in the day. Also, that's two questions. But on another level he knew that Spain would go inside, or anywhere else. Confidence was in his tone of voice. And insanity.

Victor Springer looked like someone who'd just seen the *Titanic* go down, and everybody aboard owed him money.

''I'm not liking this much,'' he told Eichord.

''Umm.''

''In fact, I don't like any part of it.''

''I hear you. What he is about is punishment. He wants revenge. He's several bricks short of a load.''

''He's also an expert, highly professional hit man, booby. He KILLS people. THAT'S what he's about.'' It was another negotiation. The lieutenant agreed to lose the tac unit, Eichord conceded to the backup and trace vans. Whatever other high-tech bullshit—just let him go in there and get it done.

The bomb squad had sent Leroys, which was what

they called their expendable technicians—a bit of tongue-in-cheek cop wit—to find and secure the grenades in the two stores. They had been there as advertised.

McTuff had factored the probabilities and rated the situation as an assessed threat that was high but acceptable—to whom? Eichord was where the buck stopped, and he tried to think of an appropriate cliché.

"Sometimes you have to fish or cut bait," he said to nobody. He was going in. He'd been adamant about the loner thing. He told Springer, "You mount people on the rooftops, Spain eyeballs 'em, not only will we lose him he'll probably scope off the coppers too—just out of meanness. We gotta try to get in and play our hole card."

Gaetano Cipriano was not thrilled. And the less thrilled he got the closer the hour drew near. It looked for a bit like Eichord was going to have to cuff him to drag him into the EGA, but in the last minutes the man fell into a becalmed state.

Oddly enough, Eichord was quite unafraid. Relaxed. Getting out of the marked vehicle and stepping over the bright-orange tape, going into the EGA, where the police seal had been broken, the chain cut, walking in and around the box-office area, then stumbling with Ciprioni and both of them tripping over something and a hoarse "SONOFABITCH!" escaping involuntarily as they found themselves staring down the center aisle into the blinding flashlight of the killer Spain.

"You scumwad," Spain said,

"Hold it, Frank, at least listen to my side," The Man began pleading.

"This is for what your filth did to my little girl," he said, and Ciprioni screamed at Eichord, "Come on, COME ON GODDAMMIT DO SOMETHING WHAT THE FUCK ARE YOU WAITING FOR—"

"Whatsa matter, MISTER Ciprioni," Spain said, and laughed that nonlaugh of his.

"YOU LOUSY FUCK. YOU SAID I'D BE SAFE. YOU PROMISED YOU WOULDN'T LET HIM HURT ME."

Spain thumbed back the hammer on his piece and Eichord said, "I lied," and jumped into the darkness as Spain blasted the life out of the man who was his mentor, Gaetano Ciprioni. Hidden somewhere in the recesses of what was once a projection booth Jeeter Oliver keyed the machine and a blinding stab of bright, yellow light tore through the darkness, the screen lighting up white as a huge image of Spain's daughter filled the back of the tiny theater with movement and a man's voice said something about "—displeasing me, you cunt—" and Eichord is in the two-handed grip and the Semi-Weaver stance and carefully squeezes. Drawing down not altogether reluctantly on the totally mad Frank Spain.

A thousand boxes of police shell casings and high-power load attest to the practice that brings him to the firing line in this thirty-minute second. That is how long it seems, conservatively, the next second takes to tick by. It is a second he will relive again and again in bad daymares, as he kicks himself for his failure and the "what-iffing" you always do when things like this happen.

The hammer begins to drop and Jack sees it very clearly, seeing it fall slowly toward the pin as he steadies controls grips the Smith & Wesson firearm just so, rigid but not too stuff, by the numbers, easy squeezy bang, and when the bang sounds, close like this, in the filth and decay of the old theater with this foul, deranged killer at point-blank range, it will be like Spain's gunshot into the head of Tony Cypriot. It will be a cartoon bang, a comic-book POW, where it requires an entire panel of artwork to phoneticize that concussive, ear-shattering, close-up explosion, and

Eichord remembers every second of this, all of it, each detail as he freezes the awful hammer fall.

Some people can do that. They can stop time. When they are very frightened or nervous or both. When they want to put off that terrible moment that they know is just around the corner they simply put on the brakes and go, Hold it! Slow down, there, time. And they nail time's shoes to the floor and nothing moves. No second hand sweeps. Nothing ticks or tocs. It all slows, drags down to a stop, and they refuse to allow it to pass through their frightened, apprehensive space. And Jack Eichord stopped it then. And he had to breathe, unfortunately, so he started time up again and let it go and watched the damn hammer fall.

Point-blank. As up close and personal as it gets and still, as the saying goes, you have to go ahead and putt it out. It ain't ever a gimmee. And you see the target fine, right there over that sight, but the thing is—shit, you can see how he's got the Russo girl. Holding her so close. Why worry, though? What hardened, practiced, supermacho cop ever missed at this range? Right? Right.

W R O N G, bourbon breath.

And now, a woman he really didn't care that much about, this stranger was depending on his skill and his coolness under pressure, and this was the frozen beat of stop-time he'd relive again and again, reddening anew each time he played it back.

What you do is you bring the top of the I, the blade, up into the U. And when the top of the I fills the U with the sight right there on your bull's-eye you stare a hole at your target and squeeze 'er off. What you don't want to do is move and what you especially NEVER want to do is blink or squint one eye shut like they do on TV.

And a thousand boxes of cop rounds ROUNDS YOU BUY, ole buddy, no they don't furnish you bullets, you BUY every damn one of those expensive babies

you blast out there on the range, and every one of fifty
thousand rounds or whatever astronomical number he'd
run through the barrel of that Smith over the years,
every one of them went right out the fucking window
as he squinted or a tic pulled his left eye shut Christ
make up some lame bullshit he MISSED HE FUCK-
ING MISSED and it was the bang of a Red Ryder
Daisy B-B gun and Spain was down almost breaking
her neck as he dragged his human shield down behind
the dirty theater seats, crawling toward his detonator
as he screamed at Eichord, "YOU'RE DEAD YOU
LUMP OF STUPID SHIT YOU'RE A FUCKING
DEAD MAN AND YOU CAN WATCH THIS WOP
CUNT DIE NOW TOO," and more that Jack could
never really remember hearing.

He could only remember his breathing and the sound
of the gunshot as Spain fired one at him over the seats
my God it was the comic-book BLAM POW
CRAKKKKKKK he'd been waiting for and it sounded
like a cannon going off. They may sound small when
you miss but when somebody fires one at you, Jack
ole pal, it sounds like Nagasaki going off in your head
and his breathing so loud, so hyper, going
"haaaaaannnnnnnnnggggggggghhhhh, haaaaaaaaaaaaaaaa-
nnnnnnnnggggghhhh," hunkered down flat against the
grime-coated cold stone floor, so afraid, and the
bright, awful, evil streak that came with the loud noise
crashing into the steel and cushion beside him and he
could never recall a moment when he'd been so frightened and he wanted to pray and he knew there was no
time now. Now, now when he *needed* to stop time, it
wouldn't stop for him, and that lunatic sonofabitch was
dragging the Russo woman away firing off another
snapped shot at Eichord and Jack knew he had to do
something and oh-God-oh-Jesus, he prayed he
wouldn't be shot. He was afraid. He didn't want to
die. It was like in combat. All you cared about was
living. Surviving. Fuck 'em all. Be on MY side, God.

You 'n' me, okay? And with that the man upstairs played Eichord's ace for him.

And he made himself come up as the little girl on the screen screamed again, and audio was up and it was loud by the ancient, cobwebbed speakers, and she saved Eichord and the Russo woman when Belmonte stabbed the metal thing into her eye and she screamed the awful scream of pain and death screaming at her father, "DADDDDDEEEEEEEEEEEE!" as he looked toward the noise, looking up at the hell of his daughter's tormentor blinding and killing her then the screams are not of a father gone mad but of a tortured animal at the cracking point and in that instant of mind-shattering recognition and agony Eichord raises his weapon in the old-fashioned way, raising the gun with one hand, squeezing the trigger, carefully taking the killer out. And the screaming of the woman and the man and perhaps Eichord and the echo of the weapons deafening blast all die as the screen returns to a blank glare, the projector—like Jack Eichord—running on empty. And a man who was once named Frank Spanhower lays rapidly dying.

Eichord sees his lips move and hears a whisper and he drops down making sure the killer holds no knife or gun and he asks him, "Please. Were there any time bombs? You don't want innocent people to die as your little girl did. Did you hide bombs?" and leaning in close to hear the stammered whisper, "M-m-m-m-mama-ma-ma-" as his life force ebbs completely. And he could have been saying anything. Mary Pat. Mama. Merry Christmas. And Eichord took the woman and put his arm around her and started back toward the street and the real world.

He couldn't make it to the bar for the obligatory two beers and the camaraderie and that wasn't like him. He knew he just didn't dare. Not tonight. He was afraid the first time somebody congratulated him he'd either cold-cock them or dive into a water glass full of Daniel's. Or maybe both, and not necessarily in that order.

The lean, mean coppers of the Special Division notwithstanding, St. Louis was typical of the police departments around the country that were, collectively, out of shape. New and stringent physical requirement minimums would mean a lot of good cops might no longer make the cut. But it was probably for the best. Fewer heart attacks would be an obvious positive benefit.

Eichord was getting too old for this shit. He went home and sat on the edge of his bed. Got up and turned on the television. Sat back down. Got up and turned it off again. Got in bed and covered his head. He stayed like that until about two in the morning when he woke up soaked in perspiration and shaking in fear. He was consumed by paranoia for a few minutes, totally disoriented, with the awful, nagging fear that the night had been a bad dream and that the one called Spain was out there in the night waiting for him. He turned on all the lights like a little kid, made himself a strong cup of coffee, and called Rita.

"I'm sorry to call like this. I need to see you." She told him to come on over and he went out the door half-dressed. By the time he got there he was a little less paranoid but still a bit shaky. She'd heard on the news earlier but she didn't ask him too much about it, for which he was grateful, and he crawled in bed with his sleepy-headed lady and they kissed a few times. Rita giving him nice, warm kisses to which he was not responding. And he held her close with his lips by her ear and said, "Hi, you."

"Hi, yourself," she said back to him, letting him squeeze her.

"Just tonight—I, uh, just let me hold you."

"Okay. Let's just snuggle."

And they did and finally he went to sleep with her

like that, holding her in his arms, his face in her soft, silky hair.

Sometime around dawn he woke up again, still holding her, and he whispered, "Hi, you."

And Rita said, "Hi, yourself," in a very tiny voice full of sleep.

And he asked her, "Are you awake?"

And she told him, "Yes. I think so. Are you?"

"Yes."

And they got each other uncuddled for a second and Eichord tried to rub some feeling back into his arms, and then they kissed some more, but hotly this time, and he finally said to her, "I want romance and I want it now," and she understood.

And it was comfortable and surprising and velvety and viscerogenic, and you know how it is. Even when it's bad it's fabulous.

Rex Miller
Slob £2.99

A slash above the rest

Death likes to drive through darkened suburban streets, sightseeing as you would take your loved ones to look at the Christmas lights on a chill and snowy December's eve . . .

He was a monster spawned from a childhood of vile corruption, nurtured in the putrefying hell of Vietnam. Six foot seven and five hundred pounds – a coagulated mountain of seething hate. But behind the soulless eyes lurked a burning intelligence – an animal cunning infinitely superior to anything on four legs.

And the monster had come to Chicago.

Homicide detective Jack Eichord had never known a psychopath like it. This was no run-of-the-mill killing machine. This was a butcher who believed in job satisfaction. A serial murderer so utterly depraved that he devoured the hearts of his victims. There wasn't a killer on earth who took life so efficiently, so sadistically – or so often. And if he gets his way, there won't be enough lives left for anyone else to try . . .

All Pan books are available at your local bookshop or newsagent, or can be ordered direct from the publisher. Indicate the number of copies required and fill in the form below.

Send to: **CS Department, Pan Books Ltd., P.O. Box 40, Basingstoke, Hants. RG21 2YT.**

or phone: 0256 469551 (Ansaphone), quoting title, author and Credit Card number.

Please enclose a remittance* to the value of the cover price plus: 60p for the first book plus 30p per copy for each additional book ordered to a maximum charge of £2.40 to cover postage and packing.

*Payment may be made in sterling by UK personal cheque, postal order, sterling draft or international money order, made payable to Pan Books Ltd.

Alternatively by Barclaycard/Access:

Card No. | | | | | | | | | | | | | | | | | | | |

_____

Signature:

Applicable only in the UK and Republic of Ireland.

While every effort is made to keep prices low, it is sometimes necessary to increase prices at short notice. Pan Books reserve the right to show on covers and charge new retail prices which may differ from those advertised in the text or elsewhere.

NAME AND ADDRESS IN BLOCK LETTERS PLEASE:

....

Name ————————————————————————

Address ————————————————————————

————————————————————————————

————————————————————————————

————————————————————————————

3/87